Praise for J

'Hyper-real noir. A grotesque r
bibliomania, doubt, obsession, w
James Ellroy

'The most electrifying debut crime novel you are likely to read all year' ***GQ***

'A feast of unsettling pleasures' ***Independent***

'A surrealistic noir epic that's part David Lynch and part Bret Easton Ellis' ***Booklist***

'Has a kind of hallucinatory fascination… amazing in its density, power, richness of detail, humour and irony… a dazzling piece of work. One of the year's 10 best!' ***L A Times***

'Mesmerizing… light-years away from your garden-variety thriller. *The Skin Palace* may remind you of *Blade Runner* or the novels of William Gibson, but O'Connell has his own dazzling tale to tell… Wickedly clever' ***Seattle Times***

'It's a measure of O'Connell's immense talent that, while creating his absolutely original and hyperbolic world, he also paints a striking vision of the haunting ways in which life and art mirror each other' ***Publishers Weekly***

'It's a helter-skelter, a roller-coaster, a ride on a ghost train – if the fairground had been designed by Philip K Dick, Stan Lee and Edgar Allan Poe' ***Independent on Sunday***

'No one does the improbable like O'Connell' ***Guardian***

'Jack O'Connell has riffed on language, fire-cleansed genre conventions, and stripped the artifice from the modern noir novel, creating a body of work both exciting and entirely original'
George Pelecanos

'A masterpiece, O'Connell's tour de force has a dose of the uncertainty of Kafka, the fantasy of Bradbury, the crisp prose of Greene, and the noir of Chandler' ***Strand Magazine***

'Brilliant writing, original concepts, emotional resonance'
Washington Post

'A brilliantly tuned, mesmerizing labyrinth of a quasi-real world as only a master artist could draw it'
James Ellroy

Also by Jack O'Connell

Wireless
The Skin Palace
Word Made Flesh
The Resurrectionist

JACK O'CONNELL

BOX NINE

NO EXIT PRESS

First published in the United States in 1993
by Mysterious Press, New York, USA

First published in the UK in 2000
by OldCastle Books Ltd, Harpenden, UK

This edition published in the UK in 2025
by No Exit Press, an imprint of
Bedford Square Publishers Ltd, London, UK

noexit.co.uk
@noexitpress

A CIP catalogue record for this book is available from the British Library.

ISBN
978-1-83501-226-0 (Paperback)
978-1-83501-299-4 (ePub)

2 4 6 8 10 9 7 5 3 1

Typeset in 11.15 on 13.75pt Minion Pro
by Avocet Typeset, Bideford, Devon EX39 2BP
Printed and bound in Great Britain by
CPI Group (UK) Ltd, Croydon CR0 4YY

FSC
www.fsc.org
MIX
Paper | Supporting responsible forestry
FSC® C171272

For Nance

ACKNOWLEDGMENTS

The author is indebted to the following works and wishes to express his gratitude to the authors: *The Cambridge Encyclopedia of Language,* David Crystal; *Bibliography of General Linguistics,* Aleksandra K. Wawryszko; *Semiotic and Significs: The Correspondence Between Charles S. Peirce and Victoria Lady Welby,* edited by Charles S. Hardwick; *Julio Cortazar,* Evelyn Picon Garfield; *Into the Mainstream,* Luis Harss and Barbara Dohmann.

INTRODUCTION

by Otto Penzler

In the late 1980s, The Mysterious Press had recently had great success with James Ellroy's *The Black Dahlia* and *The Big Nowhere* and we were expecting even more from *L.A. Confidential*. As exciting as all that was, we knew we had to do something more to keep our publishing bullet train roaring ahead.

My agent Nat Sobel (also, not very coincidentally, Ellroy's agent and, later, Jack O'Connell's as well) gave me an idea. Paraphrasing because, unlike Archie Goodwin, Nero Wolfe's assistant, I do not have a photographic memory, he said 'How about running a contest for a best first novel?'

Nice idea, and so we announced The Mysterious Press Discovery Contest with a $50,000 prize. Our mailbox instantly filled with hundreds - *many* hundreds - of submissions. One agent cleared her office of nearly two hundred manuscripts (this occurred back in the day before electronic communication was the standard), filling several large cartons. Along with my editors Sara Ann Freed and Bill Malloy, and our freelance reader, I spent months reading some truly awful books, some fairly decent ones, and a few exceptional manuscripts.

After months of filling every available hour with reading, reading, reading, we finally narrowed the possibilities down to three finalists. Making every effort to be fair, we voted for our favorites in a secret ballot to avoid influencing each other. The unanimous choice was *Box Nine* by Jack O'Connell, a decision that we never regretted as it remains as fresh and timely today as it did when it was written.

The Mysterious Press published many excellent traditional

detective novelists, including Charlotte MacLeod, Peter Lovesey, Aaron Elkins, Ellis Peters, Ruth Rendell, and Stuart M. Kaminsky, and some non-traditional authors, such as Donald E. Westlake, Patricia Highsmith, Walter B. Gibson (*The Shadow*), Peter O'Connell (*Modesty Blaise*), and Ross Thomas, winning numerous awards (and selling a lot of books). However, it was tough, hard-boiled fiction that I found appealing more often than not. Ellroy comes quickly to mind, but Joe Gores was on our list, and so was Joseph Hansen, Ed McBain, and even one-time books with Ross Macdonald and Mickey Spillane.

It was no surprise to us that *Box Nine* was destined to be published by The Mysterious Press as it was in the middle of our strike zone. It is filled with a large cast of off-the-grid characters, as unique, fascinating, and dangerous as the cast of a Tarantino film or an Ellroy novel.

They are not merely tough, however. The central character, police Lieutenant Lenore Thomas, is a borderline sociopath, and I'm not so sure of the 'borderline' part. It takes a while to warm up to someone whose first love is her gun collection and not the twin brother with whom she shares an apartment but O'Connell makes her both human and charismatic.

The action takes place in the fictional decaying New England town of Quinsigamond, mainly in an area known as Bangkok Park, so drug-infested and dangerous that most cops are reluctant to go near it. Lenore, however, is there with regularity, confident that she owns it, partly because of her insane sexual flirtation with Cortez, the dominant drug lord in town who the department is convinced will be enshrined in the Cartel Hall of Fame.

Cortez owns most of the buildings in Bangkok Park and has made his home in the Hotel Penumbra that he spent millions renovating and decorating with the superb taste one would expect of a drug kingpin. His office is virtually devoid of furniture, including chairs, so meetings are held standing.

Lenore and Cortez have a love-hate relationship but she finds it useful to keep him in pursuit, partly so that she can have a steady supply of amphetamines to feed her habit. She also wants to stay close as she is certain that he is not the top dog, he answers to someone, and that's who she wants to nail.

As bad as things have been in Bangkok Park, the police are stunned to learn that it could soon get worse when they discover the bodies of Inez and Leo Swann, both highly regarded scientists from Princeton and MIT, who invented a new drug with the street name Lingo. The police's theory is that they had planned to go into business with gangsters to make their fortune. The badly beaten and mutilated bodies of the optimistic entrepreneurs made it evident that their dreams of criminal wealth were unsuccessful.

An accidental byproduct of their experiments to find a cure for 'language delayed' children, Lingo enables people with reading difficulties to improve rapidly from slowly enunciating every syllable to a normal pace to a speed at which the sounds run into each other at 1,500 words a minute. An unanticipated side effect is that the speaker has an extraordinary sexual euphoria before falling into an uncontrollable rage.

As with today's fentanyl epidemic, in which users experience a powerful rush very quickly, Lingo is also lethal, even in small doses, convincing the police to prepare for an imminent tsunami of homicides and drug overdoses in Quinsigamond if they can't stop it before it takes hold.

Lenore and Dr. Frederick Woo, the linguistic expert brought in to help the police and the mayor understand what they are up against, think they can stop it, though the odds are astronomical, especially since they also must deal with corruption they had not previously encountered.

Corruption may be found in any city but Quinsigamond may have had more than its share and proved a rich source of material, so O'Connell based all his novels there, having modeled it on Worcester, the city in which he was born and lived his entire life.

Although he had a day job in the insurance business, O'Connell was devoted to his writing and produced some of the most original fiction of his time. He wrote noir crime novels but they pushed at the borders a good deal and were so uniquely his that an entirely new genre should be recognized to honor his unique contribution to literature.

After *Box Nine* in 1992, O'Connell published *Wireless* (1993) in which a radio talk show seduces listeners to join an underground war, spawning imitators. Detective Hanna Shaw hunts for one of the show's listeners, a former FBI agent who has evidently become part of the deadly, secret cult.

The Skin Palace (1996) tells of the greatest attraction in Quinsigamond, Herzog's Erotic Palace, reputedly the most elegant pornographic theater in America. Ripe for takeover by Hermann Kinsky, the crime king and mayor of Bangkok Park, it is Kinsky's hope that it will bring him closer to his son, who is obsessive about directing the darkest noir film in history. The ostensible heir meets a woman with a strange antique camera that offers a frightening view of the future.

In the post-apocalyptic noir thriller, *Word Made Flesh* (1999), everyone in Quinsigamond believes that Gilrein, a former cop-turned-taxi driver, is in possession of a mysterious book that some people would kill to possess. He doesn't have it but is certain that a petty fence does so he hunts for him, initiating a search that might well mean life-or-death.

O'Connell's last book was *The Resurrectionist* (2008), the story of a desperate man named Sweeney and his comatose son, who is brought to a clinic where doctors have claimed to resurrect similar patients. Although the doctors may have a solution to the boy's condition, the best hope for a cure may be in Limbo, the comic book world he loved.

Brief synopses of O'Connell's genre-bending novels cannot even hint at the richness of his prose, ranging from the occasional baroque to the snappy dialogue for which the best hard-boiled crime writers are revered.

Jack O'Connell's voice deserved to be heard when his books were first released. It deserves to be heard today, too, and for as long as talented voices may still be appreciated.

1

Talk to God. Clean up your slate. The Rapture is coming and your time is running out. Mary is doing all she can to hold back the hand of her son. All but the elect will be chastised.

Lenore lowers the orange foam headphones to her neck and shuts off the radio. Ray, the born-again Nazi from WQSG, has kicked into another screaming rant, another variation on his normal tirade against communism, Satan, and Mayor Welby's latest budget proposals.

She shouldn't have brought the radio in the first place. It's too distracting, a piece of equipment without a purpose. But the thought of spending another night listening to Zarelli debate divorce was too much. It exceeded her tolerance level. She had a hunch things could get ugly if she didn't take some kind of preventive action.

But listening to Ray rasp and suck air till he's overcome and close to vomiting is no solution.

So she sends her partner, Zarelli, across the street early, tells him to look for any surprises, and attempts to concentrate on her food. She's eating some kind of rice and raw tuna dish out of a carton. It's cold and she has no idea whether it's supposed to be served this way or if Zarelli was just suckered again, handed a cold carton of last night's house special out of a kitchen doorway. She can picture a trio of teenage Chinese dishwashers, soaked aprons sticking to their legs, pocketing Zarelli's money and laughing for the balance of their shift.

It's the Monday before Thanksgiving and Lenore is in the basement of a slaughterhouse called Brasilia Beef, sitting on a splintery shipping crate in the boiler room, hidden behind a double oil tank and an enormous, ancient monster of a cast-iron furnace. This is her third night in the basement. She's listening for sounds, distant voices. She's anticipating the noise of a business transaction, a semi-friendly deal, earnest handshakes over platters of marinated monkey livers and shooters of bourbon.

Across the street from the slaughterhouse is the Plain Jar Café, a new Laotian bar and grill. The place is owned by a new player that everyone calls Cousin Mo. It may or may not be a fresh money bin for a new company setting up in the Park. So far there's been no way to cross-check this information.

Zarelli is sitting at the bar of the Plain Jar. Zarelli's supposed to be sipping club sodas, but when he dropped off her supper, Lenore could smell booze. Now she's starting to think she should have been the one inside the bar. But Zarelli's so bad with the equipment, what he calls *the machines,* and lately he's taken to dozing on stakeout.

Earlier in the night, they managed to wire Zarelli with a voice-activated mike. The tech guys promised Lenore it was the latest thing. She didn't bother to tell them that the equipment she's most worried about is her partner. Right now, Cousin Mo and his meatboys could be sacrificing infants at the other end of the bar and Zarelli would talk right through it, choke himself spitting out his newest jokes about feminists and Orientals.

She pictures him now, her partner and lover, elbows planted on the bar, a long teak slab resting on a pedestal that's hand-carved to look like a parade of elephants, all attached, tail to trunk. She sees him fire a punch line to the barkeep, then fit his mouth around another Genesee cream ale. As always, he's dressed in this sport coat that might as well have orange neon across the back blinking *I'm a cop, I'm a cop.*

She looks down at her own lap and has to smile. She's got on the leather miniskirt that Zarelli's so hot for and a pink tank top under a denim jacket. It's a challenge finding the right outfit, hitting the perfect note between enough sleaze and not too much theatrics. Last night, sitting on the same crates, Zarelli said to her, 'Jesus, you were born to wear clothes like that.' She responded by throwing a water chestnut at him. She caught him in the eye. He said it stung all night and she said, 'It's just a reminder not to be stupid.'

But she knows no amount of eye-poking will help. Zarelli's a stupid guy. It's a fact of nature. Nothing can be done.

The problem with dressing like a hooker, she decides, is that there's no place to put the gun. You can tape a razor up high on the thigh, then spend the rest of the night hesitant about sitting down, a little worried that the only blood you draw might be your own. And besides, down in the Park a razor just isn't going to be enough. In fact, at this time of the night in Bangkok Park, a razor is probably worse than nothing at all. It's all taunt and threat and no backup. No delivery. So she's got a small .38 jammed into the pocket of the denim jacket.

She puts down her carton and fits the black department headphones over her ears. How many nights has she wasted just like this, alone in some basement or attic, waiting hours for some word, some information, a clear sentence from the mouth of another rookie broker overstimulated by speed and the legend of Cortez? Every other week it seems, some new player moves into the Park and wants to kick Cortez off the top of the hill. Last week, Zarelli gave her five-to-one odds that Cousin Mo would be dead before he could take delivery on his new Mercedes. Lenore shook off the bet.

Lenore has her own theories about Cortez, the king of Bangkok Park. She's got ideas that don't jibe with the legend, hunches she won't share anymore. Everyone in the department, Miskewitz included, thinks Cortez is headed for the Cartel Hall of Fame. Lenore thinks this may not be the case, that there's both more and less to Cortez than the current myth allows for.

Through the headphones comes the sound of a door opening and a volley of unintelligible talk interspersed with a high-pitched laugh. Lenore puts her hands to her ears and wishes she'd listened to that 'Intro to Laotian' cassette she bought mail-order. Clearly there's someone in the bar besides Zarelli who enjoys a good, filthy joke.

The sound quality surprises her. She'll have to pat a few backs tomorrow. Usually, she's trying to pick incriminating syllables out of a garbled hiss of grunts and coughs. Tonight, the words come pretty sharp and clear, and she can't translate even one into English. She thinks irony should be added to death and taxes as one more certainty in life.

'What's this? Sit? You want me to sit down?'

It's Zarelli's voice. He's giving his nervousness away like free advice.

'Is there a language problem here? I assumed we'd all speak English. Am I wrong here?'

Cousin Mo speaks English like the Queen. But he probably thinks this is a smart business tactic, rattling the customer. First sign of a short-term player. Cortez will eat this guy inside a month.

'Is there any chance of getting a translator?'

The whole room laughs.

'I say something funny?'

Finally, Cousin Mo speaks:

'Could you do me a favor, Mr. Watt?'

'A favor?'

'A very simple request.'

'Yeah. Request?'

'Could you please unbutton your shirt?'

'My shirt?'

'If you would indulge me.'

Lenore pulls the headphones off and starts running to the street, thinking, *Zarelli should come with a warning.* She stops herself from bolting into the Plain Jar, looks down the length of Voegelin Street, and sees two girls in front of El Topo. She looks to the doorway of the Plain Jar and makes her decision, runs to El Topo, and pulls a wad of bills from her jeans jacket pocket.

One of the girls is Hispanic, the other a tall Grace Jones type, all cheekbone and leg. The Hispanic girl is shaking her head, saying, 'No, honey, you want Melinda,' as Lenore counts off two hundred dollars in tens and twenties. She pulls off her wristwatch, holds it out, and says, 'Look, can't argue. This is a real Movado. You can have it and the cash. I need you for ten minutes. You won't even have to take off your shoes.'

They walk into the Plain Jar without looking at the bartender and head straight for the stairway. At the top landing is a dim corridor that breaks right and left. At the right-hand end, a meatboy in a bad-fitting suit sits on a barstool before a closed door. Lenore starts an even march toward him, as he rises up off the stool and holds a flat palm up like a traffic cop. She responds with a classic index finger to the lips, a *shush* to an excited child.

The guy puts his hand inside his suit coat and leaves it there as Lenore leans up to his ear and whispers, 'Welcome wagon gift from your new neighbor,' then she gives his lobe a small lick.

He scrunches his brow to show confusion, but doesn't speak.

Lenore smiles, indicates the girls, who've fallen in behind her, and says, 'A little something Mr. Cortez sent over. For the boss. For Cousin Mo. You know – *welcome to the neighborhood.*'

He stares at her for a few seconds, holds up a finger to indicate *wait a second,* then gives two knocks on the door and without waiting for an answer turns the knob and sticks his head inside, up to his steroid-enhanced neck. There are some low, guttural barks back and forth and before the meatboy can extract his head and tell her to wait at the bar, Lenore checks her good shoulder into his back and he falls forward onto his knees, throwing the door wide open. Zarelli is on his knees in the center of the room. Lenore jumps over the meatboy, draws out the .38, pulls down the hammer, grabs Zarelli in a headlock, and pushes the barrel up against his temple.

Suddenly, everyone in the room has a gun drawn, and Cousin Mo clearly isn't sure what's happening. Lenore knows that what she's about to do probably doesn't make much sense, but she's betting that fact won't dawn on anyone, Zarelli included, for another five minutes. She speaks fast, directly to the boss.

'Don't. This guy's a cop, for Christ sake.'

Cousin Mo raises both his hands in a weird, nervous, birdlike gesture that seems to restrain his associates.

Lenore tries for a little arrogance. 'You should really learn who it is that you're doing business with, my friend.'

A long minute passes while Cousin Mo stares and thinks, then he says, 'And you are?'

'I'm an employee of your new neighbor, Mr. Cortez. Owns Hotel Penumbra. You might have heard. You now owe him a favor.'

Cousin Mo comes forward to his desk. The meatboy is up, dishonored, shamefaced. The guy next to Cousin Mo head-signals him away and the kid closes the office door behind himself.

'Why would my neighbor be so concerned about my welfare?' Cousin Mo asks.

Lenore instinctively tightens her grip around Zarelli's neck, possibly cutting off some air. She gives a sigh and says, 'I'm sure he has his reasons. He'll probably be letting you know what they are very soon.'

Cousin Mo looks down at Zarelli and then back up at Lenore.

'He's as filthy as they come,' she says, 'but he's on Mr. Cortez's leash.'

'Are you saying Mr. Cortez wants to discuss a deal?'

She loosens up on Zarelli, steps backward, and pulls him to his feet. 'I'm saying we're leaving now. And I'm saying you should show a little more discretion in the future. And I'm saying you may be getting a call soon. Any problems with that?'

Cousin Mo looks like he doesn't know whether he's had his ego stroked or his shoes spit on. He looks around at his men, then lowers his voice and says, 'I understand.'

Lenore nods, puts the gun back in her pocket, lifts the back flap of Zarelli's sport coat, and grabs hold of his belt.

'Someone wants to talk with you,' she says to Zarelli's back. 'You try to bolt on me and I'll shoot right through your spine.'

She starts to move for the door.

Cousin Mo says, 'Thank Mr. Cortez for me.'

She marches Zarelli out in front of her, a sweaty, shallow-breathing shield, all the way back to her Barracuda. They don't speak until they cross out of the Park, at which point Zarelli smashes his fist into the dash and says, 'You put it up to my fucking head—'

She cuts him off and yells back, 'Who knows what Mo would have done if I hadn't come in. He's untested. He could have done anything—'

'—my fucking head. Right here.' He points to his temple with his index and middle fingers.

'I had to shock them,' she yells.

'Shock them? My heart. My goddamn heart.'

She pulls the Barracuda into the curb with a screech, jams it into park, and they start to slap each other around the upper torso. This is not the first time this has happened. Things escalate and Lenore loses herself, makes a fist, and comes up under Zarelli's jaw.

He drops his offense, takes his face in his hands, yelling, 'The bridge, oh no, the new bridge.'

Lenore sinks back in her seat, punches the steering wheel.

'Is it the bridge? Did I break it?' she asks grudgingly.

He doesn't answer right away, sits there stroking his jaw like a shaving cream commercial.

A few minutes go by. Finally, he says, 'You know, word's going to get back to Cortez.'

She says, 'Let me worry about Cortez.'

There's another pause and he adds, 'Thanks for getting me out of there.'

'Sorry about the gun. I probably shouldn't have pulled back the hammer.'

'You had to shock them. You had to move quickly.'

'I made a decision. I acted on it.'

He slides a hand over onto her thigh.

She shakes her head no, shifts back into drive.

'We've got a briefing in about five hours.'

He makes a face that says *please,* changes it, pitifully, into *I beg you.*

Lenore stomps the gas and thinks, *I should have popped the weasel when I had the chance.*

2

After she dumps Zarelli, Lenore cruises home to the green duplex. There's no chance of sleep, so she takes a cold shower, pops a hit of crank, and sits on the end of her bed, naked, pumping ten-pound weights and watching metal videos with the sound off. She's waiting for signs of life from her brother Ike, next door.

Lenore lives on the other side of his apartment, in the other half of the green duplex. The arrangement has worked out pretty well, all things considered. They often work different hours, but manage to have meals together a few times a week. Ike thinks their parents would be pleased to know this. They've been dead just over seven years now. They died within six months of one another. Ma went first, a coronary. Dad followed in the fall with a lethal embolism in the front of the brain. A month after the estate was settled – there wasn't much, a small savings account, and the house and car – Lenore and he went in halves on the duplex. She'd gotten a promotion on the force, and things down at the post office looked stable enough for him. They took a twenty-year fixed mortgage and moved in in the spring.

When they do eat together, it's Ike who does the cooking. Lenore, like Pa, enjoys eggs and sausages. Anytime, day or night. Ike tries to warn her about cholesterol and fat intake, but he can't talk to Lenore about crap like that. She takes her life in her hands, and in a big way, like three or four times a week. Last year, down the projects, Zarelli kicks a door in on this upstart smack dealer and Lenore leaps into his pigsty, all pumped up for a big-time collar. But the guy's been tipped, he's expecting them and he's ready around a corner of the apartment, with a gun to Lenore's head. Before Zarelli can move, the dealer pulls the trigger, but, thank God, the gun is this piece of garbage, unregistered and off the street from, who knows, like Taiwan or someplace, and it explodes in his hands – puts the bullet intended for Lenore into the dealer's own throat.

How do you warn someone about the danger of sausage after a day like that?

A guy on the TV screen with semi-permed, peroxide-blond hair grabs his own behind and makes a face like he's in agony. Lenore gets a kick out of this. Nobody could be more shocked than herself that she's become addicted to heavy-metal music. And like most addictions, she's attempted to hide this new habit from everyone she knows. She thinks she's been fairly successful in this attempt, but it's difficult since one of the inherent factors, and, yes, attractions, of heavy metal, at least for Lenore, is its deafening volume.

She thinks that possibly Zarelli is responsible, at least to some degree, for this pathetic love of the screeching sounds that issue from bands with names like Metallica and Iron Maiden. Here's Zarelli, at twenty-eight, two years younger than Lenore, and he's got this big thing for Tony Bennett. Before Zarelli, Lenore couldn't have named one Tony Bennett song besides 'I Left My Heart in San Francisco.' But when they started seeing each other, it seemed like she was slowly being indoctrinated in this Cult of Bennett. It got a little depressing. Zarelli drives this old 1972 Lincoln Continental that has the seats all ripped up from his kids and his cats. And the car still has this horrible eight-track cartridge player that should be in a museum. The back seat of the Lincoln was always filled with these old Tony Bennett eight-track tapes, those fat mothers that often cut a song off in the middle of a lyric, then picked it up a few seconds later when it clicked over to the next track. For some reason, Lenore came to despise eight-track tapes. They came to symbolize both inefficiency and obsolescence. She thinks that if you want to really teach school kids the way of the world, the laws of evolution and adaptability, show them an old, label-peeling eight-track of *Tony Bennett Sings Your Old World Favorites.*

Lenore thinks that she became addicted to heavy metal as a reaction to Zarelli's passion for Bennett. To the best of her ability to date it, the problem began about six months ago, when she and Zarelli were hitting the hottest stretch of their ridiculous romance. One night before bed, she changed the station on her alarm clock to wake herself up with something loud and thrashing. Then she began picking up some new cassettes for her own car, mainstream metal like Twisted Sister and Mötley Crüe. One night last spring, she's at the minimart leafing through magazines to bring on a dull stakeout, and unexplainably, like she was acting on subliminal orders from someone else, she buys *Metal Mania Monthly*, then reads the damn thing cover-to-cover. Within weeks she's sending for these sick catalogues from the classifieds in the back and ordering garage-band cassettes through the mail, stuff recorded on independent labels by bands too far over the line for big corporate companies to touch. They've got names like Severed Artery, and Aryan Warlocks, and Puss and the Gash. Awful stuff. They sing songs, in these weird and ironic yelling-falsetto voices, with titles like 'Tonight I Killed Her Parents' and 'I Sold You to a Guy Named Phil.' She keeps all these tapes in a bottom drawer behind her turtleneck sweaters.

Lenore thinks that no one, not even Ike, has any idea how strange she really is. But *she's* always known it. The feeling stretches back to her earliest memories. Possibly, she thinks, her father suspected it, maybe had a hunch as to some really abnormal brain activity going on in the skull of his female child. She deduces this simply from the occasional look she'd find on his face over the dinner table, a combination of curiosity and fear and confusion. Lately, she's begun to wonder if he suspected his daughter's weirdness only because it ran through his own thought patterns.

Just once she'd have liked to see that look on Zarelli's face. Anytime – sitting in his stupid Lincoln in front of some smack house down in Bangkok Park, eating the veal at Fiorello's where everyone knows him, going at it in the motel room down Route 61 – just once she'd have liked to see that he had a doubt, a vague hunch, a moment of terror regarding her, indicating the fact that he knew nothing about the way she thought or felt or why she continued to work unbelievably hard at a pathetic and ultimately useless job.

Zarelli is a guy who's done pretty well in the nine years with the force. He's never been seriously hurt, never involved himself in any real, over-the-line corruption, kissed enough ass to move up to detective but still kept some camaraderie with most of the bowling team. Zarelli, she knows, is in narcotics because, oddly, it's the department in which he can define himself and keep his compass straight. This isn't to say there aren't corrupting temptations in narcotics. Just the opposite: there are probably more opportunities to go bad in narc than anywhere else. But in narcotics, Zarelli can think and function like a ten-year-old. He can rely on the fact that all the importers, and dealers, and junkies he moves through every day are monsters. Evil. Dark. Bad. And since he is their opposition, he's goodness and light incarnate. He's the other side of the fence. Society will back him up on this. Public opinion will comply with this view absolutely.

Lenore spends all her time as an actress. She feigns belief in this same, simple moral code. Us against them, white hats against black hats. In actuality, she's not so much repulsed by this code, as she is incapable, even for the briefest of moments, of taking it seriously. Of even considering it. It rings so false. It falls in the realm of fantasy.

Not even Ike knows the real reason Lenore does her job. The real reason, or at least the best symbol of the real reason, hangs at this moment inside a leather shoulder holster, from a hook on the inside of her bedroom closet door. Lenore's weapon of choice has become, sadly, something of a cliché. She finds this annoying but not too important. Let the gangs of the Hollywood brain-dead trivialize and prostitute and unintentionally parody one of the finest examples of craftsmanship and quality she knows about. Just keep them far away from Quinsigamond and the eleven-inch length of her Smith & Wesson.

She's had experience with a variety of both handguns and, lately, more than ever, assault rifles. And she owns a small collection – a Parabellum automatic, a Gewehr 43, an original 1921 John T. Thompson .45 caliber submachine gun, all of which she keeps perfectly maintained and some of which get exercised at the shooting bunker. Her most recent purchase was an Uzi. But for reasons that have to do with instinct and aura, the gun she almost always takes to work is her .357 Magnum Model 27.

She knows about her weapons with a degree of scholarship that makes her a 'buff,' in the same way other people bone up obsessively on the Civil War or old Corvettes. Ask Lenore over a cup of coffee about the Magnum. She'll nod and start to talk slowly, in a regulated voice that almost gives away its excitement just by the extent of its suppression. She'll forget the time and infect you with her competence on the subject. She'll start in 1935, the year the weapon was introduced, developed by a pistol specialist named Elmer Keith and supported by Major Daniel B. Wesson himself. They used a .44 target model frame, then made the barrel 222.25mm long. The caliber of .357 was used to set the gun apart from all other ordinary .38s. She'll tell you how, at first, the gun was only available by special order, but demand forced it into general production. And how, because of World War II, production had to be suspended in 1941. By that time 5,500 had been forged. Luckily, she'll explain, production started up again after the Axis powers had been slapped down. Her particular gun was built in '74. It's got the shorter 3.5-inch barrel and weighs about two and a half pounds. It's got a standard six-shot cylinder and a rate of fire of 12 rpm. The last statistic she'll end on, the one she'll let you ponder and hope that you'll attach a vivid image to, is muzzle velocity. She might ask you to guess this factor and swig down the last of her bitter coffee. And when you admit your inability to do so, she'll nod again, bite her bottom lip for just a second, stare into your eyes, and spill it: *One thousand four hundred and fifty freaking feet per second, my friend, with a striking energy of nine hundred and seventy-two joules. It will detach an arm completely off a shoulder. And I ought to know...*

Lenore believes in this gun in the manner that others believe in an ancient dogma, or a concept of family or love.

Lenore adores the fact that this gun is so real, so solid and fixable, locatable in a world that seems to be more transient, transparent, and decomposing every day.

Lenore no longer believes in God. She does not believe in an afterlife. She does not believe in some fixed code of divinely transmitted morality. She does not believe in turning the other cheek. She does not believe that the meek will inherit the earth. She now believes in power and persistence. In logic and rational thought. In seizing what you need without regard to the effect of your actions upon others. She hides these beliefs out of what she feels to be wise self-preservation, out of the fact that if others knew her true convictions, it would become pretty difficult to live the way she wants.

It's only in relation to her gun that she allows herself to expose and vent the certainties at the core of her brain, the ones she thinks her father had nightmares about. Lenore has killed one person – a twenty-two-year-old Colombian who fired a shotgun at Zarelli from the shattered back window of a speeding Trans Am – and wounded three others in varying degrees of severity, including blowing the full right arm off a longtime smack broker from down the projects who made the mistake of charging her with a razor in a dark stairwell. In each of those incidents, Lenore has felt a burst of emotion that she can't put a name to, that has no definition in the heart of the average person. She approximates it every time she pulls out her weapon and draws down on a suspect without firing. It's not the same as actually pulling the trigger, but it's a step in the right direction and more pleasing than frustrating.

But on those occasions when she has pulled the trigger and sent aluminum or lead barreling into the flesh and bone of some challenging, but ultimately weaker animal, Lenore feels like she's been momentarily elevated to a state people only dream of. More than anything, she finds it ironic that she ended up a narcotics cop, since the people she's chronically arresting are in search of a similar feeling, but stupidity or bad luck has brought them to smack rather than the gun. If they only had a clue what they could feel like being on the delivery end of a bullet flying sixteen miles a minute, the streets would be pools of blood and toppling bodies. The air would be continuously filled with duos of muzzleblast and human scream. She finds it funny and appealing to think that just five seconds in the basement shooting range down at the station is about a thousand times better than the best moment she ever had in bed with Zarelli.

Over the past few years, maybe even going back as far as the death of her parents, Lenore has tried to find words that she could hang on her beliefs, her system of looking at the world and her place in it, her particular philosophy. She's never read as many books as Ike – Ike's a real reader, loves those mysteries – but she manages to dip into a dozen or more a year. She drops into the library every couple of weeks and checks something out, usually some fat book she can read chunks of, maybe an anthology of essays or something. Unlike her twin brother, she sticks with nonfiction, often philosophy and history. She knows she's smart enough so that, given enough time and persistence, she can get a handle on almost any line of thought.

What she's discovered in the course of her reading is that though many people have come close to her vision, no one's really hit the bull's-eye. She spent a couple of years on Nietzsche, boned up on a lot of secondary material, even for a time kept a small notebook to clarify positions and meanings. He still holds a warm, important place in her heart, but she feels like she somehow slid past him, as though some hidden factor – her sex, her language, the century she's living in – has forced them to part like young and bittersweet lovers.

She had a fling with Darwin that she's happy about, but which faded more rapidly than she would have bet. She tried Hegel and got bogged down, found him a little bloodless. She went through a series of liaisons with a parade of lesser, or at least less familiar, names. Sorel, Péguy, Lagardelle. Machiavelli looked like he could be a lifetime match, but last year she came to the realization that her search for a past correlation to her own system was a pathetic one. The thing to do was simply to act purely within that system. Act was the key word. Action over thought. The justification for her life could be found in the rush of feeling that lingered for a few minutes after she walked out of the shooting bunker.

Over a strong black coffee last week, coming home after a forty-eight-hour dead-end shift, she daydreamed that if only the technology existed, her brain could be monitored to find out exactly what happened at the moment she squeezed on the trigger of the Magnum and the bullet exploded out the barrel and into the body of some panicking importer. And that if it could be determined exactly what kind of chemical got secreted, just what synapse got fired, then the process could be synthesized so that she could make it happen at will. She smiled at the thought, thinking that there was probably no way that her body could really tolerate that kind of ongoing stimulation for any extended period, but that even if the feeling proved fatal, it would be the best of all possible ways to die.

For a while, after she first made detective, Lenore was the only woman in the narcotics department. This was before Peirce, and long before Shaw. Because of this, she'd often be the first person inserted into a new investigation. She could play the new hooker in town so well that Zarelli used to say to her, 'I don't know, you make me wonder.' So she logged a lot of those first couple of plainclothes years, out on Goulden Avenue, jammed into imitation-leather mini-skirts, these neon-red or lime-green cheap satin halter tops, and break-your-ankles six-inch stiletto heels. Today she would say that she knows the residents and practitioners and hawkers and brokers and generally bent mothers of the Goulden Ave block, maybe better than any cop in the city.

The area is commonly known as Bangkok Park, probably because the number of vices for sale rivals that of the memorable Asian city. Ninety percent of all the drug trade in Quinsigamond takes place in the square mile of Bangkok Park. And so in this day and age, you have to expect to find extensive, cutting-edge weaponry inside every doorway. It used to be that, just like most other medium-sized urban centers, you only had to worry about distribution and use. But you can't beat back the tide of progress that big drug money will ignite and now there are actually good-sized *production* centers right here in the city. So far, the department has found two. The first was a small lab in the basement of an abandoned brownstone on the corner of Watson and West. But the second was in a bricked-off section of the old Verner Warehouse on Grassman. Richmond and Shaw found it by accident while tailing a courier back from the Zone, Quinsigamond's try at a cut-rate East Village. The courier got wise to them at some point inside Bangkok, and managed to lose them by ducking into the labyrinth of the old Verner building. Richmond and Shaw hunted around, realized they'd blown the tail, but inadvertently stumbled onto this huge state-of-the-art setup. This was top-of-the-line, shipped-in equipment, half a million anyway, and it told Lenore just how bad things were getting.

It was after the Verner discovery that she started thinking about the Uzi.

While everyone else in the department thinks of the job as little more than a futile effort that brings them a paycheck,

Lenore pretends she's something of a zealot. She's got everyone convinced that she defines each day as a nonstop conflict between darkness and light, and this is why she's never been hesitant to draw her piece and fire away. Her fake attitude creates a problem for Zarelli, especially since the night she told him to dig some Lifesavers out of her purse and he saw the vial filled with speed. Now, every once in a while, he throws the speed in her face like it was some moral paradox that she's not clear on. In those instances, she grabs control of the argument by letting fly a derisive, condescending laugh and explaining, with a show of really strained patience, that there's no paradox whatsoever, since the issue is one of dominance. She completely dominates the drug and if she ever sees, in the briefest of moments, an erosion of her control, she'll kick and be as clean as day one. Lenore feels this is the core of truth in her act. She monitors herself. She'd like to do without the drug, but life is so goddamn crazy right now. The hours are unreal, and everyone has their limit.

She puts down the weight, leans forward, turns up the volume of the set. A voice yelps, *Get on your knees and give me your money.* She turns off the set, gets up, and moves to the bedroom wall. She presses her ear against it. She can hear the radio next door. Ike is up, probably putting the coffee on.

3

Ike opens the door with that annoying isn't-it-a-great-day smile on his face. Lenore walks in nodding and saying, 'Yeah, yeah, yeah, I know, just tell me the coffee's ready.'

She sits down at his butcherblock table and grabs the front section of the newspaper and says, 'I don't have much time. Jesus, did you burn the toast again?'

She doesn't expect an answer and he doesn't offer one. Instead he slides a brimming mug of jet-black and steaming hot coffee in front of her. The mug is green and says in bold, black letters: *Don't Speak to Me till This Mug Is Empty.* Lenore scans the headlines and mutters, 'God, these Muslims are really stepping over the line.'

Ike sits down opposite her, stays silent but drums his fingers on the table in a way he knows upsets her. Lenore knows he knows and so looks up from the paper, head cocked and smiling.

• • •

Yesterday, all day long, Ike had this crazy idea that mushroomed. He'd been thinking about a dinner he'd had with Lenore, American chop suey and garlic bread. And like most of the dinners they shared together, Lenore's plate had gone cold while she told Ike the details of a recent bust. Lenore could tell a tremendous story. She started slowly and built a solid, well-defined foundation. She gave you a quick rundown on all the key players and, though brief, her descriptions were always so unique you never had any trouble keeping characters straight. She used an impressive array of cop jargon without sounding forced or clichéd, without sounding like some 1970s TV show. She gave you a basic idea of the history of the particular dealers she was after, the cities they were out of, the families they did their bartering with, the prisons they'd done their time in. And then she'd start hitting you with the procedural stuff, how they built a case, who'd gone undercover, who'd applied pressure to whom, who was tailed and who was bugged, and who was roughed up.

But, without a doubt, Lenore's forte, her real, natural talent, was given full play when she narrated the actual arrest, when her voice would kick into that low, machine-gun rhythm and she'd manage to detail every angle of the climax, the broken-down doors, the screaming in many languages, the drawn weapons and flushing toilets, the cursing and face slapping and biting, and, of course, as dependable as Jack Webb, the reading of the Miranda card, the recitation of civil rights due all in the process of arrest.

Ike loves Lenore's stories. He could listen for hours. He wishes he had that ability to create a clear and fluid picture of confusing events. He wishes he had the energy and intelligence and, maybe, confidence to make it exciting but plausible, well paced but detailed.

And then, yesterday, while breaking down a basket of flats by zip code, the thought hit him in one quick burst: he could record Lenore's voice. He could get her stories down on tape. And, even better, he could transcribe the tapes onto paper, type them up at night. If the stories enthrall him, he's sure they would grab others. He and Lenore could turn a good buck on them. He ached for the day to go by so he could hit her with the idea and see how she felt. He'd stress that she wouldn't have to do a thing, just sit and eat and talk like always. He'd take care of the rest. He assured himself that even if she were hesitant for some reason, he'd stress the possibility of big, fast income and the things it could buy: that Porsche she mentions every week, the Soloflex machine she keeps reading about.

• • •

'So,' Ike says.

Lenore raises her eyebrows.

'Well?' he tries.

She shrugs.

'Just tell me. Did you break it off or not?'

She sighs, drops the paper to the table, sinks back into the chair, lets her mouth drop open slightly. They stare at each other until she gives in and says, 'Look, Ike, what do you want? I worked eighteen hours straight, okay? There were other people around us most of that time. I couldn't...'

'C'mon, sis,' Ike says, looking down to the table, shaking his head, 'there were people there? The whole time?'

'What I'm saying is, I didn't get the right opportunity, okay? Hey, believe me, I've ended more relationships than you've ever started, all right? I want to do this correctly.'

Ike is smiling now, looking up at the ceiling, his head bent all the way back on his neck. 'You want to keep him on the line. You want to play with him a little. And...'

He pauses to annoy her, and though she knows that's the plan, she gives in to it and says, 'Yeah, what?'

Ike brings his head up and stares at her, then he shrugs and says, 'And you're not so sure he'll be that easy to replace down at the Route 61 Motor Lodge...'

There's a long, weird pause that hangs between them, then Lenore bursts out laughing, shakes the table, spills a little coffee, and says, 'Jesus, Ike, who're you kidding?'

For a second, Ike doesn't know what to do, then he joins in, spontaneously letting out a squeal, thrilled to hear his sister laugh.

The sound dies out into long, breath-grabbing gasps and then it's quiet in the kitchen again.

'You want some fruit or something?' Ike asks.

Lenore shakes her head. 'No thanks. They'll have Danish or donuts at the briefing.' She sips at her mug, then asks, 'Hey, Ike, I was wondering, you planning on taking any vacation time? You got a lot of vacation time saved up, right?'

'I've got, like, four weeks coming.'

'I was thinking, we should hit the Caribbean, you know, some nice island. Or maybe Bermuda or someplace. We should check it out.'

Ike hesitates. 'I don't know, Lenore. We're talking big dollars for a trip like that. Two or three grand just for a week.'

She shakes her head. 'No way. Where did you hear those prices? Shaw was telling me she went to Aruba for under a grand…'

'Yeah, okay,' Ike spits out, 'but when did she go? That's the whole thing. You go in like August or something and it's a big difference. I mean who wants to go in August?'

Lenore stares, sucks her cheeks in slightly, lets them out, and says, 'Ike, you could choke the enthusiasm out of anything.'

'Look, Lenore, it's the same old argument. You never think about the future. About security. You don't have a dime in the bank, right? You make good money, but you don't save a thing. You want to buy some expensive weight machine. You want to buy a new car. You want to buy another rifle. Now it's a Caribbean vacation…'

'All right, all right,' she cuts him off. 'It was just an idea. Forget it. It was just a thought.'

Ike sees an opportunity and before he can think too much he says, 'You know, sis, you are right about me being a pain in the ass about things like this…'

'I didn't say—' she interrupts.

'No, no,' he interrupts, 'you're right. I mean, you might be a little, I don't know, impractical. But I'm just way too cautious. It's the truth. I mean, even at work, you know, it's a problem. It can be annoying.'

'You're just a little too…' She looks for the word. 'Conservative. Restrained.'

'No, it's the truth. I admit it. On the money.'

'You've just got to loosen up a little, Ike. For your own good.'

'Absolutely right,' he says.

They stare at each other, silent, Ike's head sort of bobbing nervously inside the collar of his powder-blue shirt. He runs a finger around his lips, as if he were some skier applying anti-chapping gel. He says, 'No, you're right. I've been thinking about this. Got to open up more, right? And I was thinking, you could help me on this, Lenore. And it could prove pretty beneficial to you as a bonus.'

She gives him the same look she uses on informants when she hates their story.

'What I was thinking, you know, there are ways of supplementing your income, okay, there are things we could do. Together.'

Lenore pulls her mug from her lips and spills a big puddle of it onto the table. She's laughing again, shaking her head, holding up her right hand in a 'stop' sign, trying to swallow, breathe, and talk at the same time.

'Oh no,' she finally manages. 'What? Tell me. Amway? I'm not selling Amway, Ike. No way. You'd be hiding in the other room watching TV while I was writing up orders for discount soap, right? Unh-uh.'

Ike gets a dishrag from the sink and slowly mops up her coffee.

'It's not Amway,' he says very slowly, letting her know he's a little hurt.

'Okay, good,' Lenore says. 'So what, then? You've been staying up late watching those guys in the polyester suits on those weird cable stations?'

'What guys?'

'You know. Those guys. There're all those guys. And they buy all this time on cable at like three A.M., right? They list them as "paid commercial announcements" in *TV Guide*. They've all got a gimmick and usually it's got to do with real estate. Like buying up foreclosed properties at government auctions and stuff. Though

I guess they're branching out, 'cause I've seen them do shows on like getting fifty credit cards and tapping them all for cash advances…'

'You watch this stuff?' Ike says, straightening up from the table, incredulous, the dishrag hanging from his hand.

Lenore hesitates, then says, 'Well, if I can't sleep…'

Ike interrupts. 'Lenore,' he says, genuinely astounded by her, 'you get like twenty hours' sleep a week, you know. I mean, you work ridiculous hours. So when you get to come home, I can't believe…'

She's defensive. She says, 'Yeah, well, it's not always so easy to fall off, Ike. I mean, I'm not like you…'

'I don't sleep that great, believe me,' he says.

There's quiet again. They both stare at the floor until Ike says, 'I still don't get the credit card thing. I mean, you've got to pay all the cash advances back, right? So how does that put money in your pocket?'

'I think it's what you do with the money before the bill comes. It's like some fast turnover, some quick thirty-day investment or something. I don't know. It's not like I pay attention.'

Ike considers this, then says, 'It's just, I think you could find a cooking show or something. Even the religious channels…'

Lenore rolls her eyes. 'Oh, for Christ sake, Ike, I'd rather watch a nature show on snakes or rats. The religious channels, Jesus.'

'They can be pretty interesting,' Ike says, 'you pick the right one…'

Lenore's not about to give on this point. 'They're all scumbags,' she says. 'Every one.'

'I guess,' Ike says. He knows that now it'll be close to impossible to sell her on the crime-novel idea.

'What day are you off this week?' Lenore asks.

'Don't know yet. Ms. Barnes hasn't done the schedule yet.'

Lenore's eyes bug out of her head. *'Ms. Barnes,'* she repeats, making the name sound ridiculous.

'Give me a break,' Ike says, walking to the sink to wash out the rag.

'*Ms. Barnes?*' Lenore says louder, more sarcastic.

Ike turns around and folds his arms across his chest. 'Well, what the hell should I call her?'

'Well, God, Ike,' she says, 'it sounds like she's your third-grade teacher, c'mon. Jees, it sounds worse than that. It sounds like she's your third-grade teacher and you've got a crush on her, you know.'

Ike breathes in and out through his nose and says, 'Yeah, well, it's getting late, okay?'

'Okay, all right,' Lenore says, smiling, pleased with herself. 'I'm sorry. But you've got to admit… Ms. Barnes. C'mon, Ike.'

'So what do I say, "the supervisor"? "My supervisor"? That sounds worse.'

'No,' says Lenore, 'it doesn't sound worse. What's her first name?'

Ike clears his throat and says, 'Eva.'

'Eva,' Lenore repeats. 'I like that. Why wouldn't you call her Eva?'

'Yeah,' Ike says, 'why don't you just call Miskewitz Henry, right? You just don't. God, Lenore, why don't you call Zarelli Franny? That's his name, right? But you don't.'

'I call Miskewitz Lieutenant,' Lenore says.

'Well, we don't have ranks, you know.'

'I guess,' Lenore says. She'd like to press this Eva thing, dig a little and find out what makes Ike so touchy on the subject. But it's getting late and she wants to choose her seat at the conference table before the rest sit down.

'Listen, Lenore,' Ike says, 'about this extra-income thing…'

She waves him off and gulps down the rest of her coffee. 'Save it for dinner, okay? I'm running late.'

She jumps up from the table like someone had sent a jolt of electricity through her spine. She moves toward the back door like her feet were on fire, kisses Ike on the forehead, pulls open the door, and steps outside. She starts to walk around the house to her car, then stops for a second.

Inside, Ike hears her yell, 'Say hi to *Ms. Barnes* for me,' in a singsong, laugh-choked voice.

He whispers to himself, 'How can we possibly be related?' and pushes the back door closed with his foot.

He moves to the counter, bobs his tea bag. He thinks it wasn't that long ago that Lenore felt like a real twin. Someone must have really known who was older, who came out first. But Ma would never tell, always pleading ignorance. Knowing always mattered more to Lenore anyway. Ike was content, happy even, being half of a set. And he liked the paradox, even as a kid, instinctively, so connected, but so tremendously different. Not in the classic sense, not any light or dark deal, where one of them was the evil twin. That'd be too easy. It was more like a division of qualities. Lenore, Ike thought, came into the world, for whatever reason, with strength, power, conviction. Ike always thought her abundance of these traits derived from his lack of them. She got his share. But in their wake there were other things. Some awful, like chronic doubt and indecisiveness, but others desirable, like an easy ability to listen and observe. In some ways, Ike thinks, he's a perfect spy. He's almost invisible to most people, but he hears every word they speak, sees every muscle contract or expand. And he can remember it all. He's got a memory like some flawless Japanese camcorder. Both auditory and visual.

Ike thinks suddenly of how many people must fear Lenore. Probably more people fear his sister than Eva, his supervisor. Lenore comes into contact with more people than Eva. She touches more lives and in a much rougher way. And Lenore carries a huge weapon with her, day and night, that could blow pieces of your anatomy into dust. She carries a badge that enables her to pull you off any street in the city, slap you on the hood of a car, turn all your pockets inside out, run her hands over every inch of your body, insult your heritage or looks, and ask questions about your habits and whereabouts on any given night. Ike realizes that, to someone she doesn't love, Lenore could be the nightmare that never ends.

Ike fishes his tea bag out of his mug, squeezes it dry against the side of the mug, then dumps it in the basket. He gets the milk from the refrigerator, empties the last of it into the tea, and tosses the carton. He brings the mug to his lips, blows over the surface of the tea for a few seconds, then sips and burns his tongue. He puts the mug down on the table to cool, and wonders who would come out on top in a matchup between Eva and Lenore. Who would he bet on? They have such different methods. Eva is so cool and controlled, she's like a machine that was built with care and intelligence, made to give the maximum work, at the maximum efficiency, and to last for years to come. Lenore, on the other hand, is all fireworks, all noise and light. She's perpetually explosive. She makes every decision on the verge of violence. Just watching TV with her can be a draining, punishing experience. Once they watched *The Exorcist* together, late on a Saturday night. Ike was a lot more afraid of his twin sister than he was of any demon. She spent two hours snarling right back at the screen, warning Satan to leave poor little Linda Blair alone or she'd 'waste his pathetic ass back to hell.' Toward the end, Ike prayed that she wouldn't go next door and come back with her Magnum, pull an Elvis, and blow his Sony into hundreds of pieces.

4

Lenore grabs a black coffee in a small white Styrofoam cup. She walks over to the window side of the conference room and looks out over the highway. The speed is bothering her a little today, making her feel slightly claustrophobic. To take her mind off this trapped, breathless feeling, she thinks about how much she despises the architecture of the police station.

The biggest problem is the windows. Back when headquarters was down on Kristie Place, there were these gorgeous old floor-to-ceiling windows with arched tops. During the May riots of '69, someone lobbed a bomb through one. It happened to land on the dispatch board. No one was seriously hurt, but radio contact with all the cruisers was lost for days. With that incident in mind, and combined with the energy crisis of the late seventies, when they finally built the new building at Tubman Square, they brought in these bizarre skinny strips of windows, maybe only two or three inches in width, bulletproof and Thermopane, but also incapable of being opened to let in fresh air.

There are a lot of days when Lenore just wants to bring her Magnum up from the bunker and empty the chamber into one of those skinny windows until it shatters and falls to the ground. Today is one of those days.

The conference room is on the top floor of the police station and from where she stands she can look at the sparse traffic rolling down the interstate. She'd love to be out there now, out of this stupid briefing, in a metallic-teal Porsche, clocking one twenty-five toward no destination in particular. Instead, she's drinking bitter coffee, which she knows will only aggravate the speed jag, and hoping Zarelli doesn't come over and try to start a conversation.

Richmond, Shaw, and Peirce are grouped next to the side table that's crowded with the coffee urn and a cardboard platter of cheese and lemon Danish. Richmond is telling the women some long, confusing joke that has to do with a hooker and a talking parrot. No matter what the punch line is, there's no way it can warrant the effort he's giving the story.

Zarelli comes in the door with his hands in his pockets, wearing a dark gray suit, a strange white shirt with a long, pointy collar, and a red-and-gray-striped tie equipped with both tie tack and collar pin. He looks like he's headed to a funeral, Lenore thinks. Why the hell did he dress like this? Who is he trying to impress?

It's apparent that everybody else is a little confused by his clothes. Shaw and Peirce break their concentration from Richmond's story and give funny, squinty looks.

Peirce says, 'You got somewhere to go after this?'

Zarelli shakes his head deliberately and says, 'I like to dress up on occasion. Problem?'

Richmond, annoyed at the interruption, says, 'You look like a Bible salesman from ten years back.'

Zarelli just says, 'Thanks, Rich,' and moves to the table to pour himself a coffee. He nods over to Lenore a little too formally as he adds packet after packet of sugar to his drink. She thinks he seems nervous and unsure of himself, nothing like the Zarelli she knows and is tired of. As he lifts the coffee cup to his lips, she can see his hands tremble. She has two responses to this. The first is to wonder if somehow he's already picked up on her plans to sever the relationship, through vibrations in the air or some unconscious telepathy. The second is to wonder how those shaky hands can possibly cover her if they get caught in any life-or-death situations.

He starts to cross the room toward her. Her curiosity is a little piqued and now talking to him doesn't seem as unpleasant as it had moments ago. He looks like he's wearing rented shoes that are a size too big for his feet. He seems to shuffle across the floor, the coffee cup at his lips the whole time. There's a sheen of sweat glowing on his forehead. His shirt is buttoned at the neck and pushes against his Adam's apple. Lenore feels like gagging just watching it.

He reaches the window and stares out at the highway and begins to talk.

'Okay, Lenore,' he says. 'This is it.'

She thinks about turning mute, not responding at all, letting him summon up all his powers of language and communication to no avail. Instead she says flatly, 'This is what?'

'This is for real,' he says, his eyes starting to blink too fast. 'I've got an appointment, all right? I've made a goddamn appointment.'

'That's swell,' she says, 'an appointment.'

'It's the truth,' he says. 'I told you I was going to do it. Today's the day. This is the day. My life changes at noon today, all right? This is for real.'

She has to ask. 'What happens at noon today?'

He clears his throat, tries to wipe sweat from his top lip with his thumb. 'I'm meeting Marie today. For lunch. At noon. Today. I'm meeting Marie and I'm telling her it's over. The marriage is over. I'm breaking free. I've given it eight years and today it ends. I'm telling her to get a lawyer. At lunch. I'm meeting her at Fiorello's, okay?'

Lenore would like to drive a knee into his groin. The man dressed up in his best clothes to walk out on his wife. She knows that Fiorello's is where he proposed to Marie. And it's where he first took Lenore for drinks. She thinks Zarelli must be the never-ending soap opera for all the help at Fiorello's.

She takes a breath and gets ready to say, 'Like hell you are, you idiot,' but Miskewitz's voice booms around the room, 'Okay, people, can we get down to business, the mayor is a busy man.'

She turns around to see three people gathered around the lieutenant, just inside the doorway of the conference room. One is

Mayor Welby, looking, as always, wise and professorial in a subtle, gray, hand-tailored suit. Welby is a tall guy with a huge dome of a forehead like a Yankee minister, but also a small, always-trimmed mustache that gives him an ethnic look. You might think this would be a drawback for vote-getting, but Welby has grown into the pols' pol over the years. He plays City Hall like a master musician, knowing instinctively when to stroke, when to kick ass privately, and when to grab headlines with a rabid bashing of department managers and city councilors. He sticks to the basics – delegation of authority, the promise of no tax hikes in election years, and a flawless eye for just the right photo opportunity. He's a fairly lean guy and he's in his mid-fifties. The department has no real beef with him, though Miskewitz says he hasn't taken a stand yet on the pending contract talks. The mayor married later in life and has two kids just now entering high school. His wife is often seen, but never heard, at various dedication ceremonies. Lenore doesn't really have an opinion of him. She thinks that, like all politicians, he's a man of often empty words, and since she considers her own life to be one based on action rather than words, she thinks they live on opposite sides of a very thick fence.

Standing next to Welby, looking cocky and impatient, is Lehmann, a Federal cop out of DEA that Lenore has dealt with once before. Once was enough. Lehmann is old-school and not too crazy about women working narcotics. He's wearing a blue standard-issue windbreaker and jeans, holding his aviator sunglasses in his hands and chewing on the end of one stem.

The third person is a mystery man. He's the tallest Oriental Lenore has ever seen. She'd put him at six two or three. He looks to be in his mid to late thirties, 175 pounds, all of it tight. Could be a runner, maybe even a marathoner. He's got a closely cropped head of jet-black hair and a long angular face. He's dressed in charcoal slacks, a pale blue button-down shirt, a navy knit tie, and a herringbone jacket. Lenore looks to his feet and proves herself right – he's got on penny loafers.

The guy is carrying a faded leather satchel that bulges slightly in the middle, and as she watches he shifts it from his hand up into his arms to cradle it like a sleeping child. She can't really guess at his specific nationality. He could be Chinese, Korean, Cambodian. She's just awful at making the distinctions, even though the Asian population of Quinsigamond has grown tremendously in the past ten years and she knows dozens of Asians personally. She's embarrassed by this weakness, but doesn't know how you might effectively cure it. Is there a reference book you could work with?

Zarelli touches her arm and she pulls away at once and moves to the table to sit down between Shaw and Richmond. Mayor Welby sits down in the head seat, Miskewitz on his left and Peirce on his right. The Oriental guy sits down next to the lieutenant. Lehmann takes the end-seat opposite the mayor, and Zarelli slides into the remaining seat.

Miskewitz sits forward and says, 'All right, people, I thank you for coming in this morning for this briefing, especially considering how some of you finished up work a few hours ago. Mayor Welby has a few things to say to you.' He sinks back into his chair, clearly uncomfortable with this event.

But the mayor picks up with a casual grace. First he smiles all around the table, lingering, a second too long, Lenore thinks, on Peirce. Then he folds his hands in front of him and says, 'Well, you all know who I am. This is Officer Lehmann out from the Boston office of the DEA. Some of you have met him before, I believe. And I'd like to introduce you all to Dr. Frederick Woo, on loan to us today from St. Ignatius, where he's a lecturing fellow in linguistics and language theory. Have I got that correct, Fred?'

The Oriental guy smiles and gives a small, modest nod.

The mayor continues, 'I know that right now you're all wondering why a bureaucrat is here to waste your valuable time battling what often, I'm sure, seems like an unwinnable situation on our city streets. I wish I could tell you I'm here to bring you some good news' – his voice drops – 'but I'm afraid that's not the situation today.'

He slides his chair back from the table and stands, a little too dramatically. He walks over to the windows that Lenore hates, and gazes outside for a moment, then returns to start a slow, awful pace, in a circle around the table. Lenore can tell Miskewitz hates every second of this.

'I suppose,' the mayor says, 'I'm here today as a symbol more than anything else, a suggestion to you of how serious a problem situation we're in.'

Lenore wonders why the man can't just say what's going on. Why does everything have to have a prologue? Why do guys like Welby always have to turn on the dramatics?

'It's no secret that over the past two years, drug traffic in Quinsigamond has increased geometrically. I've got the papers on my desk that prove it. You people don't need to see papers. You see the real thing, every day, walking around the muck of Bangkok Park.'

Lenore is cringing inside, caught in a spasm between laughter and disgust. What a pathetic actor this guy is. And what an asshole. She thinks he's taken his dialogue, heart and soul, straight from some low-rent B movie where self-righteous, renegade, vigilante cops fight ethnic, satanic dealers who lurk in the shadows of schoolyards.

'You are an underfunded, understaffed group of civil servants attempting, no, let's be honest, staking your lives in a battle against what has become in just a few short decades one of our largest, most intricate and ruthless multinational industries. To be frank, people, you are in an absurd situation.'

He takes a breath, comes behind his own chair, grips the back of it like the conference table was a speeding ride in an amusement park.

'And detectives,' he says in a fake-tired voice, 'things just got worse.'

He pauses and looks around the table as if he were waiting for people to audibly sigh. No one obliges and he sits back down in his head chair and continues.

'Now, I am not here today to break down what minimal morale you have left. But it is my duty to let you know about the extent of the problem we're about to face. And I want each and every one of you to feel that we're facing it together. You have my unlimited support in this effort. We can't pull any punches here, ladies and gentlemen. The time for polite conversation is long over.'

Lenore wants to lean over the man, scream at him in the same manner she's grilled dozens of informants and suspects. She wants to be less than an inch from his face, take in a lungful of air, and yell, 'Cut the bullshit and tell me what you know.'

'I'm sure I sound melodramatic to some of you. But what you'll soon hear about today is a worse plague than the crack explosion we suffered two summers ago. Worse than that heroin harvest out of Burma in the fall of...' he trails off, looking to the ceiling for the year.

'Eighty-three,' Miskewitz mutters, and Lenore knows he's thrown out a random year.

'Eighty-three,' the mayor repeats. 'It's a different animal this time, people.'

He takes a long pause for an effect that just doesn't pan out and says, 'At this point I think it's best to turn the story over to Agent Lehmann.'

Lehmann stays seated, but tosses his sunglasses out in front of him, like he's tired of talking before he's even begun.

'The substance Mayor Welby is talking about is a derivative of methyl-sermocilan. You'll come to know it more commonly as "Lingo," the label Dr. Woo has given it.'

Lehmann speaks like a man in a constant, simmering rage over having to walk among inferior people. He slaps a manila folder onto the table and opens it.

'These look familiar to anyone?' he asks, tossing a pile of 8 ×

10 black-and-white photos onto the middle of the table. Everyone reaches for a picture. Lenore pulls up a full-body picture of a naked woman, laid out faceup on a silver slab, photographed from above. Even in black and white, maybe more so in black and white, she has that pasty but shadowy look of the dead. There are thick welts and contusions across her abdomen. The standard tag dangles from her toe in the corner of the photo.

Richmond looks over her shoulder and says, 'Last week's murder-suicide up on Grimaldi Drive. Domestic bloodbath. The Swanns, right? He slit her throat and hung himself. Or do I have it backward?'

'You don't have it at all,' Lehmann says. 'Try to follow me on this. About six months back, some of my people based in Boston were asked to put a file together on a married couple, Leo and Inez Swann. Late thirties, both supposedly brilliant, degrees from Princeton, Cornell, and MIT, where they met. They lived here in the Windsor Hills section of Quinsigamond. Money spilling out of both their pockets. They worked, until recently, at the Institute for Experimental Biochemistry. They had a specialty that the doctor here can tell you more about—'

The Oriental guy, Woo, takes this as a signal to speak, though it's clear to everyone else that it's not.

'The Swanns were working on advanced drug therapy for treatment of what is termed "language delayed" children.'

Lehmann rolls his eyes.

'Sounds a little off your beat,' Lenore says.

Lehmann shrugs, still looking at Woo, trying to make it clear that he screwed up, that he'll let him know when it's his turn to speak. 'Like everything else it was strictly accidental. The FBI was doing some standard mob-sitting down San Remo Ave. Had a wire on a midlevel errand boy of Gennaro Pecci. Gennaro and his men go to dinner one night down Fiorello's Restaurant.'

Lenore can't help but look over at Zarelli, who's staring, unblinking, at Lehmann.

'And who are the Don's dinner guests but the Drs. Swann.'

Richmond states the obvious for everyone. 'Unusual pairing.'

Lehmann gives an indulgent smile back at him and goes on. 'The wire gave us nothing. They didn't discuss a damn thing of interest. The weather. Recent vacations. Local politics.'

Mayor Welby snaps into a practiced smile and says, 'Should I call a lawyer, Al?'

'Everyone agrees it was a size-'em-up meet. Both parties get a chance to feel each other out. Make an introduction. Establish contacts. Once the bureau got confirmation on the identity of the Swanns, they called us.'

'You think the Swanns were considering a mid-life career change?' Peirce says.

'Or at least a new sideline. There's definitely a precedent for chemical whiz kids like Leo and Inez turning a good dollar by leasing themselves out.'

'Mob chemists,' the lieutenant says.

Lehmann nods. 'Big demand for synthetic kicks lately. Big upswing. I've got the numbers. More controllable than run-of-the-mill organic crap. No importation problems. Chemical coke. Supertranqs, designer things.'

'I'm just saying,' Miskewitz says, 'two Ivy League yuppies from Windsor Hills seem like a little stretch.'

Lehmann gets annoyed. 'Today's labs, Lieutenant, are a hell of a lot more complicated than they were just three years back. But more importantly, it's unlikely the Swanns were dining at Fiorello's for the lasagna.'

It's a line that would only come out of the TV and Lenore hates Lehmann for saying it. But Miskewitz shuts up and Lehmann goes on.

'A month after the dinner meeting with Pecci, the Swanns resign their positions at the Institute. There were a lot of bad feelings. A lot of interoffice politics. A lot of fighting over grant money and allocations. The Swanns broke off and rented office space at the new industrial park up near the airport.'

'Place is a ghost town,' Richmond says. 'Developer's supposed to go Chapter Eleven any day now.'

'I don't think Leo and Inez were too interested in neighbors. They set up shop as consultants. They tried to make contacts with the bigger pharmaceutical boys. They called themselves Synaboost Inc.'

'You're saying,' Zarelli tries, 'that they were going through the motions. That the real contact was down San Remo with Pecci and family.'

Lehmann ignores him for some reason. 'Anything bother you about those photos?' he asks the table in general.

Lenore tosses her photo back onto the original pile and says, in a bland, bored voice, 'Nobody's throat is cut.'

Richmond sits up in his chair and looks toward Miskewitz. 'I swear homicide said a cut throat. I had lunch with Berkman. "Cut throat," he says.'

'Some facts about the Swann case,' Mayor Welby says, 'have been altered.'

'Within the department?' Richmond says, showing too much concern. Lenore feels like sliding a note to him that reads, *Shut up now.*

'Both bodies,' Lehmann says, 'were found hanging. The housecleaner called police when she couldn't get in on the second day in a row. Both bodies were tortured extensively, in very particular ways, before they were hung. The FBI was notified and the domestic dispute story was cooked up immediately.'

He pauses, reaches down, and shuffles the photos back into an ordered pile. 'We've seen the method of execution before. Definitely gangland. Definitely immigrant. There's some dispute as to whether we're talking Hong Kong or Panama.'

He pauses again, like he's learned an important lesson from Welby, then says, 'The tongues were cut out of both their heads. My people came in on the heels of the bureau. We sent a team in, sealed off the house, and spent two days combing it over. We found two of these' – he reaches into his windbreaker pocket – 'hidden inside a spice jar labeled "garlic salt."'

He pulls from his pocket a small plastic ball, like a bubble, like one of those clear round containers found in the candy-dispenser machines at discount stores. Sealed inside it and held solidly in place by some kind of clear gel, is a small, scarlet-colored pill, cut in the shape of the letter Q. Lehmann places the bubble on the table and gives it a roll. All their eyes follow it as it spins down an awkward, wobbly path and finally drops off the table's edge and into Lenore's lap.

She looks around the table at everyone, then picks it up, weighs it in her hand, holds it up close to her eyeball like it was a jeweler's loupe. Whatever the gel is inside the bubble, it makes everything she sees seem hyper-clear, more colorful, solid, more real than her normal vision. She turns her head till she's looking at Zarelli's pleading, anxious face popping from the knifelike collar of his shirt. She pulls the bubble away, places it back on the table, and gives it a small push. It rolls across to Dr. Woo, who lets it drop over the edge into his waiting palm.

As if taking this as a cue, Lehmann says, 'The doctor can give you some idea of what's inside the container,' and starts wiping the lenses of his sunglasses on the fleecy inside of his jacket.

Dr. Woo nods and puts the bubble back on the table in front of him and stabilizes it with his hand. It sits like some weird egg, some freak produced by a marriage of nature and technology. He lifts his satchel onto the table and takes out a stack of papers that he hands to Miskewitz, indicating that they should be passed around. Each handout has a couple dozen pages. The lieutenant takes one for himself and hands them down the table.

Lenore takes her copy and thumbs through it. The printing is too small, she thinks, it'd give anyone a headache by page two. There are also graphs, charts, columns of numbers, and illustrations. The last page is filled with a large and very intricate picture of a brain. The page is crammed with writing and dozens of black lines that stretch between areas of the brain and definitions of what the areas are called. Lenore thinks the odds are pretty good that she won't read a single word. If the doc can't give her the basics in conversation, he's in trouble. She's got a backlog of reading of her own at home, stuff that could refine the direction of her life, give her even more of an edge than she's already got.

Dr. Woo prepares to speak by making his hand into a fist, bringing it up in front of his mouth, and forcing himself to cough a few times. Lenore interprets this to mean that he'll speak too softly and be a boring pain in the ass. But as soon as the first words flow from his mouth, she knows she's completely wrong. He's got a beautiful speaking voice, low, distinct, strong but rich with hints of emotion and emphasis.

'As Mayor Welby said, my name is Frederick Woo, and I've been asked to come here today for two reasons. First, to try to give you a brief and intelligible explanation of what the small red pill that you see inside this capsule can do to the human brain. And second, because I consulted briefly with Leo and Inez Swann during their tenure with the Institute.'

He gives this sly, almost mischievous grin, and stares directly at Lenore. For a second, it seems like he's got nothing more to say, but then he slaps the table with a flat palm and, without taking his eyes off her, continues.

'Well, let's give it a shot.' He reaches into his satchel again, like a magician going for a rabbit, and he pulls out a plastic model of a brain. Like the kind you'd see in some high school science class, all color-coded and with parts that can be removed. It's about the size of a softball, maybe a little smaller. Woo puts it out on the table in front of him and Lenore thinks it suddenly resembles a small pet, something the doctor needs for companionship.

'I was formally trained as a specialist in linguistics, then took a detour at the end of my training and went back to square one to get a second degree in neuropsychology. This,' and he places his long index finger on the top of the model brain, 'is where those two fields intersect. What I've been asked to do this morning is quite impossible. So let's get started.'

He leans forward, places his whole hand over the top of the brain, and begins to talk rapidly and in a friendly, joking manner.

'Okay. We've all got one of these, I'm pretty sure. It's a very useful piece of equipment. There's a lot we don't know about it. A lot we thought we knew that was proved wrong. We guess a lot about this organ. I personally think it scares us a bit. Because so many answers are buried inside it. And we don't know if those answers will free us up, prove us to be the supermen we really secretly hope we are. Or if the answers will limit us, show us to be animals that know a lot of impressive parlor tricks and little more.'

He takes his hand off the brain and points to a specific area on the left side of the model.

'This little town here is called the anterior speech cortex. That's its official name. You, like me, can call it Broca's area. It's a hell of a town. Got quite a little industry going here. But, you know, like any growing industry, every now and then you have some kind of rough industrial accident…'

Under his breath, Richmond whispers to Lenore, 'What the Christ is this dickhead talking about?'

'Guess what happens when Broca's area has one of those industrial accidents?'

The table is silent. The mayor looks uncomfortable. He stares down at his folded hands like he was praying.

Woo looks at Lenore and says, 'Detective…'

'Thomas.'

'Detective Thomas, any idea?'

Lenore sighs and says, 'Planeload of lawyers flies in the next day.'

The table laughs and Woo loves it. He gives a huge smile, then moves his tongue in a circle, licking his lips.

'A wonderful guess by Detective Thomas. Close, but no. You have an accident in this area, you can't speak. You're an instant mute. You don't have any choice in the matter.'

He moves his index finger to an area toward the back of the model.

'This is another hot little town call Wernicke's area. They have an industrial accident here, bingo, you can't understand language, spoken to you, or written down for you to read, though you might be able to babble, make incomprehensible languagelike noise that no one else can understand.'

'You're an instant idiot,' Peirce says.

Woo shakes his head. 'No, not exactly, though you might be mistaken for one. At this point you're all asking yourselves why you had to get up this morning to listen to all this.'

He grabs the bubble and places it next to the brain.

'As Agent Lehmann told you, two red pills were found in the course of searching the Swanns' home. This is the second one. The first one we tested the hell out of. Both in the lab and—' he pauses, smiles – 'up at Spooner Correctional Institute...'

The mayor interrupts and says, 'None of you heard that, please,' and Woo goes on.

'Because of the constraints of time and other factors, I'm forced to do some inexcusable generalizing right now. Broca's area is that part of your brain where language is produced. Wernicke's area is that part of your brain where language is understood and interpreted. When you swallow that red pill, it does something very interesting to you. It makes a crazy dash straight for both of those parts of your brain. Most drugs can't do that. Your brain is usually protected by a curtain of protein that acts like a moat. Some things can get through. Like a lot of items from your line of work. Alcohol, cocaine, heroin. This red pill gets through with a vengeance, with an ease I've never seen before. And then it seems to know exactly where it wants to go. It seems to have heard all about these places called Broca and Wernicke. It seems to want to move right in, make itself at home. It gets busy right away. What I'm saying is that the drug somehow supercharges those two areas. It gives them a kind of speed and strength and flexibility, if you will, that they just don't normally have.'

Woo lets his eyes roam around the table, trying to read faces and gauge understanding.

'Now, in its quest to upgrade your standard-issue language equipment, Lingo exhibits some side effects. It sends a few fellow travelers off to the pleasure centers of the brain. I'd consider this an inherent perk in the drug's main business trip. There's a big adrenaline release, like a solid amphetamine rush, but it's very controlled, very regulated, an incremental buildup. It would most likely lack any of the jaggedness or anxiousness produced by the badly processed street speed that you people deal with.'

Woo pauses, takes a breath and smiles slightly.

'We gave a sample of the drug to two' – he pauses – 'volunteers at Spooner Correctional. I don't think I'm overstating the case to say that what I observed in one hour could have a revolutionary impact on fields as diverse as brain biochemistry and neuropsychology, cybernetics, linguistics, all the semiological disciplines, both hard and soft…'

His words trail off as he realizes the futility of trying to make this group share his reverie.

'We administered small amounts of the drug to two inmates and then sequestered them in a lab under absolute physiological and neurological monitoring. After approximately five minutes, we began to perceive certain changes in their general conditions, reflexes and motor responses, this type of thing. Their heart rates increased, but not alarmingly. Their brain activity was slightly elevated. But to cut to the chase, ladies and gentlemen, the evidence that something quite significant was happening within the confines of their skulls came straight from their own mouths.'

He stops speaking, pauses for any questions or comments, making sure curiosity has peaked. Then he reaches once again into the satchel and withdraws a tape recorder. He places it next to the brain model and the bubble, adjusts a volume knob, then hits a button. The cassette inside starts turning and there's a hiss of noise from a small speaker.

First, Woo's own voice is heard, in a whisper, saying, *'Tape three. Two-fifteen p.m.'*

Then there's a moment of quiet with the exception of some vague rumbling noise, caused, most likely, by the recorder being moved around. There's some coughing, followed by the slightly echoing sound of a metal door being opened and closed.

Woo says, *'James Lee Partridge, age twenty-four, scoring for the WAIS-R – verbal, eighty-one; performance, eighty-four; full scale, eighty-two. Scoring for the WRAT – reading, grade three-point-two; arithmetic, grade four-point-eight; spelling, grade three-point-nine.'*

There's a pause, then Woo's voice, quietly.

'All right, now, are you feeling okay, Jimmy Lee?'

A new voice, young, nervous, says, *'Just the headache is all.'*

'Do you think you can read this? Here, just take a look... yes, that page there, fine.'

Jimmy Lee Partridge goes through some awful, phlegmy throat-clearing, takes a deep breath in through a clogged nose and reads: *'When... the... day... of...'*

He reads in small, short blasts, word by word, as if they were meant to stand separately from one another. He reads them without any accent or intonation, in the manner that a sobbing, breath-grabbing child tries to speak.

On the tape, Woo's voice whispers, *'Start over, and concentrate, Jimmy Lee.'*

There's another pause and Lenore imagines the convict is trying to read the words to himself, before saying them aloud. She doesn't like listening to the tape. For one reason or another, it makes her uncomfortable. But she makes herself, tells herself that, like a lot of uncomfortable things, it's an important part of her job.

Jimmy Lee Partridge starts again, and this time the words flow together without any noticeable pause or effort: *'When the day of Pentecost had come, they were all together in one place. And suddenly a sound came from heaven...'*

Jimmy Lee breaks off into something of a cackle, his voice gets loud and thrilled and surprised and he says, *'Pretty goddamn good, huh, Doc?'*

Woo just says, *'Once again, Jimmy Lee.'*

And he reads: *'When the day of Pentecost had come, they were all together in one place. And suddenly a sound came from heaven like the rush of a mighty wind, and it filled all the house where they were sitting. And there appeared to them tonguesasoffiredistributedandrestingoneachoneofthemandthey wereallfilledwiththeholyspiritandbegantospeakinothertonguesas thespiritgavethemutterancenow...'*

Something happens. Lenore listens and stares at the recorder. She thinks something must be wrong with the recorder. But then she notices the same expression on all the other faces at the table.

Jimmy Lee is reading so fast that it seems like a joke, like those TV ads where the pitchman tries to cram as many words of salesmanship into thirty seconds as is humanly possible. And then some. Jimmy Lee's voice is going so fast he's starting to sound like one of the chipmunks from that cartoon.

'Andresidentsofmesopotamiajudeaandcappadociapontusandasi aphrygiaandpamphyliaegyptandpartsoflibyabelongingtocyrene andvisitorsfromromebothjewsandproselytescretansand arabianswehearthemtellinginourowntonguesthemightyworks ofgodandallwereamazezzzzzzzzzzzzzzzzzzzz...'

And the voice turns into something like the sound of a common summer insect recorded at a loud volume with a sensitive microphone. Something you'd hear on a nature show as you switched the channels on the TV on a lazy weekend. It's just an ongoing buzz, a harsh, nervous-making, buzzing sound, and after a while Lenore can't tell whether it's really out there or just in her ear, in her head, a product of her own sinuses and faulty eustachian tube.

Woo punches the recorder off and looks around the table at the troubled faces. He's enjoying the reaction, Lenore thinks. It allows him to feel both essential to our work and a cut above us. In that moment of watching Woo's face watching her own, she understands that the doctor has an ego that towers over the mayor's, and Lehmann's and Zarelli's combined.

'He was reading from a Bible that we happened to have handy,' Woo says. 'But it could have been any book and the results would have been the same. Let me add to your amazement, all right? If I could go back to the prison today and ask him what he'd read for me, he would repeat it verbatim, at the same speed. And our tests show that his comprehension was one hundred percent.'

He pauses, then says, 'Before I answer any of your questions, let me risk poisoning your amazement with fear.'

He ejects the cassette from the machine, flips it over, and inserts the reverse side into the bed. He hits the rewind button until the tape stops, then presses Play.

His whispered, theatrical tape voice comes on, saying, *'Tape six, four forty-five p.m. Conversational flow between James Lee Partridge and William Robbins.'*

There are two voices talking at once. They're both speaking extremely rapidly and Lenore can't separate them or follow the topic of their discussion. She thinks it has to do with women and/or sex, but she's not sure. She thinks she's pulled out the words *grab, bra, leg, kiss, Carrie, fifteen, Mustang, rubber* and *screw.* But she's not sure of any of them and the longer the tape goes on the more difficult it gets to distinguish any of it until finally all the language blurs once again into that amplified fly-noise, an endless buzz that makes the hairs on Lenore's neck stand up.

When it's clear the buzzing is driving everyone at the table crazy, Woo punches the recorder off.

Peirce is the first to speak. 'You're telling us that those two people on the tape, those two convicts, were speaking just then. Having a conversation, right?'

Woo nods. 'That's absolutely right, Detective. In excess of fifteen hundred words per minute passed back and forth between each of them. And that's not all of it. There was a level of contact, a level of understanding, passing between them that's difficult to relay to you. They were completely conscious of and continually integrating body language, changes in musculature, eye signals. There was a degree of speed and comprehension present in that dialogue that you or I...'

Lenore can't help herself. She blurts out, 'Why are we involved?'

Mayor Welby says, 'We'll be getting to that, Detective.'

There's an awkward beat, then Woo, staring at Lenore, says, 'No time like the present, I suppose.'

From the bottomless satchel he withdraws two of his own 8 × 10 black-and-white photos, places them flat on the table, and slides them to Lenore. She picks them up, knowing already what they are. She's seen too many of this type of photo. She knows this because it's lost the ability to shock her. The first picture is labeled *Partridge*. The second is labeled *Robbins*. They're both morgue shots, taken from directly above the subject, under the harsh white light of powerful fluorescents. The photos show the subjects from the shoulders up, their heads resting on plain white sheets that Lenore knows are covering stainless-steel slab tables. The subjects' heads are both shaved. In both photos, there are bullet holes in the head and face. In Partridge's case, the upper left-hand portion of his forehead has been blown away entirely.

Lenore stares up into Woo's face and passes the pictures absentmindedly to Richmond.

'Don't jump to any conclusions,' Woo says, almost under his breath.

'In tandem with this is an additional effect that I, personally, find fascinating. The pathologist's studies on both Partridge and

Robbins showed an inordinate buildup of sperm cells and seminal plasma in the testes and urethral glands and a severe retraction of the muscles around the ductus deferens.'

'In English, please,' Lehmann says without hiding his impatience.

Woo nods as he speaks. 'Both men were sexually stimulated. Very stimulated. Without the presence of any external erotic materials. Again, we were doing language tests.'

'Speed, Spanish fly, and a Berlitz course in one quick pop,' Lenore says.

'Let's not jump the gun, Officer. We don't know that these effects would present themselves in a lower dosage—'

Lenore ignores him. 'Quite a commodity. You take it to speak in tongues and as a bonus you get sex and power. Who's going to want TV anymore?'

'And the downside?' Peirce says, refocusing the table's attention on Woo.

'The downside,' says Woo, still looking at Lenore, 'is its unpredictability. At full dosage, you can end up with what you heard on the tape. Homicidal rage. And death.'

He waits until the photos have made their way around most of the table, then says, with his index finger pointed in their general direction, 'This is where you people become involved. Because of our limited testing and the complexity of the drug's chemical base, we've been unable to find out what a tolerable dosage might be. It's theoretically possible that the individual's language capacities can play a part in the drug's level of intensity.'

Lehmann pipes in with, 'Crack and ice are bubble gum compared with this shit.' Then he glances down toward the mayor and says awkwardly, 'Excuse the language.'

The photos come back to Lenore, who says, 'How'd this happen?'

Woo takes a deep breath. Lenore thinks it's for effect.

Woo says, 'This is a very powerful, but very unstable substance. From my observations I believe there to be three distinct stages of consequences to ingestion. The first you just heard, phenomenal increases in linguistic ability and comprehension. The second consequence follows directly on the heels of the first, and it's a stunning, erotic high, a sexual euphoria, a burst of intoxication to rival anything you've come across recently, I assure you.'

'And the last...' Lenore pauses, then says, 'Consequence?'

Woo gives an awful and smug grin and says, 'Probably just what you're guessing, Detective. Paranoia that increases unchecked, very likely to the borders of schizophrenia, if not beyond. Accompanied by a limitless and very shocking rage. A homicidal rage.'

There's silence until Lenore says, 'There was no way to prevent this?'

Woo shakes his head. 'It's unlikely in this extreme condition that any tranquilizer would have done much good. But to be honest with you, we were somewhat unprepared for the explosion. The guards overreacted. I'm sure in your line of work you can understand how certain tragedies can be unavoidable. In retrospect we often see options that may not have actually existed at the time.'

Lenore ignores the rest of the table and says evenly, 'I'm not sure we know very much about each other's line of work.'

Woo nods and says, in the same tone, 'Perhaps we can correct this in the days to come.'

Zarelli comes alive and asks, 'Well, what happens now? I mean, the convicts are dead. You burn their files and you burn the pill inside that bubble there, and, I guess, DEA—' he gives a head motion toward Lehmann – 'tracks down the deal on the consulting firm and all...'

'Not exactly,' Lehmann says, staring down at his sunglasses. 'When we found the pills inside the Swanns' spice jar they were wrapped in a piece of paper.' He takes a very small piece of crumpled-up paper from his jacket pocket and lays it on the table. 'Just a small piece of scrap paper. Except that it had a phone number written on it.'

'That connected to?' Lenore says.

'Hotel Penumbra.'

The detectives all look at each other and Lenore says, 'The Capital of Bangkok Park.'

Lehmann says, 'Yeah. And I don't think Leo and Inez were looking to book a getaway weekend, do you?'

'What about Pecci?' Richmond asks.

Lehmann shrugs. 'Could be a deal couldn't be cut with the family and the Swanns started looking elsewhere for connections and backers for their new venture.'

'Is there any indication,' Peirce asks, 'that any contact was made between the Swanns and any other Bangkok brokers?'

Lehmann shrugs. 'No idea. Bangkok is your sewer. We decided that step one was to get you people involved.'

'If the stuff is out there,' Lenore says, 'we'll know about it soon enough.' She slides the morgue photos back at Woo.

He collects them back into his satchel and says, 'I would say that's a correct assumption.'

The mayor stands up abruptly and says, 'I think we all know the critical nature of what we're dealing with. Now, I'm due back at City Hall. I leave you people to coordinate your efforts, but I want to assure you that if there's anything whatsoever that my office can do, please, have the lieutenant call at any time.'

He gives a bouncing, loose-necked nod around the table, grabs Miskewitz's hand, and pumps it fast. He starts to move away from the table, then hesitates and adds, in a lower voice, 'Detective Peirce, could I see you privately for a moment?'

Peirce seems to go a little white in the face. She rolls back from the table without looking at anyone and follows the mayor into the outer corridor. Shaw gets Lenore's attention and motions after them with her head.

'His little friend in the department,' Lenore says in an unhushed voice.

Miskewitz rolls his eyes, runs his beefy hand over the roll of flesh under his jaw, and raises his eyebrows. 'Well, people,' he says, 'we were getting bored.'

Shaw and Richmond laugh. Zarelli stares down at Lenore. Lenore stares up at Woo. Richmond cracks his knuckles and says, 'So how do we work it?'

Lehmann says, 'I'm bunking here for the duration. You run everything through me. I want to know every piece of information you trip over. I want to know what you eat for dinner.'

Lenore knows she's going to have problems with Lehmann.

Lehmann continues, 'Dr. Woo will be assisting us throughout because that's what my boss wants, so include him in all your updates.'

Miskewitz says, 'Put everything on hold that you can and junk what you can't. We'll work our normal partners with the exception of Thomas and Zarelli. Zarelli, you tag onto Richmond and Peirce. Detective Thomas, you're to escort Dr. Woo throughout the investigation—'

Lenore comes straight up in her seat and repeats, 'Escort?' as if she'd never heard the word.

Miskewitz tilts his head slightly and gives an annoyed smile. 'That's right, Lenore. As of today the doctor is on leave from St. Ignatius and on loan to us—'

'As in report—' Lenore begins, and the lieutenant holds up a hand.

'—As in accompanies you. As in the mayor wants it this way.'

'I can't take this guy down the Park,' she says in disbelief.

'Look, Thomas, we're dealing with a new substance here. Dr. Woo is the only one to have seen its effects firsthand—'

'I'll take pictures for him—'

'—There's no more discussion, Detective. That's what the mayor wants and that's what I'm telling you to do.'

Miskewitz turns back to the rest of the table. 'I think it's safe to say you'll be putting in a big chunk of overtime, so get that straight at home.'

Miskewitz leans back into his chair, leans his head on his shoulder, and opens his arms to his sides. It's some weird signal that the meeting is over. Richmond is the first to get up, saying over his shoulder to Lenore, 'Jesus, I got to use the can.' Shaw begins to move for the coffee urn. Zarelli and Lehmann mumble to one another with disgusted looks on their faces.

Lenore pushes back from the table. Woo approaches her and says, 'Detective,' and pauses.

'Poor short-term memory,' she says. 'Maybe you should get your hands on some Lingo.'

'Perhaps,' he says, again trying to flash her the killer smile.

'Thomas,' she says, 'Detective Thomas.'

'Detective Thomas,' he says, 'of course. I was wondering if possibly we could meet a little later. For lunch, possibly. To discuss the investigation.'

5

In her tiny office, Eva applies the last, slightest brushstroke of blush onto her cheek. She looks quickly at the smudged mirror, then closes the small black plastic case and slides it into her pocketbook inside the bottom drawer of her desk. She raises her hand to brush at her cheek and stops herself, thinking, *Leave well enough alone.* She doesn't like the idea that anyone might notice that she wears makeup, but without it she thinks she has the face of a corpse, cold as ice, white as a sheet.

She can tell already that it's going to be a beaut of a day. The *Reader's Digest* are in and she's got two carriers out sick. She's already called for a couple of floats from down the main branch, but nobody's promising anything. She'll handle it. If she has to, she'll call Gumm and ask him to forget about taking today off. And he'll give.

She pulls her middle drawer open and takes out her eleven-inch clipboard and several preprinted forms which she inserts under the clip. Then she folds all the forms over the top of the board to reveal a blank yellow legal pad. She takes a just-sharpened pencil from her cup and holds it above the pad. She breathes slowly and quiets her whole body, lifts her head, and remains completely still, listening.

Eva's office, which had once been a storage closet, borders the locker room. Eva takes notes on everything that is said in the locker room. The conversations are always the most banal, boring exchanges, but she notes them anyway. She thinks that it's a general rule of life that no information is so small that it can't, at some point, maybe in the far future, be put to good use.

So she keeps this private record in her files at home, an ongoing transcription of the locker room small talk, the complaining and swearing and taunting. Poor Ike Thomas, the bruising he takes.

Eva smuggles her legal pad of shorthand notes home every night, then, after a supper that's been planned a week in advance and is a nutritionist's dream of balance and freshness, she indulges herself. Eva's one great treat is music and last year, after making supervisor, she went out and blew a wad on a Bang & Olufsen stereo system that she'd fantasized about for months. It cost almost ten grand and she had to take a loan from the credit union, but each evening around six-thirty, when she slides in the CD of selections from Wagner's *Götterdämmerung*, which was the first piece of music she bought, she knows it was the absolutely correct decision. She sits in a corner, in a swivel secretary's chair, and types up her notes on a heavy black Underwood manual that had belonged to her mother. At times she has to take a break and sit with her head down at her knees in an anti-faint position. She thinks this is because of the incongruity caused by the banality of the words she reads in relation to the majesty and power of the music that's entering her ears simultaneously. She always has a tall glass of orange juice next to the typewriter, ready to revive her, put her back on course.

Eva read a biography of Wagner when she was an adolescent and for a time, during the heat of her mid-teen years, he was her fantasy lover, the guy she dreamed about at 4 A.M., bathed in a thick sweat.

Last week she dreamed about Ike Thomas. She's sure there's no meaning to this, but she can't shake loose from the fact that it happened, that somehow this strange and silent man, the brunt of the locker room's collective stupidity, invaded her subconscious and came to her dream-mind, trudged up her front walk with a bursting-full mailbag, every letter in it addressed to Eva Barnes, her name in an ornate, calligraphied script. And he spent all night pushing the letters into her mailbox, like some circus trick, like some magic act. The letters kept fitting in, dozens, thousands, there seemed to be boundless room inside.

She blocks out the memory, fine-tunes her hearing, waits for the first voice to come. As always, her timing is perfect. They start filing in, in the same order, every day: old Jacobi first with his ancient gray metal lunchbox that looks like it could house an entire breadloaf, then the new girl, Bromberg, in her fluorescent-red, oversized glasses and too-short skirt, then Ike Thomas, quiet, hunched over a little, his eyes on his own feet. Five minutes will go by, until the late-bell is just about to ring, and in will come Rourke and Wilson, both a mess, shirts untucked, hair sticking out everywhere, just about announcing to the whole post office that once again they've slept together. Eva thinks she should have bounced Wilson when she had the chance.

The first voice comes from the new girl, Bromberg:

BROMBERG: Hey, Thomas, I hear Stephenson is out today. Why don't you take two routes and really kiss the bitch's ass?

JACOBI: Leave the boy alone, Lisa. He just loves a woman in uniform. Isn't that right, Ike? And all this time I thought you were gay…

BROMBERG: I think they're both gay. The bitch and the schmuck. You should really ask her out, Thomas, you could be like fakes for each other.

JACOBI: Fakes? What, fakes?

THOMAS: Beards. Okay. The word is beards, Bromberg. Jees.

JACOBI: What does she mean, fakes?

[*7 a.m. bell*]

THOMAS: She's saying it wrong. You never heard of a beard? It's like when someone pretends to be, you know, involved with someone else.

ROURKE: We got donuts. Lisa, you owe two bucks to the kitty.

BROMBERG: I paid this week. Ask Thomas, he saw me pay. I paid.

WILSON: Is Stephenson really out again? What an asshole, I swear, that guy never works…

BROMBERG: Stephenson and Ogden are both out. You two just made it. The bitch would've been on you…

JACOBI: Billy, you ever hear of a beard, the word *beard*, okay, but not, like, on your face? Like another meaning.

ROURKE: What are you fucking babbling about? Jesus, it's early.

WILSON: Who had the cruller? Jacobi, was the cruller—

ROURKE: Shit! Goddammit, I spilled the—

THOMAS: I'm sorry, you should've—

ROURKE: You goddamn asshole, Thomas, you're such a shithead—

WILSON: Here, Billy, let me…

BROMBERG: You know, for two people in the sack so much, you two still bitch a lot.

ROURKE: That's gonna be five bucks to get the shirt dry-cleaned, shit-for-brains.

THOMAS: What cleaner's do you go to? Five bucks?

ROURKE: Five bucks.

THOMAS: It's like three bucks, Billy. Three-fifty, tops.

ROURKE: Aw, Christ, look at this, I'm a mess here. Jacobi, you got an extra shirt in your locker?

THOMAS: I've got a shirt, Billy.

JACOBI: Can't help you.

ROURKE: I don't want your freakin' shirt, you doink.

WILSON: Here, honey, let me wipe it. It'll be fine.

BROMBERG: Jacobi, you got the school today?

JACOBI: Haven't seen the schedule. I think Stephenson was due.

BROMBERG: You ever notice how Thomas never gets the school? Never.

THOMAS: I've taken that route plenty of times. I used to get the school and the library. And the elderly towers on Sapir.

JACOBI: I hate those towers. You ever notice how every one of those old people gets *TV Guide*? Every goddamn one.

BROMBERG: What I'm saying is, Thomas never gets the school. I swear.

THOMAS: I get the school. God.

BROMBERG: I'm saying there's got to be something between him and the bitch.

THOMAS: For God's sake…

JACOBI: That right? Hey, Ike? You all over the woman or what?

[*Locker door slams*]

ROURKE: Shithead getting pissed?

THOMAS: Look, I'm sorry about the coffee, okay? Can we just get to work?

JACOBI: Every bone in me says this is going to be a mother of a day. Billy, you going to the Bach Room after?

WILSON: Oh yeah, let's have a few, Billy, huh?

ROURKE: What's the word, shithead, you going to the Bach Room? Maybe taking the bitch with you?

[*Silence*]

THOMAS: What's she ever done to you, Rourke, huh?

ROURKE: Do you hear this? Did you hear this? This is unbelievable. I'm screwing around and he *is* all hot for the bitch. Do you believe this? Jacobi, did you hear this guy?

[*Whistle, general catcalls*]

THOMAS: No, I'm just asking, what did she ever do to you? Really, answer me. And while you're at it, what did I ever do to you?

[*Much laughter*]

THOMAS: What's wrong, Billy, can't you speak? Is there something wrong with your goddamn mouth?

[*Laughter ends*]

ROURKE: What a ballsy little bastard, defending the bitch like this. Listen, schmuckhead, it's nothing you or she *did*, okay? All right? It's what you *are*. All right, what you *are*. You see the difference there. You *are* a shithead. She *is* a bitch.
[*Laughter*]
[*Door swings open, closed. I assume Thomas leaves*]

Eva puts her pencil back into her cup. Without reviewing her shorthand, she pulls all the forms back down over the yellow sheet. She pushes back from her desk and stares up at a glossy poster of a recent stamp issue, the William Faulkner stamp. She stares at the face depicted in a green line drawing. The man looks so wise, distinguished, the small features, the pipe in the mouth. Eva wishes she could consult with him, ask some advice on what he'd do about the infighting among her people. When the stamp was issued, she'd looked Faulkner up in her old Britannica at home and was pleased and surprised to see he'd worked in a post office in Mississippi. Now she wishes he worked here and was out in the front lobby, reloading the self-serve stamp machines, or maybe tacking up new Wanted posters. She'd ask him what to do about all the hostility in the locker room. And she'd ask him what he thought about Ike Thomas, and if he was really *defending the bitch, hot for the bitch.*

Eva gets up out of her chair and straightens her skirt. She's wearing her navy-blue suit with a white blouse, and she wishes she'd worn something else, something a little less plain. It's difficult. When she went from carrier to supervisor she had to stop wearing a uniform. She liked the uniform. It identified her. Anywhere in the country, people just taking a quick look at her would know she worked for the U.S. Postal Service. But there's a statute that says supervisors aren't to wear the uniform. Eva guesses they want the supervisors set apart, differentiated from the carriers and clerks so that they're seen clearly as the boss, the authority figure. But there are other ways of signifying their increased status without sacrificing the uniform. There are always other options. Now every morning means a decision about what to wear, about how to look professional and serious without looking boring or dowdy or masculine.

She hears a last locker slam shut next door and knows they're all at their cages. She starts to write quickly on her scheduling forms and walks out into the workroom. Jacobi is the only one talking, and he's just muttering to no one in particular. She walks into the center of the room, equidistant from each of them seated atop their metal stools, stacks of banded mail in their hands.

'Okay,' she says, trying instantly to find the right modulation for her voice. 'As you probably guessed by now, Stephenson and Ogden are both out sick…'

'Yeah, right,' says Rourke. He didn't shave the past two days and Eva thinks she's going to have to mention it. He looks more like a Bangkok derelict than a carrier.

'I'm waiting for the word from the main office on my request for two subs. I think we can only count on one, and I'm not giving the towers to a sub. They'll never finish and we'll hear about it all day tomorrow.'

She sees them all tense up, waiting to see who'll get hung with Stephenson's awful route.

She hugs the clipboard up to her chest and drums on the back of it with her fingers.

'Thomas,' she says, 'you do Stephenson's. Wilson and Jacobi, you split up Ike's route between you.'

She pauses, looks around, then says, 'Okay, let's hit it,' and turns to head back to her office. She hears Rourke say something under his breath that sounds like 'heartbreaker,' and she surprises herself by stopping and wheeling back around to face them.

It's like a vacuum has rushed into the space between all the cages and sucked the air and noise away. Eva fills it with the question, 'What was that, Rourke?'

He hesitates, then says, 'Nothing, I was talking to Ike…'

She cuts him off, saying, 'Did we lose our razor, Rourke?'

He starts to say, 'What, you mean…'

And she cuts him off again, saying, 'Okay, there's a change in scheduling. You've got Stephenson's route, Rourke. Thomas, you're here for the day. At the window and sorting. I'll get the second sub from downtown.'

Rourke is stunned, shaking his head, stammering, saying, 'Oh, c'mon, what the hell, I didn't say a thing…'

But Eva has already started walking back to her office. When her door closes, everyone stays still, like a jumpy terrorist has a gun swaying over their heads. Finally Rourke turns to Wilson and says, 'What the fuck was that all about?'

No one answers.

• • •

If someone were to ask Ike which he liked better, being out on the route, delivering, or being inside at the cage, sorting, he'd have trouble giving a definitive answer. The truth is he enjoys both activities and he'd have a real problem trying to elevate one above the other. They're different. On the route, you're outside, meeting people, saying hello, getting some exercise. Inside, sorting the mail, you don't move or talk, your brain listens to the radio and kind of goes on remote control, sliding envelopes into the appropriate slots, tossing packages into the right baskets. But both activities have a definite procedure to follow, an order, a schedule, a continuous line of behavior. And though Ike wouldn't admit it to anyone, that's really what he likes about his job. So either way he can't lose. Inside or out, it's all the same to him.

For instance, in the manual they even have illustrations for how you should position yourself on the sorting stool. Ike follows the official example. Your feet, in regulation steeltoed work boots, are flat on the work floor, taking sixty percent of the weight of your body. Your buttocks are to rest not more than two inches on the edge or lip of the work stool, so that you're actually in more of a modified-leaning, rather than sitting, position. Though it isn't explained in the manual, Ike has guessed that some engineer may have figured out the most efficient way of going through an average-sized sorting load, coming up with the illustrated position that probably finds a perfect balance between speed and conservation of energy.

A day inside, like this, is a nice break every now and then. Ike thinks of it like the sick days he'd sometimes take in grammar school, a rare treat, a change of pace. He knows he'll appreciate the route even more tomorrow, approach it with renewed effort. Besides, there are no pit bulls inside the Sapir Street Station. He's never been attacked by Mrs. Vachek's pet, but there have been a couple of close calls. Last November, he was sliding her Social Security check through the slot in her front door and Milos, silent, waiting, cocked, tore the check from his hand in an explosion of noise and saliva and snapping fangs. Ike actually felt the wet, rubbery flap of the dog's mouth as he wrenched back and pulled his hand to safety. There was a pain in his chest for the balance of the day.

Then six months later, the Vachek door was left just slightly open, the slip bolt pressed against the jamb, just an eighth of an inch from its slot. When Ike began to push some pulpy religious monthly through the brass-rimmed mail slot, the door swung open enough to reveal Milos witnessing the opportunity of a lifetime. He lunged and Ike fell backward in the doorway, just managing to shield his throat with the mailbag. Milos caught an incisor on Ike's sleeve and shredded the whole arm, but missed any skin. By the grace of God, Mrs. Vachek appeared out of nowhere with some silent whistle in her mouth, her cheeks puffed out to bursting, blowing an inaudible command that Milos grudgingly obeyed.

It was Ike's only dog incident in eight years with the service, twelve years if you counted the summers he worked while squeaking through Jones University as a day student. If any of his current co-workers ever found out that he had a degree, it would be all over. They'd manage to be as blindly vicious as Milos Vachek and no whistle in the world could call them from his throat.

Now Ike wonders why nothing in college came as easily to him as everything here at the station. Like the zip codes, for instance. Ike knows every zip code in the state, and most of them in the bordering states. You could line him up on some quiz program and just start zinging them his way and he wouldn't flinch. They'd flow out of his mouth as automatically as meter stickers from the dispenser. He doesn't think about it. It's like there's a direct path from some pure center of his memory straight to his mouth, and no thinking is ever involved. A location is stated and a zip code is kicked out.

This is one of the reasons that Ike is probably the fastest sorter in the place. He can empty a full tray in half the time it takes Rourke. There's no contest. And if someone were to do a check on accuracy, Ike is confident he'd win that category as well. He doesn't see any reason for mistakes in this area. To him, a mistake in sorting means only one thing: you were talking to someone instead of looking at the envelope. Not that he's got anything against socializing. It's just there's a time for it. Can't they wait until the end of their shift and take it over to that stupid bar they all love so much? What the hell is so special about that place?

Does Ike regret not being a part of the gang? Never being asked to go along when they change back into their street clothes? Never heading across the street and filing into the bar, all loose and ready for some fun? Not really. Not usually. There have been some rare occasions – he could probably number them on his fingers – when he found himself longing for this vague idea of friendship that he labels 'camaraderie.' He's imagined, at those times, what it might be like inside the back room at the Bach Room, seated in a chair at a fat, well-worn round table, pouring beer from a pitcher into the half-filled mugs around him, actually laughing at something Rourke has said, whispering into Bromberg's small ear.

But most of the time he has no desire to be part of their group. He feels set apart from his co-workers, and he swears to himself that this gap has nothing to do with a sense of superiority. It's just a separateness, pure and simple. If he worked at the main post office downtown, instead of here at a much smaller neighborhood branch, the separateness wouldn't be as noticeable. He could get lost in the crowd. There are hundreds of people who work at the main station. But here there are usually just six or eight people and there's just no way to disappear. So his separateness has to be glaringly apparent day in and day out.

There have been a lot of moments, most often at night, like three or four in the morning, when Ike couldn't sleep, but stayed in bed and stared straight up into the darkness and admitted to himself, filled up with a vague sense of guilt, that he cherished his separateness. He doesn't think this is normal or wholesome. He has an unspoken theory that most animals, and he stubbornly includes humans in that category, have a primal need for community, a deep well of yearning to be part of a larger social group. He thinks that even outcasts, abnormals, discontents, rebels, nonconformists, whether they admit it or not, secretly long for other outcasts. He thinks that a true hermit is a tremendously rare entity. And that he has all the makings of a true hermit.

He enjoys being alone with his own mind and running it through a series of weird systems. He likes filling up on what would be considered the most trivial of information, because he thinks that there can be no standard for measurement of informational importance, that it's absolutely subjective. That it's entirely possible that for him, knowing the zip code of the smallest hamlet in the state is every bit as important as the President knowing the correct code sequence for unleashing a nuclear barrage.

Ike has a hunch that this trait has emerged straight from the Thomas genes, that it's a shared family legacy. He'd bet that Lenore is engulfed in separateness down at the police station and that she puts a very high value on it. He thinks both of their parents thought of themselves as cut apart from the groupings they moved within, in the neighborhood, at work, at church. He's decided this based on a collection of memories that he analyzes over and over again while walking the route, or eating a silent lunch, or giving in to the insomnia that plagues him every now and then. He imagines he knows how his parents felt, as if they were living an illusion, bringing off a ridiculously elaborate deception – the deception that people are connected, that they share history, biology, a common tongue.

One of the systems that Ike has spent a lot of time investigating is the post office. His interest began simply as a by-product of his daily routine, his urge to know a little more about an environment he spent most of his time in. But the irony of where he works soon hit him full force. The very idea of a post office is stunning to him. It's like this national, no, international, planetwide, series of shrines dedicated to an idea of connection, to the notion of real communication. Now Ike sees every post office he passes as a temple, a concrete symbol of insistence that we are not alone, that we can talk to anyone, anywhere, at any time, all for the price of a stamp.

A few years ago, Ike began delving into any and all aspects of the postal service. He'd done a hell of a lot of research, read most of the texts out there on the subject – the classic William Smith volume, the Walter Lang, the Ormsby and the Fallopian. What he loves most, though, is the fact that no one, not his co-workers, not the people on his route, not even Lenore knows about his interest or his knowledge. It's locked up, hermetically sealed within the vault of his skull. He values all this knowledge, oddly because he knows how useless it is, what a vain display the history of mail service is, what an exhibition of pointless ego. He can't understand why no one else he's aware of sees it in this manner. In every book he's ever read, the mail is a story of progress and practicality.

Just once, Ike would like to come across a book, maybe an old, dilapidated volume, crusted with dust, forgotten, wedged unseen on a rarely visited library shelf, the stamped date on the return card pasted in the back of it showing a day that went by decades ago. He'd like to open that book and find the one shunned author who was willing to tell the truth, like in the story of 'The Emperor's New Clothes.' He'd like to find the voice brave enough to say: *I'm sorry, people, you can make the mail system as efficient and elaborate and well connected as you want, but it won't change a thing. It won't make you any less isolated, any less separate, any less alone. You can mail an unlimited number of bulging envelopes, filled to bursting with words of every meaning and message, but that can't change the nature of things. We are alone. And all our post offices are but temples of illusion, intricate attempts to tell ourselves otherwise.*

• • •

Ike becomes aware of a presence and looks up startled and there's Supervisor Barnes, right next to him, smiling at his surprise.

'I'm sorry, Ike,' she says. 'I didn't mean to startle you like that. You've got quite the powers of concentration.'

'I enjoy sorting,' Ike says.

Eva shakes her head. 'See now, I never liked sorting. Sorting for me was like torture. Loved to be out on the route. Walking the route.'

'I like the route too. I like them both. Sorting and the route.'

'Renaissance man,' Eva says. 'I was wondering if you'd like a coffee. It's break time. I wouldn't want to be reported to the union for denying you your break time.'

'I'd never do something like that,' Ike says.

'Lighten up, Ike,' Eva says. 'I was joking. The float from the main station came in and I've got her on the counter. So how 'bout the coffee?'

Ike smiles, slides his behind off the lip of the work stool, and follows Eva to the small room at the back of the station. It's the regulation break room and it's filled with three uncomfortable, bright orange, molded-plastic chairs, and a shaky wooden table covered with an ancient coffee machine, two jars of Cremora, a Styrofoam cup filled with Sweet 'N Low packets, and a cardboard box in which everyone stores their own coffee mug. There's also a poster of the moon landing commemorative tacked to the wall. Ike has always found it an unusually depressing place. And he doesn't think there's any need for it to be that way. A little effort could do wonders, a little paint on the walls, some new chairs you could sit in without a backache, replace the moon landing with something a little more recent. But there's no money in the budget for anything as unnecessary as redoing a branch break room, and when Ike suggested to his co-workers that they take it upon themselves, he didn't hear the end of it for three weeks.

Eva picks up her mug. It's basic black, with no pictures or funny slogans or institutional logos. Normally she keeps it in her office and carries it into the break room when she wants some coffee. Ike has always thought this was because she was afraid Rourke or Wilson would put something in it if she left it with the other mugs. Spit in the bottom or something. She must have left the black mug in the room yesterday. Maybe it was an accident. But, more likely to Ike's mind, she's just gaining confidence. She knows they know who's the boss.

Ike's work mug is identical to the home mug that Lenore gave him, the *Neither Wind, Nor Sleet* mug. He liked the one from Lenore so much that he searched around until he found the second one at one of those strobe and incense teen boutiques in the mall. Sometimes he wonders if this purchase shows a lack of imagination or independence on his part, but usually he thinks it's just a tribute to Lenore's taste and intuitiveness.

Like Lenore, Eva drinks her coffee straight and black. He's always amazed that people can do this, straight from the pot, without burning their tongue and throat. Ike fills his mug a good forty percent with tap water and Cremora before he adds a drop of coffee. Otherwise his stomach is shot for the rest of the day. He stopped using sugar back in college and thinks it might be wise to cut out coffee altogether. He can imagine the problems caffeine can cause.

'How long have you been with the post office?' Eva asks, settling into a chair, her mug held out oddly in one hand as if it were the control stick of an old airplane.

'Eight years,' Ike says, with just a trace of pride sliding out with his words. 'And four summers before I started full-time.'

'Oh, you were a sub,' Eva says, sounding genuinely interested.

Ike nods, sips at his mug. 'Uh-huh. My father put in forty years. He had my summer job lined up every May. I swear, that guy knew every route in the city.'

'One of those veterans,' Eva says. 'Saw all the changes. Was carrying before the first zip codes…'

'Oh, God,' Ike says. 'He was out there in those days when people would, you know, write a name on the envelope, and "City" underneath it, and the letter would get delivered, no problem.'

'Lot of ingenuity in the office back in those days,' Eva says.

'Don't tell me,' Ike says. 'Was your dad in the service too?'

Eva shakes her head no and crosses her legs. Ike tries to stay focused on her eyes.

'No, though he did work for the government. And he was a special courier for a time. State Department. We lived all over the place when I was growing up. Spent a lot of time in South America. Brazil and Paraguay. I speak Spanish fluently.'

Ike is impressed. In an instant, he can picture Eva as a young girl, dressed in slightly foreign clothes, rattling off answers, in Spanish, to some old, dark teacher.

'You're kidding,' he says.

'Not at all,' Eva says matter-of-factly. 'We were south of the border from the time I was five until I turned seventeen.'

'Jees,' Ike says, intrigued and excited by the story. 'Then what happened? Your father get transferred back or something?'

Eva shakes her head again in that slightly clipped way. 'My father died. Massive coronary. Forty-eight years old.'

'Oh, God,' Ike says. 'I'm sorry.'

'A long time ago,' Eva says. 'I've never understood it. The man was the picture of health. Not a pound overweight. Good eating habits. Plenty of exercise. And to the best of my knowledge there was no history of it in his family.'

There's a pause that they both fill by sipping their coffee.

Ike says, 'So how'd you end up in Quinsigamond?'

Eva smiles and Ike looks down to the floor.

'My mother's family was originally from here. So it was the only place to come, really. We moved in with this bachelor uncle of mine, my mother's brother Kurt. Now, he was a character. But Mother, she was never the same after Father died. I kept telling myself that she'd come together with each passing year. Isn't that what you'd think? That the pain and the confusion would sort of ease away slowly, a little bit at a time?'

Eva shakes her head no for a while, staring at Ike until he's so nervous and uncomfortable he's ready to run from the room.

Finally, she continues. 'Mother drank. She had a problem. Quite a problem. I mean, this was twenty-some-odd years ago and you didn't confront this type of thing in the way people do today. I'm saying help just wasn't as available back then. This was something you kept hidden from the rest of the world. It took place inside, deep in your house.'

Ike wishes she'd stop telling him this. He didn't expect it of her and he doesn't want to have to change his image of her, the picture he's imagined of what she would be like if they ever sat down alone somewhere and had a conversation. He wonders how much longer the break can last.

When Eva speaks again, it's like her voice has come back to earth, regained a lot of strength and composure on reentry.

'It's funny, Ike,' she says. 'I don't know you well. I mean, I'm not sure if we've ever sat and spoken like this. But I've noticed you. Your routine, your work habits. I'm a very good supervisor, Ike. I know how all my people operate. You're on the ball. You're probably the best in here as far as taking the job seriously goes. You know, supervisor is not a position a lot of people would want. It'll cost you friends. I don't care who you are. You take off the uniform and put on the suit, they look at you differently. And that's fine with me, because first of all, I've never been very close to anyone at work, and secondly, the job comes first. The job is number one.'

'I'd agree with that,' Ike says, his voice a little higher than usual.

'So I was saying it's funny because, though I don't know you, I always thought it was funny that you weren't this family man. Married and a dozen kids and co-managing the Little League and all. You just seemed very, well, I don't know' – she smiles, raises her eyebrows – 'sort of purposeful and clean-cut…'

'Clean-cut,' Ike says, surprised, unsure of her meaning.

'Sure. True-blue. You know what I'm saying.'

'Yeah,' Ike says, 'I guess so,' though he has no clue as to what she's talking about.

'God knows,' Eva says, draining the last of her mug, 'not like the rest of the crew we've got in here.'

Ike thinks he might be on shaky ground. He wants to watch what he says here.

'I think everyone works to the best of their abilities.'

Eva lets out a deprecating laugh that's little more than a gust of air.

'You do?' she says, and it's less a genuine question than a mocking disagreement.

'Yeah,' Ike says, 'I think so.'

'Ike, please,' Eva says. 'Wilson? Rourke?'

'I'm just saying I'm not sure everyone has the same capacity.'

'Oh, I get it. "If you can't say something nice…"'

'No,' Ike says, 'not at all. It's just, how do I know their situations?'

'And how do they know yours? Their "situations" have nothing to do with it. Here's a job. How are you going to perform it? That's it. That's the only question to be debated. I'll tell you what I think is going on here, Ike. I'm management and they're labor and no matter how awful they treat you, you feel this loyalty to them just because they're on your side of the fence. Right? Does this come down from your father?'

Ike doesn't know what to say. He feels like he's been hauled out of bed in the middle of the night and questioned by some police force.

'Oh no,' he says. 'No, no, not at all. That's just not true, Ms. Barnes…'

Before he can bite his tongue, Eva bursts out with a single laugh and chokes out, 'Ms. Barnes? Ms. Barnes? For God's sake, Ike.'

'What?' is all he can come up with.

Eva collects herself, puts her hand up to her forehead for a second, like it will help her think, then lets it fall into her lap and says, 'How old are you, Ike?'

He hesitates, then answers, 'Thirty.'

'All right, then. I'm thirty-seven, Ike. I'm not exactly your grade school teacher. All right?'

'So, what,' Ike stammers, 'I should call you Eva?'

She smiles, seems pleased. 'Yes, Ike. Call me Eva.'

'Okay,' he says, forced cheerful, starting to move to get up out of the chair. Eva stays in place and says, 'So why do you put up with it?'

Ike freezes and repeats, 'Put up with it?'

'The rest of them. Your co-workers. I'm telling you, I've worked at different branches, and I've worked down the main station.

There are always a couple of people, okay, but this group. They're the worst bunch of bastards I've come across.'

Ike doesn't like her talking like this. He especially doesn't like being the one to hear it. He stays silent and Eva pushes.

'Do you disagree with me?'

'I guess there's a lot of hostility,' he says.

'You have a way with understatement.'

'If you're looking for a reason why...'

She cuts him off. 'I'm the supervisor. They'd hate any supervisor they got over here. On top of that, I'm a woman and that doesn't go down very well with Jacobi or Rourke. So I know why they hate me and I don't lose any sleep over it, believe me. But I don't understand what it is about you...'

'That makes two of us,' he says quickly.

'Wouldn't you like to know?'

'I've never been this popular guy, okay? I've never been Mr. Popularity.'

'This isn't about being popular, Ike.'

'I don't know.' He pauses, looks up at the clock. 'It's getting to be that time.'

She ignores his comment. 'What I think we should do,' she says, 'is have dinner together sometime and discuss it. What do you think about that?'

Ike looks down at his knees. 'You want to have dinner with me?'

'That's right,' Eva says, not backing down at all.

'You think that's a good idea, us working together and all?'

Eva smiles. 'It's just dinner, Ike. Sometimes you don't know if something's a good idea until you give it a try.'

Ike concedes this point. 'I guess.'

'Besides,' Eva adds, standing, 'we outcasts have to stay together. It's a lonely world out there, Ike.'

They both laugh at her last comment and it takes away some of the edge Ike's feeling. 'I guess we could have some dinner,' he says.

She nods to him and leaves the break room without another word, holding her black mug cradled at her chest.

Ike gets up and pushes the chairs back against the wall in a row. He puts his mug in the cardboard box and makes a mental note to wash it out in the men's room sink later on. He walks back to his cage feeling a little light-headed and hyper.

He sinks back into the perfect position on the edge of his stool reflexively and takes a minute to ball up his hands into fists and rub at his eyes. A chill moves up his back and he shudders slightly and takes a deep breath. *It's going to be that kind of a week,* he thinks to himself.

He looks down at the small metal lip that juts out from the wall of slots in front of him. The pile of mail he left off with is still sitting there. But next to it is a small brown cardboard box, the type of box the bank mails new checks in. It measures about five by three inches and is maybe an inch tall. It should have been put with the parcels. Ike doesn't remember seeing it when he left the cage.

The package is taped closed at both ends with several pieces of that thick, wide brown mailing tape. Ike leans over it and reads the simple, hand-printed address:

Box 9
Sapir Street Station
Quinsigamond

He reaches down and picks it up and immediately puts it back on the lip. His fingers are wet with something thick and oily, something seeping from the bottom of the package. He sees now a small puddle forming under the carton. And then he notices the smell – an awful, rotting-type smell. His coffee rises up halfway toward his throat.

Ike pulls a handkerchief from his back pocket and holds it up to his mouth and nose. Then without thinking, he picks up the package, dabs away at it, then mops up the puddle on the cage lip.

He throws the soiled handkerchief into a nearby wastebasket. Then he does something he has never done in his career. In his whole life. He uses his fingers to tear open the package. He breaks open the tape at each end and runs his finger along the inside edge of the package, touching something moist inside. His heart starts into a rapid and painful pump, like rubber bullets being fired at the inside of his chest.

He rips the entire top of the package open and tosses it on the floor. He looks inside. And he looks away for a second, unsure, then brings his eyes back again.

It looks like the chopped-up remains of a small fish. There's a tiny section of the face left, one eyeball still visible. The smell is horrible. And then he sees the parasites – tiny mites and worms crawling through the terrible remains.

A sweat breaks instantly over most of Ike's body. He makes himself move slowly, to create the illusion of control. He makes himself walk, not run, to the men's room. He steps inside and bolts the door and turns on both faucets in the sink. He takes a breath to keep himself from vomiting.

Then he cups his hands, lets a pool of water fill up, and begins to splash his face, repeating the procedure over and over, trying to steady himself, wash away the sweat, clear away the smell, obliterate the image of decay and cruelty that's just smacked him like a hit-and-run car on a familiar street.

He knows already that he can use all the water in the city's reservoir, but he'll never be successful. It's too late. The image is there to stay.

6

Peirce is in the parking lot, unlocking her Honda, when Lenore moves up next to her.

'Never a dull moment, huh, Charlotte?' Lenore says.

Peirce balks and drops her keys to the ground and Lenore says, 'Didn't mean to startle you.'

'It's not you,' Charlotte says, stooping. 'I hate these briefings.'

'Yeah, well, we can't let things get boring.'

Peirce smiles, but it's clear she wants to get going. Lenore leans her behind against the Honda to show she's not finished talking.

'They teamed you with the professor,' Peirce says. 'Zarelli will go nuts.'

'Screw Zarelli,' Lenore says, pauses, and adds, 'What'd Welby want?'

All Charlotte can say is, 'Huh?'

'At the end there. When he asked to speak with you.'

Peirce straightens up, tries to square her shoulders. They stare at each other for a few seconds.

Finally, Charlotte says, 'Look, Lenore—'

But Lenore cuts her off and in a low but still-friendly voice, says, 'Look, Charlotte, I couldn't care less who you sleep with, okay? I think you know that. If Welby was telling you where to meet him or what to wear tonight, great, have a goddamn ball. Doesn't concern me.'

Charlotte nods.

'But if he was asking you about any of us… about me or Richmond or Zarelli or even the lieutenant, that's a different story. And I won't put up with an inside mouth. You know I won't.'

'Put up with?' Peirce repeats.

'You know what I'm saying, Charlotte. We stay out of Welby's way and he stays out of our way. That's how it's always been. If he's saying he wants to suck on your neck, great. Get what you can. But if he's asking you to talk about fellow officers, if he wants to know about narcotics...'

She trails off shaking her head and Peirce says, 'Yeah, what?'

Lenore says, 'Then you and I have a problem, Charlotte.'

There's another round of staring, then Charlotte steps forward and sticks her key into the door lock. Without looking at Lenore, she says, 'He asked me to wear this black chemise tonight. He bought it for me.'

Lenore holds back a laugh, raises up off the Honda, and says, 'That's what I thought.'

She touches Charlotte on the shoulder and takes a step away, then turns back and says, 'Remember who broke you in, kid.'

Charlotte gives her own smile and says, 'How could I forget, Lenore?'

She climbs in behind the wheel, kicks over the engine, and watches Lenore walk to her Barracuda, then she pulls out of the lot and takes a left toward Main Street. When she's a couple of blocks from headquarters, she pulls the Panasonic microrecorder from her bag and thumbs the On switch.

> Victor, Victor, Victor. Master of persuasion. How'd I let you talk me into this? Okay. Professional voice. It is Monday. November twentieth. Ten A.M. I'm sitting in my Honda at a red light on LeClair Ave. That digital sign on the front of the Quinsigamond National Building says it's thirty degrees outside and there are thirty-three shopping days left till Christmas. Which reminds me, I've got to make a withdrawal today. It's that time of year, Victor. So what are you getting me? [*Giggle*] Your favorite narc, Charlotte Peirce, and I've been such a good cop all year. Have you made your list, Victor, checked it

twice? Okay, I've got the green. I'm not exactly sure what you want from me here, Victor, Mr. Mayor. Should I call you Mr. Mayor on this? How official is this, boss? That's the bitch about this thing. Not like talking on the phone. Or pay phone in your case. No one ever answers you back. It's just talking to yourself. The guy in the red Camaro in the next lane is staring at me, Victor. Thinks I'm nuts. Nowadays you see people talking to themselves in their cars all the time. Take a picture, schmuck. He just blew past us. It's an '81 Camaro. Vanity plate. Mass reg L-I-N-K. Link. Like that black guy on *Mod Squad*, remember? No, you wouldn't remember. That's the big thing about couples like us. The difference in ages. We refer to different TV shows and the other guy never gets it. I'm turning left onto Main. I'm heading for the highway. [*Pause*] Back again, dearest. Just rolled off the expressway and onto Kimble. I've decided to start with the Institute. You never said whether you wanted me to tape interviews. Should I try to hide this thing in my bra or something? You know, it's small but not that small. Are any of these things made by American companies? Jesus. It just hit me. This isn't it, Victor? This better not be it, Victor. It's nice. Great. Panasonic. Voice-activated and all. But it's not going to cut it for a Christmas gift. Not from you. Not after the past six months. That would be just like you, you know? And you probably took the money out of office expenses. Probably had that secretary buy the damned thing. I don't know what to make of you lately. After the briefing, you say 'my personal input' and – what was it? – 'the investigation within the investigation.' You use these words. You're always using words. That should be the big requirement for mayor. Forget voting. Get the guy who's best with words and make him the boss. I don't know why I'm going along with all this. I figure I've got two choices here. Either you're, like, paranoid over the edge, or you just want to hear my voice all day. Which would be sweet. Number two would be nice. But I've got this feeling that you're just one more guy with a little more power than he's comfortable with. Okay, so back to the briefing. Obviously, there are people you don't trust. You want a cop's perspective, right? But it's got to be someone you can trust. Why are you so scared, Victor? [*Pause*] I'll tell you one thing right off the bat. I looked around that conference table this morning and I listened to that weird-as-they-come Oriental guy, Woo, the language guy there, and you know what hits me most of all? I'm bored. I'm bored to tears, Victor. Sorry, but that's from the heart. Anyone with the brain of a five-year-old can see that this Lingo stuff is just one more log on the fire, you know? To me, it's just not that interesting or different. Maybe the way it hits the brain and all makes Doc Woo all hot. Great for him. To me it's just one more product that no one's supposed to have. A controlled substance. That's the term. That's supposedly my job. Stand between the public and the product. They've got no right to it. Protect them from themselves. I don't want to get into a big discussion here 'cause that's not what this tape is for and I know how you get and it would only annoy you. But you're right to ask my opinion. 'Cause the fact is, you and I can't help but look at this thing from two different places. So, from my point of view, where does that leave us? The same boring vicious circle. The same system, over and over again. I'm not the smartest cop in the world, Victor, but I can't help but think every now and then about how both sides, the dealers and the cops, live off each other. And what would happen if it really ended? If you eliminated the product? What would they do and what would we do? Someone would have to think up something else. Forget it, I'm babbling. You know what's scary? I'm realizing that this is how my brain always works when I'm driving. Listen. The most likely way to distribute a new product is to run it through already-opened channels. Give it to the marketers to market. They're already set up for business. They know what they're doing or they'd be shut down already. They've got liquid capital. They've got experienced personnel. They've got distribution centers. They've got a pipeline to the customer. The customer's already trained, already running to them. Just bring in the spring line and hang it on the rack. They'll buy. If they liked designer A, they'll love designer B. So that gives us the Park, of course. There's no question. Bangkok is where the stuff is going to end up. So, it seems to me, this should run just like a normal investigation. We get word on a new shipment, something larger than normal. And you know, like they say, we round up the usual suspects. The system takes over. There's some fireworks, maybe. Some gunplay. The newspapers run a real sweaty story, a lot of front-page pictures, bodies facedown on the sidewalk, half covered up by blankets. And on Monday you come back to work again. But you seem to think there's something more here. You want to say the difference is the capacity for violence that the drug triggers. But please, don't insult me. I've seen almost ten years of people wired over the edge. It's just a matter of degree after a while. You think we've got a problem here. You say everything's still too vague, we don't have enough information yet. But you know what I think, Victor? I think that you think that there must be someone, maybe *someones*, that you suspect aren't exactly on the right team. And in this case, that bothers you a lot more than usual. [*Pause*] All right, Victor, I'm not saying yes or no. I've got some thoughts on the subject. Just opinions, you know. I'm pulling up to the visitors' parking lot at the Institute. There's a little white shack and a gate. I'm shutting off now. I've got to talk to the guard. Later, boss.

7

Rollie's Grill is a classic Quinsigamond Lunchcar Company diner circa 1925. It now rests on the original site where it was put down years ago. It was moved twice in the course of its life, but now it's back where it belongs on the corner of Frenchman's Boulevard and Fourier Avenue.

The current owner, a Cambodian who calls himself Harry, has done pretty well since he hauled ass out of his homeland in '75, just steps ahead of the bloody knives of the Khmer Rouge. Improbable as it might sound, he married a Puerto Rican girl named Isabelle and they've got quite the family now – four little girls who are always playing in the last booth next to the exit. Harry has trained them to scream when someone tries to bolt on a check.

Harry and Isabelle own an ark of a house, a sprawling three-decker crammed with people spanning almost a hundred years in age. It sits like a mirage behind the diner in a state of perpetual renovation. Harry's rounded up a few cousins who managed to escape genocide and he's trained them, made them into solid short-order cooks, though he thinks Lon is a little inconsistent on the omelettes. Isabelle, for her part, has a huge extended family, all of whom seem to work at irregular intervals, in one capacity or another, at the diner. The air during the dinner rush is a wild mixture of Spanish, Cambodian, and a fractured but street-hip English. The menu, scrawled at the start of each day on an enormous chalkboard that hangs by a chain from the barreled ceiling, often features an unlikely combination of paella, Kompong Som soufflé, and franks and beans.

Isabelle has done wonders with the diner. She's got a real knack, a genuine instinct for design and color. The Grill had become tired and shabby when Harry picked it up from its previous owner. In the past year the place has come back to life. While Harry secured iffy bank loans and scrounged for secondhand kitchen equipment, his wife retooled the whole of the diner. Isabelle swears she had no plan in mind besides restoring cleanliness and order, but one look inside Rollie's and you're forced to doubt her. She went back to the basics, scrubbed and rescrubbed the tilework and taught herself how to regrout. She stripped an awful yellow paint job from the booths, brought them down to the original wood, and then stained them into a subtle sheen. She recovered the torn stools, sanded down windowsills, spent hours scraping grease from the grill's backing wall.

And when everything passed her severe standards, she took the diner a step further. She branded it with the stamp of Harry and Isabelle, personalized it, made it unquestionably theirs. She went about this last step with the devotion and scrupulousness of a borderline fanatic. She mined their native cultures and combined the results for a weird but pleasing style. Two framed and matted maps of Cambodia and Puerto Rico now hang over each doorway. Shelves are crammed with carvings, curios, talismans from each homeland. The cash register is watched over by statues of both the Buddha and St. Anthony. It's as if Isabelle has formed a tiny new nation composed of artifacts from two very different worlds. And it's as if this minute, barrel-roofed nation immediately transcended its origins and wound up stronger and more peaceful than its forebears.

Dr. Woo has been waiting ten minutes, studying the decor, when Lenore comes through the door. She'd given him directions that were a little more vague than was necessary and she'd wondered more than once about whether he'd make it. She says, 'How goes the war?' to Harry's cousin Lon as she walks past the counter and slides into Woo's booth. Lon closes his eyes, grows a huge smile, and nods rapidly. Lenore thinks he's got a monster crush on her.

'Any trouble finding the place?' Lenore asks, sliding out of her jacket. The diner is always a little bit overheated.

'Not at all,' Woo says too fast. 'You give excellent directions. One of the benefits of police experience, I suppose.'

Lenore grimaces and makes a fast, reflexive shushing sound. She realizes she'll have to explain this, though she doesn't want to.

Woo looks around and asks, 'Have I said something wrong?'

Lenore raises her eyebrows. 'It's just that nobody here knows I'm a cop and, I don't know, I'd rather keep it that way.'

Woo looks interested. He lowers his voice conspiratorially. 'You think that their attitude toward you would change if they knew you were a police officer?'

Lenore shrugs. 'No idea. Probably not. I don't know. I just like this place. I kind of stumbled upon it and so far it isn't real popular. It hasn't been profiled in the newspaper yet. It's still mine right now. I just don't want to endanger – what is this?'

Woo doesn't know how to answer the question. This woman suddenly seems a lot more erratic than he'd thought at the briefing.

'What is what?' he finally says, trying to show the confusion on his face.

Lenore lets out a deep breath. 'Look, I'm working on a few hours of sleep here. A few hours out of like the past twenty-four. I mean, you asked me to lunch, remember. I assumed there was something you wanted to discuss regarding the briefing. I knew this wasn't a good idea.'

'I didn't mean to upset you, Miss Thomas,' Woo begins, but Lenore interrupts, saying, 'It's Detective Thomas,' then she hesitates and softens slightly, 'or Lenore. Just call me Lenore, okay?'

'And you may call me Fred,' Woo says.

'Are you serious?' Lenore asks.

'I don't understand,' Woo says.

'Whatever you say. Freddy it is. Your friends call you that?'

Woo is on the verge of being affronted. He says simply, 'That is my name.'

By way of a semi-apology, Lenore mumbles, 'Tell you the truth, I've never been crazy about "Lenore," you know?'

There's a couple of seconds of silence as they both stare sideways up at the menu board. Then Woo asks, 'How did you find this place?'

Lenore smiles, indicating that she likes the question, and Woo is pleased. 'Okay,' she says, 'my old man was a mailman, right? This neighborhood was one of his routes. And a couple times a week he'd eat lunch in here. Always the same thing. Cup of ham and bean soup and a grilled cheese sandwich. Back then it was owned by Rollie. The original Rollie. From the name, you know? So my father took us, my brother and my mom, here once or twice. I was pretty young. Then Rollie died and the place closed down for a while. Then it reopened and changed owners about every other year. Got real run-down. Got to look like a place you just didn't want to eat in. Then Harry and Isabelle bought it and cleaned it up again. I was working one night, over a year ago I guess, and I could *not* stay awake. I usually don't have that problem, but this one night, Jesus, I was just out. I was working, stakeout, you know, about a block away from here. Down off Ironhouse Avenue. And I came in here for a coffee. And that was it.'

'That was it,' Woo repeats.

Lenore nods. 'Yeah. The coffee was great and the place was great. And Harry was wonderful. I mean, charming. That's the word I would have to use. Charming. So I started coming in a couple of times a week for lunch...'

'Just like your father,' Woo inserts, pleased with himself.

'Yeah, right,' Lenore says. 'Just like my old man. And I got to know Isabelle, and then a bunch of the relatives.'

'And now,' Woo says, vaguely gesturing with his hands, 'you're a regular.'

'I guess so,' Lenore says flatly, secretly pleased by the comment.

'So what's good?' Woo asks, and it's a second before Lenore understands that he's referring to the lunch menu.

'Oh,' she says, 'just about anything. I'm going to go with the Monday Special and a black coffee.'

Woo raises his eyes to ask for more details.

'It's sort of this fried-rice goulash. Mostly vegetarian. Water chestnuts, onion, pepper, pineapple. You know what I'm saying?'

'Do they use MSG?' Woo asks.

'Yeah, I'm pretty sure they do,' Lenore says.

'Doesn't affect you?'

'I think it gives me a boost.'

'I think I'll have the tuna melt,' Woo says.

Lenore calls the order over to Lon, who starts putting it together immediately. She wonders if he's upset about her bringing another man into the place. She's never taken Zarelli here. Now she's glad about that.

'The reason I asked if we could have lunch,' Woo says, lowering his voice substantially to indicate his seriousness, 'is because I sensed a certain degree of, perhaps, hostility, at the briefing.'

'You did?' Lenore says blandly, showing a real disinterest. She wonders as she answers if a guy who's an expert on language can figure out what she's really thinking.

'Yes,' Woo says. 'I was thinking that, possibly, we could talk about that. In light of the seriousness of the situation and the fact that, whether either one of us likes it or not, I'll be consulting on this case, and most likely spending a good deal of time in your company, well, I was thinking that the way to proceed at this point might be to clear up any acrimony right at the start.'

'Acrimony?' Lenore says.

'Let me make a guess here,' Woo says. 'Permit me some groundless speculation for a moment, please. I was watching you this morning and I was wondering how many reasons could there be for your distaste of that meeting, and the presence of Agent Lehmann and Mayor Welby and myself…'

'Lehmann I know,' Lenore interrupts. 'Believe me, I've got my reasons for being hostile to Lehmann.'

'All right, fine,' Woo says. 'That still leaves the mayor and myself. Let me just tell you what I was thinking on the drive over here. I was thinking you'd be justified in some resentment. That some resentment of this morning's proceedings would be only logical. I was thinking how I might feel in your position. This is your line of work, your expertise, your city. You've got a long and proven history in dealing with narcotics and Bangkok Park. You've taken quite a few risks over the years, done what was asked of you and then, perhaps, a bit more. And this morning an image-obsessed politician and an ivory-tower academic come into your life and tell you what's new and what you're to do about it. It's patently unjust.'

Lon brings their food to the counter and Lenore, without taking her eyes off Woo, leans out and grabs the plates and brings them down to their table. She's got a frozen and bemused look on her face. She grabs the pepper shaker and puts a blanket of black powder over her rice, then mixes it up with her fork, still staring at him, until Woo starts to fidget and clear his throat.

'What?' he finally says. 'Have I offended you somehow?'

Lenore shakes her head no, slowly, a logy swing from side to side. Woo finds her bizarre, decides the lunch date was a mistake.

'You are slick, Dr. Woo,' she says. 'Very sharp, a very slick character.'

'I don't understand,' Woo says, fingering his tuna melt.

'No, no,' Lenore says, 'don't get me wrong here. This is refreshing. Trust me. I could tell you stories. The men I've known. God. No one has made this much of an effort in ages. I mean, I'm used to Zarelli trying to tease me like a sixteen-year-old, for Christ sake. I mean, this is an event. Really, Doc, you've achieved the effect you were going for. The closest I come to being flattered these days is from the Spanish pimps down Club 62.'

'I'm not sure I…' Woo begins, but Lenore waves his words away.

'No, I swear to you, Freddy, this is a compliment. Hey, this is the high point of the month, you know.'

Woo says, 'Lenore…' then just leaves his lips open slightly and she can see his tongue resting like a pink carpet in the valley of his mouth.

Lenore begins to laugh quietly, a low, guttural, staccato laugh that actually scares Woo a little. She takes in a mouthful of rice, sits back in her seat, and chews slowly, nodding and staring at him. Then, finally, she swallows and says, 'Here's how I see it, Freddy. I don't really care one way or the other about you or the mayor being at the briefing this morning. Just doesn't matter to me. I have other things to think about. The mayor just wasted a little of everyone's time, but no big deal. And you, I guess, might actually prove useful. At least that's what Lehmann and DEA seem to think. And Lehmann is an asshole, but he's not stupid. I'd like to say he was, but it's just not the case.'

She takes another helping of rice and pineapple, chews, swallows, breathes, and continues.

'But your version of things is very workable. You've got logic on your side and you bet that that was enough. Good bet. I would have sized things up in roughly the same way if I were in your shoes, so to speak. You figure you'll call me hostile, then, before I can get defensive, you'll acknowledge the correctness of my hostility, sort of putting us on the same side of the fence. Instant-comrades kind of thing. It's a nice maneuver. Got a lot of things going for it. It's kind of compressed, you know. Uses a domino effect. You call out a personality flaw in me, defuse it by labeling the reasons it's justified, disarm my reaction to it by allying yourself on my side of the fence, and come off like a real sensitive guy, all in one shot. Very good. Let me ask you, is that your standard approach for picking up women? Because I'm sure, God knows, it's effective, but it just seems like a little bit of overkill, you know. Like using a howitzer to kill a housefly. Haven't you ever just offered to buy someone a drink? What got to you, anyway? What, did you figure that same "hostility" that annoyed you so much in the briefing room would be a real different thing in the sack?'

She stares at him. She holds her fork out, halfway across the table, like a crude weapon. She can almost see his brain struggling to make a fast decision, whether to continue trying to feign innocence or turn the whole thing into a laugh on him, a 'you've got my number,' 'we can be buddies now' strategy.

He tries a third ploy. He says, 'You're a stunning woman.'

Lenore says, 'Yeah, I'm a real piece of work.'

Woo picks up his tuna melt, takes a tiny bite, puts it back on his plate, and wipes his mouth with the paper napkin. They're both quiet, sizing up the situation. Then Woo says, 'What I mean is that you're correct. I thought I was telling the truth about the nature of your feelings toward the outsiders at this morning's meeting. I honestly did. But, more importantly, that was secondary to my hopes of seducing you…'

'Seducing you,' Lenore repeats, too loud. 'God, listen to how you talk. You're a real winner, Freddy.'

'Fred,' he says. 'Just Fred, please.'

She ignores him, spears a water chestnut and a pepper with her fork.

Woo takes a breath and goes on. 'But what I find thrilling, right now, exciting, significant, is the fact that you intuited the actual intention, the hidden meanings, behind my words. You peeled back the first layer, what you wish to think of as a facade, though, again, I promise you it was an honest opinion on my part, but you stripped it away to expose the primary meaning of my message, the core of what I was attempting to communicate. You're a natural, Detective Thomas.'

'My head is just growing by the minute.'

'What I mean to say is you're the perfect person for this case. You appear to have a highly evolved sense of what I would call semantic intuitiveness, or, maybe, semiotic intuition, or...'

She cuts him off. 'Look, Fred, whatever you think, I'm not a very intuitive person...'

'I beg to differ...'

'I'm just not, okay. I'm the ultimate pragmatist. That's why I'm great at my job, if you want to know the truth. I find the easiest, most effective way of getting something done, then I just carry that out, follow it down the line. It seems simple to me and I don't really understand why everyone doesn't behave in this manner. Right now, what we've got to get straight is that fate has thrown us together. Well, fate and Mayor Victor Welby. Now, I don't know why. Standard procedure would be that you leave us your phone number and we call you up when we've got a question. Maybe you make an appearance at a progress briefing. But Miskewitz made it clear that the mayor has other ideas. He wants you and me together on this. He doesn't share his reasoning with me. So now I've got Mr. Ph.D. taking a field trip to Bangkok Park, with me as the tour guide. And there's nothing I can do about it. I just have to deal with it, figure out what might be the best, most efficient way to achieve our mutual end. Our end is to find out if this Lingo shit has found its way to my street, and if it has, to neutralize its effect on the local environment. You agree with that?'

Woo smiles, pushes his sandwich away. 'I like the way you talk. I like the rhythms of your natural speech.'

Lenore shakes her head. 'Jesus Christ, you don't catch on, do you? You know, in your own way you're a real moron.'

'No, no, Detective,' he says. 'I'm very clear on the fact that, from a romantic avenue, you've shut me down...'

'A romantic avenue,' Lenore repeats. 'Jesus.'

'But from your side of things, you have to try to keep in mind that my life revolves around language. So when I make the statement that I love the way you speak, I'm commenting on a professional level.'

'I'm sure.'

'Now, as to your summation of our mutual problem, yes, I agree.'

'You agree?'

'That our first step is to determine the presence of the drug, to find out if there was any mass production or marketing. Let me ask you. It's known I consulted with the Swanns while they were still at the Institute. Why aren't I a suspect?'

'Don't worry, you are.'

'Then let me say, here at the start, that my contact with them was very brief. We met three or four times at the most. I simply gave them my opinion on certain theoretical questions. If need be, Detective, I can certainly account for my whereabouts at the time of their deaths.'

'Yeah, well, believe me, Freddy, you're a long shot right now. I'm more inclined to start piecing things together from the distribution end. Down in the Park.'

'Bangkok Park?'

'You ever been?'

'I'm afraid not,' Woo says.

'Not even a drive-through? Little tourist peek?'

'My time is fully claimed, I'm afraid.'

'Yeah, mine too.'

'I've heard many of the stories, of course…'

'Of course,' Lenore mumbles.

'Younger colleagues who've ventured down…'

'A little excitement, a little spice, little break from the scholarly grind.'

'Exactly.'

'They lose a week's pay and their Blaupunkts and they think it's worth it.'

'I wouldn't know.'

'I would. Middle-class tourists in the Park piss me off.'

'Of course.'

'Place is a cesspool. Tell your people to stay in the Canal Zone with all the bohemians. They can get their kicks hitting on teenage lesbians with purple-dyed hair and snake tattoos.'

'Now, the Canal Zone I've been to…' Woo begins.

'I bet. Listen, Fred, the Zone isn't the Park. The Zone is all these kids playing artist in the run-down factories that their grandfathers broke their backs in. And that's fine, that's okay, I don't care. If they want to pretend that the Zone is loaded up with truth and danger, great. As far as I can see they're not hurting anyone. They play zipperhead music and write bonehead plays…'

'Actually, I've seen some of the performance pieces and…'

'And read dirty poetry. Super. Have a ball. But Bangkok Park isn't the Canal Zone. It's a whole different world. You know that the mortality rate in the Park is four times greater than any other square-mile area in the county? Probably in the whole goddamn state. Are you aware there's an entire economy that's completely independent from the rest of Quinsigamond and I'd bet its own little GNP works out at about ten times the city's total budget? You can't imagine the kind of cult crap that goes on in there. There's just a whole culture, a whole different set of… I don't know. You just have to taste it, you know. Words aren't going to do it.'

Woo sits back. He folds his arms like he's the one who's made some point, waits a beat before quashing an almost condescending smile, leans forward, right in line with Lenore's face, and says, 'That's always the case, isn't it?'

8

'All right, now just calm down, take a breath, you feel faint? You look a little green, you want to put your head down? Just try to relax for a second, you're just a little queasy. It happens.'

Eva closes the door to her office and pulls a battered green shade down over the window. Ike sits in the dull-metal straight-back chair, the weight of his upper body resting on his forearms, which rest against his thighs. He's breathing heavily.

Eva moves behind the chair, puts her hands on his shoulders, lets them rest there for a second, then begins to rub them in small circles down to the shoulder blades, then back in close to the neck.

Ike mutters, 'I'm really sorry about this. I just got a little nauseous.'

Eva repeats, 'It happens.'

Ike clears his throat. 'What should I do? Should I head downtown, tell the postmaster?'

Eva stays silent. She walks to her desk, looks down into the small package laid open for inspection on top of yesterday's newspaper. She looks at the package's contents dispassionately, maybe even a little bored, as if she were an aging pathologist and the contents were just one more in a series of autopsies she's run through year after year. The smell, however, is difficult to ignore.

'My job right now,' she says, 'is to be brutally honest with you.'

Ike comes upright in his chair, nods, and says, 'I understand that.'

'What you did in opening that package is a big offense. We both know this. Procedure would have been for you to bring it to me. To let me make the determination. You acted on impulse and that surprises me.'

Eva pulls a long black-handled scissors from her pencil cup and makes one slow, deliberate poke at the mess in the center of her desk.

'Still, we're dealing with a very unusual set of circumstances here. And experience has taught us all that it can be quite costly to march to the letter of the law. We all remember Shipley.'

Ike nods, staring at the floor. He doesn't actually remember Shipley, but he knows the story that gradually, as time goes by, is being upgraded to legend. It goes back maybe twenty years now, when Quinsigamond was caught in an unusual wave of civil unrest. Shipley was a nighttime sorter down the main station who came across a suspicious package that was making a ticking noise. He was a by-the-book guy and as he walked the long corridor to the supervisor's office, the bomb went off and Shipley lost his hands.

Though Ike doesn't know it, Eva has always hoped for a day when Shipley's common face would grace a commemorative, a sad and noble set to the eyes and two hook arms crossed over the chest.

Eva sits down slowly in her chair, her eyes on Ike the whole time. 'I'll level with you,' she says. 'I've got a tough call to make here, Ike, and I've always found in situations like this that it's wise to allow a good bit of intuition into the weighing process. Now, nothing I say here goes outside that door, agreed?'

Ike lifts his head and gives a series of fast, short nods.

'Okay,' Eva says. 'Then I don't think there's any reason to go downtown on this one. It was a freak, a onetime occurrence. Let's learn from it and move on. I don't think I need to mention, though, that if it had been Wilson or Rourke, the paperwork would already be in the typewriter. You're clear on that, right, Ike? I'm letting your past record and your general character carry the day here. You're aware of my reasons for this decision?'

'I'm aware,' Ike says.

'Now, it might be a little sticky tying up loose ends, but I've handled worse. First of all, let's get the log and see who's the tenant of box nine.'

She rises out of her seat with a visible burst of energy. Ike is pleased to see her in good spirits, all upbeat and ready to move ahead. He knows that Eva likes him, but he's also had a small suspicion that she had this weird thing, sort of a fetish maybe, for discipline, for the idea that if you act out of line, there are absolute consequences that must be paid.

Eva pulls a small gunmetal drawer from the index file cabinet that rests on top of the battered green bookcase. It's identical to the card catalogue file in a library, but the post office uses it to record all the box tenants and their rent payments. Eva lays the box down next to the decimated fish remains and starts to flip through the first cards in the drawer. She stops, grabs a pencil, and writes something down on an old envelope, then she replaces the drawer in the cabinet and sinks back into her chair.

Ike wishes she'd say something, but she just raises her eyebrows, grabs the receiver off the phone, and punches in a number. While she waits for an answer, she tosses the envelope to Ike. It reads:

Loftus Funeral Home
388-3757

and somehow, to Ike, the dead fish in the package makes a little more sense. He thinks up possible answers: some family member displeased with the appearance of their deceased relative, some former embalmer who got fired…

'Hello,' Eva says, in a voice that sounds older than it is. 'This is Supervisor Barnes at the Sapir Street Postal Station. May I speak with Mr. Loftus, please?… I see, well, either one, whoever handles the mail… thank you…'

She puts a palm flat over the phone and says to Ike, 'You know that place?'

He nods. 'My parents were both buried out of there.'

She pulls her palm away. 'Yes, Mr. Loftus, this is Supervisor Barnes, Sapir Street Station, how are you this morning?... that's great. I'm sorry to bother you, but I was just doing the monthly review of our files here and I just noticed that there's no notice of rent paid on your post office box since last year... oh, I see... would you know the exact date on that by any chance? A ballpark guess... is that right? Well, again, I'm sorry to bother you. You can imagine how the bookkeeping can get from time to time, clerical errors and... yes, sir. And how is your service now? Any problems with your carrier?... very good, then... all right, then. You give me a call if we can be of any assistance... sorry to disturb you... all right, thanks again... goodbye.'

She hangs up the phone. Ike wishes she'd get rid of the fish. The smell is filling the office and who knows what kind of parasites might be crawling onto the desk.

'They canceled box nine over a year ago, just like it says on the card.'

Ike doesn't want to hear this. The idea of a twisted, disgruntled ex-employee was helping to clear everything up for him.

'Who's got the box now?' he asks.

Eva shakes her head. 'Unless there's a mistake, the box was never rented out again. According to the log, it's been empty since Loftus Funeral Home let it lapse. I suppose it could still be intended for them. Sent by someone who didn't know they'd canceled.'

Ike says, 'I guess.'

'But it's odd it's not addressed to them. It was addressed to the box. There's no mention of Loftus anywhere on the package.'

They're silent for a minute, then Ike says, 'Lot of messed-up people out there.'

'In here too,' Eva says without any hesitation.

Ike thinks she must be making a reference to Wilson and Rourke and maybe even Bromberg. He thinks she's really hung up on these people, really a little overconcerned. He's disappointed to think Eva's perspective could be so biased or obsessive. He wouldn't have thought she'd be someone to waste a lot of time thinking about the likes of Wilson and Rourke. They're small concerns, little aggravations. They're like a pothole in the street you live on – you just learn to navigate around them. Pretty soon it just comes naturally, reflexively, no thinking involved.

Finally, Eva gets up and dumps the whole package into the wastebasket. She goes to the supply closet and takes down a full bottle of generic ammonia, uncaps it, and pours a little into the basket. She puts the ammonia back in the closet and says to Ike, 'You never know when you're going to need that.'

He thinks that in a few minutes the room will be suffocated with the burning reek of ammonia, but at the same time he likes the idea of all of the parasites and germs being poisoned into oblivion. He guesses Eva has made the right choice.

'Who do you think sent it?' she asks.

Ike says, 'The fish?' even though he knows she means the fish.

Eva stays mute.

'No idea,' Ike finally says. 'There's no way of knowing. That's the thing about mail. It can come from anywhere, out of the blue. Without a return address there's no way to know where it came from…'

He almost bites off his own tongue. What the hell is he saying? Twelve years with the service and he can make a statement like that? The fish must have shaken him on some deeper level that he's not even aware of yet.

'The cancellation stamp,' he moans.

'Don't bother to look,' Eva says.

Ike wasn't really thinking about looking. 'No,' he says.

Eva shakes her head slowly and emphatically. Ike thinks she'd look perfect right now if she took a long, thin, foreign cigarette, already in an antique black holder, and inserted it between her lips.

'There was no cancellation mark,' she says. 'There was no postage stamp at all. No meter sticker. No indication of origin whatsoever.'

'I was so taken back,' Ike says, 'so surprised and all that I didn't…'

She cuts him off with a single and unconvincing word. 'Understandable.'

He pauses, thinks, and says, 'So how did it get here?'

Eva puts her hands together and moves them to crack her knuckles, but no sound issues.

'Two possibilities,' she says. 'At least two that are most likely. Someone got in here when we were closed and deposited the package.'

'Or?'

'Or one of our own brought it in.'

9

'It's a beautiful car,' Woo says, honestly admiring Lenore's restored Barracuda.

'Yeah,' she says, not knowing why she's annoyed by the comment. 'I'm saving for a Porsche.'

'Expensive car.'

'Expensive is a relative term.'

Miskewitz spoke to her once about the Barracuda. With its ten-coat black paint job and its perpetually gleaming coat of polish, he felt it was a little too conspicuous down in the Park. Lenore didn't give an inch. Without coming flat out and saying he was an office boy who didn't know gak when it came to the Park, she made the point that where there are smack dealers, there are flashy cars and that the Barracuda was as appropriate as she could get on her insulting salary. It was a tense moment. Miskewitz sensed there was a line he could cross over, that there was an intricate balance between getting what he wanted and holding on to experienced field people. Lenore carried the day and since the incident there's never been another word about the car.

Woo pulls a cassette from a built-in pocket on his door and reads the title aloud. '*Discount Lobotomy* by Goebbels and the Woofers.'

Lenore refuses to be embarrassed. 'It's cutting-edge stuff,' she says. 'It's the music of tomorrow. It's not for the average person. The average person couldn't handle it.'

Woo has enjoyed her reaction. He starts pulling out other cassettes, mumbling their titles.

'*Your Aryan Masters Sing Songs for the New Order.*'

'These people are artists…'

'*Drop the Bombs, I Want to Get Off.*'

'You have to look past the limitations of history…'

'*Genocide Rag* by Stalin's Moodswing.'

'Shock is a freeing-up tool, a device for liberation…'

Woo smiles and raises his eyebrows at the same time. 'Quite the music library, Detective.'

Lenore smirks, decides not to waste her breath, and says, 'What do you know about it?'

'Not too much,' Woo says. 'My taste runs to Gregorian chants.'

'You're kidding me,' Lenore says, half interested.

'Not at all. There's real power there, believe me. An overwhelming confidence. I could give you some tapes. I really think you'd like it if you gave it time.'

'Yeah, well, time is a problem these days.'

They're sitting in an unused delivery alley on Voegelin Street in the heart of Bangkok Park. Across the alleyway and a half-block north they can see the rear of Hotel Penumbra. Lenore is waiting for an olive-green Jaguar XJ with customized, heavily smoked, and bulletproof windows to roll up and park in the private garage below the hotel. Cortez is late and that's a bad omen. Cortez has a penchant for being on time.

Lenore speculates that maybe it was Mingo Bouza's fault. Bouza is Cortez's chauffeur/valet/comedian, the latest in a series of aides who seem to chronically disappear without any notice or explanation. Maybe Bouza was late picking Cortez up at the masseurs, where he goes three times a week for a rubdown.

Cortez has been the proprietor of Hotel Penumbra for a little over a decade now. There are a good many people, and Miskewitz is one of them, who regard Cortez as the main reason for the blindingly rapid and catastrophic downfall of Bangkok Park. Not that the Park was ever a garden spot, but there are still a few people alive in Quinsigamond, in some dim, forgotten nursing homes, who could tell you about a neighborhood of blue-collar but upright immigrant people, a place where you could walk the streets day or night and children grew up in enormous numbers. The Park fell into a common ghettodom in the postwar years and gradually, drugs, gambling, barterable perversion and weaponry moved in more and more. But it wasn't until about fifteen years back that Cortez came to town and the Park became an official war zone and any atrocity was an ongoing possibility.

Lenore is one of the few people who will not lay blame at Cortez's feet. She's seen more than most of the others, and she knows he's up to his elbows in a kind of limitless and surreal, postmodern vice, but he's a player like the rest. She's sure there are people above Cortez. They don't come near the Park. They may not even venture into the county. She has no idea of their names or identities, their ages or positions, creeds or lands of origin. There's not a shred of physical evidence that they exist. But Lenore is absolutely certain of their existence. It's one of the few principles that reside in the vague and shifting cortex of her brain she silently calls *faith*.

Lenore has labeled these suspected higher-ups, these alleged invisible handlers of Cortez, 'the Aliens.' She does not discuss her belief in the Aliens with anyone. She thought about broaching the subject one night over dinner with Ike, but he fell into a coughing fit as she began to open her mouth and by the time he recovered, the moment was gone. Lenore's highest goal in life is to discover the Aliens and annihilate them. This is not because she finds their exploitation of the Park morally abominable or ethically unacceptable. She can no longer debate things in these terms. It is because she views their unflinching refusal to show face as a sign of ultimate cowardice. They want unlimited rewards without any risk. They want complete bounty without exposure or effort. Lenore views this mode of behavior as an affront. She feels her future destruction of the Aliens will simply be a lesson to them in the ways of nature, in the city of Quinsigamond.

To achieve her hidden goals, she's had to use a substantial amount of savvy and deception. Her sole connection between herself and the Aliens is Cortez, so she's had to walk a line that grows finer each passing week between practically protecting a known if elusive felon, and appearing to perform her job not only correctly but aggressively. Her major ploy, and she fears it's growing thin, has been to continually hint at major future arrests, the leveling of Cortez, Hotel Penumbra, and the entire network of illicit activity that flows in and out its doors. She has had several uncomfortable conferences with Miskewitz, told him she's building an elaborate investigation that will lock Cortez up in Spooner Correctional for life, rather than the pitiful wrist-slap he'd serve if they grabbed him on the small-time charges they're already sure of. Luckily, Zarelli backs up everything she says. She knows that's because he believes it. He's accepted the fact that Lenore cannot live by the good-partner rule of shared information, that she's a reservoir of secrets. Zarelli doesn't even care anymore that he's left in the dark. His world has narrowed until its boundaries consist solely of Lenore's neck, breasts, hips, thighs.

Does Lenore find Cortez attractive? There's no question. Often, as Zarelli clumsily climbs on top of her, smelling of Fiorello's garlic and cigars, she's made him into Cortez, lean, foreign, murderous, a slightly hyper nervous system under rigid inner control, a huge and twisted sense of humor, daring in bed up to the line of perversion. Maybe sometimes darting over the line.

She has dreamed of Cortez, the images very faded and confusing now, but involving, among other things, a bed of fresh poppies, leather, gunpowder smoke, scarred dark flesh. She would like, just once, to taste him, to run her tongue from his Adam's apple slowly down to the imagined patch of jet-black hairs near the navel.

What does Cortez think of Lenore? It's possible, maybe even likely, that he knows she's a cop, though neither of them has ever communicated the fact and both continue to play at the vague cover story that she is either a misplaced and rootless, existential bohemian walking foolishly into the dark world of psychotic outlaws and anarchy, or a mysterious, very smart and tough hooker-cum-pimpette looking to advance into the world of narcotic brokering. Or, possibly, some weird mutant, an anomaly with an untold story, moving into Bangkok Park for reasons no one is quite connected enough to grasp. In his heart of hearts, at the unstable core of his self-honesty, he is intrigued by Lenore to the point of foolishness. He finds her the most exciting woman in his memory. And Cortez has had more women than Elvis.

Lenore and Cortez have never spoken. All of the communication between them is suggested, implied, an almost too-subtle blend of gesture, attitude, eye movement. She thinks he's aware that she's protected him from serious harm for over a year now. He thinks she knows he's placed her off limits for the normal Park harassments and shake-downs that fall under his domain. They've both extended these cloaks of safety for a common, simple reason: they both want to see what will happen in the course of their future interactions.

Cortez secretly refers to Lenore as 'the Widow' because of her penchant for wearing black when visibly in the Park. No one understands the intricacies or delicate logics of their relationship and, in fact, though unbeknownst to her, it is Lenore who has been the cause of so many of the right-hand men getting the sack. Already Mingo Bouza, wise in his own way, suspects this. He treads lightly when the boss makes obscure comments about the Widow from the backseat of the Jaguar.

Lenore and Cortez have never really come into direct contact. They see each other from a distance, on the street late at night. They have winked to each other across the packed dance floor at Club 62, in the lobby of Hotel Penumbra. They communicate solely through the written word. They seem to leave humorous and taunting messages for each other in odd, exposed locations

– graffiti scrawled in telephone booths and on the walls of dingy unisex rest rooms. Cortez has Mingo drive to strange spots in the middle of the night, run to a designated area, and copy down words off a wall, into an expensive leather notebook. Sometimes, Mingo's instructed to leave behind some words he doesn't even understand.

• • •

'How much do you know about this Cortez character?' Woo asks.

'More than anybody else,' Lenore says.

Woo's presence is more than an aggravation. It's a kind of personal insult. There's no way the mayor can know what he's doing to her, forcing on her the presence of Dr. Woo. It's an intrusion on the one area of life, the few continuous moments, where she's satisfied. And in this way, it's like a subtle rape, a forcing of an alien will. But the rapist isn't Woo. It isn't even Miskewitz. The attacker is Welby and Lenore won't forget that.

She decides to talk, to lay out what she knows. It isn't that she has any interest in appeasing Woo or being polite or helpful. It's simply that she loves talking about Cortez and is frustrated by the limits she's imposed upon herself. Talking about him makes her feel more connected to him, more a part of his world. She wonders, given the right set of tragic circumstances, could she ever draw down on Cortez, grip tight on the Magnum, and fire death into his chest? Unfortunately she knows that she could, that there would be little question about what to do, that self-preservation would carry the day and she'd leave the King of Bangkok in a bloody, gasping heap outside the revolving doors of the Hotel Penumbra.

'The big fact that you have to know,' she says to Woo, 'is that Cortez is the King of Bangkok.'

Woo nods, feeling hip, feeling like he's ready to slide into the swing of things. 'He's the top dog,' he says.

Lenore raises her voice. 'That's not what I said. I said he's the King of Bangkok. Inside Bangkok, he's the King. But Bangkok isn't the whole world, is it? There's a lot more terrain to this planet than Bangkok Park, right?'

Woo is at once cut back to a fumbling humility. He goes quiet and Lenore, content in his silencing, begins her story.

• • •

Cortez's history begins the day he got off the bus in Quinsigamond. Logic and the nature of life tell Lenore that he obviously came from somewhere, that there is more information, probably stored somewhere south of the border, in bulging police files in Colombia or Bolivia. But that ancient history is incidental.

Lenore became involved the second that Cortez's snakeskin-booted heels touched down on the asphalt of her city's Greyhound station. She wonders if, on that particular day, she felt a change in the atmosphere, noticed some unexplainable rise or dip in the barometric pressure around her body. At the time there would have been no way to ascribe a relevance to it, but today, she swears, she can feel the flux in the air when Cortez's Jaguar gets within a block of her.

At first Cortez was just one more player in the overload of aspiring brokers feeding off the decay of the Park. Now, his displaced contemporaries will say he had no blueprint, that he tried a little of everything – pimping, extortion, the smack trade. Lenore finds this very hard to believe. She thinks it's an impression that grows out of the fact that Cortez is so good at thinking on his feet in continually changeable, pressurefilled situations that associates start to decide this indicates a lack of long-range planning skills and backup contingencies. Lenore thinks that the two virtues are not mutually exclusive. She finds them both in herself.

Whatever his endeavor, Cortez started cornering markets within his first six months as a Park resident. His unique intelligence and personality and ability to judge character combined with an innate sense for reading the marketplace that would have done just as well on Madison Avenue or Wall Street.

Cortez reaped huge cash profits in his first year as a 'no-holds-barred entrepreneur.' Like an old-time Yankee baron with a sense for building solid and conservative foundations, Cortez plowed big chunks of his income into real estate. Virtually every piece of land was for sale in Bangkok Park and Cortez seemed to gobble most of it up. At the Quinsigamond Registry of Deeds, his company, Rayuela Realty Trust, vied with an ancient Boston banking conglomerate for most titles recorded in the shortest period of time.

Ironically, Cortez considered his finest acquisition that first year to be the old and decrepit Hotel Penumbra. He loved the look of the place, its weird, monstrous façade. The building had been put up back around 1900 by an architect with a sense of the threatening and the theatrical and a strange love for a mutant design that was part High Gothic and part art deco.

Cortez made the building his home and business headquarters and then he went a step further. He set about to invest the old hotel with his own character, to will it into a perfect representation of his personality, a signpost of his Olympian goals, a chronic, granite reminder of his very presence and force on the landscape. He wanted a dark and frightening shrine to his power, his essence as defined by real estate.

The transformation turned the hotel, already something old and interesting, into something bizarre, a surreal stationary carnival injected into the heart of Goulden Avenue.

Now, as before, the building sits five stories high. But in clearing away a century of grime and dust, it came to look taller, to stretch wider on the block. The outer face of the building is an illogical mix of marble, sandstone, granite, and a copper that oxidized within the first ten years and settled into a sea-green color. The whole ark is a maze of jutting angles, most set at forty-five degrees. The main entrance is a row of revolving doors, which means that luggage must be brought in through a side door. Above the entrance is a flat awning-overhang made of hand-scrolled copper and electrified with hundreds of glowing bulbs. It's held up above the sidewalk by four sets of enormous linked chains that stretch up into the air like the fat lines of a whaling ship, then mount into the side of the hotel in black iron sockets that look like portholes. Three sets of windows run up the front of the building, the middle set recessed slightly and the set on either side protruding like enclosed medieval kings' balconies, ornamented with tiny copper catwalks with iron-bar railings. The top of the building rises up with two towering octagonal spires with hideous gargoyles running around their bases. Lightning rods with silver-ball tops rise out of the spires and Cortez has made them into twin flagpoles from which he flies huge flags bearing his family crest. At night, he illuminates them with unreal blue-white beams from a row of antique, Broadway-style klieg lights mounted on the roof.

At midnight, the Hotel Penumbra looks like some cursetinged, truly haunted fortress, pulled from the soaked and wormy earth of an Eastern European mountain community and transplanted, intact, into the drug-crazed terrain of Bangkok Park.

The inside of the hotel, however, is a different story. No one but Cortez knows for sure, but there are rumors that he's dumped anywhere from two to five million into restoration and renovation. On the first floor, where the Standish Lounge and Supperclub were once located, Cortez has modeled, out of a gutted cavern, the now-infamous Club 62, by many estimations, the darkest, hippest, most dangerous nightspot in the Western world. Club 62 is more like an upscale, outlaw flea market than a nightclub. Everything is for rent or sale. What is not readily available can be procured and delivered within an hour.

The interior walls of Club 62 are high-quality red brick and mortar, painted a cool white. Cortez has had them customized so that a continuous stream of red-dyed rainwater runs down the walls into a sewer grating. One regular is said to have thought the walls looked like 'an autopsy-room floor turned sideways' and that this is the exact effect Cortez was going for. Certainly, the furnishings and decor do not emphasize comfort. Though there is no need for them structurally, huge black iron beams with endless rows of rivets and studs run through the air. The tables and seating follow this same iron-and-steel/heavy-industry motif with enormous I-beams laid down as benches and small, mock conveyor belts mounted here and there as cocktail tables. Lighting comes from a continuous row of industry-sized, high-intensity, neon-green bulbs trapped inside wire-mesh caging high up near the ceiling. It has been said that the mixture of the green light playing off the rushing blood-water of the walls can give the place a Christmassy feel, but Lenore finds this hard to believe.

The cocktail waitresses are all Amazons. There are minimum height and shoulder-span requirements for hiring. Their uniforms consist of black leather motorcycle pants with red stripes down the side, neon-green suspenders, and black, pointy, steel-toed boots with odd cowboy spurs mounted on the back. The hostess is signified by the wearing of a black miner's hard hat with inset flashlight.

The floor of the club is simply a bed of crushed gravel. This makes for a constant *cushing* background noise.

It is rumored that people disappear into the bowels of the club for weeks on end, emerging with skin paler than the dead and eye pupils so small they can barely be seen.

It is rumored that the drugs of choice are a synthetic designer amphetamine called Opie, short for Oppenheimer, and an antique hallucinogen called Rucksack Ho. It is rumored that these goods are sold openly, by waitresses moving from table to table with large trays supported by a thick strap around their necks, old-time cigarette-girl style.

It is rumored that on Tuesday and Thursday nights, orgies of unspeakable shape and length are regularly scheduled and executed, and that often Cortez himself will direct the activities, barking out acrobatic instruction, from a hidden balcony, with an old-fashioned police bullhorn.

On the second floor of the Hotel Penumbra is Cortez's brothel, what he calls the Secretarial Pool, and what customers know as the Deer Park. It is rumored to house a dozen girls in a blend of royally pampered Euro-luxury and subtle Oriental beauty. It is rumored to capitulate to any fantasy a customer can call up or refund 110 percent of your money. It is rumored that no one has ever requested the refund.

On the third floor are the living quarters of Cortez's staff. There is Mingo Bouza, newest member of the group, chauffeur, valet, and companion. Cortez likes to laugh often, to be entertained. Mingo is something of an amateur stand-up comedian. This was his main qualification for the job.

Next to Mingo's suite is Jimmy Wyatt's. Jimmy is the hotel's resident muscle. He lives on steroid injections, raw eggs, and a mystery liquid that he keeps in a silver pitcher next to his bed. Jimmy was born and raised by a schizophrenic ex-nun just outside of Las Vegas, Nevada. He killed his first man in a dispute over who would purchase the last newspaper at a drugstore. He was sixteen years old. He can bench-press over 250 pounds, run the mile in 4.4 minutes. He spent three years in Korea sleeping under burlap, perfecting a martial art that has yet to be named. Jimmy is a mute, having had his tongue cut out during the '76 prison riots out at Spooner Correctional. Jimmy considers himself something of a natty dresser, which Mingo finds a riot. All of Jimmy's clothes are made of spandex or leather. Jimmy serves as Cortez's personal bodyguard and, rumor has it, traveling assassin.

The last of the third-floor trio is Max, a local kid, about fifteen years old, born in the middle of the Park, a native in every sense of the word. Max is the houseboy, the gofer, the collector of loose ends. He never seems to sleep. He has lived in the hotel for over three years now. He's all dark skin and thin bones and a wild head of bushy jet-black hair that tends to wave, like some southwestern American Indian. Max dresses in army fatigues and high-top sneakers. He takes a chronic but good-natured ribbing from the Secretarial Pool. One rumor has it that Max is Cortez's son. Max is not sure one way or the other. So far there is no rumor about him being the Widow's snitch.

The top two floors of the Hotel Penumbra make up Cortez's penthouse residence. They are connected by an authentically restored gilded-cage elevator. The rumor is that most of the renovation money went into the top of the building. Cortez has more square footage in, say, his bathroom than most of the houses of immigrant families of Goulden Ave. The rumor is that Cortez went through two architects, three interior designers, and an uncountable number of contractors before he got his home the way he wanted it. He lives alone. Very few people have seen the inside of his place, the Sanctuary, as he calls it. The regulars at Club 62 play games, making up details about the place. They say his kitchen has a separate electrical system for the sea of cutting-edge appliances, that his master bedroom could house a regulation running track, that his closet space would throw Princess Diana into a rage of envy. Though no one can come up with any logistics, the favorite notion is that his living room floor somehow retracts into the walls to reveal an Olympic-sized pool.

Cortez seems to be spending more and more time within the walls of the Sanctuary. The latest rumor is that he's got some kind of special library up there. That it takes up most of the top floor. That he's had the whole place fireproofed. That little Max is the only one to have seen it. And that it consists of either the world's most extensive collection of pornography, secret histories, or occult material.

For some reason, Lenore finds it easy to picture Cortez as the sole figure in a huge, dim, exotic library, perfectly postured in an ancient, uncomfortable wooden chair for hours, days, head bent slightly and hovering six inches above the pages of some enormous and weighty book, an atlas or an original philosophical treatise from fifteenth-century Italy, all worn-out purple leather and red vellum and smelling of oceans and the deepest caves of Europe, with all the words hand-printed, calligraphied, and illuminated by obsessive, virginal, paranoid monks.

She can picture Cortez unmoving, dressed in a floor-length maroon robe with loose cowl hanging down the back, subsisting on cold bitter coffee, his hair becoming tangled and matted, sweat breaking from the hairline to the eyebrows, his lips opening and closing, twisting in new ways to learn an unfamiliar language, conquering yet another risky frontier—

• • •

'The irony is,' says Woo, 'that I actually have family in Bangkok. The real Bangkok. In Thailand. Distant cousins. Some branch of my mother's side of the family.'

'Just one crazy world,' says Lenore, keeping her eyes on the back door of the hotel.

'I don't know Mother's side very well, actually. Very diverse. Very spread out. Father's people were from Hong Kong. He was something of an electronics wizard. He emigrated in 1935 with his new bride.'

'Adventurous guy.'

'He did well. Classic story from that generation. Poverty to the good life in thirty years. He ended up the head of Research and Development at Yen Labs.'

'Still alive?'

'He died two years back. My mother's alive, though. She's at the McLaughlin Home. Fine place.'

Lenore says nothing, but lets out a long sigh. Her speed kick is fading a little and she knows that within the hour her nerves are going to get a little raw.

'How about your people?' Woo asks. 'Your parents?'

Lenore stares straight ahead, tries not to blink. 'Both gone.'

'Your father was a mailman.'

'For about forty years. Ma kept the house. They were nuts for each other. One of those deals.'

'I like the way you talk,' Woo says.

'Shut up,' Lenore says.

• • •

The Jaguar rolls into the garage. After a few seconds Mingo and Max emerge. There's no sign of Cortez. Lenore figures he took the private elevator straight up to his place. She watches as Mingo pulls a wad of bills from his pocket, peels off a couple, and hands them to Max, talking the whole time. She wishes she had brought a high-powered lens and the ability to read lips. She thinks for an instant about asking Woo if he can read lips, but stays quiet.

Mingo steps back into the garage and the door rolls closed in front of him. Max pushes the money into his army-pants pocket and sets off down Goulden Ave, probably, Lenore guesses, to pick up some groceries or household supplies. She waits until he's out of sight, a good block up the road, then cranks the Barracuda and pulls out of the alley.

They pull to the curb slightly in front of Max and in her side-view mirror she can see him raise his bushy eyebrows. She lowers her window, waits a second for him to approach the door, and says, 'Maxie, honey, I've missed you like crazy.'

'What a wiseass,' Max mumbles, and climbs in the back.

10

On the ride up to the penthouse, the elevator speakers play a scratchy rendition of an old tango. Cortez concentrates, tries to recall its name, gives up when he reaches the top and the doors slide open. What he wants, more than anything, is solitude, to be isolated in his library, to leave word with Jimmy Wyatt that no one is to come upstairs under any circumstances. That when he wants food or tea he'll buzz the kitchen and Max can leave a tray outside the library door.

It's not that he wants a long stretch of time to read. His capacity for reading is diminishing daily. Not long ago, he was a record-breaking reader. Often, he consumed a book a day, first page to last in one sitting. It's been almost a month since he finished a book, a novel, written in an archaic Uruguayan dialect. It had started off like some kind of occultish mystery story, but changed at some point. There were passages he couldn't completely understand, and he got in the habit of supplying his own action at those junctures. It was the story of an indentured slave and his master, the descendant of European adventurers. They're the last inhabitants of an ancient family castle in some unnamed mountain region. The master is growing decrepit. He's the last of his bloodline and with each passing day it seems his cruelty toward his loyal servant grows geometrically. Cortez had the most difficulty with the last chapter in the book. It appeared to be a dream sequence, but there was no way to be sure. So he assigned his own meaning to the strange words on the last five pages, and turned the book into a revenge tale with the abused servant finally gaining the upper hand, avenging the pain of all his slave forebears, and in a bloody orgy of repressed hate set free, severing the old aristocrat's head and rolling it down the most jagged face of the mountain.

Cortez wishes he were better with languages. He's not bad, but he yearns for a natural facility, an innate talent that would give him foreign tongues with the ease of a reflex. What he really needs is time to concentrate, hours of uninterrupted study.

He lets himself into the library, unbuttons his double-breasted jacket, pushes a hand halfway into his pants pocket. He starts to walk around the outer edge of the room, next to the walls of empty shelves. He pulls an index finger across the length of the waist-level shelf and draws a line in a deep layer of dust. It's not the staff's fault. Everyone, even Max and Mingo and Jimmy Wyatt, has strict orders to stay out of the library. The library is for Cortez alone.

Months ago, the shelves were loaded, crammed with books, mostly fiction, a surprising number of whodunits. Packing all the volumes into those reinforced cartons took days, but Cortez did it by himself, late at night, looking blandly at each novel for just a second before laying it in its box.

He's not sure why, but he has always held the belief that a successful man must own a library. Where did this gauge of status come from? He can find no trace of it in any books and movies he was exposed to as a kid. It's doubtful it came from his mother or any of the dozen aunts who moved in and out of their small homes during his youth. It must be something that sprang, independent, into his still-forming brain. Just some weird, random spasm of development.

The buzzing noise begins to sound. When did phones trade in the ring for the buzz? He takes a deep breath, holds it, and watches the phone, a cordless black science-fiction prop, ring from on top of the mantel. Then he starts to walk toward it in slow motion. He makes foolish, time-distorted, exaggerated motions. He pretends he's an Olympic sprinter, shown on television from a distant country, crossing the finish line in a slowed-down instant replay, all arms and legs pumping.

He lifts the phone off the mantel as he exhales.

'Cortez,' he says, all gasp and wheeze. 'Yes, sorry, time got away. I was at the other end, ran the whole way… I'm sorry, could you speak one at a time? The connection… I understand. I thought it might be best to have my driver hand-deliver it… yes. Yes. I see. Very well, I'll see to it. I'll just mention again that we do have the testing facilities here and we could fax—… yes, of course. Certainly. The matter has had my utmost concern… well, he tried to say the sample went light on my end… my feeling is that we're dealing with a first-time middleman, a broker with too much ambition and not enough experience. I would—… yes, of course, I know. And I have. Very traditional message. He can't mistake our intentions. The first box is a warning. The next step is his… well, the problem, as I see it, is we have no alternate sources. This is a prototype. There is no competition. I've looked at the most recent reports from all the relevant networks. The Triangle isn't even aware. General Gow in Burma hasn't even heard rumors yet. I think it's safe to say one hundred percent domestic. Hard to believe—… uh-huh, uh-huh, that's right. An accidental by-product. All the great products arrive this way… oh, please, must we? Must you insult me this way each time? That's a legitimate expense. My car is the purest sign of my stature in the community. And I wouldn't have those neighborhood monkeys fill the gas tank. They couldn't tell a Jaguar from a Volkswagen… we agreed on this… all right, fine. Fine. I don't wish to argue… yes, I'll be here… yes. Yes. Goodbye.'

He looks down at the face of the phone, all the small, rubbery, yet illuminated buttons. He presses down on the Off button as if it were a detonator. As if this simple, solid touch could demolish the whole of the Hotel Penumbra, the walls crumbling inward and down, like an ancient yellowing newsreel of a firestorm in a long-forgotten war.

11

Peirce gets dizzy standing in line at the Burger Bonanza. She actually has to step to the side and lean against the stainless-steel shelving where big plastic tanks of mustard and ketchup, molded into the shapes of frontier water towers, sit dripping condiment from their spouts.

She doesn't know what's wrong with her. She makes herself get back in line, then she starts to suspect that this morning's briefing has affected her somehow. Not the photos of the murdered Swanns. And not the prospect of wartime in Bangkok Park. Those are standard elements in her work.

No, it was the unusual event, the presence of Dr. Woo and all his talk, his attempts to be funny and simple when nothing he was talking about was either. Parts of the brain being villages. How we make words. Why we understand them.

She's never really thought about this before and she still doesn't see a need to. But now, in line waiting to order lunch, it's as if just hearing this Woo guy, just being exposed to him, has somehow *affected* her. And so, when she takes in the whole scene here around her, it's suddenly too much.

All these teenage or elderly clerks, dressed in cowboy gear, polyester vests and chaps, and kerchiefs around their necks, lined up before their computerized cash registers that are made to look like covered wagons. Everyone talks at once in the same mechanized-polite voice. The clerks' hands push buttons on the computers as the customers speak. The fry-persons and assemblers behind the front row all wear mini-headsets with curved wire microphones that twist to the corners of their mouths. Voices issue from hidden speakers somewhere, lists of food and beverage orders coming from drive-through lines outside.

It suddenly strikes Peirce as an immaculate beehive customized for the production of processed circles of beef and moving faster than anything should.

She can barely stand giving her order to the geriatric cowgirl before her, and when it comes she grabs the bag and runs out to her car.

Once inside she locks all her doors and begins to take deep breaths. After a moment, her panic subsides. She punches a straw through the lid of her soft drink and starts to unpack her burger. Once she's set up, she grabs the tape recorder from under the seat and hits the On switch.

> Yo, boss, I'm back. It's Charlotte, the light of your life. I hope the chewing noises don't disgust you too much. I'm sitting in the parking lot of a Burger Bonanza over on Turnstein Boulevard. Any chance I might be reimbursed for a Rodeo Cheese Melt, large fries, and a medium Diet Coke? I mean, I'm still working and all. [*Pause*] The Institute was a trip, boss. I realized, walking into the place, that I'd been there once before. Are you ready? Seventh-grade field trip out of Brown Street Public School. Mr. Zamenhof. My science teacher. First crush. They took us on a tour. Some people in white lab coats. They brought us into a room, showed us pond water under a microscope. I was so impressed. We got to keep the slide. [*Pause*] Excuse me. [*Pause*] Oh, I'm going to pay for this thing. I'm getting too old. The body can't handle the grease. I've got indigestion already. Anyway, I flashed my badge to the front desk, this woman with a real attitude. She made a comment about phoning first, but she buzzed a manager and directed me down to his office. A Mr. Weston. First name, Booth, can you believe it? He's about thirty-five. A real smoldering yuppie type. Gray pinstripe, flaming red tie. Hair short but moussed. Body

of an eighteen-year-old marathoner, not that I noticed, Victor. The office was small but immaculate. Not a speck of dust. All gray and, what's that color, mauve? You know what I mean. The guy is not a scientist. More like an M.B.A. type. His official title is Director of Communications, but basically I think it's the public relations job. He keeps on top of the Institute's image. Takes all the weird crap they work on in the labs and translates it into nice Sunday newspaper feature stuff. 'We're about to crack leukemia' crap. He makes sure we hear about the Nobel Prize winner they've got on the payroll. He coordinates the dinners where the banks give plaques to some guy who cloned a tomato, you know what I'm saying? He invites me into the office, all controlled smile and calculated handshake. I'm doing my best back at him. He starts off in his friendly but professional voice about how he's already spoken to both the police and the FBI and the DEA and even some of my own people. I liked that last part, like the local cops were lepers or something. He's all nods and chuckles about how it's all in their notes already. So I'm smiling and nodding right back, mimicking his whole act, and I say, 'Yes, but it's not in my notes.' Just to let him know I can be a bitch if that's what he wants. Which we both know I can, right, Victor? So basically, he runs it down just like I expected from the briefing. Except that he keeps throwing in that the Institute has had no dealings with the Swanns since they left to form their own consulting firm, Synaboost, a good nine months ago. He says he knew the Swanns only slightly. He interviewed them, separately, when they first signed on board, that's how this guy said it, right, 'signed on board,' like he's a cruise director. He interviews everyone, makes a file on them for any future press releases, or that kind of thing. I asked to see the files, which were basically just what he said. Black-and-white studio glossies of each, good-looking folks, Victor. Leo, he's like a gracefully maturing surf Nazi, all blond hair and ten-inch teeth and tiny, gold-rimmed round granny glasses. Sort of a cross between William Hurt and Warren Zevon, if that helps. Forget it. I forgot, you wouldn't know either of those names, would you, Victor? Inez is another looker, but just the opposite of her husband. Darker, Old World look, big deep brown eyes, sort of a Spanish look to her. A Natalie Wood type. That's got to be a name we intersect on. I hope. The profiles were basically fill-in-the-blank stuff. They came to the Institute last year. Came as a team. One package, all or nothing. They'd both just finished up a two-year grant at someplace called Teller Labs Limited in Jemez Springs, New Mexico. According to the paperwork, this Teller place is a workshop under the direction of Uncle Sam, and the Swanns' grant was one hundred percent Federal money. Their project down there was listed as— [*pause*]. Hold it. I took notes. Yeah, here, 'Pinpoint Stimulation of the Anterior Speech Cortex Through Linguavoxide-Two Therapy.' [*Pause*] And you wonder where your tax dollars go, Victor. Anyway, the Swanns left New Mexico halfway through their two-year stay. The P.R. man said it was by mutual consent. Something like they got tired of the Southwest, and the army got tired of their pet project. But our own little Institute back here was all hot for it and made them an offer. Now, most projects at the place are worked on by teams of five to seven researchers. But the Swanns work alone. Just the Mr. and Mrs. Touching, huh? I guess it was one of their requirements before they'd take the position. [*Pause*] Oh, God, I feel awful. Why do I eat food like this? Why do I do this to myself? Jesus, Victor, you know I live on Zantac these days. You feel responsible for that at all? I'm done, that's it. I can't eat the rest of this. [*Pause*] Anyway, another requirement was no progress reports. The Institute has this hierarchy system where each project team has a group leader, just like chem lab in high school, you know. The first of each month the group leader is supposed to file a progress report to the board of directors. How the work is going, any breakthroughs, any setbacks. The Swanns said thumbs down on this. There was a note in the files that quoted Herr Leo as saying that this type of thing wastes his time and inhibits his imagination. I get the feeling this was a cheeky couple, you know? The Institute said okay, I guess they wanted these two. There was a small compromise. Leo and Inez said they'd let the BOD know whenever they 'turned a corner.' Those are Mr. P.R.'s words. But whether they turned any corners or not, in the whole time they were at the Institute they never wrote up a report. At least there's nothing in their files. They were very reclusive during their whole stay. They nodded hello in the morning and goodbye at night. They made no friends among the other researchers. No one ever socialized with them, was ever invited out to their home. These bastards even brought their own coffee in this huge thermos so they didn't have to go into the cafeteria. Fun couple, huh? Regular Rob and Laura Petrie. How 'bout that one? Did you get that one, Victor? Weston said that a few months into their work, the Swanns started staying late at the lab, and he's spoken to people who say that there were occasions when they worked all night. I've got to figure something was up. According to him, it was around this time that they made the request for some extra cash for an outside consultant. The boys with the checkbook weren't crazy about this. As a rule the Institute likes to work internally. They've got a farm team at various universities around the country. They like to bring people along, tap the bench. But the Swanns had a very specific request. Dr. Frederick Woo, a language theory expert right across the city at St. Ignatius. I guess there was a little tug-of-war, but as usual the Swanns got their way. Woo came on board in a limited capacity, just for a short period of time. I guess they wanted to bounce some ideas off him. But you know more about this guy than I do, boss. He's on your team now. And I'm not here to look into the technical crap. I could barely cut up a frog as a teenager. I'm just here to find connections and to do you a favor. [*Pause*] I'll be back soon. I feel like I could barf. God.

12

'So'd ya bring it?' Little Max says, making a halfhearted, unambitious grab for Lenore's breast. She swats his hand away, tired, but tied into the ritual that Max loves.

'I brought it,' Lenore says.

They're sitting in the Barracuda in the parking lot of the old Quinsigamond airport. The airport is deserted and abandoned, a mini ghost town of aviation. Weeds have grown up in the middle of both runways. Windows are smashed in and doors missing from the old wooden, Colonial-style terminal.

There's a new, modern airport a few towns outside of the city. Lenore hates the new airport, though she's never been there. She made a small vow to herself never to fly out of that 'abomination in the name of progress.' The old airport sits on the very top of one of the city's seven hills, and though this made it ridiculously susceptible to dense fog, it also gave it a strong quaintness and a view that extends for miles and, on some autumn days, all the way to Boston.

Woo has relinquished the front seat to Max and sits silent in the back, his hands folded and resting in his lap like a monk at prayer.

'So c'mon, c'mon,' Max says, 'let's see.'

Lenore reaches under her seat and pulls out an oversized black leather portfolio. She unzips the top, reaches in, and pulls halfway out what looks like a stiff piece of drawing paper or posterboard. It's filled with colorful cartoons framed in square panels with inked-in dialogue balloons. Woo leans forward to take a look. Max mumbles, 'Jesus,' with a real and humble reverence.

'What strips?' he asks quietly, his voice suddenly sounding much younger, even prepubescent.

Lenore suppresses a need to grin, a feeling of triumph. She acts bored and says slowly, as if attempting to remember bothersome facts, 'Two *Ripped-Up Man* and a *Prince Natema*, I think.'

'Oh, Christ,' Max says, and he sinks back into his seat, then snaps forward and says, 'Lemme see,' and tries to grab the drawings.

Lenore stuffs them back into the valet and holds it at her side.

'You're forgetting your manners, Maxie.'

Max breathes out a lungful of air and his head bobs fast and loose.

'How'd you get 'em?' he asks. He can't help himself.

'C'mon, you dink,' Lenore says to him. 'You know better than that. I ask the questions. That's how it works. My game from here on in.'

Max starts to drum on his legs with the palms of his hands and Lenore says, 'Look, Max, I own these now, okay? You want, you can get out of the car, and I can go home and burn them in my fireplace. They're mine. I possess them. I can do what I want. So don't waste my time and don't piss me off. You want some original Menlos, great. Tremendous. Start talking to Lenore.'

'Just one thing,' Max says. 'I really need this, okay? Do you know Menlo?'

Lenore says, 'I know people who know Menlo.'

She waits a beat while he digests this, then says, 'Now, your turn.'

Max nods, trying to be adult about the situation he's put himself in. He takes a breath and begins.

'Some shit is definitely up. Cortez is acting like a freakin' loon, okay? He can't sleep for shit. We hear him all night, me and Mingo and Wyatt. We hear him above us, in the library, I guess, pacing all night, walking around in big circles all freakin' night long. It'd drive you nuts.'

'He's expecting some merchandise?'

'That's what we figure. He's always uptight before a big delivery, but never like this. He's got us all running these dipshit errands, anytime at all. Three A.M. and he's buzzing on the intercom in this high-pitched voice, telling Mingo to go get ten cloves of fresh garlic. Yeah, you tell me, you know. Where do you get ten cloves of garlic at three A.M.? Mingo busted in the back door of this bodega down on Billings and cleaned them out. This isn't good shit for the neighborhood, you know?'

'Any visitors? Any phone calls?'

'Nobody new's come around. Phone calls, who knows? Cortez has got a dozen private lines up there. It's like the freakin' White House or something...'

'What kind of shipment are we talking? We seem to be saying this isn't any normal smack deal.'

'I'm just telling you the guy's on the edge, okay? I mean, you want me to guess, then okay, yeah, I'd say you're right. This is something new. This is something different.'

'But no sign of the Aliens...'

'Look, lady, I don't know the Aliens from shit. You think there's somebody over Cortez, but I'm telling you, no one else thinks so. He's gone big for a while now. He's got his own pipe to the Southland and the Triangle. Maybe there's some generals in Colombia or some big-time slants in Burma or somewhere that he's got to rely on. But here in the U.S., I mean, I'm telling you again, Cortez is no one's errand boy. He's independent. You give the guy ten more years and he'll own the whole East Coast. That's what Mingo says anyway.'

'Any weird shit at Club 62?'

Max lets out a wild, child's laugh.

'Stupid question,' Lenore admits. 'I mean anything weirder than normal?'

'Well, I'm not down the Club much, you know, except in the mornings when I help out with the cleanup. But Wyatt was telling me, I mean, you know, signing to me, how there was some crap last week.'

'Shooting?'

Max nods. 'Bad news, according to Wyatt. Two guys went apeshit. Started as this regular men's room brawl, two dorks all twitchy on speed. But they went at it like they couldn't die. Knuckles, then knives, finally they pull pieces. Now, this is from Wyatt, and usually he's okay, he's on the money, not like Mingo, you know? Wyatt says they each had like four or five bullets. In the arms, legs, in the freakin' neck, okay? And they kept goin'. Wyatt says like this was beyond like a coked-out numb or something. He says it was like you could see fire coming off their backs, whatever that means. He says they were fucked up in a way he's never seen and he says he's seen them all. You gotta remember, this is a guy who lived in Korea for a while…'

Max pauses, turns toward the backseat, and says in a lowered voice, 'No offense to your friend here.'

'I'm not Korean,' Woo whispers.

Max turns back toward Lenore. 'Wyatt says you couldn't even understand these guys. That this weird fuckin' clickin' and buzzin' sound was like comin' from their throats.'

Lenore and Woo catch each other in the rearview mirror.

'Are they dead?'

Max scrunches up his face and says, 'You kiddin'?'

'What did Cortez do with the bodies?'

'Wyatt and Mingo took the truck. Hauled them up to Galloway and dumped them in the Passaconaway River. Listen, the fish are gonna be buzzing from those guys…'

'Any of the girls been acting strange lately?'

'The secretaries?' Max asks, delighted, like it was a new and filthy word. 'They're all strange to me. You should hear the crap they say to me.'

'Nothing out of the ordinary?'

'We had a runaway last Thursday, but that's not like out of the ordinary. You know, one of them bolts every couple of months. Wyatt brings them back most of the time…'

'She have a name?'

'Called herself Vicky. She was probably like a couple years older than me. Redhead. She was really into those Harlequin books, those paperbacks, you know, at the supermarket. I talked to her a couple times, just joking around.'

'Vicky have any relatives in the city?'

'No, I don't think so. Not in Quinsigamond, I mean. She had a sister back home, she said. Darleen, I think. She was southern, from some small town in Mississippi.'

Lenore stares at Max for a long minute, then looks away, out over Quinsigamond. She studies the landscape, tries to pick out monuments, buildings, and streets she knows. Max fidgets, twists his neck around like it was stiff, scratches at his nose.

'That wasn't bad, Maxie,' Lenore says finally. 'That was okay. We'll call it okay. Not great, not quite what I needed, but it'll do for now. There's always tomorrow, right?'

'I guess,' Max says, unsure and nervous.

Lenore pulls the portfolio into her lap and takes out one of the drawings. 'What do we have here?' she says, seemingly to herself. 'We got a *Ripped-Up Man*. Oh, dammit, you like the *Natema* strips, don't you? Doesn't it figure?' She sighs and nods to herself. 'I'll tell you what, Max, you take the *Ripped-Up Man* print here, you take this one and I'll hold on to the other two. Then when you find out something more, something pretty specific about Cortez's shipment and plans and all, we'll get together again and you can pick up the other two prints…'

Max's jaw goes rigid. He bites in on his lips and stares at Lenore. He says, 'That wasn't our deal. You said three Menlos. Three originals…'

Lenore matches his heat. 'Things change, you little brat. You just calm down this second. You'll get the other two. I just need a little more information…'

'But this isn't what you...'

'Forget what I said, Max. This is how it is. You get the one print now. You get the rest later. That's it. End of discussion. Just do what I want and you'll have them all. And you know a smart little bastard like you might have thought for just a second that if I can get my hands on these, I can get my hands on others. Smart little bastard like you might have thought about the future a little.'

Max shuts up, slumps in the seat, and sulks for a second, then says, 'Just drop me behind Gomper's station, I'll walk home from there...'

'You got a stash there? You'll want to keep that clean...'

'Hey, don't worry so much,' Max says. 'I know how to take care of things. I'll need at least twenty-four hours. Look for me about this time tomorrow. I'll see what I can get.'

'I'll bring the prints.'

Max spits the words out like seeds from a piece of overripe fruit: 'I bet.'

Lenore kicks over the Barracuda and drives down Symon's Hill. Max hops out at the burned-out remains of the old train station and Woo climbs back in front. They idle for a second, watching the boy disappear inside the Gothic rubble of cracked marble and broken hunks of granite, into the rail pits where the trains used to roll in, away to some labyrinth of hiding places with his new joy protected inside his coat.

Lenore wonders as she watches: could he really be Cortez's son?

13

Eva locks up her office door, even though she knows the next shift-supervisor is in the locker room talking with the night sorters. She walks out of the station without a word to anyone, gets into her Volkswagen, starts the engine, looks in the rearview, applies the too-red 'Summer Flame' lipstick she picked up this morning. She pops the cassette of Wagner's *Götterdämmerung* into the tape player, pulls a harsh-bristled brush from her pocketbook and runs it through her hair, and shifts the car into reverse.

She pulls out of the station parking lot onto Sapir Street, takes her first left onto Breton, her next immediate left onto St. John Court, and another left onto Fairlane. She drives halfway down Fairlane and parks, locks up the car, and walks a block until she's on Sapir again.

She heads for the Bach Room, starts to walk past the entrance, then wills herself to move under the awning, to take a breath and pull open the front door. Lyons and Wales, whom she worked with downtown, come walking out, both talking at the same time. She holds the door for them and looks down to the ground. They move past her without a word, but as she lifts her head, she sees Lyons glancing back over his shoulder, still talking but staring at her with a puzzled and slightly sad look on his face. She hesitates, watches the pair move down the sidewalk, then steps inside.

The place is completely empty. She wishes her eyes would adjust to the dimness more quickly, but she knows they work at their own speed, and so she calms herself, walks slowly to the bar, and takes a seat.

Marconi walks to her slowly as if he's not sure what to do. She knows who he is from the mail-burning scandal, but they never worked at the same station at the same time, and she thinks it's unlikely he'd recognize her. He dips his head toward her and raises his eyebrows like they could communicate fully and with just gestures, muscles contracting and expanding.

When Eva doesn't speak, he says, 'Can I help you?'

She begins to order a drink, a shooter of schnapps maybe, but before the words come out, she changes her mind and says, 'I was wondering…' She pauses and looks behind her. She registers that one table in the room is covered with empty glasses and beer bottles. She turns back to a confused Marconi and says, 'I need some directions. Do you know how to get to Umberto Ave?'

Marconi just stares at her for a good ten seconds like she's spoken in some archaic tongue that he has vague and troubling memories of. Then he says, 'Jesus, I thought I knew every street in this city, but that's a new one on me. Is it 'round here? Is it supposed to be near here or something?'

Now it's Eva who pauses, until finally she volunteers, 'Yes, I mean, I think so. I mean, that's what I was told.'

'Umberto Ave?' Marconi repeats, giving the words an almost Italian accent.

'Umberto,' Eva says.

'Do you have anything else? Do you know what street it's off?'

'No idea. I think it might be a new street, though. Is there any new development going on around here?'

Marconi nods vigorously, thrilled that they've found some common ground, some sort of clue. 'Okay, that helps. You've got some new condos going up off of Eagleton. Pieces of crap really, but people are idiots, right? Then there are some duplexes, maybe a dozen new duplexes, being tossed up over behind the ball field off Sheary. Both of those are within a couple of miles.'

'Eagleton and Sheary,' Eva says as if she were trying to memorize the names.

Marconi nods and slaps the bar lightly. 'I've got a street directory around here somewhere. Only about a year old. Where the hell…'

'Is there a ladies' room?' she asks suddenly.

'Absolutely,' he says, 'of course. Right in the back.'

She slides off the barstool and heads in the direction he motions with his head. At the back of the bar is a small doorway that leads into a tiny alcove. Inside the alcove, smelling of an oily disinfectant, are two brown wooden doors, one labeled *Gents*, the other *Ladies*. She enters the ladies' room, a single toilet and sink. She locks the door with the small slide bolt and looks at herself in the oval-shaped mirror on the wall. She pushes some stray hairs into place, moistens her lips. Her heart is pounding, so rapid and forceful she feels a growing, frightening ache. She runs some cold water in the sink, lets the stream wash over her fingertips, then runs them across her forehead. She takes a series of deep breaths, tries to calm herself. She moves to the wall, touches it, then brings her ear to it.

She hears voices on the other side, and though she can't be sure, can't at first pick out any discernible words, instinct tells her she's listening to Rourke and Bromberg. Up in the corner, at the ceiling's edge, she spots an old brown metal grille, some sort of vent. Before she can think, she slides out of her shoes and climbs up on top of the toilet. She rises slowly toward the grille, holds her breath, then brings her eye close to look.

It's a small, bland room. There's a round wooden table in its center with five chairs pulled around it. One chair is empty. At the bend opposite her, Eva can see Wilson, still in uniform, holding a bottle of beer up near her chest with both hands. Jacobi is to her right, Bromberg to her left. That means the person with his back to her is Rourke. They each have something on the table in front of them, what looks like a tiny manila envelope, like a miniature pay envelope, maybe only an inch long.

Eva gets nervous and brings her head down below the level of the grille. She listens:

ROURKE: Don't be an asshole, Jacco. You let me worry about the Paraclete. You don't trouble yourself about it.

BROMBERG: Have you got a location picked out yet? We've got what… how many days?

ROURKE: We've got plenty of time. Jesus, would you people get a grip, take a few Valium or something? Goddamn.

BROMBERG: Screw you, Billy. It makes sense to be nervous. You've never worked anything like this before. You've never even come close.

ROURKE: Will you relax, for Christ sake, it's a broker situation. You've brokered one deal, bang, you know the ropes. You bring people together, you arrange the terms, you find the common ground.

WILSON [*laughing*]: Common ground? You been reading a book or something?

JACOBI [*laughing*]: He's been watching cable. He's been watching those guys in the shiny suits with the cassette tapes…

BROMBERG: You ever deliver a set of those things? Those home study things? Weigh a ton…

ROURKE [*yelling*]: Shut up… will you all shut the fuck up? Goddammit, this is serious here. For Christ sake.

BROMBERG: Why don't you tell us how serious, Billy?

There's a few beats of silence, then,

ROURKE: What do you mean? What do you mean, how serious?

BROMBERG: Well, I don't know about Wilson these days, but Jacobi and I, we haven't seen dime one for all this serious business…

ROURKE: You're an impatient little bitch, you know that, Lisa? Huh?

BROMBERG: Just didn't know if you only gave a cut to the people you were drilling.

WILSON [*yelling*]: Oh, screw you, you jealous little brat.

ROURKE [*yelling*]: Hey! Shut up! Just everyone shut up! Right now.

There's a couple of seconds of silence.

ROURKE: You keep this up and nothing's going to work out. Now, I've brought us this far, am I right? I've got both sides involved here. I've brought them to the table. I've made the connections, communicated the offer, communicated the negotiations, complimented everyone, kept the wheels turning, kept the cogs free. Now it's about to come together. Don't screw us up now. Jesus. This will be the sweetest move you've ever walked into, if you just let it happen. You've just got to learn some patience. All of us have to learn patience. You people don't understand the kinds of people we're dealing with here, the type of mentalities. There's a whole cultural thing going on here. From both sides, both directions. That's why we've got to be extra careful, make sure no one gets accidentally insulted, rubbed the wrong way, culturally, you know. Now, Lisa, you're all tight about the money end, which I understand. You've put yourself at risk, like the rest of us. We've got to remember, we've all shared equally in the risk. That was part of the price of admission. You've got to be a risk-taker to achieve anything in this world, right? Okay, today is a little preview. A little advance, a little look at what the future holds for everybody…

BROMBERG: You're kidding me. You've got some cash? You really got some cash?

ROURKE [*laughing*]: Relax, Lisa. What I've got is something better than cash. What I've got you can't get out of your all-night teller machine…

BROMBERG: No money, do you believe this?

JACOBI [*quietly*]: Let the man talk.

ROURKE [*quietly*]: You can open the envelopes now.

Eva raises her head slightly until she can see out the grille again. Everyone at the table is busy ripping open the flaps of the small envelopes. Jacobi gives himself a paper cut on the thumb and says, 'Oh, shit,' and plugs the thumb into his mouth and starts sucking.

Bromberg is the first to spill the contents on the table. Eva can't see much, just something tiny and reddish, smaller than a dime.

'Oh, you stupid mother,' Bromberg says, her voice so low and halting, Eva thinks she might fall off her chair.

Rourke seems to be dancing slightly in his seat. There's another uneasy silence, as if no one knows what to say. Eva gets nervous and ducks again to listen.

ROURKE: Yeah, yeah, so I scammed a little off the top. Who'll notice? They've all got enough to worry about. Think of it like we're these quality-control guys, okay? We've got to randomly sample some of the merchandise before we can vouch for it.

BROMBERG: No one's asked us to vouch for it.

ROURKE: Relax. Think of it like the way you read *Playgirl* before you deliver it. Or how I've seen you take home those detergent samplers when the people are on vacation, right? Relax.

WILSON: Weird stuff. Kind of like a noodle, you know. Like the noodles in soup or something.

JACOBI: Little harder than a noodle. But just a little. A little more rubbery.

BROMBERG: Is everyone's in the same shape?

JACOBI: The letter *Q*?

ROURKE: Like alphabet soup. Like one letter plucked out of a bowl of alphabet soup.

WILSON: Why the letter *Q*?

ROURKE: Who freakin' knows? These chemist guys are weird mothers. Who knows what reasons they got?

Eva lifts her eye to the grille and watches them all studying the substance in their palms until Rourke says, 'Since this is our first time, I think it might be a good idea here to go easy, if you know what I mean. Why don't we just break them in half if we can?'

'Just half?' Jacobi asks.

'Better make it a quarter,' Rourke says, hunching over the table and going to work on his Q. The others follow his example. Someone says, 'Not that easy to break.'

When they're all done, Rourke says, 'Cheers,' and brings his hand up to his mouth. Then they take turns swallowing while the rest watch, no one swallowing at the same time, as if a capacity audience were needed for the ritual to be legitimate.

BROMBERG: How long does it take to kick in?

ROURKE: Guess we'll find out. We're explorers.

WILSON [*upset*]: What about the beer? What if it doesn't mix with the beer? Maybe we shouldn't have drank the beer.

ROURKE: Knock it off. Don't you think they would have taken that into consideration?

WILSON: Who? Who're you talking about?

ROURKE [*exasperated*]: The chemists. The freakin' doctors who invented the shit in the first place. You think they're morons? You think they've got no feel for their market? For the social settings this thing will be introduced into? They think crap like this out. They take stuff like this into consideration. You people have got to learn to relax or you're not going to make it—

WILSON [*interrupting*]: Not going to make it? Do you mean like in general, in life in general, we're not going to make it, or do you mean right now, when the thing takes effect, like if we're tense or nervous or upset it will have some awful side effect—

ROURKE [*yelling*]: Just cut it out right now. Knock it off right now. Let's just take it easy here and give this thing a chance.

There's a second of silence and then,

BROMBERG: Yeah, okay, I feel something happening already.

WILSON: I think I feel something too.

JACOBI: Is it getting hot in here?

ROURKE [*cutting him off*]: Now, everyone calm down. We're not—

BROMBERG: Oh yeah, I've got a rush starting here. I've got—

WILSON: Jesus, Billy, I feel—

ROURKE: I know what you mean. I know what you're saying.

JACOBI: I'm getting a little, ah, Billy, you feeling kind of—

ROURKE: I know what you're saying—

Bromberg gets up out of her chair suddenly and knocks it over. Eva watches her face as she cranes her neck out a bit and starts to look quickly around the table, an odd smile spreading over her lips. There's a small flutter of her right eyelid, but either she's not aware of it or it isn't bothering her. She runs a hand around the back of her neck, comes around the front, and runs her index and middle fingers down the line of her Adam's apple and into the shallow cavity below, then further inside the front of her blouse. She says, 'I am fucking buzzing,' in a quick, clipped voice that raises slightly in pitch with each word. Her free hand starts to slap against the side of her leg.

Rourke leans over to Wilson, gives out a quick, high laugh, sticks his tongue into her ear. Wilson starts a rolling giggle and Rourke tries to whisper, 'I'm hard as a freakin' rock,' but it comes out fast at full volume and suddenly the whole room is convulsing with laughter.

'That's what I'm saying,' Jacobi chokes out. 'That's what I'm trying to tell you.'

Wilson slides out of her seat and into Rourke's lap and they start kissing, a weird, birdlike peck around the proximity of each other's mouth, their tongues suddenly taking on lizardlike movements, darting in and out of the holes of their mouths like enraged snakes. They begin to lick each other's face as Jacobi, still in his seat, begins to spit out filthy limericks that get unintelligible after the second one. Jacobi's head starts to jerk in unexpected directions, as if someone had harnessed it and was tugging in random directions with too much force. The motion doesn't seem to bother him, though. He smiles a big idiot's grin as the head leaps side to side, up and down in jagged Tourette-like seizures.

Rourke starts to unbutton Wilson's blouse, his fingers flying, either unaware or uncaring of the others' presence.

Bromberg's the only one who seems to be growing unpleased with her condition. She's squatting against a wall, on the verge of hyperventilating, talking to herself. Eva tries to make sense of the sounds, but between Jacobi's singsong babbling and the sucking noises issuing from the tangle of Rourke and Wilson, she has no success.

All she can do is watch as Bromberg's mouth starts to move open and closed, faster and faster, until the lips, tongue, teeth, gums, and black and pink interior are a blur, a messy haze of spastic tissue. An arena of muscles stimulated past known kinetics and into a world of helpless speed. It's as if a point will come where the mouth will be forced to explode, where the tongue's absolute, maximum capacity for movement will not be enough.

Eva looks away from the sight and climbs down off the toilet. She doesn't want to witness the arrival of that point. She stands rigid for a moment in the small confines of the stall, puts her hands against the cool green metal wall to steady herself, and closes her eyes.

But she can still hear the sound, the awful, scratchy, buzzing sound, as if a high-speed motor had materialized in all their larynxes. As if a minute hive of unclassified insects had formed in the throats of all her carriers.

14

The Barracuda flies through the five-way intersection at Hoffman's Rotary, a new lesson in speed, congestion, and odds. Lenore maneuvers the car like she was the last fighter pilot left to hold the line against a barbarian aggressor. She comes inches from impacting half a dozen cars. Horns blowing the full range of the scales fill the air.

Woo is almost on the floor. He screams, 'Shouldn't you have one of those flashing red lights mounted on the top?'

'Probably,' Lenore yells, yanking the wheel to her right and missing the bumper of a Lincoln by a breath.

They cross into the Canal Zone in minutes. There's already a crowd down past the main boulevard that the locals insist on calling Rimbaud Way. The woodcutters and calligraphers have even made their own street sign. A block down Rimbaud, two patrol cars have blocked off the small alley that leads to the burned-out remains of the old Seward typewriter factory. Behind them are three other black-and-whites and a growing pocket of black-clad, one-hundred-pound zombie artists that the uniforms are trying to disperse or at least keep at a safe distance. Red and blue lights are flashing everywhere. There's a plainclothes guy, Lenore thinks his name is Dennison, squatting behind one of the blocking cars with a bullhorn in his hand.

Lenore pulls off the street onto the sidewalk and kills the engine. She yells for Woo to stay put, but he immediately follows her out of the car. She hauls her badge out of her back pocket and flashes it ahead of her body as she runs past the patrolman hoarding the bohemians into order.

She squats next to the guy with the bullhorn, her back against the patrol car, and says, 'You're Dennison, right?'

He just squints, waiting for an explanation of her presence.

'Lenore Thomas, narcotics. My lieutenant just radioed me down here. Said you've got a situation I need to know about.'

Dennison stares at her like he's trying to decide if he should challenge her authority, then he looks around and starts talking. 'The initial patrolman, Carson, he responded to reports of gunfire from down the old Seward shop. Figured it might be some more of those gallery freaks, those kids that load the old breech shotguns with paint pellets and blast away at reinforced plywood…'

'The Black Hole Group.'

'Yeah, them. So Carson comes down the boulevard and turns down the alley, and bang, his windshield is blown to shit by a forty-four slug. He manages to pull out and call in backup. It's a girl, for Christ sake. Young kid. She's up the goddamn telephone pole, climbed up the spikes right to the top. She's got a bird's-eye view and she's cranked on some badass speed. Over the edge. She's babbling away up there a mile a minute and you can't understand a word of it. Every now and then she lets a bullet fly. We don't know if she's aiming for us or not. We don't know if she's even aware she's here.'

'Anyone in the crowd identify her?'

'Not yet, but she doesn't look like she's from down here. She looks more like Bangkok material. Street thing. Burned up. Seventeen years tops. Big head of red hair.'

'That's my girl,' Lenore says, 'and I need her in one piece.'

Dennison looks away and gives a sarcastic bob with his chin. 'Wish I could promise delivery, Detective, but as you can see, it's kind of a volatile situation. We don't know how much ammo she's got up there.'

'Whatever was in the chamber. Nothing more. Guaranteed.'

'Oh, thanks, I'll just charge right in.'

There's a pair of department binoculars on the ground near Dennison's feet. Lenore gestures to them and asks, 'Can I take a look?'

Dennison nods. Lenore picks up the binoculars and crawls back toward the trunk end of the patrol car. She comes up over the edge of the car and peers down the alley. It's an unsettling feeling, the eyes suddenly on top of the weird, decayed remains of the Seward factory, charred ruins from one of the hottest fires in the city's history. It was an arson case, never solved. The property was sold to a company that went bankrupt. The city condemned it, but each year failed to come up with the funds to tear what was left of it down. Now the Canal Zone's various art groups and fringe sets use the place for everything from Black Masses to audience-participating theaters.

At the very end of the alley, about thirty yards from the entrance to the boulevard, sits the telephone pole. Lenore starts at the street and follows it up to the big, gray metal box mounted near the top and the thick black cables that run off into the air.

Then she centers her vision on Vicky, Cortez's runaway hooker. Vicky's bare feet are planted on the top climbing spikes and she's got one arm hugging the splintery wooden pole. She looks like a graphic symbol of hell, a child possessed and tormented beyond descriptive words. She's dressed in a floor-length, satiny, black nightgown. She has the remains of the bottom half, torn and shredded most likely on her climb upward, haphazardly pulled together, sort of gathered up slightly and held against the pole. Above the waist, the gown is form-hugging and sparse, held on her body by a single thin strap around her neck. Her left breast has fallen out of the gown and is exposed to the air and the public. But it's Vicky's face that captures and assaults Lenore's eyes. Lenore knows, from the moment she sees it, that it will perpetually define, give image to, maybe even devour, the word *torment*, for the balance of her life.

The face is a masterpiece of the pure lines and curves of horror, of a primal fear. The eyes are bulging and yet sunk back a full inch into the skull. The skin is unblemished but sallow and taut to the point of ripping off the bone. The cheeks protrude at the sides of the nose, as if casting a furious vote for skeleton over cartilage. But it is the mouth that is the center of everything, opened into an endless-seeming hole, a bottomless O. It appears never to draw breath but moves ceaselessly, so fast that its motions begin to blur within the lenses of the binoculars. Vicky is forming words faster than her tongue, lips, full mouth can handle. It's as if they're all instruments pushed suddenly far beyond the limits they were designed for, as if they were inadequate substances, forced to the point of shattering under immense and unnatural forces of speed and gravity.

'I have to talk to her,' Lenore says.

'You know her number,' Dennison jokes, pleased with himself, searching through his sport coat for a cigarette.

'I need to speak with her,' Lenore says slowly, enunciating each syllable as if Dennison were an inattentive child.

'Hang in,' he says, mimicking her voice. 'This could take a while.' Then he goes back to his own voice and says, 'My guess is she'll go over the top in a while and drop like a stone. Whatever crap she's on is going to burn her down sooner or later. We'll just wait for the fall.'

'I'm going down there,' Lenore says.

'Like hell you are.'

'I need to ask her some questions.'

'Then you better hope she can still talk after she hits the ground.'

Lenore looks to the ground, waits a second, cocks her head, and smirks at Dennison. 'You want to do this your way,' she says, 'then great, we can do it your way. But I've got to tell you I've got weight on this, okay? I'm with DEA on this. Maybe others. If you want I can go back to my car and call it in. I can say I'm getting no cooperation and we can wait five minutes for some Federal boys to come down and insult the way you dress. They'll pull your authority in front of all your people. If you want it that way, fine with me.'

Dennison's head is rigid, and Lenore thinks a good wind would cause it to fall from his shoulders in a pile of heavy dust. His jaw is thrust out toward her and finally he opens it and says, 'You are a real bitch.'

'Absolutely,' she says. 'Now're you ready to help me out?' He stares at her and she says, 'I'm going to advance from the left side of the alley. Our left. I'm going to want the bullhorn to start out with. I want a line of your best shooters – what've you got, four, five guys with rifles – I want them in position, fully focused, but absolutely no firing unless she lets one fly...'

'You could be dead by then,' Dennison says.

'Odds are I'm safe. She's a teenage hooker. Even on her best day she's not a sharpshooter. In this condition she'd need a miracle to get anywhere near me.'

Dennison shrugs and turns away, snapping his fingers to reposition his men. Lenore looks around to find Woo at her shoulder and says, 'You should really wait at the car, Freddy. Play the stereo till I get back.'

'I should probably go with you, don't you think?'

Lenore just laughs.

'Seriously. I'm the only one who's witnessed this before. Out at Spooner. If she can be talked to...'

'Her mouth was moving like, out of control. I wish I could hear what was coming out.'

Woo shakes his head no. 'Very unsettling noise,' he says.

Lenore lowers her voice and says, 'The two guys out at the prison, when they went nuts, could you talk to them at all? Was there any communication?'

Woo breathes out heavily. 'Hard to say. My guess is they understood me, but it was as if they couldn't...' he trails off, pauses, picks up – 'slow down, slow their nervous systems. Maybe their brains, their language centers, couldn't slow them down enough to make it a dialogue.'

'If the girl has gotten into some Lingo, and I'm certain that's the story here, we don't know the dosage or anything…'

'It's all up in the air, Lenore. That's why I suggest—'

She cuts him off. 'Just go back to the car. Just wait for me at the car.'

She turns to Dennison and says, 'We all set?'

A beat-up Lincoln Continental screeches to a stop at the police line, lights and sirens engulfing it.

'Oh, shit,' Lenore says, infuriated.

Zarelli jumps out and runs toward the blocking cars waving his badge and gun high in the air. Lenore hears at least one uniformed officer say, 'What an asshole.'

Zarelli practically dives to the ground between Dennison and Lenore and says to Dennison, 'Zarelli, narcotics.'

'Another one,' Dennison says, and rubs at his eyes.

Zarelli turns to Lenore and says, 'It's all right, honey, I'm here.'

For a second, Lenore doesn't know what to do. She's astounded by his presence, let alone his words. She opens her mouth, but nothing comes out. Then she decides to forsake language entirely. She lifts her pants leg and pulls, in a furious motion, her secondary weapon, a .38 revolver, from an ankle holster. She sweeps her hand upward and presses the side of the barrel, not the front, to Zarelli's forehead. She leaves it there for only a second, but it's long enough for him to flinch brutally, fall sideways toward the ground, snap his eyes shut, and scrunch his face into a grotesque expression of shock.

Dennison lets out a bubbly, surprised bark of a laugh. Before Zarelli can recover any composure and speak, Lenore is gone.

She moves around the trunk of the patrol car, the bullhorn in her hand, out in front of her like a gun. She moves to the exposed corner of the car's bumper, squats down, raises the bullhorn to her lips, and says, 'Vicky, honey, where are you?' in a bad southern accent, made bizarre by amplification.

She looks up to see that Vicky has heard her call. Her head juts from one side of the pole to the other, insectlike. Her free arm shoots straight up into the air, waves a weapon, a Magnum, Lenore thinks, like a flag.

'Vicky, child,' she tries again, 'it's your sister Darleen. I've been looking everywhere for you.'

Though Vicky's mouth continues to move at its unnatural, blistering speed, her head and eyes seem to be moving separately, trying to focus on the direction of the voice, trying to lock on something familiar.

Lenore starts to take small, slow steps down the alley, her left hand holding the bullhorn up, her right hand gripping her gun, held slightly behind her back. 'Why you hiding from me, Vicky?' she yells. 'I need to talk to you now.'

She continues down the alley, and after the halfway point she starts to hear the noise. At first she thinks it's coming from the telephone pole itself, from the gray metal box and the wires. It's a humming sound, slightly electrical, a weird buzzing noise, sort of like a hornet, Lenore thinks suddenly, or a whole swarm of hornets, recorded on tape and played back a bit faster and louder. And then she remembers Woo's tape of the inmates, Jimmy Lee Partridge and William Robbins. She knows the buzzing sound is coming from Vicky's mouth. The buzzing sound is Vicky pumped on an unspecified amount of Lingo and turned into something horrible, a monster out of some child's nightmares, a demon out of some fanatic's fantasy. And with a language, or at least a sound, a noise, so disturbing it makes Lenore want to run to the other side of the city.

But she doesn't. She continues to approach the pole at a consistent pace, void of any jarring motions. She feels waves of a heavy nausea pass over her and a sweat breaks on her forehead.

She wonders if this is caused by Vicky's noise or her own fear or lack of a hit of speed this afternoon.

'Why did you run from Darleen, honey?' she says. 'You know Darleen wouldn't hurt you.'

She starts to walk across to the pole side of the alley in an angle, talking the whole way.

'I'm your sister, Vicky. I'm here to help you, sweetheart. You don't need to be afraid no more. I'll take care of everything.'

She slows to a wedding-march pace for the last ten or so steps to the base of the pole.

'Now, come down here right now, Vicky. C'mon. Darleen is waiting.'

If Max is wrong about Vicky having a sister named Darleen, she'll take some action against him. At this point she doesn't know what it will be, but there'll be some retribution, something to help him remember his mistake. But even if there is a legitimate Darleen, Lenore has no way of knowing if Vicky is far enough gone to think she's speaking with her. Normally, she enjoys a big gamble, a pure tough-odds situation. But her heart isn't in this one. She thinks if she'd just gotten a chance for a quick hit of speed, a little crank to reheat the system, she'd be on her game, in full control of both rational thought and instinct. But right now the buzzing sound is bringing her close to vomiting.

She advances to the pole, stops, and stares up at Vicky. 'You took some bad medicine this time, sister,' she says. 'You come down and Darleen will help you.'

The buzzing noise halts and is replaced by an awful combination of muted grunt and raspy breath. It's as if the girl on the pole has had her tongue severed and is making a horrible effort to speak through her throat or nose. It's as if there were some awful confusion in the prenatal stages and she never developed the skeletal structure necessary for speech. Lenore cringes listening to her pull air into the lungs, then try to pump it back up and out of her body, transformed into words she once had no problem producing.

Vicky starts to go through a series of terrible sounds, mostly choked-off, spastic explosions of wind and spittle. Then she starts to hyperventilate, exhaling more air than she's taken in.

Lenore starts to panic a little and fights against it. 'Just calm down, now, Vicky. Just do what Darleen says, now.'

But Vicky gets worse, her arms start to flail and her body seems to buck away from the pole like she was losing all motor control.

'Who gave you the medicine, Vicky?' Lenore yells, now frantic. 'Who gave you the drug, Vicky?'

Vicky hangs out from the pole with one hand on a spike. Her head is quaking on her shoulders. Lenore sees a small thin stream of blood seeping slowly from her right ear.

'Who?' she screams.

Vicky's full mouth starts to vibrate, the tremble of the lips and all the skin within about a half inch of the lips, begins to increase geometrically, until the bottom half of her face is a sickening, surreal blur.

Then the vibration ceases all at once and her tongue comes in and out several times, complete with a white, foamy cover. Lenore takes a step forward, her eyes focused in on the mouth. It opens, trembles barely, comes together, and opens again to form a single word: *Mingo.*

Then, immediately, the convulsions set in again, and this time the whole body is affected. A hand flies up into the air and the gun explodes. Lenore sinks into a shooting crouch, arms extended up, gun sighted and ready to fire, but she realizes before squeezing off that the girl is just helpless to her own muscles and firing harmlessly in the air.

'For Christ sake,' she hears, and then Zarelli is beside her trying to yank her backward.

'You dumb fuck,' she screams, and refocuses on the pole just in time to see Vicky unconsciously drawing down on Zarelli. Then she hears that unmistakable noise, that one-in-a-million sound, gunshot. Lenore takes air in and before she can think, she pumps out two bullets. Both of them enter Vicky's chest left of the breastbone. Heart shots.

Vicky's body heaves, weaves backward away from the pole, hangs a second, and then drops, dead weight, a mute stone, to the ground.

Things seem to start moving in a spastic, slow motion for Lenore. She hears a voice from the police line behind her yell, 'Hold fire, hold fire,' and it sounds like it's coming from the top of a third-world mountain, hundreds of miles away. She looks down at Zarelli, who's lying flat on his back, arms crossed and up, covering his face. There's no blood. He's unharmed.

Lenore runs to the body, instinctively puts her fingers to Vicky's throat, waits the useless extra half-minute. There's no beat, no pulse, no trace of an even fleeting life. The body is in an odd position, as if Lenore had discovered it in bed, in the middle of a humid night, trying any placement of arms and legs in an effort to find comfort.

Lenore ignores procedure and rolls the body onto its back so that she won't have to view the gaping hole of the bullets' exit path. She can't help seeing the two entrance's bull's-eyes, however. And then she sees something else. Situated in Vicky's cleavage, lodged securely between her breasts, is the letter *Q*. It looks like a jewel, a small charm that fell from a broken and lost necklace.

Lenore hears the running footfall coming down the alley behind her. She takes the Q from Vicky's chest, hides it in her hand, feels the rubbery, shiver-making texture of the item. She swallows hard, rises to her feet, and turns to face the troops.

15

Peirce sits in the Swanns' library, surrounded by books. The room is in darkness. She hasn't bothered to turn on a light. She finds herself wondering what will be done with all the books. Will they be donated to some library or one of the city's colleges? Will they be inventoried and appraised and then sold off to some dealer, the proceeds given to the state?

She'd like to think of the books as orphans, but their size and bulkiness and lack of color prevent her. They have the look of textbooks, tomes that only a dozen people in the world can read the whole of.

The Swanns had no other family. Just each other. Why did two people need such an enormous house? A house like this should be filled with a noisy, multigenerational clan. It should be filled, regularly, with the sound of huge dinners that take hours to prepare and even longer to eat.

The silence in this place must have been awful.

Then again, maybe she's got it all wrong. Maybe the house was like a huge fortress for the two of them. Leo and Inez locked up in paradise, every need taken care of and plenty of room to spread out.

It's possible. She can picture herself making a home in a place like this. With Victor. Rolling around on the oriental carpets, foolish in this enormous private palace. The thought makes her reach for the recorder.

A little Alka-Seltzer and the girl is as good as new. You're not going to believe this but Charlotte is getting hungry again. You're either home by now or on your way. The Mrs. has supper on the table, right? What'll it be tonight, Victor? It really doesn't matter. She's such a great cook, everything's wonderful, huh? [*Pause*] I said I wouldn't do this. And besides, now that I think of it, you've got a City Council meeting. So you're probably grabbing a quick sandwich in the office with the amazing Carol, secretary of the decade. It's getting pretty pathetic, Victor, when I'm losing it over your wife *and* secretary. Swear to me that all you guys are doing right now is going over new budget proposals. [*Pause*] I'm sitting in the library of the lovely but dead Leo and Inez Swann, in the Swann mansion up on Grimaldi Drive. In the ritzy Windsor Hills section. I knew I should've been a real estate broker, boss. Let's see – 'This charming fifteen-room Tudor…' No, wait. 'Charming' is the wrong word here. 'Stately.' You'd have to use 'stately.' I read the Sunday real estate ads. Sometimes they call the houses up here 'magnificent.' It's a kick just walking through a place like this. A little spooky in this case, you know? I was a poor kid, Victor, grew up on the south side of the district, all those good blue-collar folks that return you to office year after year. Now and then, my old man would drive me and my brothers and sisters up around here. We'd take a quick look and bang – out again. You always had the feeling up here that there were servants looking out the windows at your old broken-down station wagon, that there were these butlers, hidden behind enormous drapes or something, with a gold-plated telephone receiver in their hand, calling the cops. Like 'Intruder alert. South-siders trespassing in Windsor.' This was where all the Yankee doctors and judges and the publisher of *The Spy* lived. It was like another world. A place I was always curious about, but scared of at the same time. This place where all the power in the whole city lived. And as a kid, maybe I got this from my dad, I don't know, but it was never good power. Never something that was going to make things better. At least not for us. And sitting here now, in this house that's ten times too big for the Swanns, I feel the exact same way. All over again. [*Pause*] Have you ever been in this house, Victor? Well, I guess you've been in a lot like this one. I know you've had dinner up at *The Spy* publisher's house, what's his name, Welch. My old man used to say about him, 'More money than God and a whole lot slicker.' You know, for a second I thought it was funny that you didn't live up here. Mayor of Quinsigamond and all. But then it hit me. You're really just a civil servant like me. We're in the same class, Victor. There's one thing we've got in common. I felt like a criminal just walking up the path to this place. I clipped my badge to my belt in case any neighbors were watching. We've still got the yellow police line practically wrapped around the whole house, roping it off. I ducked underneath instead of breaking it, but I'll tell you, something about that yellow plastic material. I hate touching it. It's like it's infected with death or something. It's like this glaring symbol, you know. Don't cross this line, stiff on the other side. [*Pause*] I'll tell you one thing, these two had expensive tastes. There had to be money in at least one of their families, and I'm betting Leo. He just looks the type. And you don't live like this by being a researcher or scientist or whatever. At least I don't think so. I know there've been three different investigations through this place and teams of lab guys and all, but I wanted to take a look for myself. It's weird, Victor. It's like living in some old English movie, I swear. How do you live in a place like this? Yeah, I know the answer to that. But it's like, you walk into this huge, I mean enormous, foyer and it's all this shining ancient wood everywhere. Walnut or mahogany. I don't know this kind of crap. But the walls are so glossy you could go blind. And on either side of the foyer are these two stairways, wide enough for about six people across. And they both run up and meet at this balcony. And out in front of the balcony is this gigantic chandelier. I mean they had to have gotten this thing out of some landmark hotel in

New York. [*Pause*] Listen. I got here hours ago, Victor. And I spent the first hour just wandering through. Not touching anything. Not even looking for anything. Just taking it all in. Just trying to see if I can get a better feeling for what kind of people Leo and Inez were. For me, it's always best to work from instinct. I know you probably disagree with that. You're the ultimate manager, right? Everything scheduled. Look at all the options. No, all the proposals. Weigh it all. Use a system. See what fits best. Maybe you're right. I mean, look how far I've gotten in this life by following my feelings. I can bitch and moan with the best of them, Victor. I'd like to live in this house for just one week. With you. Like a married couple. Like Leo and Inez. Me, in the gourmet kitchen with the butcher-block island and the overhead copper rack for hanging pots and pans that don't look like they've ever been cooked in, and I'm in a white terrycloth robe, and I'm packing the kids' lunches for the day, straightening your tie, giving you a little tip on how to deal with the school committee. [*Pause*] The Swanns both had a library, a study. I'm in Inez's right now. I spent an hour in Leo's. A man's room. Big power desk. Dark leather chairs. The walls lined with books. Inez's room is different. In all the ways you'd guess. Pastels. Antiques. Her desk is so small. Too small for me. Prints on the walls. Who's that guy? French, I think. Painted all the water lilies? Anyway, I've been sitting here, my legs curled up underneath me, on this small uncomfortable couch. I've been trying to picture them, Leo and Inez, alone, late at night, in this ark of a house. Two people alone in this giant house. They're in their studies. They're separated. They're reading, writing down notes, trying to think. Figuring out work problems. And then I think about Lehmann telling us at the briefing about their dinner with Gennaro Pecci. At Fiorello's. And it doesn't make sense. Doesn't go together. I think Leo and Inez were the type of folks who would have turned up their noses at a local wise guy like Pecci. Even if he is second or third generation. And I know drugs and money make the weirdest kind of bedfellows. But the Pecci angle doesn't make sense to me. Even if it fills in a lot of holes. [*Pause*] I pulled every book down off Inez's bookshelf, Victor. A lot of old books alongside new ones. Some of them might be rare or something. I don't know books. They have names like *A Psycholinguistic Study of the Angkor Wat 'Wild Child'* and *The Berlin Symposium on Hyper-Kinesics* and, yeah, here's a good one, *A Statistical Analysis of Leberzunge-Therapy, Buchenwald, 1943*. Plus a bunch of stuff in German and French and maybe Russian that I can't even pronounce. Real page-turners. Best-sellers. Now, I'm taking it for granted that somebody already did this, looked through every book. But in one book, love this name, *Deconstructing the Fifth: Advances and Abuses Within the Cohn-Group's use of 'J.M.'s Langley-Catacomb Cocktail,' 1949–1950*, there was a bookmark, actually just a stub of paper used as a bookmark. It looks like the bottom half of one of those little pink 'While You Were Out' slips. Printed, in pencil, in these small, perfect block letters is the word 'Paraclete.' I don't know if that rings any bells for you, but I've got nothing. [*Pause*] It's getting creepy in here, Victor. I'll talk to you later.

16

Ephraim Beck's Mystery Bookstore has operated in the same location for over one hundred years. It has not always been exclusively a mystery-book store. It has, on the other hand, always been owned by the Beck family. The Becks are something of a local myth in Quinsigamond – the bloodline cursed with the incurable affliction of bibliomania.

Ezekiel Beck, Ephraim's grandfather, started the store around 1890, according to the myth, when his Victorian home was structurally threatened by the sheer weight of his library. He was a genuine book nut, manuscript mad, addicted to bound paper and ink. The floors of his house were buckling, the walls beginning to bulge. His wife warned of divorce and scandal. Zeke quit his growing law practice, moved the family to the second and third floors of the house, and set up shop on the first. His logic was that this would stabilize and maybe even reduce the number of volumes under his roof.

He did not physically alter the family home in any way. In some instances, he did not even bother to move furniture. The dining room, for instance, was turned into the philosophy section, and Locke, Hume, Berkeley, and the rest overran the tables, china cabinets, and buffet. The pantry was devoted to poetry, and Shelley, Keats, Wordsworth, and Whitman lined the shelves that had housed sugar and flour and coffee. The small music alcove was crammed with theology. The front parlor loaded with contemporary fiction, a rolltop proprietor's desk, and a tin-scrolled cash register.

Ephraim, the grandson and last of the bloodline, fifty years old now and still a bachelor, lives in three rooms on the second floor of the house. The top floor is used for storage. And the first floor, still outfitted in its original Victorian decor, houses an extensive and often idiosyncratic collection of mystery literature, from rare Poe first editions to fading pulp paperbacks. Ephraim switched to an exclusively mystery stock the week after his father died. He issues a catalogue twice a year that he mails to customers 'as far away as Melbourne.'

Now, drinking a European tea spiked with a cheap rye, Ike studies Ephraim's attire and attempts to calm himself. Whenever he's rattled, Ike has found that an hour's browse through the rooms of Ephraim's home will settle him down, give him perspective. He has known Ephraim for almost ten years and he has recently given up on determining if his chronic manner of dress – black wool pants, threadbare white shirt with tiny turn-down collar, maroon suspenders, maroon bow tie, cowl-collared gray cardigan – is natural or an affectation, a manifestation of Ephraim's *idea* of how an eccentric Yankee bookseller, feigning pennilessness, would dress. Now, when Ephraim lights up a bowlful of tobacco in one of his grandfather's ancient, hand-carved pipes, Ike just smiles and takes in the pleasant smell of apples.

Over the years they have engaged in hundreds of hours of battle over the merits of the classical English puzzle-box mysteries of the elite class versus the more character-oriented morality plays of the desperate American individual. Ephraim is the Anglophile. Ike, surprisingly, likes his book crimes hard-boiled and urban. Neither one of them knows what to make of the new wave of *déco noir* books from France where there is no hero, little plot, and just page after page of random, bizarre violence.

'Did you try the book idea out on your sister yet?' Ephraim asks offhandedly, jamming a felt cleaner into the end of one of the pipes.

'Haven't found the right moment,' Ike says.

The shop just isn't having the calming effect today. He feels jittery, tentative. His lungs feel constricted. He should have taken the mutilated fish as an omen.

A phone upstairs begins to ring and Ephraim pulls himself out of his chair and starts up the stairs, saying to Ike, 'Tend the shop for a second.'

Ike finishes his tea and rye with a single, long swallow, then gets up and starts to pace. Eventually, he begins to walk in a large circle through the whole of the first floor, dining room to pantry to kitchen to parlor to music alcove to living room to front hall, back to the dining room. He wonders as he walks what it must have been like to grow up in a house that was literally filled, wall-to-wall, with books. Do you end up appreciating them in a way that the average person cannot? Or do you take them for granted, expect their continued presence the way debutantes expect money and attention?

He moves through the circle again, pausing this time in the parlor, inspecting, again, all the first editions inside the now-antique, glass-door mahogany bookcase that rises as high as the eleven-foot ceilings. Most of the books in the case have been for sale as long as Ike has been coming to the shop. They're very high priced, mint collector's quality, fairly rare. Ike has suggested that Ephraim alarm the store for the sake of these volumes alone. He stares at the spines of the ones he'd love to possess, reads the authors' names – Chesterton, Collins, Hornung, Futrelle, Morley.

Ike takes a step back from the case, stands silent, and listens. He rarely gets moments alone like this and though he knows Ephraim wouldn't be pleased, he tells himself that possibly handling one of these treasures might turn things around for him, salvage the day a bit. Besides, his hands are clean and all the money he's spent in the shop should entitle him to at least hold the first edition of *Red Harvest* for a minute.

He slowly pulls open one of the doors and is impressed by its weight. He reaches in and pulls down a Chesterton – *The Club of Queer Trades.* Written in 1905, Ike guesses, and opens the volume to prove himself right. He hears Ephraim move upstairs, gets nervous, slides the book back into place on the shelf, and closes the case door. He hasn't felt this kind of jumpiness since he stopped taking that asthma medication fifteen years ago.

He walks into the huge kitchen, lined recently with library-style shelving to create cramped mini-aisles. Ephraim has pulled the 'True Crime' section out of the basement where it was getting a little musty, and given it a full aisle in the kitchen. Ike browses it now and just the names off the spines make him uneasy. They're all here, all the famous and most depraved murderers in the collective history of our worst fears – Torquemada, Jack the Ripper, Lizzie Borden, Richard Speck, David Berkowitz, John Wayne Gacy, and, of course, Manson. Manson gets almost an entire shelf to himself.

Ike does not read true crime books. He doesn't see the entertainment, can't understand how someone could squeeze any enjoyment out of them. But he continually browses them, pulls them down off the shelf and studies the dust jackets. Sometimes he'll force himself to open to the photographs and take a quick peek. It's become a small test he makes himself endure every few visits to the shop.

He settles now on a title he's never seen before: *Matamoros – Devil's Playland*. It's a fat volume, maybe two inches wide at the spine and jacketed in glossy black with blood-red block lettering. Ike would bet his life that there are plenty of photos and more than one will be ridiculously lurid.

He reaches up and grabs the volume, pulls it out from its neighbors with a little effort, and lets out a shocked scream. Through the space left between the books he can see Eva's head.

Eva screams back at him.

Ephraim's feet come running across the upstairs floor and he's yelling, 'What's wrong? What's happened?'

Eva comes around to Ike's aisle and they face each other, breathing like they've finished sprinting a lap around the city.

'For Christ sake,' Ike heaves.

Eva has her hand plastered over her mouth, but as air comes into her lungs and seconds go by, she begins to smile and shake her head.

Ephraim rushes into the kitchen, finds them in the aisle, and just stares, eyes bulging a bit and lips pulled in.

Ike lets out a long, heavy breath, slowly reshelves the crime book, nods to both of them, and says, 'I'm sorry, sorry, really. God. I didn't hear Eva come in and when I looked through to the next aisle, I don't know, I just...' He shrugs the rest of his explanation.

'I'm sorry I startled you, Ike,' Eva says. 'Your message said to come over here and the door was open and no one was at the front desk out there so I...' and she repeats his shrug.

Ephraim, seeming a little offended that the tranquillity of his shop has been even temporarily broken, frowns at both of them. 'This is a friend of yours, Ike?' he asks.

'I'm sorry,' Ike says again, and before he can make any introductions, Eva grabs Ephraim's hand and pumps it and says, 'Eva Barnes, very nice to meet you. I work with Ike. Very nice place you have here. I've always intended to come in.'

Ephraim stares at Ike and says, 'Very nice to meet you, Ms. Barnes.'

There's a beat of edgy silence between the three of them until Ephraim says, 'If you two will excuse me, I've got some things to tend to at my desk,' and leaves.

They both watch him walk back to the living room, then they look at each other and Eva says, 'Are you all right, Ike? I'm sorry, again, I didn't mean to startle you like that...'

'I'm sorry I yelled,' Ike says. 'It's just when I looked through and saw your face on the other side of the stacks, I just...' and again he shrugs.

'I got home and heard your message on my answering machine,' Eva says. 'I came right down here.'

'Yeah, I appreciate that. That's really nice of you...'

'It's not a problem, but what is it you needed to speak to me about? And why here?'

At the opposite end of the kitchen are two old rocking chairs, overstuffed and low to the ground, the backs covered with Ephraim's grandmother's handmade quilts. Ike leads Eva, by the hand, to the two rockers, settles down into one, and indicates with a hand gesture that she should do the same.

Eva sits and sinks deep into the chair, finds it, surprisingly, just as comfortable as it had looked.

'I come down here,' Ike says, 'when things are bothering me. I come down here to hang out. Think, read. Drink a little with Ephraim. It's just a great place to be, you know? Some people go to bars, right?'

'So I'm told,' Eva says.

'My sister has this weird old diner she hangs out at, you know? She's never offered to take me there and I've never asked to go. It's her place. Place to think. I just think everyone should have some certain place, some designated area.'

'It would be nice.'

'You have any place like that, Eva?'

'Nothing that comes to mind right away. Why did you ask me to come down here, Ike?'

'I'm really sorry to bother you like this. I really shouldn't have called, I guess. Those machines. Those answering machines. I think you hear this machine and you think, okay, it's like this middleman between you and the person you're calling and you can say things that…'

'What am I doing here, Ike?'

'I'm really sorry about this, Eva. I think it was that fish today, seeing that fish, and nobody claiming box nine. I'm feeling a little over the edge, if you know what I mean.'

Eva comes forward in the rocker, leans the top part of her body over her lap, holds her chin up with clasped hands, and stares at Ike.

'This will sound, you know, not only dumb,' he says, 'but, I guess, sort of childish.'

She stares.

'I was wondering if you could tell me, talk to me, tell me why the others hate me so much?'

'The others?'

'The other carriers, the others at the station.'

'Rourke?'

'Rourke, Wilson, Bromberg, even Jacobi. I swear I never did a thing to them. I've always tried to be friendly, even help out, you know. I'm union, I pay the dues. I don't shirk the bad routes. I'm not some loud, insulting guy.'

'They hate me too, Ike.'

'Yeah,' he says sheepishly, 'but, forgive me and all, but you're the supervisor, okay? You're the authority. You're the boss. There's a whole tradition there. This is what I mean. If I were in your position, which, by the way, I wouldn't want, not in a million years, but if I were in your position, I'd be able to understand it. I probably wouldn't even give it a lot of thought. It'd be – bang, okay, I'm the boss and they hate the boss. But I'm not the boss, I'm just another carrier, and it's starting to drive me nuts. Why?'

'I think you're looking at this the wrong way, Ike.'

'I think what I want is, like, what's the word? An overview. Am I using the right word? I want an overview of my personality. I mean, let me come out and say it, I think you're one of the most intelligent people I know' – Ike smiles – 'and don't let Ephraim hear me say this, right? I'm asking for some help. I'm asking you to identify the problems for me.'

'The problems?'

'With the way I act or speak or move. Or whatever. That's got to be the first step in changing things.'

Eva sits back in the rocker and it makes a loud creaking noise.

'I was very pleased when I heard your message, Ike. I took it as a sign, as a good omen, a signal that I wasn't alone. On my way home from the station I had been thinking about calling you.'

'Calling me?'

'Is there any other reason you asked me here today, Ike? Let's face it, we're both in that pretty awful position of not knowing how many cards to play.'

'You've lost me.'

'My guess would be that we're both operating completely on instinct at this point. We both have information that we're anxious to share, we're dying to share, but we don't know who to trust.'

'Information about what?'

'We're dying to trust someone, and I think that we've both got a hunch that at some point, if this thing continues, there'll come that moment, that leap, that cutting of all nets, when we have to trust someone, it's an imperative, there's no alternative.'

'What thing?'

'All right, take this moment, right now. My brain has a few avenues it can go down. A: everything is as it seems and you know nothing and you called me to discuss some inferiority problem. B: you're so scared and confused and justifiably paranoid about what you do, in fact, know, that you're hesitating over sharing your information with me until you can confirm that I'm on your side or, at the very least, unaware and innocent and *not* on their side. And then there's C, which, if it's the true avenue, I've made the big mistake right here in the beginning and the whole thing is over. C Avenue says you, Ike Thomas, are in on it, are part of their group, and you've been positioned as an apparent outsider to see how much I know, if anything.'

Ike squints at her and says, 'I don't get it. I don't know what the hell you're talking about.'

'That doesn't tell me anything, does it?'

'I guess I've made a mistake here…'

'You ever been to the Bach Room, Ike?'

He starts to breathe heavily again. He wants to call Ephraim. He says, 'I'm sorry to have bothered you.'

'What's the story on the back room at the Bach Room, Ike?'

'I think maybe you'd better go, Ms. Barnes…'

'Ms. Barnes,' Eva says, her voice going high and loud. 'Oh, please, can we at least address each other properly. Ms. Barnes?'

'I'll show you to the door now.'

'What's the story, Ike? You call Rourke now? You tell him there's a new problem?'

'I'm not feeling too well, really…'

'You're going a little green in the face there, Ike. How good an actor are you?'

'I don't, I don't, I have to…'

He bolts out of his rocker and runs across the room to the stacks. He darts into a random aisle and starts to hyperventilate.

Eva comes after him slowly and when she finds him, her voice is like that of an older, calmer doctor, reassuring, soothing, a wife's voice of hope and control and protection.

'It's all right, Ike,' she begins, measured, unrushed, slightly above a whisper. 'Just sit on the floor here. That's it, down on the floor, okay, good, now lower your head a little, to your knees, just like that, fine, you're okay, you're fine, slow down now, let the air come in, there you go.'

She ends up on her knees, holding his head against her breast, stroking his damp forehead, pushing back the hair, creating a rhythm with the calm sweep of her palm against his skull. His breath begins to come normally and after a few more minutes, he raises his head from her chest and mouths the word 'sorry.'

They both lean back and sit, cross-legged, campfire style, facing each other in the quiet of the narrow aisleway.

'Something's happened,' Ike says.

Eva just nods.

'I don't know anything. I swear to you. But I can't think of any way to prove that to you.'

'Neither can I,' Eva says.

Ike reaches across the space between them and takes her hand. He holds it lightly, lets his thumb run over the skin, the ridges of the knuckles.

'Tell me anyway,' he says.

17

'The thing I hate most,' Lenore says, 'is when I start breaking my own rules. And that's what's happening here. I vowed I wasn't going to start having conversations with you, okay? I don't want us to get to know each other. I'm going to get very tense if this continues.'

Woo gives the same smile she's seen on his face too many times already. It never varies and it's one of the most prominent items on the list of reasons she dislikes him.

They're back in Bangkok Park, back inside the confines of the Barracuda, and though that's exactly where Lenore wants to be, it also makes her uneasy. Standard procedure after a shooting would be for her to be relieved at once of any and all field work and start filing endless forms concerning her every move, submitting to hours of internal-affairs interviews, probably having to do ten hours or more with the department shrink for the relief of post-shooting trauma.

In fact, she feels no trauma at all. She has replayed her actions and decided she acted correctly. Zarelli was in the line of fire. Vicky had to be disarmed. She accomplished her objective. It proved to be a fatal shoot. There's little control over these things. Though she didn't ask, Woo has said that the odds are the dosage of Lingo running through Vicky's body would have proved lethal anyway. If additional consolation is needed, she knows she can consider the fact that, given Vicky's current lifestyle and environment, her life expectancy couldn't have been gauged any higher than another year or so. Eighteen months tops.

Ten minutes after Vicky's body is loaded into the ambulance and hauled off for autopsy, Dennison is on the radio with Mayor

Welby, of all people. Then Miskewitz gets on the horn and, as Dennison raises his eyebrows so high they could tear, the lieutenant tells Lenore to 'proceed with the investigation.'

So she and Woo end up back in the Park, staring out at the rear of the Hotel Penumbra from her favorite alley, waiting, as long as is necessary, for Mingo Bouza to show his face.

'Very simply,' says Woo through his smile, 'all I'm attempting to ask you is if you've given thought to the consequences of your actions.'

Lenore slouches in her seat, her eyes glued to the Penumbra's garage. 'There's something about you that's not right,' she says to Woo. 'You just witnessed me blow away a seventeen-year-old girl…'

'Yes.'

'… and you want to know, your big question is, if I've thought about what I'm doing bribing Little Max the snitch with some drawings by some local cartoonist. This is what you're asking me?'

'Exactly.'

'Jesus Christ, you are a goddamn idiot.'

'You are so hostile.'

'That's right, that's correct, and you shouldn't taunt a hostile person. The danger is enormous.'

'I'm not trying to taunt you. I'm curious if you've carried your actions to their logical ends.'

'My actions concerning Max and the drawings?'

'That's right. I'm looking for an insight into the police mind…'

'Oh, what is this shit? "Police mind"…'

'I'm sure this will sound trite to you, but, in fact, didn't your enticing Max with the artwork constitute a corruption of innocence, something you hate Mr. Cortez for?'

Lenore can't believe what she's hearing. She shakes her head and turns to him. 'Woo, I have to know this, you're thought of as a bright guy, right? You're a freaking expert in your field, correct? But I sit here and I listen to you and, for Christ sake, to me you're as dumb as mud. Really. This isn't just a way of insulting you. This is how I feel.'

Woo isn't upset at all. 'Continue,' he says.

'First off, who said I hated Cortez? Did someone hear that come out of my mouth? Mr. Expert on Language? Did you hear those words? Did I fall asleep behind the wheel here and say this and I'm not aware of it? No, sorry, never said it. You've made a huge assumption – Lenore hates Cortez – enormous goddamn assumption. Now, beyond that, you, of all people, again, Mr. Freaking Language, Dr. Language, right, you say I'm a corrupter of innocence. Listen, excuse me, I've got to say this – Mr. Asshole, okay, Little Max may be young, I'd say he's fifteen or so, which, I'll grant you, is traditionally thought of as relatively young here in Quinsigamond. But where does it say youth and innocence are the same thing? You're Mr. Language, right? Youth. Innocence. Two very different words as far as I can tell. Yep, I bribed a young kid. I manipulated him beautifully, I'm great at that. But I had no dealings with any innocence. Little Max has been a stranger to innocence for quite some time.'

Woo nods his head, tries to indicate that he's impressed with what she's said. 'Very good,' he says. 'Point well taken. But beyond this, you did use him as an informer. We can agree on this small, simple fact.'

'We can agree. He's an informer. I received information from him. I do it every week. I'll continue to do it. It's how the job is done.'

'I'm just wondering how you feel about informers in general.'

'In general, I think that they're pieces of garbage that can't be trusted and are wrong as often as they're right. I know what you're looking for here. How do I morally perceive them? That's what's underneath your question. Don't bother to answer. I think they're contemptible. In general. But I like Max. I would exclude Max from that answer. At the moment.'

'At the moment?'

'Things change.'

'I'm having trouble placing you, Lenore. On the political compass.'

'You've got a hunch I'm sort of this paranoid, McCarthyist creep, a loaded gun. Ticking bomb. Fascist hypocrite. Nutcase libertarian...'

'I honestly don't know quite what you are.'

'Well, let's leave it that way for the time being. So much more romantic.'

'Do you use drugs, Lenore?'

'Of course not. Narcotics officer, remember?'

'I was wondering what percentage of the enforcers, the policers, were guilty of the crime themselves.'

'No idea. I don't know of any. You could probably find a study somewhere.'

'No doubt. Why have you never married?'

Lenore can't help but laugh. Her face crumbles into a huge smile, then she dissolves, laughter coming full from the mouth, shoulders and stomach actually shaking. She pulls her noise into a closing whine and says, 'Oh, Freddy, Freddy. I think you have a real attraction to violence. You just push and push.'

Woo loves the reaction he's gotten out of her. He folds his arms across his chest, pleased, a little proud of himself, she thinks.

'You're being wasted in academia. You should be one of those all-night radio guys. Syndicated. Open lines to all of America. Get them on the line and open them up. An audio incision from head to toe. Push and push and get every twisted insomniac to confess all their sins and crimes to the public. What entertainment. You'd be a phenomenon. Ratings history.'

'I will admit, I've always had a strong love of radio.'

'That would have been my guess. You're a radio guy if I've ever seen one.'

'You are quite a package of contradictions, Lenore. I suppose it's no secret at this point that you fascinate me.'

'I'm trying to picture that sentence coming out of anyone else's mouth. Can't do it.'

'Could we admit a mutual attraction here? Could we both extend ourselves to risk and vent these hazardous feelings?'

Lenore goes quiet and just stares at him. She opens and then closes her mouth. Then she opens it again and says, 'You're either the most pathetic guy I've ever met or you're over the top, you're tooling with me and I don't even know it, you've got capacities that I'm just blind to.'

'And aren't you curious to know which it is, Lenore?'

She wishes she had some perfect, hateful line. Instead she says, with little conviction, 'You tell me.'

'Like you said before – things change. I think that's the bottom line, really. I think everything is in constant flux. I think that nothing in this world is stable. I think maybe the difference between being pathetic and being overwhelmingly in control is a difference of perspective. And that perspective, like a pendulum, will swing from one extreme to the other.'

He reaches across to her and just barely touches the skin on the back of her neck. He runs a finger lightly down a cord of knotted muscle. If it were Zarelli doing this, a man she's spent the past several months sleeping with, she'd be driving an elbow into his chest and curing his stupidity. Now, shocked at herself, she comes up with a weak, heartless 'Don't.'

Woo doesn't stop. He shifts a bit in his seat, draws nearer to her side of the car. His voice goes low and he says, 'My guess is you drink far too much coffee. The tension is just gleaming off your body. You could do with a month of massage and hot baths.'

His fingers slide around the curve of her neck, around the front to below her jaw. He has a delicate touch that surprises her, like a kind doctor, a combination of professional, learned knowledge and instinctual sensitivity. His index finger travels back up her throat to below her earlobe and probes softly at the hinge of her jaw.

'You clench unconsciously. I would guess that you grind your teeth in your sleep.'

She keeps herself from looking at him. She stares at the Penumbra garage and mumbles, 'I don't sleep.'

'No surprise there,' he says, his fingers moving down soothingly over her Adam's apple.

'Stop,' she says, but her body stays rigid, her eyes frozen forward, unblinking, then closing up.

She feels him unfasten the first button on her blouse. Her eyes open, but she doesn't speak. He frees the second button. Her breath starts to come heavier and she makes a loud swallowing noise. The third button comes loose.

And the garage door swings open and Mingo Bouza pulls the Jaguar out into the street and rolls off, headed west.

Lenore shifts the Barracuda into gear and Woo's hand hesitates for only a second and then falls away from her chest. She waits a moment to give Mingo a safe lead, then pulls out of the alley and begins the tail.

They both stay quiet and Lenore's glad for this. She leaves four and five car lengths between herself and Mingo. She'd rather risk losing him at a red light than give themselves away. They drive for close to an hour and, for Lenore, that leaves only two possibilities – either Mingo is in love with the Jag and logging time behind the wheel just for the kick, a fairly innocent fix, or Cortez has told him to watch for a tail and he's making a safety arc, driving a huge circle around the borders of the city.

But if Mingo expects a tail, he's not doing a thing to lose it. He drives long stretches of speedway – Chin Ave, Hooey Road, William Brown Hill. He keeps at a constant rate of motion. He stays in the same lane for long stretches of time. It makes Lenore more than a little suspicious. She wishes she had the time and appropriate conditions to give this some thought. She wishes she could take a half hit of crank and pump some weight in a dim and deserted gym with the latest underground speed metal playing off a portable Bose and echoing off soundproofed walls. Then the truth would come to her. Her intuition could combine with the limited facts and tell her the most likely answers to the questions *Where is Mingo headed? Is he aware of my presence or just stupid? Is this a trap?*

Eventually, Mingo winds toward the west side of Quinsigamond and Lenore is unsure of whether or not to feel comfort now that she's on home turf. Woo stays silent in his seat, possibly sulking over coming so close to what he wants so badly. How far would she have let him go, she wonders, and is hit instantly with a picture of herself, naked and hungry for a little more air, in the cramped backseat of the Barracuda like some high school girl with an encroaching curfew. She puts the picture out of her mind, only with difficulty, by thinking of Vicky in her long black nightgown, swaying like a limp branch up the telephone pole.

Lenore watches Mingo take a left onto Sapir Street and her stomach tightens up. She's not sure why, but she doesn't want to consider the possibility that Ike could see her with Woo. The Jaguar slows, pulls into the curb just beyond the post office, and Lenore pulls into the parking lot of a convenience store on the corner of Breton and Sapir. She sinks in her seat and Woo glances at her, then does the same.

Mingo climbs out of the Jag carrying an oxblood briefcase, looks around as he fumbles with the keys to lock the car door. Then he crosses the street with a small jog and heads into the Bach Room. Lenore watches the screen door swing closed and then, absentmindedly, she begins to rebutton her blouse.

'You play gin rummy?' she asks Woo, still staring at the Bach Room entrance.

'Excuse?' Woo asks, but Lenore ignores him.

'We've got to make a couple phone calls,' she says, 'and pick up a thermos of black coffee.'

18

'I've done everything you've ever asked… this *can't* be necessary. I've done everything—… no. I'm *begging* you—… no. Then it's best left to me.'

Cortez brings the cordless phone down from his mouth to his chest and holds it there for a moment, his eyes closed, his hands trembling. Then he moves the phone away from his body, looks down into the small cradle of illuminated rubber buttons. He pushes on the Open Speaker switch and sets the phone gently down on the fireplace mantel, mouth-grid faced up toward the library ceiling.

He walks over to the black steamer trunk, the only thing left resembling furniture in the whole room. He grabs a leather handle and eases the trunk down until it rests horizontally on the floor. Then he drags it to the center of the room.

There's a shave-and-a-haircut knock on the library's double doors. He takes a breath and yells, 'Come in, Max.'

The door opens slowly and Max, looking smaller than usual in his green camouflage army clothes, enters with a single step, then stays put.

They stare at each other until Cortez says, 'Is it what you expected?'

'It's a little… empty.'

Cortez smiles. 'I don't like to be crowded. You know that.'

'Yeah, but a chair. A table, maybe.'

'Creature comforts.'

'Yeah, well, ain't we creatures?'

Cortez laughs. 'Right again, Max.'

'I never got what the big thing was with this room. Nobody could go in this one room.'

Cortez hand-motions him to come closer and says, 'Well, Max, there always has to be one exception to any freedom. Like the apple in the garden.'

'You know, I only get about half of what you say.'

'I think you're doing better than Mingo and Jimmy.'

'Big challenge.'

Cortez nods, clears his throat, looks down to the floor.

'So why'd you want me up here now?' Max asks.

Cortez lets out a heavy sigh. He sinks down to sit on the steamer trunk as if it were a bench and he slaps the top of the trunk to indicate that Max should do the same.

'I've been giving some thought to your future, Max.'

'My future?'

'I've been considering the best avenues for you.'

'Avenues, yeah.'

'I'm very upset with myself, Max. I honestly think I've been quite lax in regard to your education.'

'You mean like school?'

'I mean, like, the development of your mind, the forging of a sturdy personal aesthetic.'

'Aesth—'

'We can't let our origins limit us, Max. We can't become content with our situations. That leads to decay. Try to remember this always.'

'Was there some errand you needed run? Something from the store?'

'You've done very well around the hotel over the past few years, Max. You performed your duties, done all that was asked of you.'

'I don't do all that much.'

'And in return, I've slighted you. But you must know it was never an intentional slight. A man gets involved in business,

Max. In the planning, the telescoping, the contingencies. The day-to-day pressures mount. A man begins to forsake the truly important goals. It happens to most men, I think. I had hoped to hold myself to a higher standard.'

'You know, I think Mingo could really use a hand down in the kitchen…'

'Here you are now, already in the midst of adolescence. There's so much I should have showed you already. I'm sure I'd be appalled with myself if I knew the depth of your ignorance.'

'Jees, don't be so hard on yourself, Mr. C—'

'Just now, for instance, my reference to the Eden story. Right over your head. A primal metaphor like that. But of course, how could you have known it? Spontaneous generation in the brain? It has to be passed down. The oral tradition, Max.'

'Oral tradition, sure.'

'There are so many stories I could have told you by now.'

Cortez rises off the trunk, but holds out a hand to indicate that Max should stay seated.

'So many nights, up in my balcony at Club 62 with my bullhorn and spotlight. And I could have been with you, Max, lights out, seated in a rocker next to your bed, yes? I could have told you stories until you fell off to sleep.'

'I was with you in the balcony a lot, boss—'

'And the funny thing is, it would have proved even better training, I think. I truly believe that.' Cortez starts to walk a small circle around the steamer. 'Better even than observing my actions firsthand. We could have sculpted the imagination. Taught you to think in terms of legend and myth. Larger than life. Wouldn't you have liked that, Max?'

Max hesitates, then mumbles, 'Yeah, I guess,' and Cortez reaches from behind him, places his hand on the boy's forehead, and pushes him slowly down until he's reclined on top of the trunk.

'It could have been just like this, Max. You're not quite ready for sleep. I'm tired from an endless day, but regenerating, finding a second wind in what's to come. Close your eyes, Max.'

Max looks up at Cortez, visibly uncomfortable, but not knowing what to do. He closes his eyes. His legs hang over the end of the trunk. Cortez continues his circle.

'I could have transferred all the classics to you, Max. Chronicles of war. Stories of gods and monsters and long ocean journeys. We could have learned together. Just a voice in a dark room. A father's voice. Comforting. Protecting. Full of hidden knowledge and ancient stories. Homer, Max. Hesiod. Terence. Virgil. Ovid. All the names, Max. And the Bible. All the stories. We could've worked our way through. From "In the beginning" to the last "Amen" of Revelation.'

Cortez talks and walks another circle, comes to rest at Max's head. The boy's eyelids are fluttering. He wants to open the eyes, but he doesn't dare. Cortez squats down, puts a hand on Max's forehead, lowers his voice.

'I could've taken you from the six days of creation to the visions of John. But there's a price for everything, son. And some opportunities only come our way once. A single chance.'

Cortez reaches inside his jacket and pulls from an inner breast pocket a long, pearl-handled dagger. An antique. Handmade. A gift from people whose faces he's never seen. He grabs the handle tight in his hand, raises it above his head, squeezes it as he leans down and kisses Max on the forehead.

The boy's eyes come open, shocked and wide. They stare at each other for an aching, impossible second.

And then Cortez brings the dagger down. Plunges it into the steamer trunk all the way down to the handle. He pushes Max up to a standing position and yells, 'Get out!'

The boy runs, stumbling, out of the library. Cortez stands up and runs to the fireplace, grabs the phone from the mantel, holds it up to his mouth, and yells into the receiver, 'Two words. Fuck you,' then heaves the phone like a speedball, the length of the room, until it smashes against a wall in an explosion of black plastic and colored wires.

He takes the dagger from his pocket and places it on the mantel, then puts a hand on either side of it to steady himself. He takes a few deep breaths, swallows, and says aloud, 'I'm a dead man.'

19

Lenore would give almost anything to know what Woo is dreaming about. She wishes there were some process she could tap, some gift of science that would allow her to bring in a Sony Trinitron, strap a few cables and electrodes from TV to forehead in the manner of every cheaply made 1950s science-fiction movie she's ever stumbled upon at 4 A.M., sitting cross-legged in her bed, zapping through the cable channels with the remote control and pumping a ten-pounder with her free hand, her Magnum in her lap.

If she could make the connection, adjust the volume, and hone the contrast, what would she see among the static and sparks of Woo's synapse pictures? The stale air and dull faces of a college classroom as Woo's hand draws root words and clever, pointy symbols on a slate blackboard? The milk-white skin of the latest eighteen-year-old co-ed he's seduced on the couch of his linguistics office? Or just maybe her own face, spitting smug insults his way as his hand slides inside her silk chemise and cradles her breast and his fingers run over a rapidly hardening nipple?

Maybe it's nothing like that. He's breathing easily, not making any noise. Maybe it's some simple pastoral dream from his grandfather's narrated past. Something about rice paddies or the slow lapping sound of water against the sides of a sturdy junk bobbing near a shore, riding out the mild, endless waves of the family village. Maybe she should wake him suddenly and ask him, demand that he spit out his imagery before it fades. Interrogate him for every detail he can save from the deteriorating land of REM sleep.

Lenore's own dreams were horrible and she's grateful to be awake. The first thing she did after opening her eyes and getting a bearing on her surroundings was to pull a hit of crank from her pocket and pop it. There's no water available, so she had to swallow it dry. It went down hard and her throat still aches.

But she's happy to be awake and even this filthy basement is better than what she went through in the nightmare: she was the sole passenger on this endless subway ride. The subway car was this broken-down bullet, windowless, graffiti-covered, floors filled, for some reason, with old, yellowed, crumpled-up newspapers. The graffiti was in either code or some new inner-city slang or an obscure foreign language, but there were crudely drawn illustrations next to it that gave her an idea of its meaning. Like some subterranean Rosetta stone. Both the forward and rear doors were jammed shut. Every now and then the lights would go out and she'd sit in the darkness for what seemed like an hour. The car seemed to be gradually but consistently picking up speed. Her feet vibrated on the floor and her hands, gripping the edge of her seat, began to shake. There was an awful and incessant electric-sounding hum in her ear. At one point she panicked and ripped open her coat to look for her gun, but her holster was empty. Cold air began to fill the car. Every now and then she moved to the front and back doors and yelled, first calling out full sentences like *Is anyone down there?* or *Can anyone stop this thing?* Then she shortened to calls for *Help*, and finally, just before giving up, she made guttural, animal noises, howls and barks. She collapsed back onto the cream-colored molded plastic bench and began to imagine the cinematic possibility that some bomb had fallen and decimated the city. That the radiation had seeped into the tunnels and killed the driver, the only other person in the subway, in this terrible strangulating manner. She fell sideways on the bench, curled into a fetal hunch, and wondered which would be worse – to be choked out in the near future by the radiation making its way toward her, car by car, or to be immune to the radiation and live, trapped on this perpetually moving vehicle, circle the city over and over, until dehydration alone turned her car into a mobile grave. She could probably have hurled herself out of one of the shattered windows and under the wheels, but suicide was out of the question for more than one reason. As she crowded in further on her own body, the hum in her ears increased until it became painful. She woke from the dream with her hands at the sides of her head.

She and Woo are in the basement of the Sapir Street Postal Station. Miskewitz, through Mayor Welby, had the postmaster let them in during the night so they could get in position and set up operations before any of the mail carriers, or even the branch supervisor, knew of police presence below their feet.

They brought with them two sleeping bags, a bag of convenience store food – potato chips, candy bars, packaged donuts – a double thermos of coffee, and all the electronics needed to listen to and tape any phone calls coming into or leaving the Bach Room. At 2 A.M., Miskewitz had a lineman setting the tap on the pole behind the bar. Lenore and Woo moved into the basement just before four.

Now Lenore is kicking herself for not bringing something to read. Woo brought a small paperback, without any cover illustrations, titled *Aztec Tongue* in big white block letters. She'd like to ask him if it's fiction or some difficult textbook but she knows she won't. She hasn't given any thought to the question of why she allowed this dorkwhite, whom she doesn't even like, to unbutton her blouse, control the situation. The fact that she didn't set an initial, unforgettable example – inflict some physical punishment, draw a little nose blood – bothers her tremendously. Had it been Zarelli, his index finger would be in a splint right now and he'd be explaining to the wife and the lieutenant how he slammed his desk drawer on it.

She's set things up in a tiny alcove at the back of the basement, away from the sidewalk-level windows covered with black wire grilles. There's a small semi-room, set off from the rest of the cellar by two brick partitions, housing the old furnace, the water main, and the electrical board that's updated with a box of circuit breakers. Lenore and Woo pulled an abandoned worktable into the alcove, dusted it off, and placed on it the receiver and tape machine.

Though the alcove is much roomier than the inside of the Barracuda, Lenore would much rather be in her car. She feels slightly claustrophobic in the cellar and she hates the thought of breathing in years of dust and soot. The idea of rodents doesn't thrill her, but it's below the cooped-up feeling on the list of things that annoy her. Ike, she thinks, would probably love it here, secluded, forgotten, dim, an extreme version of his side of the duplex. Ike dislikes bright lights, and, she suspects, has some latent agoraphobia brewing in his psyche. They're exact opposites in this regard and she wonders if anyone has done a study of this in twins. *We're dizygotic*, she thinks, *two different eggs*, and then she envisions herself and Ike as small gray rectangular magnets. Turned one way, they repel away from one another. Ends reversed, they slide together helplessly and mesh. She considers the fact that some days she dwells for hours on Ike's lack of a girlfriend and considers women that she could introduce him to. Other days, she knows, his singleness pleases her and she wants him to stay forever alone, on the opposite side of her walls.

She's dressed in her oldest black jeans, a teal cotton turtleneck over a light-thermal undershirt, black Reeboks, and a secondhand leather bomber jacket that she bought off a Cambodian with an eye patch at the refugee flea market one Sunday morning. The market was set up weekly out at the old train lot on Ironhouse Ave. It wasn't until she got the jacket home that she found a small 3 × 5-inch drugstore notebook in the breast pocket. The notebook contained only three pages, all the others had been torn out. The pages were filled with foreign writing, Oriental-like, and from the way it was set on the page she guessed that it might be poetry.

She debated for three weeks whether or not she should return it to the merchant. Her biggest argument against its return was her reasoning that he was just a salesman, just a broker, that he'd gotten it elsewhere and the notebook didn't belong to him any more than her. She never discussed what to do with anyone. Not Zarelli, not even Ike. After a month, she went back one Sunday morning to the flea market and managed to locate the booth where she'd gotten the jacket. But the Cambodian with the eye patch was gone. In his place was a Nicaraguan selling old eight-track tapes. She purchased *Vic Damone's Greatest Hits* for a quarter and gave it to Zarelli at work the next day. Zarelli shrugged and said, 'He's not Tony B, but he's okay.'

She wishes she'd brought the notebook with her to the cellar. Most likely, Woo could translate it for her. Then she changes her mind and is pleased she didn't think to bring it. Whatever her imagination has made those obscure symbols into would be wiped out the second Woo opened his mouth and changed them into English.

Woo's eyes begin to flutter a bit, tiny mutant birds, and then they go into a series of full blinks. He stares up out of his army-green sleeping bag and Lenore thinks he looks like he's been swallowed up to the neck by a sentient vegetable that's invaded the planet.

'How long was I out?' he asks.

'Just a couple of hours,' Lenore says. 'Sleep well?'

'Strange dreams,' he says through a yawn, and pulls his arms free from the bag to stretch.

'Join the club,' Lenore mumbles.

'What time is it?'

'Little before seven. Want some coffee?'

He nods, shimmies out of the bag, and climbs to his feet. 'Yes, please.'

Lenore unscrews the thermos cap and pours a cupful. 'It'll have to be black,' she says.

'I normally drink it black,' he says, taking the cup, sipping, and burning his lips.

'It's steaming,' Lenore says too late. 'Sometimes these thermoses work too well, you know?'

Woo nods and dabs at his singed lips with his fingers. He's dressed in a pair of old pleated chinos with slightly flared legs, a too-thin brown leather belt, a cotton baseball shirt with blue three-quarter-length arms and a picture of Ezra Pound silk-screened on the front, a fraying navy cardigan, and low-cut white sneakers void of a brand name anywhere on them. Lenore thinks he's an illustration for a men's magazine on 'how *not* to dress for a date.'

'For breakfast,' she says, unrolling the top of a paper bag on the table, 'we've got a choice of cream-filled chocolate cupcakes, mini sugar donuts' – she rummages – 'chips, licorice, graham crackers…'

'Excuse me for saying so,' Woo says with a guilty smile on his face. He blows on his cup of coffee and continues, 'But it surprises me that you eat these things. I mean, you've got such a stunning figure—'

She cuts him off. 'It's all metabolism. Don't listen to any of the experts on this. Trust me. It's metabolism. I've got a digestive system that won't quit. I burn up food like you read about. It runs overtime. Just really aggressive.'

She pulls out a bag of salt-and-vinegar potato chips, tears it open, puts one in her mouth, and offers the bag toward Woo. He reaches in, takes a chip, bites into it, and, after a beat, makes an awful frowning and squinty face.

'So sour,' he says, his tongue caked with small pieces of chips. 'And this early in the morning.'

'I thought you people loved sour-tasting food.'

Woo makes an exaggerated, gulping swallow and says, 'Where did you hear this?'

'Just one of those things you hear.'

Woo makes small, pecking sips at the cup of coffee.

'That book you brought with you,' Lenore says, 'that Aztec tongue book? What is that? That's not a textbook, is it?'

'Not exactly, no,' Woo says. 'It's a very obscure novel from the early 1900s, I believe. Written by an Argentine who chose to remain anonymous. It's been out of print for years. I picked this edition up, used, last year, and never got to reading it. It's really a mystery novel, of a sort.'

'My brother loves mysteries. Reads them all the time. Nonstop. Like peanuts, one after another. I can take them or leave them.'

'I have a colleague, a woman in the literature department, she says that the mystery, or, no, I guess, the detective story, that's it, the detective story, is the most fitting mode for expressing our contemporary situation. What did she call it? Very clever woman. Something about – post-God, post-humanist, post-holocaust, post-literate, numbing void. Something like this—'

'Actually, I was a criminology major.'

'Of course.'

'And that was a hell of a long time ago.'

'Another symptom of our times. We live longer than any humans to walk the planet, yet we start thinking we're elderly soon after adolescence.'

'I don't think I'm elderly. Believe me, I know where I stand. I've got a good grip on my age. I'm better at thirty, both mentally and physically, than any rookie the department took on this year. I guarantee that.'

'I don't doubt you, Lenore.'

'But the fact is, I work at it. I mean, there's an awful lot of effort.'

'Self-evident.'

'I think, you make the effort, your body responds. And the things you can't change, they'll follow along. You see one gray hair in my head? Go ahead, look close. Not a one. Now, it's not like I use any coloring or anything, but my brother, Ike, okay, same exact age, we're twins, okay, you should see all the gray ones he's sprouting. Another five years and forget it. That'll be the whole head. Now, same age, same genes, for Christ sake, and look at the difference.'

'Perhaps it's stress. Is your brother in a very stressful environment?'

'More stressful than narcotics? Jees, Freddy, c'mon.'

'You have a point.'

'You know where Ike works? You'll love this. Directly above our heads. I'm not kidding you. He's a letter carrier. Mailman. Right here at Sapir Street.'

'Such a coincidence.'

'Maybe. I don't really believe in coincidence.'

'You know, Lenore, for some reason I didn't think you would. What is it you go for? Fate? The karmic wheel?'

'The thing I hate most with you is I really can't get a bearing on when you're making fun of me.'

'I can't recall one instance since we've met when I made fun of you. The mistake you make, Lenore, is to overcomplicate things. You can take me at face value. I'm a very simple man.'

'I've heard that said half a dozen times before and it's never been true.'

'Think about it, Lenore. You see in front of you a man who's spent nine-tenths of his adult life inside enormous libraries. In terms of theories of language, well, perhaps, maybe, possibly I'm a bit involved. But, I swear to you, in terms of just day-to-day routine, these common dynamics of meeting and speaking with people – waitress, I'd like a cup of coffee; Bill, good to see you; Ms. Dixon, how's the new baby? – I'm so ill at ease, I'm constantly second-guessing myself, overpreparing for every minute encounter.'

'God, that's terrible.'

'I don't sleep well.'

'Oh, c'mon. You were deep into dreamtime the past two hours.'

'Well, pardon me, but, again, that just shows how comfortable I am in your presence.'

'Now, that's something I don't hear very often.'

'You're out to confuse me, Lenore. One compliment will bring me an insult and an obscenity, the next you let pass.'

'You just don't get it. We're a little out of sync here. I don't think you always pick up on sarcasm or irony or, I don't know.'

'Yes, this is true. I know what you're saying. There's sort of an urban hipness – self-deprecation, detached absurdism, mock horror set next to a bored complacency.'

'Whatever. Now you're the one thinking too much. I had this nun in grammar school used to try to teach us French. She'd always say, "Let the words wash over you." I always took that as – don't think so much, get the flavor, get the rhythm. You think too much, you miss the forest for the trees.'

'You speak French?'

'No way.'

'Too bad. I always enjoy a little practice.'

'Practice?'

'I speak six languages. I'm working toward eight.'

'Ambitious guy. You've impressed me.'

'I didn't mean. I was simply…'

'Take it easy, Freddy. I'm serious. I'm pretty serious. That's an achievement. I'm not running you down here. Ease up.'

'Both my parents were fluent in a variety of languages. I was somewhat destined for my field.'

'Are you saying there was a lot of pressure? You were pushed—'

'Not at all. I had an extremely happy childhood. A very happy family life.'

'I feel that way too. I look back and just can't remember any bad times, which is ridiculous. All I can see is my parents in their living room chairs and Ike and me on the floor. All of us staring at Ed Sullivan or something.'

'I'm saying that due to both genetic and environmental influences, I was predisposed to language.'

'Yeah, well, that has its advantages. A lot of people flounder around looking for something to do. Most people fall into something.'

'But I get the impression this is not the case with Lenore. You knew what you wanted, yes?'

'Not from birth, but yeah, I knew pretty much what I wanted. Let's say I knew exactly what I didn't want.'

'Tell me.'

Lenore pauses, looks up toward the lines of piping near the ceiling, then says, 'This will be strange to you, a word guy like you, but sometimes, a lot of times, I hate putting words to feelings you've known for a long time, feelings you've known forever. It's always so inexact. It's worse than that.'

'Tell me anyway.'

'I didn't want to be controlled. I didn't want to be dominated. I didn't want to be restricted, directed. I didn't want to be dominated. Forget it.'

'No, that's good. That has to be close.'

'That's like ten miles from home. And then some.'

'It's a starting point.'

'It's like pretending you have a starting point.'

'Not meaning to be rude, Lenore, but this is my specialty.'

'Then you give me the word.'

'It's *your* feeling.'

'Bingo.'

'I just can't help but wonder, though—'

'Think about what you're about to say here. Ask yourself, "Would a normal person take what I'm about to say as insulting?"'

'You're saying censor myself, think before I speak.'

'I just feel something bad coming.'

'I was simply going to ask if you'd ever considered the fact that many would call police work the most restrictive job of all. The policeman becomes a tightrope walker and all. Dominated by her ostracism from the masses. Controlled by ever-increasing rules and regulations.'

'That's good, Freddy. That's what I would want you to believe.'

'This is not the case.'

'Not for me. It's a state of mind. It involves the imagination. If you're stupid, forget it. You're exactly right. Take Zarelli. A genuinely stupid man, okay? He's a walking definition of constipation. He's an absolutely controlled man. He's totally dominated from all directions. Family, job, the general population, Lenore. But Zarelli's an idiot. He's the cause of his own condition.'

'You're saying you can outwit your condition?'

'I think I manage.'

'It's an idea with promise. Imagination as the key to freedom.'

'Okay, let's not take it too far. You'll deplete the whole thing. I'm just wondering, at the dinner table growing up, you're sitting there with the folks, you ask someone to pass the rice, right? What do you say? What language do you use?'

'Usually, English. English would be the norm.'

'Boring.'

'I'm not saying this is hard-and-fast. This was the norm. You might hear French. You might hear Spanish.'

'Keep going.'

'German, Russian, possibly Yiddish, and, of course, Cantonese.'

'Get out of here. What's with this Yiddish?'

'My father studied the Kabbalah. Taught himself. A hobby.'

'Get out. Say something in Yiddish.'

'*Voorshtlekh mit gehbahkehnch beblekh.*'

'Translate.'

'Franks and beans.'

'Great. You'll never starve.'

Woo takes a deck of cards from his coat pocket and Lenore is about to say, 'I don't play pinochle,' when she sees a skeleton figure pictured on the box and realizes it's a tarot deck.

'Wouldn't have picked you for a guy who'd have much use for occult crap,' she says.

'Strictly for amusement purposes,' Woo says, again with the

put-on smile that makes him look like an annoyed maitre d' in Chinatown. She watches his hands and is surprised by his skill and comfort with the cards. She wouldn't have expected it. If she'd been giving Zarelli a rundown on Woo she'd have mentioned an awkwardness, a clumsiness that's clearly not the case.

'Have you ever used a tarot deck?' he asks.

'High school, I guess,' she says. 'Sleeping over friends' houses.'

'It's a system like any other. For me, it's not a question of whether I give credence to its occult history, whether or not I believe in prophecy through the cards. It's just a system to me, and fascinating within that realm. I don't have to be as affronted as my colleagues in the hard sciences. I can confront the cards on different terms.'

'So you're going to tell my fortune?'

'Let's have a look.'

He hands Lenore the cards and she starts to shuffle. They stare at each other as her hands move, then he nods and she hands the cards back. Woo pulls the top card up and lays it down.

'This is Lenore,' he says. 'Interesting. The High Priestess. Learned and practical. A challenge to many men. But she has difficulty forming lasting relationships.'

'Real deep. You couldn't get hired by a carnival.'

He smiles and turns over several cards, laying them down in a definite pattern. He seems to be concentrating. On the turn of the fifth card, he stops.

'The Moon,' he says in a hushed voice.

'What's wrong with that?' Lenore asks.

'The Moon is a card of warning. It falls here to show what has occurred in your recent past. It shows danger. The chance of having made an error is great.'

He goes on spreading cards without looking up at her. She wants to laugh, but can't force it, and instead stares down at Woo's hands. They hesitate and he looks up at her and says, 'I think we should stop with this next one.'

'Which is?'

He flips it over. There's a picture of an angel blowing a horn, possibly Gabriel, and a naked person emerging from an open coffin.

'It's the card of Judgment,' Woo says. 'This is the future. The future shows a time of judgment will come. A great deal of sorrow. And a calling to atonement for a wrong committed. Something hideous and uncalled-for.'

Lenore's upper lip begins to quiver and the motion shocks her. It's a tugging, nervous twitch that she once felt while trying to move a refrigerator, a signal, located randomly in the lip, that the weight of the appliance was much more than her body should be handling. It's as if a dentist had given her a weird, double injection of both novocaine and some untested muscle stimulant. The tiny nerves in her upper lip first seem to go dead-numb and then tear away, out of control, spastic, and shoot north toward her right ear. She starts to tell herself that she's having a stroke, a seizure of some kind, but she knows this is a lie. What's happening to her lip is the result of an overstimulated nervous system, a psyche bullied into a cold, fear-ignoring willfulness, a diet of coffee and screeching music, a year without a normal night's sleep, and, most of all, the issuance from her gun of two aluminum and lead bullets that tore down a Canal Zone alley at four hundred feet per second and entered the hysterical heart of a redheaded teenage hooker named Vicky.

Woo just stares at her. It's clear he can see what's happening to the lip, but he makes no comment, offers no assistance.

Her right hand comes up to her face. She attempts to push the lip physically into place and hold it there, but it's a useless effort. The lip is locked into its numb then spastic routine and no amount of force from the hand can stop it.

She feels that ceaseless burning pressure behind the eyes, and tears start to come. Immediately, she descends into the breathing pattern of a child half woken from a horrifying nightmare, that choking, irregular, suck-and-heave pattern. Within seconds she's hysterical. She's sobbing, choking, keening, moaning, her head slightly flailing around her neck in a jagged circle, a fist pounding into her thigh, her dull fingernails managing to break the skin around her ankle through her socks.

Woo grabs her by the wrists, pulls her hands away from herself. He's even-voiced, moving moderately, deliberate.

'Lenore,' he says, then he repeats her name, over and over until it takes on the ring and rhythm of a chant.

After a minute he pulls her forward so that her body awkwardly falls, then leans into his. She lets her face, her eyes and the bridge of her nose, find a mount at the juncture of his neck and shoulder, and she collects herself up into a more regular, consistent sobbing.

He moves his fingers slowly through her hair, strokes the back of her neck, whispers into her ear, 'Lenore, there are people upstairs now. They'll hear us, Lenore. They'll know we're down here.'

She's surprised at how much this quiets her. They stay in a rigid and uncomfortable position for several minutes. Lenore thinks of an old movie version of *The Diary of Anne Frank* that she saw as a child. She and Ike watched it together. She thinks of herself now as Anne Frank, holding herself motionless, waiting, perpetually breathless, for Nazis to kick in the attic door.

Finally, she pulls away from Woo, positions herself back on the floor, cross-legged. She begins to rub at her eyes and says, 'I'm sorry.'

Woo simply reaches forward, touches then lightly squeezes her leg.

'Vicky,' she says, as if the name were a word without any assigned meaning, as if she'd read it off the wall of a cave.

Woo nods.

A small red light begins to flash on the receiver on the table. Woo stays silent but starts to point rapidly at the table. Lenore stares at him for a second, then jumps up and moves to the table, grabs the headphones, and brings them to her ear. She hears the traditional phone-ringing sound, reaches out, and turns on the reel-to-reel recorder. The two large wheels of tape begin to turn and the needle in the sound meter box jumps up into view, shocked alive. The phone rings a few times, then there's a click of a pickup and she hears:

VOICE: Yeah, I'm here.
VOICE: Very good. I hope I didn't wake you.

Lenore's heart bucks. She'd bet all her memories of her parents that the second voice, with its accent and confidence, belongs to Cortez.

VOICE: I don't live here. I've got a life besides this shit, okay?

CORTEZ: Relax, Mr. Rourke. There's no reason we can't be civil with one another.

ROURKE: I'm not so sure about that.

CORTEZ: Were you offended by my package, Mr. Rourke?

ROURKE: What package? What?

CORTEZ: You'll find, in this business, Mr. Rourke, there's a line of demarcation, a pivot of sorts—

ROURKE: I hate it when people talk like this. Too many fucking words—

CORTEZ: There's a certain savvy needed in these endeavors, a definite, innate self-discipline, belief in standards. There's an instinct that's needed, Mr. Rourke, and I'm not entirely sure it's the type of thing that can be learned. In this, it's like a very useful form of grace.

ROURKE: Jesus. Just talk to me like a human for once.

CORTEZ: For instance, regarding my little package—

ROURKE: I said – didn't you hear me? – I said, what package?

CORTEZ: —you have to know how serious to take such a

thing. You have to innately know from the very moment that you smell the stink, that you see the dismembered remains, the tiny parasites moving in and out of the host, you must be hit with understanding in that instant. You must know that this is very simply a symbol, a literal suggestion, a method of effective and concise communication, that it delivers a very important message in the most dramatic and instantaneous and lasting of ways. It's a work of art, Mr. Rourke. A thousand words, as the saying goes.

[*Whistling noise from Rourke*]

CORTEZ: And your reaction must be astute. You must know how to gauge your response. To take the message seriously enough to correct any aberrant behavior, but not so seriously that you rupture the whole relationship.

ROURKE: You can be an infuriating guy. Has this ever been said to you? Has anyone, maybe in passing, made this remark? You get a person's juices going, you know? You bring me to the edge of saying shit, I don't want to… like 'talk normal, you fucking beaner.' You see, there you go. I said it. It's out. Can't suck the words back in. They're out there and you heard them.

CORTEZ: Racial slurs have very little meaning to me, Mr. Rourke. Meaningless. No meaning. In this instance, it doesn't even apply. My understanding is that 'beaner' refers to a Mexican, or more likely, a Mexican-American. I'm an Argentine. Born in Brussels, to be honest.

ROURKE: Oh, for Christ sake…

CORTEZ: You say you didn't receive my package. I'm left with a choice as to whether to believe you or not.

ROURKE: What was in the package?

CORTEZ: It's no longer pertinent. You weren't sorting yesterday?

ROURKE: Bitch put me on a route. I'm telling you, luck is not with us.

There's a pause and Lenore starts to wonder if the tap's been discovered.

CORTEZ: My assistant said you were a bit uncooperative during his visit.

ROURKE: Guy's a freaking comedian.

CORTEZ: You continue to dispute our claim?

ROURKE: Look, mister, the sample I gave to your man had three units—

CORTEZ: Unfortunately, only two units arrived in the Park. I paid for three sample units.

ROURKE: I sent three. There were three. Think about this, why would I screw you before the main buy? Think about this. I got my neck so far out now. Think about my position for just one freaking second, okay? I'm in midair here. No one wants to be visible. I've got a producer whose name I don't know, won't show his face. I've got a purchaser who wants me to do all my talking to his goddamn funny-guy driver, for Christ sake.

CORTEZ: This is pointless. We've all got problems, Mr. Rourke.

ROURKE: I've fronted money. I've taken some risks here. You know, my own people don't have some banker friend in the Caribbean they can tap with a WATS line, okay? These people sold their cars, mortgaged houses—

CORTEZ: You saying I should be sympathetic because the broker in this transaction is an ill-equipped amateur. This is what you're saying? I should show mercy and patience and ignore my instinct because you're still trying to learn a new trade. I think you've made a huge mistake, Mr. Rourke—

ROURKE: All right, listen, forget it, we'll kick back on the missing unit, even though for all I know your driver Bozo—

CORTEZ: Bouza.

ROURKE: Bouza, Bouza, for all we know he lifted a Q.

Okay, forget it. Everything's still on. Everything's perfect. It's all set to go.

CORTEZ: My confidence is shaken, Mr. Rourke…

ROURKE: You've got to be kidding me here. You're pulling my chain here, right? I talked to the Paraclete this morning. This A.M. He's ready. Everything is packaged. The whole wad. Your final offer is still A-OK. We just need a time and a place.

CORTEZ: You spoke to him?

ROURKE: I swear to you he called this morning. At my place. Like four A.M.

CORTEZ: The Paraclete? Himself?

ROURKE: Yeah… well, his people. You got people. I've got people. Of course, he's got people. His main guy called. Guy with authority. Speaks for the Paraclete. You got Bozo—

CORTEZ: Bouza.

ROURKE: Right, right.

CORTEZ: He's agreed that I name the spot?

ROURKE: He could be happier. But he'll live with it.

CORTEZ: Fine. We'll go with his original location.

ROURKE: Okay. I know right where you mean.

CORTEZ: Is 2 A.M. agreeable?

ROURKE: Couldn't be better. Could not be any better.

CORTEZ: I'll be deducting the cost of the third sample from the payout. There won't be a problem with this?

ROURKE: I'll cover it. It'll come out of my commission. Off the top. Everyone'll be happy.

CORTEZ: Then I'll see you, Mr. Rourke.

ROURKE: Done.

There's one hang-up click, a pause, then a second click. Lenore waits a beat, then shuts off the recorder and removes the headphones.

Woo stares at her and she holds the headphones out to him, indicating that he can listen to a replay if he wants. He shrugs, but takes the headphones, puts them on, and spends several seconds adjusting their placement on his head. Lenore rewinds the tape for him and when the counter numbers fall back to zero, she hits the Play button.

Then she steps back and leans up against one of the brick walls and watches Woo's face closely as he listens. She's not sure what she's looking for, but she knows it's important that she watch. Possibly, some look will kick in at the eyes, or the whole head will shake upon hearing something significant. She knows she's being ridiculously greedy. She's gotten every piece of information she needs in one call. She's gotten Cortez as a buyer. She's gotten someone named Mr. Rourke as a broker. She's gotten someone named the Paraclete as the producer. She's gotten the time of the transaction. But she wants more. This doesn't surprise her. She knows, no matter what she came away with from the tap, no matter how wise and prepared she emerged from the cellar, she would want more.

Woo's face gives her nothing. He sits in a rigid schoolboy position, eyes straight ahead, focused on brick and mortar, lips primly together. He's even got his hands folded on the table in front of him. He's a blank sheet.

There's nothing to read.

20

Ike feels as if he's in a high school play, maybe a drama club production of *Twelve Angry Men*, done in the gym, a hundred parents trying to get comfortable on the wooden bleachers. He feels like he's missed every rehearsal since the play was cast, but they've kept him in the role anyway. Now it's opening night and he doesn't know a line. He can't even seem to find a script.

Eva knows her role. She's a born actress. She walked into the locker room like it was any other day. She read routes and names off her clipboard. She told Rourke if he had a problem to spit it out. She stared Wilson down in seconds and walked back to her office like her mind was already on requisition forms for a new bulletin board in the rental box area.

Ike's having more trouble being convincing. When Bromberg tossed him the first insult of the day – something about dogs on his route running from him – he just froze and stammered until he felt like he would choke. Wilson got a real kick out of this, spitting out a laugh and slapping Rourke's shoulder, but Rourke just stared at Ike without a word, then squatted down to retie his boots.

When Eva assigned Ike to sorting again, Rourke said, in a quiet voice, that his foot still wasn't completely healed and he'd go to the union if she refused to give him indoor work. Eva said that was his right and she'd wait for the call. Rourke organized his trays like a mute, sulky, but hyperactive child and was out on route before any of the other carriers.

There's no float available today and Ike is thankful for this. It means he'll have to sort and handle the customers at the counter, but he'll be alone with Eva and he needs to talk. He waits a few minutes after the last carrier, Jacobi, leaves, then moves to Eva's office.

'What do you think?' he blurts. 'You think they know we know? You think we're in trouble here? You decide who we should talk to?'

Eva smiles and raises her eyebrows. 'Number one. You calm down. I don't care how. Find a way.'

'Okay, all right. You're right. I'm sorry. I'm not good under pressure. I've got a terrible gag reflex.'

'Deep breaths. Over and over.'

'Takes a lot of concentration.'

'Did you sleep?'

'No way. Not five minutes. Terrible. My sister was working all night. Never got home. I watched *Johnny Belinda* on cable, then about an hour of rap videos till I was going nuts, then I put in a tape and watched *The Frozen Dead*.'

'You should've come over. I drank a dozen cups of tea and watched Orson Welles in *The Stranger*.'

'So what have you decided?'

'I'm not sure who—'

'We've got to talk to someone—'

'What I'm saying is we've got very little information.'

'What are you talking about? *You* told me, remember? *You* said they're selling some weird drug—'

'We don't know what they're selling. It could be some pathetic gimmick Rourke dreamed up. *The Mailman's Miracle Diet Program*. Starch blockers and vitamins.'

'This isn't what you told me. This is *not* what you said.'

'The other thing is, you tell someone on this, you're an informer.'

'Oh, for God's sake.'

'Tell me you're not. It makes you an informer, Ike, you've finked on co-workers.'

'I don't believe this.'

'I'm just saying. I'm playing devil's advocate. You want to review all the information before you make a crucial move.'

'They're criminals, for God's sake, Eva.'

'You don't know that, Ike. You don't know anything. You're going on what I told you.'

'Exactly. What you told me. Listen, I still think the thing to do is to call my sister in. We call Lenore. We say, "Lenore, this is what we know." We let her decide what's what. She's a professional. She's my sister. She'll know what to do.'

'I don't know.'

'I'll be honest with you. This surprises me. I'm pretty surprised here.'

'What do you mean?'

'To be honest, nothing personal, but I always thought you were like the picture of good judgment, clear thought. You knew what to do. Take-charge person. Responsible—'

'I think I'm being responsible. We wait and we see. I think this is the responsible route.'

'I'm as scared as you are, Eva.'

'This has nothing to do with fear.'

'Yeah, it does.'

'I'm asking for a little time.'

'How much?'

'Things just don't seem as black and white to me.'

'C'mon. Please.'

'That's the truth. Sorry, but it is. Give me today. I'll work it out today. Tonight I'll come by your place. We'll talk with your sister.'

'Tonight?'

'Let's just get through the day. Let's just act like it's a normal day. Like any other day.'

Ike pauses, breathes, nods, starts to walk backward. 'I'll be at the cage. Sorting.'

Eva nods back, looks down at her desk blotter, and says, 'Thanks, Ike. Will you close the door going out?'

He walks to the cage and turns on the fluorescents mounted over the sorting boxes. He thinks that with the lights on, the cage looks like a miniature baseball stadium during a night game – the main wall of slots and its two hinged and angled wings are the bleachers. Sometimes he thinks of each letter that he sails into the correct slot as a home run. But he never thinks of himself as the batter, more like some unknown contest winner, called upon to croak out the national anthem.

He knows it's going to be a long day. He doesn't understand Eva's hesitation. Sometimes things *are* black and white. If what she says she saw at the Bach Room is true, then Rourke and the others have gone into the drug-dealing business. And it's probably pretty likely they're even using the post office in some way. What's there to debate about? Ike doesn't consider himself some hard-line law-and-order dork, but wrong is wrong. Illegal is illegal. The proper people should be contacted and talked to. Like Lenore. Lenore's job is to deal with this situation. It's what the city pays her to do and she knows how to do it well. What the hell could be going through Eva's brain? Is there some subtlety that Ike's missing? Is there information he hasn't been given?

He suddenly feels more like an outsider than ever, like someone who, no matter what time they leave to go to the theater, walks in ten minutes after the movie has started. And every question whispered to the person in the next seat is met with an avalanche of the *shushing* noise.

How do you remove that feeling? How do you inject yourself into the ordinary track of life? How do you become common, a typical part of a greater whole, just one more guy who belongs to dozens of groupings without any thought to the process, immersed so mindlessly into roles like husband, father, son, neighbor, alumnus, local barroom crony, civic committee chairman, church member, Elk, Rotarian, Knight of Columbus, Red Sox fan, Red Cross volunteer, poker team member, Tuesday's car-pool driver, citizens' crimewatch associate, Big Brother, one of the block's nightly eleven o'clock dog-walkers...

Ike stops, a long manila envelope in hand, hovering before a slot. He can't think of one thing, one role, one activity, that defines him as a member of something. As belonging to anything. Then he remembers *brother*, but it's an empty, uncomfortable word. His closeness to Lenore has diminished every day since adolescence. And he's helpless to stop the erosion. It's like an ugly side of nature, not pleasant to talk about or think of, but truthful, provable, a fact of life. He's sure that some of this growing distance is Lenore's fault. Her behavior and attitude and general personality have grown harsher and tougher since they turned teenagers; they took on something like a barbed-wire coating after Mom and Dad died. But Ike knows probably more than half of their distance is his responsibility. It's only logical. It follows the same pattern as his relationships at work, in the city, walking through the supermarket, pumping gas at the self-serve station. Ike knows he makes people feel hostile and aggressive. Maybe there's a doctor somewhere in Quinsigamond who could take on the case, study the facts, and make a few basic determinations. But Lenore is his sister. His twin. It shouldn't have to come to that, help from some cold outsider. That's why he's thought of the police novels they could write together. The idea was a tool, a possible device for pulling them back toward a feeling, a surety, a blanket called family or blood-love.

What would he do when he finally told her the cop-novel idea and she smashed it without a trial, without even an exploratory breakfast discussion? Ike's given the idea more than a month of thought. He's sure it has some genuine merit, and in more than one area. Ike's big wish in life is that Lenore was still someone you could talk to. But it's as if she's starting to give up on the concept of dialogue, to become an apostate to the idea of exchange, slowly being converted to the church of the monologue. At least as far as Ike is concerned. He wonders if this is what she's like with the other cops. In a lot of the mysteries he reads, cops are famous for their short tempers and misguided self-righteousness. But Lenore's perpetual anger, this heated, seething, ongoing outrage, seems like a mile beyond the day-to-day petty nastiness found in those novels. It feels like it comes from a more dangerous place and like the enormity of the possible damage it could cause is too large to measure. At night, lying in bed, sleepless, while his sister lurks in alleys around Bangkok Park, Ike says unfocused, nondenominational prayers, not that Lenore will change, but simply that her wrath is universal, not meant for him alone.

He's tried to make vague suggestions that might or might not change her. He's mentioned news articles that prove the connection between loud music and hearing loss. He's spoken of talk shows that detail the results of long periods of time without vacation. He's mentioned casually the fact that he might switch to decaffeinated coffee. But he knows he's probably just too close to the problem to be able to identify it. And Lenore's response to all the seeming small talk is the same cutting sarcasm and annoyed interruption.

Ike thinks back, pictures his mother. She's like an opposite image of Lenore, cell for cell. Like Lenore was formed out of some negative mold of her mother, received all the counter-qualities that Ike remembers in the woman. She was soft-spoken, contented, serene, endlessly compassionate, at times joyful, with a deep vein of humor and a love of the quiet. Now it's as if somecne stole her away, inverted all of those traits, and placed her back in his presence in the form of Lenore.

But Lenore wasn't always this way. That's the thing. That's the killer. He's not deceiving himself. She was always tougher, capable of being more cutting, always a little quick, in motion. But it was a strength, and it was only part of the total package. She was also the funniest person Ike had ever met. No question. And way back it had seemed like, in her own way, she'd had her own well of mercy. And if she was always capable of violence, Ike thought it could be triggered only by an assault on the people she loved, that the two sides of her were absolutely connected, and rage could only be tapped by an aggression against himself or Ma or Dad. In first grade, when Dennis Lamont bloodied Ike's nose at recess, Lenore waited for the end of the school day, then went after the kid with a vengeance. She blackened both his eyes and left lumps all over his head. Ike felt more than a little ashamed, but he both acknowledged and appreciated Lenore's motivation. A Thomas had been harmed. Retribution was like a simple reflex. The next day she had noticeable contempt for the principal's lack of understanding. It was one of the first of her many childhood disputes with authority.

Although he can't be certain about the chronology, Ike thinks it was a decade later that Lenore began to change. It was as if in entering puberty, some natural biological event kicked in, and Lenore's tendency toward aggression took leave of its natural trigger. One day it was just not necessary for a family member to be affronted. Lenore's hostility had a life of its own. But it seemed within the boundaries of normalcy until their parents died. From that point on Ike started to fear her a little. There was something about Lenore that was not there before. There was an irrational menace; an unhealthy predatory feeling surrounded her. When she came to his side of the duplex now, Ike expected her to be wearing a black hood and carrying a sickle.

Ike despises the fact that she collects weapons. He's sure it's not something the other cops do. He's aware that narcotics is one of the most dangerous jobs in the department. Especially lately. If he has to, he can understand the Magnum, rather than the standard-issue .38. But Lenore has something like an armory on the other side of Ike's walls. It just isn't necessary, and it's a sign of something wrong. She also seems to love the weapons, to dwell on them inordinately, take them out and clean them incessantly. She keeps small cans of oil on her end tables the way other people keep candy dishes. Ike knows there are tubes of graphite and bristle reamers in the slots of her silverware drawer. She spends more time in the depths of the shooting bunker than most women her age spend at the latest downtown clubs. Ike thinks he'd be shocked if he just knew the percentage of her salary that went to bullets.

What's the thing with guns? Where did it come from? There was never a gun in the house where they grew up. Dad wasn't a hunter, didn't believe in it. If he was in front of the TV on the weekend and some hunting segment came on the sports program, he'd get up and turn to anything else. Bowling, cartoons, a cooking show, whatever. As long as he didn't have to watch guys in forests up in Michigan or swamps down in Louisiana, big guys who spit phlegm a lot and kept their rifles broken open, hinge on the arm, barrels hanging limp to the ground until they spotted duck or deer or moose. Ike remembers his father saying they had 'little brains and less heart.' Now the man's daughter keeps things like an AK-47 and an Uzi in her bedroom closet. Something's gone wrong in the family.

What would Eva make of Lenore? They're both professionals, very conscientious in their respective jobs, proud of their competence, confident in their abilities. Is that grounds for mutual admiration or competition? Would they recognize each other's proficiency? Would they miraculously fall into this ardent conversation about slacking standards and the general decrease in the intelligence of the population? Or would a terrible hazard take over the room, Ike's kitchen maybe, as they summed each other up and felt unconsciously threatened? Would insults be mouthed, slanders shouted, push degenerate into shove? And Ike has to admit that he's interested enough to wonder, if the worst happened, who would win the war. Clearly, Lenore has the superior weaponry and the training to use it at maximum efficiency. But there's something in Eva. He'd have to give Eva big points for control, more control than Lenore, a genuine coolness in the face of anything, a type of dispassionate reasoning you can't learn, a fierce ability to calculate that has to come through the genes, through generation after generation of cold, often brutal logic, winning out over emotion, primal sentiment, and bloodlust. Ike suspects Eva's got it. And realizing that makes him startled to think she's hesitating, debating what to do about Rourke and the gang. Ike should be the one hesitating, weighing options, stalling for time. Eva should have it straight from the start. It's one more thing that adds to this constant feeling of displacement, this general sense that rules are melting and order fading away.

He'd like to stop, go home, spend the day in his bathroom throwing cold water in his face. But he knows this would be the worst thing he could do. When this feeling blankets him, the only solution is to find the most common, routine, instinctual activities and walk through them. And right now that would be to continue sorting, continue with the repetition, the hand-to-slot motion, the pattern of reading an address and filing a letter. What could be more mechanical than this? More rote and mindless?

He hears the customer bell ring at the front counter. Has Eva opened the doors already? He checks the wall clock and sees that it's after eight. The station is officially open. He puts his handful of letters back in their tray and walks to the counter, but there's no one waiting. He looks beyond the waiting area, out the window to the parking lot, but there's no sign of anyone. There's only a small box wrapped in dull brown mailing paper and tied with twine. It's about the size of an average donut box and he doesn't want to touch it, doesn't want to go anywhere near it. His stomach goes into a spastic knot and he wishes he could just radio for some official men in space suits, bomb squad guys with huge bulky gloves, boots twice the size of their feet, special metal boxes hooked up to obscure canisters full of disarming, defusing chemicals.

But he can't do anything like that. He has to reel in his panicking imagination and act normal. He has to approach the package, hold it in his hands, read the address off the front. He has to do this or admit to being well on his way to lost, out of touch, inconsistent with the majority's view of reality.

He steps up to the counter, puts a hand flat against either side of the package, turns it around. The smell starts to hit him. It's not the same as the stink from the first package, but it's just as bad in its own way, if not worse. He brings his head forward slightly until it's hovering above the top of the package. He knows before he even reads:

Box 9
Sapir Street Station
Quinsigamond

He can't well up any fluid in his mouth. It's as if all saliva has evaporated in an instant. There's an odd burning ache that flashes through his groin and then disappears. His ears start to throb as if he's been out in a winter cold for hours without a hat. He can-taste a disgusting, acidic bile in the back of his throat. His breath becomes so labored, he thinks his lungs are in the process of a slow-motion collapse.

He bites on his bottom lip, hard enough to break skin and draw a run of blood to the surface. And then he moves past all these horrible symptoms, these oppressions from his own body. He freezes them, steps out of them, wills them past perception, and reaches beneath the counter for the cool handle of the gray X-acto knife.

He knows he should call for Eva and turn the box over to her, but something makes him push the edge of the blade into the package and before he can stop himself, he's cutting. He goes to work on the twine like a surgeon at his peak, one slice and the string is limp on the counter. He runs the blade through the skin of the wrapping paper, finds a lip at the edge of the box, and slices Scotch tape. Then he sets the knife to the side and cautiously begins to lift the top off.

Inside is stuffed with crumpled newspaper – some edition of *The Spy*. He removes all the newsprint and drops it to the floor near his feet. He comes to a single sheet of white typing paper. In calligraphied lettering, like some enlarged strip from a fortune cookie, it reads:

You are a man in need of a warning

Something moist is blotting the typing paper from underneath. Ike reaches in and lifts it by a corner, has to seemingly peel it away from the box's contents. He lets the paper loose and it floats downward toward the small pool of crumpled newspaper.

He looks in.

In the first second, it's hard to tell. It looks like a platter of those small cocktail hot dogs that are served as hors d'oeuvres, basted with a thick tomato sauce.

And then the realization grabs him and there's no mistaking the truth: they're fingers. Human fingers. Dozens of severed human fingers bathed in the residue of their own shed blood. The nails, still attached, are black on maybe half of them. There are all sizes, adult and child, and types, pinky to index. There are no thumbs.

Ike knows what should follow is a scream, a siege of vomiting, a faint. Instead, he's hit with a violent trembling, instant Parkinson's. It starts with his hands but shoots out to all extremities almost instantly. His head becomes a bobbing, brainless clown head.

He steps back from the counter and lets his body do a slow fall backward until he finds himself in an awkward, still-vibrating, sitting position. An image takes over. A picture of his deceased parents, wrapped in the rags of their best clothes, looking like decaying movie zombies, pale blue mailbags draped over both their withered, bone-visible shoulders, pounding on his front door at the green duplex, driven to deliver something unknown.

And then, thankfully, he blacks out.

21

The new office park next to the old abandoned airport is a small ghost town. Rows of cookie-cutter office condos reveal whitewashed windows as the headlights of Peirce's Honda move across them. She expects to see plasticized sagebrush blow across the parking lot as she pulls up to the boxy guard shack where the rent-a-cop is watching the Celtics on a portable black-and-white TV.

She shows her badge, and rather than leave the shack, the guard grabs the keys to the Synaboost office and tosses them to her.

In five minutes she's inside the lab and talking into the recorder.

It's quarter to nine at night, Victor. You're saying, 'Doesn't this girl ever go home?' No, you're not. You're not thinking of me. You're in the middle of a City Council meeting, hoping the cable TV cameras pick up your good side. Which side is that, boss? [*Pause*] Sorry, I'm just feeling a little tired. And I am about to head home. Once again I've pretty much come up with zero. Sorry, again. I'm sitting in a brand-new teal-blue leather swivel chair in the ridiculous offices of Synaboost Inc. up at the about-to-go-bust airport industrial park and ghost town. Flashed the badge and had one of the security guys let me in. Whatever happened to those old donut-eating, heavy-eyelid guys with beer bellies and walkie-talkies? Or was that just how they always showed security guards – night watchmen, right? – in the movies? I judge everything by the movies. Have you noticed that, Victor? This guy, this guard, he could have been a surfer out in Malibu. Probably about twenty-two with these magazine biceps just about ripping in two the gold insignia on his shirt sleeve. Am I making you jealous, Victor? I didn't think so. The truth is, the guy had ordinary arms and I think he was stoned. [*Pause*] I guess I'm officially off duty, Mr. Mayor. I hope so, 'cause I'm sipping the Swanns' B&B out of the Swanns' Waterford crystal, listening to the Swanns' Bang & Olufsen stereo. That new local talk-show guy is on, the one who thinks there's someone hiding under everyone's bed. Maybe he's right, huh? Let me tell you, Victor, he has *not* had kind words for you. Words like *puppet, tool,* and *pawn*. He won't come clean on who supposedly holds your strings, though. [*Pause*] Thought I'd take a swing by here before calling it a day. You should see this place, boss. Synaboost Inc. What kind of a name is that? Did they try to picture what it would look like in tiny print in the back of *The Wall Street Journal*? I don't like it. I don't know why. Did you take a look at the report on this place, Victor? Or better, did you see any photos? Good old Leo and Inez. Not exactly misers, you know what I'm saying? The office is sandwiched between two larger businesses. Steinmetz Neon Sign & Sculpture and Martinez Operations Research Inc. I think they've got the smallest square footage in the place. But they made up for it. There's a reception area outfitted like they made the Fortune 500 last year. Then, behind that, a huge shared office for the loving couple. Get this, they used a partners desk – like one desk with both sides equipped for use. I'm guessing the teal chair, the one I'm swiveling in this very moment, belonged to Leo. Inez's looks antique with this cream brocade back to it. Weird. They've each got a personal computer and they look brand new. Oh, and I found a little private bar. Looks like the Swanns had a weakness for champagne and brandy. There are these little weird touches, like they made this attempt to put their own stamp on the place and it went all wrong. If you ask me anyway. There are these weird microscopes all over the place. All different sizes. They look like they're antiques. Where the hell does someone buy antique microscopes? But they're using them for decoration, I guess. Like sculpture, maybe. Okay, behind the office and running to the back of the building is the lab and it's just what you'd think. Bright overhead fluorescent lights, long white worktables. Tons of beakers and test tubes and all this mad-scientist crap that I couldn't put a name to in a million years. Plus a back wall full of technical books. The killer is that the place had been opened less than a month. What a waste. [*Pause*] Maybe you think I'm wasting time, Victor. I know this isn't how you do things, but I always find that sooner or later, whether I'm cleaning out my refrigerator or setting up a sting in Bangkok, I've got to just stop and step back and look everything over. So, while you trade lame insults with Councilor Searle, I'll sit here in Leo's new chair and see what we've got. Okay, the brilliant and rich and beautiful Swann couple work long and hard on a new drug treatment for 'language delayed' individuals. In the process, their shining personalities piss a lot of folks off and they bounce from a government operation in New Mexico to the Institute for Experimental Biochemistry to their own profit-motivated lab called Synaboost Inc. It looks like they made some breakthroughs, but they're so secretive and closemouthed about everything it's hard to say. By accident one night, the Swanns are spotted swilling pasta with Mr. Mafia himself, Don Gennaro Pecci, sometimes local banker for those suffering from bad credit or some wild business-venture ideas. Next thing you know, the Swanns are found smacked in their Windsor Hills mansion in a style known to be employed by certain international drug cartels, i.e., their tongues are missing from their heads. And because of the tongueless corpses, the big shots like yourself and Lehmann throw a media blanket over the whole mess and call it a murder-suicide of the domestic violence variety. Meanwhile, a search of the crime scene finally reveals a weird little red pill in the shape of the letter Q and you call in a consultant to do a little unauthorized testing out at the Spooner resort for our favorite sociopaths. We find out two things about the Q-drug, now called Lingo. First, the language skills of recipients shoot off the scale. To the point of no control. And second, all of the pleasure centers are massaged, you end up like a cat in heat, and there's a major adrenaline rush. And third, if you pop too much, there's the little side effect of absolute, homicidal rage. So we're left with a pretty huge problem – the possibility that the Swanns were able to set up production before the cat got their tongue. Sorry, must be the B&B. Now, the Fed report I read says that the lab here was wiped clean. No trace of anything. Not even a stray Swann fingerprint. To me, that says some work was done in here that no one wants us to see. But I'm a pessimist at heart. Look at the men I date, she said. I can't help it, Victor. You didn't know what a weapon this little Panasonic would be when you gave it to me. Better be more careful when you pick out my Christmas gift, you know? Let's say Leo and Inez cooked up a couple of batches of Lingo before they got smacked. It follows that whoever's holding the stuff wiped out the whiz kids. Big-M time. Motive. [*Pause*] I say business partner of some kind. Silent or otherwise. The most visible suspect, again, is the Pecci family as financial backers of a new product with big Bangkok market potential. But I vote 'no.' Here's the thing: we know the big immigrant wave has grabbed massive chunks of Pecci's Bangkok power over the past five years. And Pecci has pretty much let it go. He's got a nice, long-standing arrangement with the city fathers, no offense, boss, and Bangkok is more of a sewer every week. Pecci is ready to turn the whole place over to the Jamaicans and Cambodians and every other refugee party off the boat. He's diversifying into real estate, buying up hotels and waiting for the day the Commonwealth legalizes gambling. I say thumbs down to Pecci. That leaves a clean slate for investors. Okay, we have to consider Mr. Bangkok himself. Mr.

Colombia. Cortez. It's a possibility, but he's normally a retailer, a distributor. Could be branching out, stretching his arms farther up and down the ladder. Let's leave him a possibility. Could be there's a new player in town, someone who saw this as a perfect way to make a name, really explode on the scene, get a rep. I've spent a little time on the new Narc-Linc base we've bought into for the department computer. I can imagine what I'll have to do for that little appropriation. Anyway, there's sort of this after-hours electronic bulletin board that narc squads around the country use casually, sort of a hobby thing. You input tips and street talk and narc gossip, stuff like that. Lately, I've punched up rumors about a Honduran named Arnello who was coming in to test the water. But remember, information like that is never very reliable. There was also talk about a Cuban hotshot headed north named, I think, Fante. And there was a trio of Hawaiians, all brothers supposedly, sweeping east with some impressive display cases, but, again, supposedly, they're strictly icemen. I could go on for weeks with this kind of thing and we wouldn't get very far. Now, if you want to look at the problem in terms of the Swanns' connections, rather than the product's likely connections, you hit a brick wall almost immediately. No family, no friends. No one but each other. There were people at the Institute, names like Blonsky and Iser and Daleski. Older men and women. Seems like a real long shot. Then there's Woo, the consultant. More likely, but still… [*Pause*] Then, of course, we have to turn the tables on ourselves and take at least one hard look. This is a rule of mine. In the middle of a case, turn a hundred and eighty degrees and see what's there. Question, Victor: is it possible that the missing tongues and the Lingo-in-the-garlic-salt are just ways of focusing our attention in the wrong direction? [*Pause*] No, I didn't think so either. I'm almost out of possibilities. Except for the unspoken one. The most unpleasant one of all. [*Pause*] Why do I have this recorder, Victor? Huh?

What's the real deal with the tape recorder? With my little investigation within the investigation? What is it you know or think you know that you won't tell your mistress? I hate that word, Victor. Mayor Welby. Sir. I hate the fucking word *mistress*. Let's say instead – the narc you're screwing behind Mrs. Mayor's back. [*Pause*] I'm a problem to you, Vic, old friend. And the sad part is, I wouldn't have to be. But it's situations like this that just start me thinking and then the more I think, the more pissed off I get. 'Cause if I'm worthy enough to sleep with, Victor, then I'm worthy enough to share your miserable suspicions with. [*Yelling*] Especially when they concern my goddamn department. [*Long pause*] You've got information I don't, right, Victor? And you want to add to your information through my efforts. Without sharing what you've already got. With me. Without talking to me. [*Pause*] You think someone's dirty. And by that I mean over the top. I mean filthy. I mean more than an occasional look-the-other-way. I hope you've got something hard to back up your suspicions. [*Pause*] Okay, let's give it a rundown. I'll eliminate myself, since even if you think I'm a suspect, I know otherwise. Unless I'm a multiple-personality case. And if that's true, I want to know, do you date us all? Do any of us know about each other? [*Pause*] Might as well finish off poor Leo's bottle. Don't worry, it was almost empty to begin with. Let's see, now, who can we smear tonight? I think I'll kick free Detective Shaw. She's the new kid on the block. Not that that gives her clearance, but she's still learning the alphabet, you know. I don't think she'd know who to extort from yet, or on what days of the week. Richmond is a more likely choice. But where's his motivation? I mean, sorry, but I don't think this guy's ambitious enough to work both sides of the street. He's an old bachelor waiting on his pension and not exactly a scholar, if you follow me. Lieutenant Miskewitz? Interesting. I've never quite known how to read the guy. He's never made himself clear to me. Is he brass or still a street cop at heart? Depends on what time of the day you talk to him. He's changeable. I've always felt he was in over his head, got a few promotions he didn't really expect and feels uneasy about it. But the big point is, if Miskewitz is in on anything, it's got to be with a lot of help. He's an office man. He's only down in Bangkok when *The Spy* is shooting a cover photo. A lot like you, Mayor Welby. So if Miskewitz is involved he's got a partner. Then there's Zarelli and, believe me, it's a distinct possibility. Wouldn't surprise me in the least. This guy could justify anything. 'What, the Nazis? A little loud, a little flashy, but not bad guys at heart' – that's Zarelli. I've got no facts here, but I know the guy's heart. And I'm pretty sure it can be bought. And that brings us to Detective Thomas. Lenore. The woman who showed me the ropes. [*Pause*] Lenore is unique. I don't know what to say about Lenore. The words don't come. She's complicated. I don't know anyone like her. The thing is, she's been down in the Park for a long time. She's made friends. She's got her nails deep into some informants. One problem is that the Park's a different world. Everything's painted even subtler shades of gray than the outside. All the words and numbers take on different meanings. I think it's very easy to get confused. At least it would be for me. I just don't know about Lenore. It's almost impossible to read her. I've never felt close to her, for all the time we've spent together. I don't think anyone has. Richmond tried to tell me he thought something was up between her and Zarelli, but that's more than ridiculous. Lenore would eat a guy like Zarelli for a midday snack. She'd break him in two. She'd leave him shaking in the men's room. The thing is, you could give this quick portrait of her, okay? You could use words like *isolated* and *precise* and *cold* and *willful*. You could go on. But that's absolutely surface. And I don't know what's underneath. I've always thought of Lenore as one of these people who end up doing something shocking with their lives. Something unbelievably good *or* bad. Like they disappear into Calcutta one day to care for lepers. Or they walk into a Burger Bonanza and wipe out everyone inside with an Uzi. Then afterward, the reporters go to all the neighbors and friends and they say, 'I just don't know, she was very quiet, I had no idea.' I think that everything Lenore Thomas is, she carries around inside herself. Sealed. Impregnable. So does that mean she could be filthy or not? [*Pause*] I don't know. You tell me. Victor. [*Pause*] I think it's time to go home.

22

Woo finally finds the right key on his chain and unlocks the loft. Lenore has a tremendous need to stretch, to push out the muscles of her arms and shoulders, arch her back, roll the whole trunk of her body in a great circle. But she represses the urge and simply huddles inside her coat.

A lot of people have moved into rehabbed sections of all the old Quinsigamond mills in the past decade or so. His apartment is a middle floor, above a tool and die outfit and below a printing firm. Both shops are out of business, and it appears that Woo might be the only person using the building. Lenore thinks this must give the place a mausoleum-type feel. It doesn't help that the place is so huge. He's got about eight hundred square feet of living space, all of it wide open, undivided.

'The rent is cheaper than what you might think,' he says to Lenore as he pushes two enormous, reinforced metal doors open. They're like barn doors for housing mechanical horses of some smoggy future. But once she steps inside, she sees a different story. She's impressed. The room is void of any of the dimness and griminess that always seem to haunt converted lofts. There are three trackways of recessed lighting hidden high in the steel I-beams of the twelve-foot ceilings.

'Your electric bill must cost a fortune,' Lenore says, staring upward.

'Not so bad,' Woo answers, locking and bolting the doors with levers and chains. 'And it's well worth it. Gives it a much warmer feeling.'

Lenore can't agree with this, though she nods her head. The

place is immaculate and scrupulously stylish. It could be the centerfold of some aggressive new architectural magazine for well-educated musicians. But *warm* is not a word that comes to mind. The ceilings are so high, the gulf of open space so huge, that there's a hint of a gymnasium feeling. Despite herself, Lenore smells for sweat and old towels.

'You must have sandblasters come in weekly,' she says, and Woo looks at her, smiling and cocking his head to show he doesn't quite understand the comment.

'I mean it feels so clean. So fresh,' she explains. 'I've been in a few of these redone places and there's always this feeling. Like there's a century of grit and brick dust hanging in the air that no amount of scrubbing can get rid of.'

Woo nods wildly, seeming thrilled with her comment. His arm sweeps upward and his hand waves toward the ceilings. 'I had an air quality control system installed when I bought the place. Essential. I'm very happy with it.'

'You own. So it's a condo setup.'

'Something like that,' he says, starting to walk toward a long wall unit of high-gloss black cabinetry made of some material Lenore can't identify. It doesn't look like either metal or plastic. There's a double sink set into the middle of a countertop that juts out, slopelike, wavelike, from below the cabinets. Its faucet is black and bizarre, rising maybe a foot and a half into the air before the head curves over and faces downward. It's like some sleek water-spewing rattlesnake. Rising out of the floor a few feet in front of the sink is a cutting-block island that holds what looks like a customized built-in espresso maker.

'I'll make some tea,' Woo says, and starts to work.

Lenore follows him to this kitchen area, leans on the island, and studies the rest of the room. Though the walls are all classic red brick, you can't see much of them. They're almost all lined, as high as the ceiling supports, with endless sections of bookshelves. It's all constructed out of the same weird high-tech black material as the kitchen. After every few shelves, up near the top, is an arcing lamp, resembling a streetlight, with its industrial, metallic housing and its *War of the Worlds*, lined, wide-eyed bulb. Every other lamp is lit and they give off an eerie bluish gleam. Lenore notices one of those old-fashioned wrought-iron rolling ladders found in old libraries. Though she can't see from this distance, she's sure it's workable and she flashes on an image of a naked Woo riding the ladder across his enormous collection of books, arching his body outward away from the walls, letting out a war whoop, possibly drunk, acting like an ass in the privacy of his own factory-home.

She knows she's probably seen more books gathered together in one place. But never like this. The local library, for example, must have more books. But they're arranged in short spurts, aisles, around corners, divided up into separate rooms. Here it feels like Woo has actually used books as his primary building matter, that books make up the walls, house him, keep him safe from the elements. No matter what happens here tonight, she'll find a way to look at a run of spines, commit a bunch of titles to memory.

'Did you decorate yourself?' she asks.

'Mostly,' he says.

Steam starts to rise out of a kettle built in the shape of a perfect triangle.

'Let me ask,' she says, 'though I know it's not the case with you, let me ask anyway, all right, you know how you go to some old Colonial restaurants, any of them, there are a dozen around here, five minutes outside the city. You know how you go and they seat you in, say, "the library room," "the study," right, they always call it something like that. And they bring you into this big, high-ceilinged room lined with natural-wood bookcases. And your table sort of comes right out from the bookcase. So that while you're eating you can look at the titles, right? And then there's that moment, right after you're seated and they hand you the wine list and leave you alone, and you put the wine list down and turn your head to the bookshelf.'

'Yes,' Woo says, eyes squinting at her, intrigued.

'And you see that all the books, every one of them, are like these *Reader's Digest* Condensed volumes, or like old high school trigonometry textbooks. And you know, again, that they just bought these things gross, right, bought them in carton loads from furniture stores or something. Bought them by the pound. And it just takes something away from the whole place.'

Woo stares at her while he fills two triangular-shaped mugs to the brim with boiling water, then he smiles and says, 'I've not had this particular experience, but I assure you, Lenore, every book you see here was purchased with my own hand. Nothing bought by the pound.'

'Must have cost you a small fortune.'

'Spread out over a period of years. I follow the wisdom of Gertrude Stein. "If you have money buy books, if you have any left over buy food." Or something like that.'

'Most of them on language? Linguistics?'

'The majority, yes.'

He pushes the mug in her direction. 'Best to drink it just after boiling,' he says. 'It's a special blend from the homeland. I have cousins who are kind enough to ship it over.'

Lenore takes a sip. The tea tastes a little bland after all the coffee she's had, but it's warm and she thinks it might settle her stomach.

Woo holds one hand on the side of the mug and places the other over the top. Lenore thinks this must be burning him and she starts to wonder if he's some sort of fellow control freak, ready at all times to go beyond the limits of pain and good taste in order to prove a point. Or it could just be that he's got a chill and has a high tolerance for tactile heat.

He stares down into the black of his utility island and says in the low voice of an actor, 'You know, Lenore, I was more than a bit surprised when you agreed to come back here.'

Lenore stares at him, lets a few long seconds drag by, then, sucking back any sarcasm or anger, she says, 'Yeah, well, don't count your chickens, you know, Freddy?' She takes a sip and shrugs. 'I was feeling way too closed in in that cellar. We'd gotten what we needed off the tap. I had to get out of there, come down a little. And I really didn't want to go back to my place.'

'I see.'

'You see what? Besides, I was pretty curious how a guy like you lived, what your setup would be and all.'

'And do you approve?'

'Beautiful place, if you can afford it. St. Iggy's must be paying sweet these days.'

'I have to say there have been a few grants. But I can't believe in all these years no one's ever told you it's rude to inquire about someone's income.'

Lenore lets out a sharp bark of a laugh that almost echoes at the other end of the loft.

'Give me a freaking break, Freddy. This is America. Twentieth century. Income is all we fucking talk about now that sex is dead.'

'My mistake. I thought it was God that was dead.'

'What do you think killed him?'

Woo smiles, takes a deep breath, finally takes his hands off the mug and sips his tea. 'Lenore,' he says, 'you are truly unlike any woman I have ever known.'

'You've got to get out more, Freddy.'

'You want to know what I think? I think you have a problem turning off, what shall we call them, certain police traits, investigator's characteristics—'

'—Gestapo tendencies, Nazi reflexes.'

'No, no, no. That's not what I said.'

'Comes pretty damn close.'

'I apologize, then. I should have been more clear. What I meant was that you look at me and you see a typical academic—'

'You're not so typical, Freddy.'

'—and you see my home and a spark goes off, a little buzz sounds, and your brain is already ahead of you, doing the math, saying "teacher's salary, great big loft, something is wrong," and you're off and running the possibilities.'

'So which one is it?'

'Which?'

'Possibility?'

'Oh. Yes. The most obvious one, of course.'

They stare at each other, mouths closed, shoulders squared.

Woo smiles first and says, 'My parents had some money.'

'First guess,' Lenore lies. She'd had an offbeat suspicion that Woo had twenty over-the-limit credit cards in his desk drawer and a shaky and stupid mortgage destined to fall on him when the first grant ran dry.

'So, now, let me invade you for a while,' Woo says.

'Excuse?'

'This man, Zarelli, when did things start to go wrong with you and him?'

'Ooh, I'm impressed. Let me guess, you did body language seminars in the seventies.'

Woo is genuinely thrilled and amused by her comment.

'Closer to the truth than you'd think.'

'I think I'm pretty close. We Nazis are like that.'

His smile fades. 'Lenore, honestly, I'm sorry if you misinterpreted—'

'C'mon, Freddy,' she says, calm, still friendly, 'I didn't misinterpret a thing. But there's no need for an apology. Really. I know the truth about my beliefs. You know me for a matter of hours and make a judgment. You know I've done the same about you. Big deal. Happens every day. It's how adults live. It's practically our right. So enjoy your opinion. It doesn't change the truth. I'm the one who knows the truth. There's no fascist inside of me, Freddy. No way.'

Woo gives up on apology and says, 'Confident woman.'

'Oh yeah. Read "bitch."'

'Oh no. This I reject. The chauvinism charge I reject. Absolutely not. I don't even acknowledge the word *bitch* in its colloquial sense.'

'Good word. I use it all the time.'

'I'm a little sensitive about being clear on this point. Yes, I've made a judgment concerning your natural aggressiveness. No, I do not regard that aggressiveness in terms of your sex.'

'So, if I was standing here, minus breasts and plus penis—'

'—I'd be a very disappointed man.'

'Scuse me, we'll get back to the jokes and the flirting in a minute. If it was Zarelli's body with Lenore's personality, Lenore's character, the fascist implications would have still come out.'

'First of all, I reject the fact I implied fascist tendencies. I did not. You want to think I did. Not the case. Plain and simple. The word *police*, the word *investigator*, does not equal fascist or Nazi. Not even close. Not in the context I used. But, to your point, yes, had you been a man, and *had* there been an implication, it would have come out. I would have thought the same thing. And no bitch word. Vocabulary of the oppressors.'

'Okay, truce. These kinds of arguments can never be won.'

'And winning is quite important—'

'Here we go again, you don't quit, Freddy.'

'Liability of the profession.'

'There you go. Every profession has its dangers, right?'

'Absolutely.'

'Isn't it exciting when we agree?'

'So how long have you been popping speed?'

'Excuse me?'

'What's today's phraseology? Crank? Meth?'

'You're a loon, Freddy.'

'Please, Lenore. I acquiesced on the money question. You balked on Mr. Zarelli. It's still my turn.'

'What does a guy in your position know about crank?'

'Ignorance of history is a dangerous flaw, Lenore. Before speed was seized by the working class, it was certainly graduate student domain. How else does one read almost two hundred very dense texts in less than a year?'

'You did that?'

'Nineteen eighty. The year the assault on language began.'

'What makes you say—'

'To be honest, I wasn't completely sure. I took a learned guess. My big question is... I can't believe the others, Zarelli, Shaw, Peirce, I can't believe they haven't noticed.'

'Please, this is narcotics. Sooner or later, everybody has a hobby. If it's not crank or crack, it's shoe boxes full of hundreds and foreign cars. I think you know what I'm saying.'

'Zarelli? Shaw?'

'Zarelli, yeah. Shaw, I don't think so, but she's young. Give her time. See, Freddy, I'm not a Nazi, I'm a cynic.'

'You're saying the whole department is corrupt?'

'No, you're saying that. I'm saying that a blanket statement like that, in a situation like ours, like mine, like the department's, I'm saying it's completely gray, I'm saying every day is relative. No, I don't use the word *corrupt*. I don't think it applies. I don't think it's like anyone is on Cortez's payroll. Unless even I'm totally blind. I'm saying there's a huge system that employs both our side and Cortez's. And we both work for it. We maintain a pathetic balance. We play yin and yang and keep the wheel turning. Bangkok is a pinball machine, Freddy. Zarelli and Shaw and Richmond and me are the flippers and Cortez is the silver ball—'

'Oh, please.'

'Screw you, you don't like the way I talk. I'm saying mostly we keep Cortez and company bouncing within their borders. And sometimes someone is slow on the flipper and the ball rolls through.'

'And is that someone ever you?'

'I've got my own problems. According to you anyway. And I've got my own theory about Cortez.'

'Which is?'

'Puppet. Total, willing puppet. He's a smart guy and a better actor. He's probably even a pretty good manager. Maybe he knows how to move money. And maybe there are connections back in South America. But I don't care. There's someone above him. There's someone who never walks into Quinsigamond. They can shred and shove every file from Interpol to the FBI to Lehmann and his Federal walking egos at DEA. There's somebody else. I call them the Aliens.'

'The aliens?'

'You really popped crank, Freddy?'

'Through all of graduate school and for a year after.'

'How'd the nervous system do?'

'How do you think?'

'How'd you deplane?'

'Rough but intact.'

'No, I mean, was there a method or anything?'

'As a matter of fact, yes. I walked about ten, twelve miles a day. Fast pace.'

'Around Quinsigamond?'

Woo nods. 'Went through a half dozen Adidas in a little over half a year. And I poured gallons of this tea through my body. I drowned in tea. Honestly, I choked on it, I drank so much, but it washed everything out.'

'Must've made it tough walking.'

'Again, it's easier for a man. There's usually a tree to step behind.'

'I lift weights.'

'It's not the same thing. It's not aerobic. Do you still think you're in control?'

'Absolutely. Have I looked rattled to you? I'll know when the compass swings.'

'A classic cliché. Where do you buy?'

'C'mon, Freddy.'

'Oh, of course. Bangkok. Little Max?'

'He's been helpful on occasion.'

'Curious drug, speed. I really fell in love. Head over heels.'

'Mine's much more a working relationship.'

'Sure. You'll be chasing it around the desk before you know it.'

'It's all a matter of will, Freddy.'

'How long have you been a regular abuser? Do you find you can still think clearly? I found I could for the first year, almost two. Then things shifted. It was really as fascinating as it was terrifying. The brain images started coming faster than my ability to identify and label them. Like race cars at the Indy 500. Have you ever had a seizure?'

'That's pleasant. No, never. Listen, enough on this topic. Why don't you show me the rest of this place.'

Woo smiles, brings his mug up to his mouth, and stares into it as he sips.

'All right,' he says. 'Let's have a look.'

She follows him deeper into the room. Somehow, it seems to get wider as they approach the library area. There are books, most of them big, thick volumes, oversized and without dust jackets, lying in stacks on the floor. The books look like old, obscure encyclopedias. Some of the stacks are eight and nine volumes high, rising up three and four feet high like models of ragged skyscrapers.

On either side of the library area are two identical couches, both covered in black leather and looking inviting, like you'd continue to sink deep into the cushions a full five minutes after you lay down. There's no sign of chrome or wood on them and Lenore thinks they look like weird twin animals, some mistake in genetically controlled husbandry. She stares from one to the other and thinks of a flabby, glossy black cow lying down in a rainy field at night.

The only other piece of furniture in the room is an enormous monstrosity of a desk that almost spans the width of the building. It's actually several desks and tables cobbled and bolted together to form a startling new creation. And it is genuinely startling. It begins at either end of the room with two old-fashioned rolltops complete with an assortment of cubbyholes and tiny drawers. They face each other and jut out perpendicular from the back wall of shelving forming two secretarial L's, two right angles turning at either end of the main desk body. The main body is comprised of two conventional mahogany executive desks, each bolted to its adjoining rolltop, and then joined to an eight-foot conference table that runs between them.

Stationed behind the table, in the center of the whole setup, is the largest swivel chair Lenore has ever seen. She decides it must have been custom-built. Of course it's black and leather with a subtle pucker design, but it's the back of the chair that's so attention-getting – it rises up, narrowing as it goes, almost five feet tall at the top of its curve. Lenore thinks the height is a foolish mistake. It's humorous and ends up detracting from the rest of the power look of the office.

Stationed on top of the two conventional desks at either side of the main table are state-of-the-art reel-to-reel and compact disc players. Lenore spots three different sets of headphones hanging from hooks in the rolltops. In the center of the conference table sits an oversized computer monitor and the longest keyboard she's ever seen. It looks more like a musical keyboard, a synthesizer keyboard, than one for a computer or word processor. There's no logo that she can see on any of the equipment, but she can tell in a glance it's not Apple or Wang or IBM. It's got to come from someplace she's never heard of.

Taking up every bit of surface space around the sound and computing equipment are small versions of the book stacks on the floor. There are several stacks of paperbacks with plain white covers and a couple foot-high blocks of typing paper, the top sheet of which is covered with tiny type that seems to run off the page in all directions, marginless. Lenore isn't close enough to be sure, but it's possible the words are in another language.

She steps up next to the main table and knocks on it like it was a door.

'So,' she says, 'you tell me who the Nazi is.'

Woo squints at her and pulls his head in like a turtle. 'The desk,' he says.

'A desk Goebbels and Göring would fight over.'

Woo gives a small smile. 'The last time I checked, furniture choice was not a characteristic of the Nazi.'

'We could argue about that, Freddy.'

'I need a great deal of room. I need to spread out when I work.'

'Ship this baby down to Latin America. There's a whole bunch of petty dictators who'd kill for this monster.'

'You find it offensive.'

'Overwhelming. It's the biggest desk, if you can call it a desk, that I've seen. You should coin a new word, Dr. Woo. This kind of thing requires an addition to the language.'

'All I can tell you is it suits my needs. Form follows function perfectly.'

'Yeah, and there's a lot more going on there besides.'

'There's so much room here. I decided, why not use it?'

'Uh-huh. Where do you sleep, Freddy?'

'The couches are tremendously comfortable. They fold out into beds. Often I don't even bother pulling one open. I'll sleep right on the couch.'

'Okay, Freddy, let's think about this for a second. You've gone to the trouble of making Godzilla's desk in here, because there's so much room, as you say, but you don't own a bedroom set.'

His voice goes low and his eyes shift to the floor.

'My work is quite important to me, Lenore.'

She realizes she's offended him and she's a little surprised that she regrets what she's said. Whatever mood of sparring and playfulness was between them feels gone and in its absence she's aware of how much she enjoyed it. She wants to get it back, reinstall it at once. She reaches up and places a hand on Woo's shoulder and says, in an apologetic voice, 'I'm sorry, Fred, I was just teasing. I stepped too far there. I just got caught up, carried away a little, you know. I was just riding you a little and I just… I don't know.'

Without lifting his eyes he takes her wrist and pulls it to his mouth and plants a long kiss on the inside span of skin just below the border of her hand.

She doesn't say a word and she doesn't pull away. She wishes only that she had a moment to swallow some crank. She wouldn't even need water for the wash-down.

He moves his way from wrist down the inner arm to the bend at the elbow. She knows she should find it funny, a caricature, a sloppy imitation of John Astin in a long-ago sitcom. But she doesn't react with a laugh or a comment. She lets him go, lets him work on the inner skin of her arm, kissing it slowly, wetting it barely. Her breath starts to come a little heavier. He makes the jump to the neck beautifully. He kisses below the ear and starts to suck and lick and really taste her skin, take in her salt and maybe a bitter drop of left-over perfume. She pushes herself closer to him, works her way into a tighter embrace so that their bodies press together in longer, unbroken spans.

His mouth drops lower on her neck and he hits a spot that makes her buck slightly. He feels it and speeds up, his tongue gets more aggressive, his lips pull on her and in spite of herself she lets out a noise, a breath-grabbing sigh and it comes out as a moan and she hopes, for a second, that he doesn't mistake it for a laugh, and then the thought is gone and their hands are at each other's clothing, feeling for buttons and zippers where there are none, furious at working so blindly.

His hands fall to the rim of her jeans and start to unbutton them, but she grabs them at the wrist and pulls them up underneath her turtleneck, but on top of the thermal undershirt. He starts to alternately squeeze and rub her breasts, like he can't decide which he wants to do, and while his hands move she takes a second to pull the jersey off and drop it to the floor. Then she pulls his hands away and places them at the sides of his legs. His head comes up from her neck and he looks like a horrified child, but she smiles and calms him and mouths the word *slow*, then she starts to unbutton his cardigan and pulls it from his arms. He makes no motion beyond the visible rising and falling of his chest and a smile that he can't suppress. She knows she now has full control and it sets her off, gives her a charge almost as heady as a swallow of meth. She goes slowly to her knees and unties his old sneakers, getting playful, improvising, dipping fingers inside the elastic band of his socks and tickling just above the ankle. He doesn't say a word, but his body seems to tremble a bit and she loves it.

She lifts each foot and removes the shoe and the sock, slowly, with an almost detached air, like this was her profession, like she'd worked a lifetime at Kinney's. She rises back up and strips him of his Ezra Pound shirt. She steps back for a second and stares at his chest. It's neither hairy nor completely void of hair, but rather has a few single curly strands in a dozen or so random places.

Now she steps back up to him, very aggressive, with the same body English she'd use just before a cuffing, or better, a full-blown strip search. He seems to love it. His breathing gets more obvious. His head does a stutter on his neck. She reaches around his back, drops her hand, and squeezes his ass with all her strength. There's a part of her that would like him to shout out her name, but she controls herself as well as Woo, lets go, and comes back around front to unfasten his chinos. They're held at the waist by a small metal clip and she releases it fast, but takes her time drawing down the zipper. He's got a continuous tremble going and Lenore finds it both disturbing and satisfying. For less than a second she questions the sincerity of the tremble, but she lets the thought go and pushes the pants down over his hips.

He's wearing white boxer shorts underneath. They have a gray pinstripe in them. They feel a little brittle, starchy, as she grabs them at the sides and yanks downward. When they touch the floor, she pats his hip and he steps out of all the clothing around his feet.

He's naked now, but she keeps her eyes on his eyes as she reaches forward and takes him in her hands. His mouth drops slightly and he makes a noise and takes some air. She squeezes very lightly and he grows. She releases and steps backward and motions that he should lie down on the floor.

He complies, moving carefully, finding a narrow strip of space between the mountains of books. He stretches out on his back, his hands folded behind his head for a pillow, his legs bent up at the knees. She likes him on the floor, likes the picture of him. She wants to remember it, press it into her memory, saved vivid for the distant future, for times when she's void of a partner and less in control of her life and herself. She wants to save the image in her mind, not as some mild, personal pornography, but more as a symbol, a suggestion of this feeling that has no title she knows of. It's a feeling beyond the words *power, control, dominance,* or *will.*

She walks a full, dramatic circle around Woo, taking giant steps over the smaller book piles. His eyes follow her path, stay on her face. She stops when she arrives back at his feet. She knows there'll be no speaking, no communication using the spoken language. They'll exchange messages, or rather, she'll indicate what she wants and he'll respond, a simple and efficient cause-and-effect equation.

She starts to give him the full show. She brings her feet together. She grabs her undershirt at its bottom and pulls it up slowly so that it forms loose ribs, bunches of ribbed material, she holds for a minute, arms crossed and prepared to pull, under the bottom rim of her breasts, gives him the hesitation tease she knows he wants, stares at him. Then she pulls the shirt free, up past the neck and head and simultaneously off the arms. Her breasts bob as the shirt rubs past. Her nipples are hard and she brings her fingers up and runs them around the areolas. It's a show for his benefit and his body continues to visibly respond, but it also feels as good as it looks.

She begins to unbutton and unzip her jeans. She gauges her speed to a midpoint where he's on the verge of frustration and fulfillment. She pushes the jeans down her legs and steps out of them. She's wearing white cotton panties, not bikinis, but close enough. Woo doesn't seem to notice the difference. She smiles at him, places her right hand over her navel for a minute, then inches it downward until her fingertips dip into the waistband. She waits, then teases him with a few more inches of finger sliding downward into still-invisible hair.

He lets out a garbled *Oh*, starts to rise up to a sitting position, but she gives him a stern shake of the head and he settles back into place.

She bends forward slightly, hovers over his legs. She says, 'Don't speak, Freddy. Don't open your mouth. No words at all.' She pauses, then says, 'Now, do you want me down there? Do you want me on the floor? Do you want me on top of you?'

His mouth opens, then at once snaps closed, all jaw, alligator-like. His head takes over with a jerking, too-fast nod and she loves it. It's just the effect she was going for.

'We're going to need some music,' she says, and turns to the desk area. Woo makes a throat-clearing sound that she ignores. She likes being almost naked in this place. She likes the idea of the huge, open space and the coldness of the brick. She thinks if she lived here, it'd be an effort to throw on clothes and leave each morning.

She fingers the toggle switches at the bottom of the reel-to-reel machine and says, 'Let's see what the doctor likes.' She hits the Play button and the reels start to turn smoothly, at a precise speed, the opposite of Woo's head. A single, high-pitched electronic tone sounds and she realizes for the first time that she doesn't know where the speakers are. The tone is followed by silence. She assumes there are probably several speakers, mounted in hidden spots in the study for the best possible acoustics. A guy like Woo would be concerned about sound quality and proper speaker placement.

'Guess we've got a blank tape,' she says, but Woo has stopped nodding and now he just stares up at her, maybe impatient, maybe doubtful, insecure.

Lenore slides out of the balance of her underwear, tosses them on top of the desk behind her. She comes down on her knees, in front of his feet, relaxes into a sitting position, ass on heels.

'I've always considered getting a tattoo, Freddy. Always wanted one. I've debated the question. They're considered cheap in this country. Biker women. Junkies. Hookers. Every hooker I've ever known has had a tattoo. I'm not sure the general public is aware how many tattoos are out there. More than most people would think. But, as you well know, in the Orient it's a different story. At least for the men. I don't know what the tattooing standard is for women over there. But with the men it's considered an art form, right? An enhancement of the skin. And I've got to concur. Got to agree with that. I've considered placement and for some reason I'm drawn to the erotic areas. I know about the pain involved, but I'm good with pain. No problem there. And, of course, I've thought about the design. What would I choose? We can rule out the typical red rose or butterfly right off the bat. I want something unique. Something custom-drawn and more suited to me. And I can't quite come up with what it should be. So do me a big favor, Freddy, if you would. Give it some thought. Not right now. Don't say a word right now. But sometime in the future, in the days ahead, give it some thought and tell me what you think would be the best sign for me. Something that would just scream *Lenore* permanently. From underneath my skin.'

She sits silent for a few seconds and then rises up on her knees again. She makes him spread his legs apart by slapping his feet.

When they've opened to their widest stretch, she lies down between them, her belly to the floor, and very slowly, with her eyes locked on his face, she takes him in her mouth. He lets out a high, sucking sound and the question kicks in – *is it possible no one's ever done this to him before?* She sucks very slowly, with gradually increasing pressure, for almost a minute, then she climbs forward on her knees and straddles him, first sitting too high, on his stomach, teasing him, licking his chest.

'Remember,' she says, 'you speak and it's all over.'

But it's not clear whether he hears her or not. He's letting out these hardly audible whines, his eyes rammed closed. Lenore thinks he sounds something like a miniature dog, quaking near the back door, asking to go out.

When she thinks it's been long enough, she moves down, pulls him inside, and starts to ride. She's wet enough and then, in a minute, much more wet, and they fall into a rhythm that she sets but he responds to beautifully, perfectly, without any instruction, without words or gestures.

And then a voice barks into the room:

Ngaatojai

She jolts upright, sits rigid, but leaves him inside. His eyes spring open and an awful terrified look spreads on his face. He can't speak. She doubts that even if she commanded him to, his vocal chords would respond. It's clear he wants to tell her something, but he can't shake the silence.

The voice barks out again. The word sounds foreign. The voice has a slightly clipped, mechanical sound to it. And then it hits her what's happening: the tape. The reel-to-reel machine. The tape she's turned on has come to life, hit the recorded stretch, only it's not music. It's words. Or maybe one word. All in different languages, a long pause between each loud, crisp, elaborated pronunciation.

'I get it,' she says softly to Woo, trying to be reassuring. 'It's not *Teenage Deathcamp*, but it'll do.'

Slowly, she brings them back into their swaying rhythm.

Imperio

His legs come up and cross around her back. They pick up some speed.

Kuhilani

He starts to buck slightly underneath with this flawless timing, as if he could feel exactly what was happening inside her and knew how to facilitate the experience, deepen it, elongate it, intensify it.

Dominante

He reaches up, eyes closed again, searches with his hands until he finds her breasts. He squeezes, just the right force, positions the nipples between the notches that separate his fingers, pulls, twists, just slightly.

Vorherrschen

Lenore's heart suddenly heaves, gives what feels like an extra, wider pump. In spite of herself she lets out a sound, a nonword, void of attachment to anything physical.

Przewaga

She picks up the speed. A new noise starts to issue at the slapping together of her thighs and ass with his pelvis. His legs around her make a new effort, bear inward, hug her like a sweaty and trembling vice.

Dominio

Woo starts to breathe out through his nose in harsh short bursts, a dragon from his own childhood nightmares. His head is snapping from left to right, his eyes shut so tight that his forehead shows a plain of creases and folds. He's biting his lips and pushing air in hard between his gums and inner mouth.

Cumhachd

Lenore's hands slap down onto his chest, palms flat, and she starts pushing off his breastbone like he was some accident victim on the highway. Her toes are curled up to the breaking point. A slick coating of sweat has broken everywhere and streams run down from her neck, over her breasts, over his hands squeezing her breasts, rubbing her nipples. A weird, old Three Stooges-type noise comes out of his mouth. She leans forward, inclines lower and lower over his chest, pumping her hips faster as she moves. Her hands go to the sides of his head, just above his ears, and she grabs two fingerfuls of hair and holds tight, pulling, shaking her own head now side to side.

Dominari

He's the first to let out a yell as he comes, but within seconds she's joining him. She had hoped to dismount and dress as soon as he was satisfied, but that isn't an option anymore. She lets her own eyes close, lets the noise pour out of her mouth, meaningless, passionate babble. Her hips buck in a last spastic set of spasms. She comes up as far as she can on her knees and still keep him in, then rams down, draws in air, and falls completely forward onto his chest.

Time seems to pull into the breakdown lane. Her sense of taste overwhelms her. Everything is salt. Woo stays quiet, but his lungs continue to work overtime. Neither of them attempts to alter their position.

The light seems a little dimmer to her. She keeps her eyes closed, realizes she's hugging him around the shoulders. She becomes aware of a sound, a slight, almost inaudible hiss, probably from the hidden speakers.

She's too loose to brace herself, though she knows it's coming, so she waits, willing listener, suddenly submissive.

And then the bodiless voice says: *Dominance.*

23

Mingo likes this street, tree-lined, middle-class, relatively stable. He rolls the Jaguar at a creeping pace and studies the old houses, all Victorians, many of them painted in bright pastel colors. He finds the architecture amazing, finds it hard to believe there was a time when men would put this much effort and detail into a building. Just for the sake of the way it looks. 'They must have been fanatics,' he mutters, without any explanation to his train of thought.

Cortez sits next to him, preoccupied, eyes closed, his thumb and index finger rubbing over the bridge of his nose.

'The first time I came down here, I figured this couldn't be it. This doesn't look like a place with stores, you know…' Mingo says.

'Commercially zoned,' Cortez tries, without opening his eyes.

'Exactly. This looks…'

'Residential.'

'There you go. First time out, I figured you'd given me the wrong directions. Then I practically broke my back carrying all those boxes up there.'

'A little suffering is good for the soul, Mingo.'

Mingo raises his eyebrows, picks up a little speed, until Cortez says, 'Okay, pull over and wait here.'

He gets out of the Jaguar and stands on the sidewalk looking up at the building. A pastel-yellow Victorian. Turrets, cupola, odd angles and jogs everywhere. There's a carved wooden sign hanging over the archway that leads up onto a wraparound porch. It reads 'Ephraim Beck's Mystery Bookshop.' Simple, Cortez thinks, tasteful. He walks up onto the porch where a long redwood picnic table holds a row of seven old-fashioned orange crates. The crates are all packed to capacity with paperback books. A small sign, propped on a tiny antique-looking easel, reads 'Any three for a dollar.'

He looks back down to the street and sees Mingo behind the driver's wheel, in a world of his own, talking to himself. He thinks to himself, *Everyone I draw around myself is defective in some way*, then moves inside the shop.

A bell rings as he pushes open the storm door and steps into the foyer. It's warm inside. The lighting is soft, but bright enough for long-term browsing. He stands in one spot and does a full scan. He loves what he sees. The place is so different from Hotel Penumbra, evokes a different era. Different concerns, importance placed on different priorities.

In the front room off the foyer, a middle-aged man is sound asleep on a small couch covered with a paisley quilt. He has salt-and-pepper hair, clipped gray mustache, wire-rim glasses pushed up onto the crown of his head. He's dressed as if he's playing the part of the kindly, old bookseller at the community theater. A white cotton button-down shirt covered by a brown, unbuttoned cardigan sweater. Suspenders barely visible. Corduroy pants. Penny loafers over heavy argyle socks.

He looks to be in an uncomfortable position, neither sitting nor lying down, but an unusual blend of the two. His head is cocked backward on the back edge of the couch, his face pointed up to the tin-plated ceiling. His mouth is open slightly. His hands are gripping a book spread open in his lap. Cortez would like to read the title without waking the man.

Instead, he takes a step to an elaborate walnut bookcase with a sign resting on top that reads 'New Arrivals.' He starts to reach out to pull down Harry Keeler's *The Book with the Orange Leaves,* but stops himself and simply looks. He feels uneasy, like the confused kin of a young mother who's given her infant up for adoption, and now returns to his school yard to simply stare at what was once hers. He turns away from the bookcase, annoyed with himself for the dramatics, ashamed of the conceit of this idea. But he can't help one last thought – *I'm not much more than the fictions I've sold.*

The entrance bell did nothing to disturb the sleeping man and Cortez is unsure whether to ignore him and begin browsing or to try to wake him gently and announce his presence. Then the thought hits him that it's possible the man is dead, a heart attack in the middle of the book's climax, maybe a murder scene or a chase.

Cortez leans forward slightly without taking a step. He wants a sign of breathing. The chest to rise. The eyes to flutter.

But there's nothing. He has to confirm the worst. He begins to move toward the couch and the man's mouth opens and says, 'You're a first-timer.'

Cortez stops and instinctively squelches any show of surprise. The man hasn't moved his head or opened his eyes. Cortez finds this rude. Especially to a potential customer. The guy obviously has no business skill. It's amazing the place has stayed in operation so long.

'Excuse me?'

Now the head comes up and the body straightens itself into a normal sitting posture.

'Ephraim Beck,' he says, extending a hand that Cortez walks toward and shakes. 'I doze sometimes. When it's slow. I find it very refreshing.'

'I'm sure.'

'What I said was, this is your first visit to the store. Most of the customers here are regulars. That's the way it is with specialty stores, you know.'

'I can imagine.'

'You from out of town?'

'Here on business.'

'Saw the ad in the yellow pages?'

'Actually, I asked the desk clerk at the hotel for some of the better bookstores in the city.'

'I see. Are you a collector?'

'Really, a beginner. An amateur.'

'We've got something for everyone. Any author you're especially interested in? You look like you might be a Chesterton man. Am I right?'

'To be honest, I'm going to be doing a great deal of traveling in the near future. A lot of time on planes. Trains. I'm looking for some titles that will keep my interest. But at the same time I don't want to load myself down.'

The man squints his eyes a little and makes a noise, sucking air through his clenched teeth. His manner suggests he's weighing a difficult decision. Finally, he shrugs and says, 'I think you're going to want to go with paperbacks.'

'Paperbacks,' Cortez repeats.

The man nods. 'I know, I know. It's like you can feel the decay in your hands as you're reading the first line. But you've got limited luggage capacity, correct? And if you're going to be on the road for any length of time... let's just say you stuff a first-edition Chesterton down into the Samsonite before you turn it over to the airline people. Come the end of your trip, I don't want to look. I mean, it's a question of respect.'

Cortez decides this is the kind of man who could wander off into endless oblique stories with no apparent meaning. He says, 'Do you have any Hammett?'

The man takes a breath and smiles indulgently, as if to say, *please, think about your questions before you ask them.*

'Okay, how about the obvious choice?'

'That's not so obvious to me.'

Cortez nods. 'Sorry. *Maltese Falcon*. Any paperback edition.'

'I've got one by Vintage. Two ninety-five, plus tax. Good-sized print.'

'Sold.'

Mr. Beck smiles and starts to move for a wall of paperbacks toward the rear of the store. He throws his voice back over his shoulder as Cortez follows. 'Now we're moving. What else can we get? You said it would be a long trip.'

'Yes, but now that I think about it, that one title should do it. There'll be some books waiting for me at my first stop.'

The clerk stops at a shelf, runs a finger parallel to the books' spines without touching them, stops, and pulls down a black-covered book with green lettering and a picture of the famous bird sitting like an Egyptian sphinx.

He turns back toward Cortez and presents it. 'First published in '30. Still tremendously popular today.'

'I've read it before.'

'I would think so,' the man says, and then seems to regret it.

Cortez lets him off the hook and says, 'There's a part of this book that gets to me. One particular scene. A small bit. You know what I'm talking about?'

The man smiles as if they'd just become conspirators. As if they'd sealed some kind of mutually beneficial agreement.

'You know the scene? With Spade and Bridget O'Shaughnessy? At Spade's place?'

'The story of Flitcraft,' the man says.

'Exactly,' Cortez says. 'I knew you'd know.'

The man's head slopes to the side a little. His lips stay together.

'I've always wondered what other people thought about that.'

When the man realizes that Cortez is waiting for a response, he says simply, 'Of course.'

'Why do you think that scene is in there?'

The man lets his head roll slightly. His tongue slides out of his mouth and wets his lips. 'It's a great story,' he says.

They stare at each other for a few seconds, then Cortez reaches into his pocket and pulls out a roll of bills. Without looking, he fans them slightly, lets his fingers run through the fan, in decreasing denomination, until he stops and yanks loose a five. He hands it to Beck and says, 'Keep the change.'

24

Ike has left the clock radio on and now, as he sleeps, the talk-show host warns the public about the dangerous epidemic of skinheads, racist teenage males who shave their scalps and engage in hideous violence in our urban cesspools. These skinheads, according to the talk-show host, are one of the greatest dangers facing our society today, a horrible blight on the landscape of freedom and truth, a perversion of all the values that America has fought and died for in bloody wars on foreign shores. They are monsters, beasts, scum of the earth, and must be dealt with as such.

HOST: Thank you for waiting, you're on WQSG, tell the city what's on your mind.

CALLER: Ray? Hello? Ray?

HOST: Yes, ma'am, you're on the air.

CALLER: Hello? I don't… hello?

HOST: Go ahead, dear, we don't have all night. You're on the air.

CALLER: Oh yes, thank you, love the show, listen all the time.

HOST: Thank you. Your question, please.

CALLER: Yes, well, I was wondering, this skinhead problem, this problem you've been discussing, I was wondering, is this an inherited problem, what you would call a genetic problem, because my husband's brother – oh, I was going to say his name, but never mind, he has no hair, he lost all his hair, all at once, just gone, not even any left around the ears, like, you see. Now, they called that, the doctor he went to called that alopecia, and his hair never came back, but he was always the same man we've known, wonderful man, nothing like these people you've described, he had none of these side effects...

HOST: Okay, one of those nights. All right, dear, now listen to me closely. These young men shave their heads, they don't lose their hair, they shave their heads. Voluntarily. You understand? They do it to themselves. It has nothing to do with any disease. It's a way to identify themselves as part of a hate group. And I'll take a moment to say that I wish people would listen just a little more carefully before they call in. Next caller.

CALLER: Hello, Ray. It's Johnny Z calling.

HOST: Johnny, haven't heard from you in quite a while.

CALLER: You're a popular man these days. Tough getting through those lines.

HOST: And what does my friend Johnny have to say about tonight's topic?

CALLER: Clean and simple, Ray. Long as we're castrated by the liberal courts in this state it's up to each man to protect his family in whatever way necessary.

HOST: Amen, brother. Amen to that.

CALLER: These faggots are one more reason we got to protect our constitutional right to bear arms. I've got a beautiful double-pump Winchester I keep right on the back of the bedroom door, loaded and ready to go. I say, come on in, skinheads. Come on and visit. I'm all ready and waiting. Wouldn't think twice.

HOST: I hear you, Johnny.

CALLER: Just wanted to say it.

HOST: Thanks for calling. Next caller, you're on the air.

CALLER: Yes, Ray, just wondered if you people down at the station would like the real truth about all this?

HOST: About all what, caller?

CALLER: About how these skinheads are just one branch in Mayor Welby's secret army and as we speak they're mapping out the final details in their plan to round up all the blacks and Jews and—

HOST: Next caller, you're on the air.

CALLER: Yeah, Ray, this is Vin from down San Remo. I thought this was going to be UFO night? What happened to UFO night?

HOST: Next Wednesday, Vin. Next caller, you're on *City Soapbox.*

CALLER: Raymond, what's gotten into you? You sound as bad as these skinhead people you're complaining about. 'Throw them in a pit and bulldoze the earth right over them.'

HOST: This is Mrs. G, isn't it?

CALLER: You know my voice, Raymond.

HOST: Poor Mrs. G, we're never going to see eye-to-eye. But let me tell you, dear lady, when you're out there, day after day, the way I am, and you see this constant erosion of everything that was once good and pure in our town, well, I'm sorry, you start to think that maybe drastic measures are called for before it's just too late and we wake up one day and the whole thing has been taken away from us. History tells a sad story, Mrs. G, believe me, it's happened before. And we'll be back in a short minute after this word from your friend and guide in your darkest hour, Loftus Funeral Home over on Patterson Ave.

Ike is dreaming an awful vision of his mother and father in the kitchen of the old family house. He's standing in the center of the room, ashamed of something unclear. And his parents are walking in circles around him, equidistant from each other. They're furious with him, berating him for this unstated failure or transgression. He's sobbing, begging forgiveness, promising repentance, but it's useless. Whatever he's done is so heinous, they won't even listen to his sorrow. Ike's body trembles in his bed, the dream is so clear and real.

Outside the green duplex, Eva looks at both entrances and finds Ike's – 91B. She moves first to his doormat, squats down, and lifts it, but there's nothing underneath. She stands back up, steps to his mailbox, opens the lid, and looks inside to find it empty. Then she runs her hand along the underside of the box and pulls a key out of a small metal lip. She lets herself into the apartment and stands silent inside, letting her eyes adjust to the darkness.

She moves through rooms, steering herself with her fingertips on the edge of furniture, walking in tiny, comical steps to avoid tripping. She finds her way to the back bedroom and stands in the doorway for a few minutes watching Ike's body quake. It's a horrible sight, like looking on a helpless child in the midst of a dangerous fever.

Before she can rethink her actions, Eva walks into the bedroom, sits on the edge of the bed, and begins to stroke Ike's forehead softly and whisper, 'It's okay, now, I'm here, it's all right, Ike,' as if she were his dead mother come to life out of his nightmare, but bearing a radical change of heart.

Ike's eyelids flutter, flip open, and his whole body bolts backward on the bed as he lets out a scream of *Ma, Ma, Jesus,* loud enough to be heard three houses away.

Eva jumps up into a crouched position on her feet, her hands and arms balanced on the mattress. She's yelling back at him, 'It's Eva, it's Eva, stop it, it's me.'

Ike knocks a glass off the nightstand, then manages to turn on a lamp.

'For God sake,' he chokes, hand on his chest, then up over his mouth.

'I'm sorry,' Eva says, backing up. 'Are you all right? I'm sorry.'

Ike takes a second to breathe and look around the room. 'How'd you get in here?'

'I looked until I found a key. There's usually a key.'

'You almost gave me a heart attack.'

'I'm sorry, Ike. I thought it was a good idea at the time.'

'You always go breaking into people's homes?'

'Really sorry. It was a stupid thing to do—'

'What are you doing here?'

'I need to talk to you, Ike.'

'I've got nothing to say. I don't want to talk to anyone. Just dock me for today. Whole day.'

Eva comes forward again and sits back down on the edge of the bed.

'Why did you run out today, Ike? What happened?'

'I just wasn't feeling well. I think I'm getting the flu. I'm probably contagious right now.'

'Did something happen while you were sorting, Ike?'

'My God, I'm having chest pains, I'm having actual chest pains.'

'Now, take it easy. Calm down.'

'Calm down. Calm down. This is it. I'm having chest pains.'

'What kind of pains? Should I call an ambulance?'

'I don't believe this. I'm thirty years old. This is unbelievable.'

'Oh, Ike, what have I done? Should I get on the phone? Should I call?'

'Wait a minute. Wait a minute. Hold on.'

Ike sits up in the bed, leans forward, tilts his head to the side. His cheeks balloon out a couple of times. He makes a fist with his right hand and very lightly thumps his mid-chest. It's possible that he belches, though Eva hears nothing. Then he comes upright and takes a breath and says, a little sheepishly, 'I think it's okay now,' as if he were speaking about something other than himself, 'I think it's all right.'

Eva sighs her relief and shakes her head. 'Please forgive me, Ike. I didn't mean to scare you like that.'

'It's just, you wake up, someone's standing in your room.'

'I don't know what I was thinking.'

'I just had no idea who it was. It could have been anyone. I had no idea.'

'It's just that things feel like they're on the verge of getting out of control.'

'Listen, Eva—'

'And I don't feel like I can trust anyone else.'

'I'm not sure I want to talk about this anymore.'

'I know that something happened today.'

'I'm starting to think that maybe you should go home.'

'I think you should tell me what happened at the station, Ike. You were sorting and then something happened.'

'I don't want any problems here, Eva.'

'At the bookstore you were all for going to the authorities. What happened, Ike? What changed your mind?'

'Forget the bookstore, Eva.'

'I thought we were going to talk to your sister.'

'Forget my sister. Forget everything.'

'What did you find in the mail, Ike?'

'Would you please get out?'

'Where did you put it, whatever it was?'

They stare at each other. The room fills up with the sound of the talk-show host lecturing:

> HOST: All right now, I've had enough of the stupidity. I've had enough of the inarticulate talk. Very simply, I'm asking you to frame your questions before you dial the number. There is no need for this. But what it does display for me, in crystal clarity, is the depths that this once-great country has descended to. By allowing Marxism in our schoolrooms, by allowing unchecked immigration across our borders, by allowing a blatant, flagrant abuse of a welfare state designed to propagate lives of drug dependency and casual sexuality, by allowing, allowing, *allowing* would be the key word here, my friends. Where has discipline gone? Where has consistency escaped to? In what dark bowels does respect for law and order and our unique system of democracy now reside? Let me mention

a phrase here, people, a phrase that blazed a fire in the minds of men like Washington, like Jefferson. That phrase is *new world*, my people. A world that once, long ago, was untouched by the decadence of the Continent, of a Europe so in love with itself that it fell, as long-told prophecy said it would. This very land, the soil, the physical earth that stretched in a rich and wild run from Atlantic to Pacific, was once the last bastion, the refuge, the last possible paradise on an orb gone sick. It was a pure and final chance to forget the past and try again, start anew, build a civilization based on a consensus of values and good *family* morals. And what did we do in this damnable century of blinding technological advancement? We spit on it. We balled it up and tossed it down like a piece of festering garbage. We said *NO! We shall not be pure! We shall not fulfill the dream!* We handed the promises of this green land over to a satanic horror with many names: Liberal Humanism. Moral Relativity. Leftist Ideology. Castrating Feminism. Darwinistic Thought. Socialistic Atheism. New Age Heathenism. I could go on. Believe me, I could continue all night and into tomorrow. But I need no further proof of the futility of my cries than your phone calls. The pathetic ramblings of my audience tell me to throw in the towel, abandon the good fight. How much further can our intelligence be eroded? Will we move back into the caves of our forebears, draw on the walls, live with the wild dogs, eat with our fingers? [*There's a small breath of dead air, and then*:] While you ponder the answer to those questions, I'll take a short break for a word from tonight's sponsor, the Loftus Funeral Home, specialists in your prepaid burial needs. Remember, there's no need to burden those left with your final duty.

The advertisement begins with the whine of maudlin violins and Ike looks at Eva and says, 'Listen to me. There was a box in today's mail. Just like last time. It was addressed to box nine. It was wrapped in plain brown paper. There was no return address. I cut it open.'

He pauses. A voice from the radio is saying something about *when the time comes, we'll be ready.*

Ike takes a breath. 'Now listen to me. It was a box full of human fingers and blood.'

'Jesus Christ,' Eva says, hands going up to her mouth.

'The sight of it made me faint. I was on the floor for a few minutes, I guess. When I woke up, the box was gone. And there was no one else in the room.'

'Why didn't you come and get me?'

Ike stares at her.

'You think I took the box?'

He doesn't say a word.

'You think I sent the box? You think I'm involved in this?'

He sinks down slightly into the bed.

'For God's sake, Ike, how can you suspect me? Don't do this, Ike. I can't be alone on this.'

'I'm going to try to sleep now,' Ike says, drawing the covers up to the fold between his neck and shoulder.

Eva stares down at him. The ad on the radio finishes and the host comes back on, his voice sounding refreshed.

HOST: We are back and our caller is Lois.

LOIS: Yes, hello, Ray. Let me tell you a little story about how these skinheads accosted my mother downtown last week, right on the common, near the reflecting pool…

Eva eases her shoes off her feet. She stands and begins to undress. She quickly folds each item as it falls away from her body and places it in a neat pile on the floor. When she's naked, she takes a corner of the sheet and quilt and yanks it back from the bed.

Ike's eyes snap open and she lets him take a long look at her. She drops hold of the bedclothes, places her hands lightly on her hips, model-like, and does a very small twist from side to side, to indicate she's on display, to give him a full chance at observation.

'Eva?' is the only thing he can manage to say and it comes out as a stunted question.

She raises an index finger to her lips and gives the ancient *quiet* sign.

'You don't want to talk,' she whispers, 'we won't talk.'

She climbs into the bed and advances at once, pulls her body across the mattress until its full length is parallel with his. Then she puts her arms around him, cradles him, pulls their chests together, flattening herself. She intermingles their legs and can already feel him growing against a thigh. She's pleased, bordering on being something like proud, comforted by the fact that he's getting hard in spite of his shock and depression and paranoia and confusion and terror.

They fumble, pull him free from sweatpants, T-shirt, underwear, all the while kissing, wet, breathless, tongue-crazy.

The only noise beyond their breathing and muted, guttural groans is the talk-show host, Ray, starting up again, voice rising in both pitch and volume, building another ranting theory, preaching his endless warnings of decay.

25

Lenore sits in the Barracuda for a few minutes. She's parked across the street from Rollie's Grill. It surprises her how much she can see through the front windows of the diner. It's like a little diorama, a small scene enclosed in a porcelain-framed case. An intricate picture of dozens of interacting parts becomes clearer the longer you look. She can see that half the booths are filled. She notices an enormous customer in mechanic's coveralls perched on a counter stool. She spots one of Harry's cousins, possibly Lon, clearing the empty tables. She can see Isabelle behind the counter stirring the contents of the big kettle. And Harry is next to her, his mouth moving, jabbering a story as he chops peppers.

She thinks that Harry and Isabelle have always struck her as an odd but instantly appealing and attractive couple. And now it dawns on her why. At first glance, their glaring disparateness, most obviously, but not limited to, their racial difference, makes them seem like such separate entities. But then, constantly on the heels of that observation, there's the indisputable fact of their togetherness, this plain happiness of their mutual attraction and love, and it burns away the separateness and acts as a billboard for the possibility of *family, wholeness, belonging.*

An image forms in Lenore's mind. She hates it, instinctively, but like an annoying and persistent daydream, she can neither eliminate it nor alter it. She's stuck with it: herself as Isabelle tending a pot filled with an exotic stew. And here's the tough part: Woo as Harry, dicing up vegetables and babbling the pleasant fables of his grandfather.

A fact becomes apparent that's so bizarre it makes her dizzy. *She could love Woo.* There's the genuine possibility that she could care for, pledge herself to, undertake a life with this odd Oriental linguistics professor. The Barracuda is full of the smell of him. And she knows this is why she lingers, why she doesn't want to get out.

He had suggested that they shower together. That she call Miskewitz, tell him she needed some sleep in order to keep going. That they push book piles aside and have a postcoital picnic on the floor of his library. He'd said he could make a huge gourmet omelette for two, something special, a surprise. He'd stroked her forehead and said she had to sleep soon, that it had been days since she'd really slept and that something could *happen* to her, emphasizing the word so that it conveyed a childlike fear, a dread of inconceivable monsters.

She'd lain in his arms and listened to him speak, kissed his chest, run her fingers over his bony cheeks. But she'd left the loft, still wet, her legs a little undependable, her nervous system shorting out slightly, sending small blue flashes before her eyes as she found her way back to her car.

She knows she should have gone back to the green duplex, searched for a Valium, called in to the lieutenant for a break, collapsed into bed, and crashed. But instead she drove to Rollie's Grill, intent on black coffee and overspiced food. And something else. Now, staring through the boxy, rectangular windows, she's intent on studying Harry and Isabelle, on paying attention to their gestures, their mannerisms, the number of times they touch one another. She wonders about the sound of their voices as they speak to one another. She wonders if there's a signal that two people give off when they're bound together, committed in some old-time, superstitious way. Do they learn some difficult, shared language, some bizarre and insulated code only understood by the two bound parties? At night, in bed, at the end of the once-endless day, do they dispense with language entirely, fall into a lazy, sleepy telepathy? Do they utter sounds on a frequency that outsiders can't hear? Do their inner organs vibrate when their mate comes within a certain perimeter? Like some birds, do they have an ability to will their own death when a spouse dies? Like swans? Like her parents?

There has never been anyone that Lenore felt this way about. She's been involved with a number of boys and men over the past fifteen years. She has never felt rejected. Normally, she was the one who decided to sever a relationship. But even when she wasn't the one who called it off, she always felt relief, never rejection. It was always like a great weight had been lifted.

But now images she can't eliminate or adapt to are coming into her head, stuff so alien that she doesn't know what to do with it: she sees herself moving into Woo's cavernous loft, preparing to bake bread on his gleaming black counters, folding her freshly washed sweaters on the couch as he works at his ridiculous desk, instructing burly, ethnic moving men on where to put down the new bed. She sees herself and Woo hosting a small dinner, a homey, old-fashioned casserole of some kind, dense with noodles, cheese, multicolored vegetables. Woo sits at one end of the new teak table – *we've got to lighten this place up a little, honey* – and Ike, their sole guest this evening, sweet Ike, still having trouble renting out the empty half of the green duplex, sitting at the other end. And Lenore in the middle, equidistant from each, closest to the kitchen area so she can run the show, pull things from the oven and refrigerator, grab a new bottle from the wine rack. She sees her own mouth opening. Words come: *Fred, honey, you should really take Ike up to the new courts with you next week. Ike, they've built some beautiful new racquetball courts up on the hill. Fred could show you the basics. It would really do you a world of good...*

'What the fuck am I doing?' she says to herself, aloud, inside the Barracuda.

She jumps out of the car, starts to walk to the diner, then turns back, pulls open the door, and grabs the keys from the ignition slot.

A gust of steamy air hits her as she pulls open the metal door and steps inside the diner. Lon almost drops his rubber tub of dirty dishes trying to say hi to her. She slides into the first booth and nods hello. The table is littered with the debris from the last customers. There are two breakfast plates coated with the hardened yellow remains of fried eggs, large glasses with grainy traces of tomato juice, side bowls dusted with the last brown crumbs of Harry's secret-seasoning home fries, toast crusts, orange rinds, coffee mugs. She guesses that both customers were men, probably truckers, possibly in their mid to late forties. Then she stops herself, annoyed that she can't even take a seat in a lunchcar without reflexively analyzing the landscape like a crime scene. She can't turn off being a detective, looking for the tiniest evidence that might reveal something more. But what? What is ever revealed that's truly of use? It's the process, the breaking apart of the immediate environment, sifting it fragment by fragment and looking at each particle from all perspectives, dusting it, photographing it, putting it down and picking it up again – this is what has become important to her. The method. The technique. The system. The idea that she can no longer sit in Rollie's Grill without her mind taking over, shifting into an inspect-and-analyze mode, reconstructing a common diner-booth's previous occupants – she finds this pathetic beyond words.

Behind the counter, Harry raises a full coffeepot toward her and she nods again. Lately, she's noticed that inside the diner, communication is often assisted by the gesture and the hand signal accompanying normal, audible words. She assumes this is because of the number of different primary languages that all the inhabitants speak. As far as she knows, only Isabelle is terribly fluent in a second language.

Isabelle manages to get her instructions across to everyone. She snaps Spanish at her own extended brood, handles a beautiful, rhythmic English with the customers, and cuts what, by her own admission, is a broken, sometimes humorous Khmer dialect. She is the translator through whom all interracial communication must pass. She referees the fights between her Uncle Jorge and Harry's cousin Lon. She relays Harry's words about a clean grill to her sister Luisa. She's able to barter with both of the odd, lanky 'sales reps' from both the Mekong Market and the New Ponce Bodega. And she's able to keep Karl, the redneck milkman who calls the diner 'the town's own goddamn United Nations,' harmless and under control.

Lenore watches Isabelle now as she comes out of the storeroom wiping her hands on her apron. She's a large woman, but she moves like someone half her weight and age. Though Lenore has to admit, she has no idea how old Isabelle actually is. Lenore envies her grace behind the counter, not just in the way she moves, the ease and agility of her body – Lenore thinks she could match that – but her easy manner of dealing with people. Lenore has never seen her blow up and yell. In any language. She's never seen her grab the front of someone's shirt or throw a water glass or serving spoon across the room. Even in those moments when the diner is packed to capacity during a dinner rush and boothfuls of college kids are screaming rude insults about their wait and cousin Lon has burned a second omelette and the dishwasher has started to leak again, Isabelle just dances through each crisis, attending to one thing at a time, cajoling the college boys with refills of coffee and her smooth voice, patting Lon on the back with a soft word to relax, even taking a monkey wrench to the bottom of the old Cleansomatic.

Lenore feels that put in the same position, she, too, could handle all the problems. But it's the method that differs and how things are left in the wake of the job's completion. It's not a comfortable thought, because her method for dealing with all problems arises out of the core of her personality. Her schematic is simple – confront the problem and take the shortest, most direct route toward its solution. Every other consideration is superfluous. She's never doubted this before. It's been the first holy truth. The truth of truths. But in looking at Isabelle, she sees a woman – and it's an important fact that she's a woman – capable in an all-pervasive, almost primal way. And yet there's no blood left in her wake, no jumpy casualties, no pockmarked landscape.

The disparity of their jobs is no answer. Lenore can actually see the diner as a microcosm of Quinsigamond. It's not that much of a stretch. A bunch of unassimilated people side by side, droning and bitching from time to time in a native tongue, serving drunks and head cases and average hungry schmucks, passing time. The fact is that even behind the counter, in a much more insulated and controlled world, Lenore would be bullying her way toward the last clean plate and the end of the day.

Lon appears with a dish bin and an embarrassed smile. He clears the table of all the dirty dishes, wipes it down with a damp rag, and heads back behind the counter with this endearing, scampering run. Isabelle walks up in front of her and slides a black coffee onto the table.

'Don't you ever get tired of this place?' she asks.

Lenore shakes her head. 'This is my free zone, Isabelle. This is where I relax.'

'Free zone,' Isabelle repeats, smiling. 'I like the words.'

'Got a free minute?' Lenore asks, and Isabelle rolls her eyes like some old-time Hispanic soap opera star. Then she slides in on the other side of the booth.

'Busy day?' Lenore asks.

'Average. They're all average.'

'You ever get away from this place? You ever take a vacation?'

'I don't think that word goes into Cambodian.'

They both laugh and Harry eyes them suspiciously from the chopping table at the other end of the counter. Then he can't help himself and breaks into an approving smile.

'Does he understand what you say?' asks Lenore.

Isabelle shrugs. 'When it's convenient.'

Harry calls something down to her, a series of short high-pitched syllables. Isabelle laughs and makes a long kissing sound back toward him.

'It must be strange sometimes,' Lenore says. 'Two different cultures and all.'

Isabelle smiles. 'My grandmother used to say it's good to mix the blood. Keeps things bubbling. No dead water.'

'Dead water?'

'What's your word? Stagnant?'

'Yeah. That's it. I think I see what you mean.'

There's a pause. Lenore sips coffee and Isabelle watches her, then says, 'Everything okay today?'

'Isabelle, I hope, I don't mean to…' She stops and starts again. 'Is it possible to love someone you don't really understand?'

Isabelle shakes her head, bites away a smile, lowers her voice. 'Who do we really understand?'

Lenore shrugs, tries to ignore a chill rolling up her back. 'Too easy an answer.'

Isabelle lets out a long, heavy sigh and makes a hedging, slow nod. 'You never been married, have you?'

'You know,' Lenore says, 'this is an area I really want to make people clear on. I really believe, firmly believe, okay, that there are people who, for whatever reason, are not suited to the married life. And I've always thought that if these people let themselves go out and fall into a marriage, enter a legal arrangement, because of pressure or doubt or whatever, I've always thought, how goddamn unfair to everyone in that picture. So no, I've never been married. And the reasons are that first, I value independence above almost anything else, and whether anyone can accept it or not, I honestly enjoy long stretches of solitude, of just being alone. And secondly, I don't know, maybe I've got these ridiculous standards or something, but I've never met anyone whose company I'd want to be in for more than a couple of months. Tops. More than two months is pushing it. You start to go brain-dead. You start to have conversations about the color of his socks.'

Isabelle leans back in the booth, looks at Lenore, takes a sip from Lenore's coffee, sways her head slightly from side to side, like she was giving herself time to think about this speech she's just heard.

'Maybe,' she finally says. 'But for me, Lenore, there's this time, sometime, every night, midnight maybe, when we' – she gestures toward Harry with her skull – 'get out of here and we're gone upstairs, we're lying down, we're watching the black-and-white reruns of *The Honeymooners*, we're drinking from the bottle of Riunite, my head's on Harry's chest and he's laughing, which you really don't hear him do down here, and my head's going up and down with the laugh… I think, this is it, Isabelle. This is the island. You're safe now.'

They stare at each other, then Lenore can't help herself and she says, 'Safe? That's it? You want safe?'

'That's part of it. You're lying if you say it isn't.'

'Part of it. Bingo. Part.'

'And then there's the rest.'

Isabelle straightens up a little and then leans back again. She seems to be getting a little angry. She says, 'What are you asking? You asking do I love Harry? Yes. Simple answer and it's yes. You can believe that or not. You don't have the last word on anything, girl.'

'I didn't mean to offend you—'

'There's no offense,' she says, an edge clear in her voice, 'but, for your own benefit, I've got to say, you're a vain girl, Lenore, girl, woman, a vain woman.'

'I have to disagree, Isabelle. I'm a realist. I'm a pragmatist. I know what my abilities are and I know my limits.'

'Vanity.'

'I guess we define the word differently.'

'Suddenly, you think you want love—'

'Excuse me, who said that? Did someone say this?'

'I, too, know my abilities, Lenore.'

'Simple statement. I place a high value on independence, Isabelle.'

'Independence? This is the reason for the twitches? The chills?'

'Jesus, everyone's a guidance counselor today. I'm coming down with a cold, is all.'

'Listen to me, Lenore. There are many diners open in the city. They all serve hot coffee. But you're sitting here. And *you ask me* about Harry and loving someone without completely knowing them.'

'Friendly discussion, Isabelle. I didn't mean to set you off.'

'I'm not set off. You're a very smart woman who I know almost nothing about. Harry and me, we fix your meals for the past year. Fill you with enough coffee to swim in. You smile and you talk. You make Lon's day every time you come in the door. You know that, don't you? You pay your check and you tip our people. But we don't know you, Lenore. We don't know you at all. Isabelle's been around a little bit longer than you. She knows some things. Harry too. You've got some problems that are not going away. Like that chill and the twitch. No aspirin going to take that away, Lenore. Smart woman like you knows that.'

'Oh, for Christ sake,' Lenore mutters, looking out the window at her car. 'You always talk to people you don't know like that?'

When she looks back, Isabelle is shaking her head no.

Lenore gives her a forced smile and says, '"One of these days, Alice…"'

Isabelle starts to slide out of the booth.

'I've got a stew to put on,' she says. 'Your coffee's on the house.'

Lenore watches her move behind the counter and start to pull vegetables from the refrigerator. When her arms are full with carrots, onions, celery, peppers, scallions, she dumps the heap on a cutting block and draws a huge chopping knife down from its holder mounted on the wall. She goes to work with speed and precision, hacking the vegetables, making a rhythmic chomping sound. Lenore finds the noise oddly pleasing, reassuring, almost peaceful.

She watches Harry at the other end of the diner, writing up a check. She knows he still writes orders in his native language and she wonders what happens if he hands *#2 breakfast plate,* written in Khmer, to Uncle Jorge, who still speaks only Spanish. Has enough time passed for Jorge to know that the odd lines and slashes scratched on the green pad mean *two eggs, scrambled, and a side of bacon*?

She thinks about where she can establish a new free zone. It's getting harder and harder to find an unspoiled hole in the wall that's fairly clean, uncrowded, cheap, family-owned, and open all night. It's not that these places don't exist, just that it's become trendy, especially among the Canal Zone crowd, to find and usurp them, make them into clubhouses for whatever the ideology of the month might be.

There was a place over near the vocational school that had been shut down for about ten years. She's heard someone – Shaw or maybe Peirce – mention that it was up again and running. She'll find time to swing by, make an inspection, see if it fits her basic needs.

She glances out the window again and sees a motorcycle pull up behind the Barracuda. It's one of those glitzy new models, a bullet bike, controversial because of its too-powerful engine and the absurd speeds it can reach. It's an import, all metallic red and gold with silvery, speckle-paint lightning bolts slapped on the bulging gas tank. The rider, of course, is dressed all in leather, pants as well as coat. Zippers everywhere. He's got one of those enormous high-tech helmets on, matte black and smoked visor. It makes him look like a robot extra in a pricey science-fiction movie.

He's sitting on the bike as it idles. He seems to be looking at the back of the hand he's just pulled a glove off of. He raises his head for a second, looks at the back of the Barracuda.

Lenore's stomach starts to tighten a little. She raises herself up slightly off her seat, leans closer to the window. The biker pulls his glove back over his hand. He starts to pull down the zipper on his coat. Lenore is half standing in her booth, her nose almost touching the glass of the window.

Then she sees it. It's hanging from a black stretch-strap around the biker's neck. She sees him cradle the main body against his chest as he starts to pull out from the curb.

'Everyone down,' she screams, trying to lunge from the booth and at the same time pull her weapon from its holster.

The biker screeches into the street. He's got enough distance to pick up a head of speed before coming parallel to Rollie's Grill. He angles his Uzi straight out from his body like some new mutant appendage, a third arm that can pump a projectile at over twelve hundred feet a second.

The barrage hits the diner like the sound of a long string of wired-together firecrackers, amplified to some awful level as they pop off one after another in perfectly timed microsecond intervals. The bullets come in at window level, glass shattering, shards raining in a line down the wall of booths. The screams seem to come a second too late and they're all that Lenore can hear as she jumps down the three small brick stairs to the outside pavement, sinks into a leg-spread stance, and manages a single burst from the Magnum, before the untouched biker rounds a corner and is out of her vision.

She stands frozen for a second, then reholsters the gun and bounds back into the diner. The screaming continues, but it's degenerated into a more common jag of hysterical crying. Customers are sitting in shocked, breath-grabbing hunches, glass still resting on their shoulders and laps. Uncle Jorge is already on the wall phone screaming in Spanish, '*Ayúdenos! El está muriendo!*'

Lenore focuses on him for a moment, then makes herself approach the counter, lean her torso over the marble countertop, and look on the sight of Lon cradled on the floor in Isabelle's arms, blood flowing down from pathetically small openings in his neck and chest. There's a gurgling sound that's achingly clear through the collective moan and cry of the diner. Harry is on his knees at Isabelle's side, his hands held together, flattened into pathetic pancakes, pushing down gently and futilely on his cousin's chest, blood oozing between the spaces of his fingers no matter how firmly he presses them together.

Harry's head is shaking in short but violent jerks. Isabelle's eyes are closed. Someone has grabbed the phone from Jorge and is yelling an address in English. Lon is motionless. His hand grips a spatula. His blood has made it down his waist apron to his knees.

Now the gurgling begins to come and go and the change makes the noise even more awful. Sirens begin to become audible in the distance. Harry pulls his hands up from the wounds and covers his own face. His mouth opens and he lets out sounds, maybe words. It's still a language that Lenore doesn't know.

26

There's a logic that says that the last thing a mailman would want to do in his off hours is walk. But like everything else, this is not always the case. Ike enjoys walking on the good days. On the bad days, he needs it like food and shelter, a condition of survival. But today has gone beyond the definition of a 'bad day.' Today has become something that just a week ago his imagination couldn't conceive of. Today is a living horror story, a nightmare all the more sickening in its clarity, in its total sensual capacity. Today is like the vision of hell that every black-habited nun warned him about in his innocent childhood. *Terrors your small brain cannot even picture, Mr. Thomas, terrors that are never-ending, eternal and absolute, pain and revulsion and sorrows beyond anything anyone who ever walked this sinful planet could ever concoct.*

The one thing the nuns were wrong about, the one thing Ike would actually find amusing at any other time in his life, is their idea that most of this terror and horror and sorrow was caused directly by carnal thought and deed. And this just isn't the case. The sex came after the horror, Ike thinks. The sex came later. It didn't cause anything. It was caused. By, he doesn't know, confusion and desperation and plain fright.

Afterward, neither he nor Eva knew what to do. She disappeared into the bathroom. He went to the window and peeked through the blinds and when he didn't see Lenore's car, for some reason he was relieved. When Eva came back into the room she was dressed. Ike sat in bed, silent. She leaned over to him, one knee up on the mattress, kissed his forehead, and said, her voice sounding like someone else, someone in a movie unsure of whether to cry or laugh, 'I'll call you when I know what I'm going to do.' Then she left and he was alone in the green duplex again.

And rather than be alone he decides to walk. He heads for downtown thinking he'll hang around the mall, eat something fried at a kiosk, read magazines in the bookstore. But when he reaches the mall entrance, he goes past it and veers toward the Canal Zone.

When Ike was in college, the Canal Zone was just getting its start as a self-segregated neighborhood for the local art crowd. Back then it was just one more rundown industrial section in another northeastern town on the slide. Each small manufacturing operation that packed up and headed for the Sun Belt left the Zone with one more unused, century-old, redbrick mill. At the time, there was little call to turn the old factories into hip, upscale condos, and they sat empty until one by one, small art groups, each with a different axe to grind, began to move in and stake claims.

Now, a decade later, the Canal Zone is Quinsigamond's own East Village. It's got half a dozen theater groups, performance-art clubs, countless galleries and boutiques and gritty little cafés. There are political-fringe headquarters and all kinds of subterranean co-ops and communes. There are constantly weird, ragtag parades being run through the streets, bizarre posters being slapped up on stop signs and mailboxes in the middle of the night. There's a lively, if not yet hard-core, drug trade. And on every corner there's at least one character who, in another, older time, might have been referred to as a hipster.

Ike passes them by like they were phone poles or parking meters. They're all in mid-spiel about something, speaking in a throaty whisper, preaching a gospel of detached weirdness, a speedy-Zen commentary on the constant irony of this world. And as he passes, Ike wonders if he listened, would he hear a continuous story, a coherent patter carried from beacon to beacon, one mouth picking up the tale as the last one leaves off? Maybe they're all part of some modern guild, a vocation filled with mentors and apprentices, fathers and sons, passing down, intact, the difficult art of hyperesoteric mumbling, idiosyncratic, stoned to the gills, living Burma Shave billboards, one-man Greek choruses, clad in last year's suit and working in the new medium of insinuation and gesture.

They come in both sexes. They perpetually leer, like they've just heard a joke that Ike wouldn't understand. Their hands move like first-base coaches, touching themselves on the arm, neck, behind, groin, forehead, mouth, lighting for barely a second and moving onto another body part. Their heads twitch in a countermeasure to the movement of their eyes. They all seem to have studied ventriloquism at one time in the foggy past. Their mouths don't seem to move in relation to the volume of words that erupt into the air around their shoulders. They give Ike the creeps and he hurries down the street, eyes focused on the pavement, head hunched in toward his shoulders.

Between the growing cold and the Zone hipsters, he feels a need to get off the street for a while. Ahead, he sees a green and orange neon sign suspended out over the sidewalk. It reads 'Bella C's.' He does a quick shuffle toward the place, tries to look in the window, but it's obscured by a handmade poster taped to the glass that shows a crude picture of a sailboat and what Ike guesses, from the stick-figure palm tree, is a desert island. Underneath the drawing are the words:

Bella C Presents
Tonight Only
'Shake-It-Up in the Zone'
A Jolly Rotten Players Production of
The Big Storm Story
tix inside/3 drnk min.

Before he can think, Ike pulls open the door and steps into the dark.

He stands in the doorway while his eyes begin to adjust. The bar has a big, open feeling to it, like there's more to it than can be seen, a back section for banquets and private functions that runs on forever. The immediate barroom has a gutted feeling, like partitioning walls were once knocked down to make some more space for swelling crowds.

But there are no crowds here tonight. The room is empty except for a large old woman behind the bar, a thin cigar wedged just barely into her mouth. The curls of smoke obscure her face, but as Ike moves closer to take a stool, he can make out features. There's a huge pinkish boil bubbling out on the left side of her jaw. Her hair is pulled tight and high on her head and pinned into a severe bun. She looks slightly simian, large-eyed, long-jawed. Her ears wing out from her head and stray wisps of dyed-orangey red hair shoot out among them like they were failed efforts at trying to wire the ears back to the skull. She's dressed in what Ike's mother would have called a housecoat. Looking closer, he sees it's covered in this odd print of tiny tongues, something like the old Rolling Stones logo, but smaller, more common, less caricatured. Ike thinks her housecoat is one of those instances of someone reaching too far for a joke. The comic's version of the law of diminishing returns.

The woman is intent on the crossword puzzle from today's *Spy*. She hunches over the paper, removes the cigar from her mouth, inserts a stubby pencil, sideways like a horse's bite. She's kneading her forehead with her fingers as if the action will cause synonyms to form in her brain.

'I'll have a beer,' Ike says, and his voice comes out too high.

The woman ignores him.

He waits a full minute and says, 'Ma'am, a beer, please.'

She sighs, takes the pencil from her mouth, and says, 'I can't hear you,' in a standard, singsong, child's tone.

Ike looks around the bar and back at the door. 'Are you closed?' he asks. 'The door was open and the sign was on, so I came in. Is that the story? You closed?'

'Can't hear a word,' she says in the same maddening lilt.

'You're asking me to leave,' Ike says. 'You want me to go?'

'Levi's,' she barks, the word sputtering out of her mouth. 'L-E-V-I-S. Type of blue jean. Levi's. That right? You'd say so?'

'Does it fit?' Ike asks.

She gives him a spastic little nod. Her mouth falls open and he sees what few teeth she has are caramel brown. She writes in the word, places the pencil behind an ear, and slides the paper under the bar. Then she grabs a mug from a back shelf and pulls Ike a beer.

'Can't talk when I'm doing the puzzle,' she says. 'Everyone knows they have to wait until I finish the puzzle.'

'Sounds fair,' Ike says, taking the mug and digging into his pocket for some bills. He lays them on the bar to indicate that she can run a tab, that he'll be here a while, but she snaps up one of the bills and rings it into the ancient cash register at the end of the bar.

'I'm Bella,' she calls down to him. 'The original.'

'Hello, Bella,' Ike says, trying for his friendliest voice. 'I'm Ike.'

'I've never seen you in here before, Ike. I don't know many of the names, but something about most of the regulars sticks out. A shaved head or half a shaved head. Or a tattoo. Everybody's got a tattoo today, you ever notice that? They've made a real comeback. My husband had tattoos. He was a sailor. Most sailors get a tattoo, you know. That's the business we should have gone into. Everyone wants to be marked up today.'

'I'm not a regular,' Ike says. 'I'm not from this part of town. I'm just out walking.'

'Nobody walks anymore. There's the difference. Everybody wants to get marked up, and nobody wants to walk anymore. They all sit and look at the tattoos.'

'I guess,' Ike says, and starts in on the beer. He's starting to like the place. As weird as Bella is, he feels something maternal off her. Her place is starting to relax him. He wishes he had brought a mystery book and could settle in for a while.

'You come down here for the show?' Bella asks, walking back toward him as she mops the bartop with a rag. 'It's four bucks. And that's on top of the three-drink minimum.'

'Yeah,' Ike says, 'I saw the poster in the window. What's the story on that?'

'The story,' Bella says, leaning in over the bar, pressing her chest down on her arms, lowering her voice conspiratorially, 'is two bucks for Bella. Before we agreed, one of the little bastards says, "But you get to see the play for free." I almost spit in the little shit's eye. Now they don't let him do any of the talking. And they pay Bella her fifty percent gross.'

'This would be the theater company. The Jolly Rotten Players.'

'Is that an idiot name or what?'

'It's got a ring. It's got something.'

'A ring. Sheesh. I know what you expect. You expect me to be an understanding little old bitch under the skin, right? You expect me to say, "You know, Ike, under all the green hair and skull tattoos and leather and chains and drugs and sneering, they're really good kids, just kids after all."' She throws a hand out from her side like she was swatting away some invisible insect. 'Well, that's not Bella and that's not them. They're exactly the little shits they seem to be.'

Ike shrugs. 'So why let them use your place?'

'Bella's was here a long time before these little bastards were even born. You're from the city, then you know business down here had some rough years. We were hand-to-mouth now and again. Then Archie has the heart attack and I'm all alone. I had license problems. I had break-ins. You're too young to remember the riots down here.'

'I remember hearing—'

'Hearing's nothing. This place was a goddamn war zone. Now it belongs to the artists, and all the trash has supposedly moved over to Bangkok Park.'

'Supposedly?'

'These wise guys with the earrings in the nose, in the cheek. Enormous pain in the ass, my friend. You'll never know.'

'But they help you pay the rent.'

'Bingo. We play out this little lie. I pretend that they're like my black sheep, my kids who went to Europe and came back all wrong, okay? They pretend like I'm the stone age mommy, all out of it, but a good heart and genuinely lovable. It's all shit. We're both… what's the word? It was in Sunday's puzzle. Like a heartworm… something inside of you—'

'Parasite,' Ike says.

Bella slaps the bar. 'There you go. Parasite. Eight letters. Fits perfect. They get a cheap place to do their plays, read their books. I take what I can off of them. I never ask where they get the money. They manage.'

'You both get what you need.'

'Well, that's about the best you're going to do.'

'Amen. How about a shooter to go with the beer?'

'How about the four bucks for the performance?'

Ike pulls all the money he has out of his pocket, finds a twenty, and lays it on the bar.

Bella doles out a shot of the house bourbon and says, 'Show should begin anytime now. Hope those aren't your good clothes.'

Ike looks down at his legs hugging the legs of the barstool and then back up at Bella.

'The special effects. You could get soaked if they start to cut up. I was nuts with the bastards at dress rehearsal, but then I realized the floor's cleaner than it's been in years.'

Ike picks up the shooter and asks, 'Where's the rest of the audience?'

'Looks like it's just you and me tonight, darling. But you'll love it. Well worth the price. It's a classic. Or so they tell me. I don't remember ever seeing it and I was crazy for the movies when I was young. Raul, he's the leader, the head guy, he says,

"It's restructured, Bella, reinvented." Reinvented. Like it was a machine. Jesus. These kids could talk the ear off a goddamn dead dog. So much horseshit.'

Ike fires the shooter, and a bell, like an old school recess bell, starts to ring from some back room.

'That's it,' Bella says, and starts to shuffle out from behind the bar. She moves to the front door and locks it, then yanks the heavy, dark green pull shades down to the windowsills.

Ike rotates on the stool to follow her.

'What's all that for?' he asks.

'Part of our agreement,' she says. 'Once the bell rings, that's it. No one else gets in. They say you got to be here from the start.'

She gets back behind the bar and her head starts to nod and she says, 'Oh, and I'm supposed to pass this,' and she pulls out an old black felt top hat from under the bar and slides it down to Ike. There's an index card secured in the hatband that reads: 'Fund for the Preservation of Dangerous Art.'

He throws a dollar in, slides the hat back to Bella, and asks, 'What's so dangerous?'

She ignores him and sinks down into a small, rickety, wooden rocker wedged in behind the bar. The yellowish lights from the room's chandelier begin to flash on and off. Garbled noise starts to sound from the same direction as the recess bell. It's a few seconds before Ike can determine that the noise is supposed to be wind and thunder. It sounds like it's being played off his mini-Panasonic. Then, sounding slightly closer, he hears two male voices yelling over the storm.

1ST VOICE: Son of a bitch, we're going down!

2ND VOICE: Bogus shit, dude, death city!

1ST VOICE: Where's the big Kahuna?

2ND VOICE: In a crouch, man. Behind you. And it's the waves that's the big Kahuna in a storm like this.

1ST VOICE: Bad shit, man, we'll never surf again.

KAHUNA: I heard that, you little weasel. We pull through, I hope you get herpes.

The owners of the three voices start to appear from the double doorway at the back of the room. They're three young men, maybe around twenty years old. They're all dressed in those longish California swim trunks, 'baggies' Ike guesses they're called, all hot pinks and lime greens and Day-Glo tangerine. Though he can't see too well from this distance, they seem to have perfect golden tans and Nautilus-pumped bodies straight out of a muscle-magazine ad. And all three are posed, arms out at their sides, shoulders hunched forward slightly, bodies crouched a bit, knees bent, one leg pivoted forward, the other set at a ninety-degree angle. They're standing on surfboards. They're pretending to surf.

The wind and thunder noise suddenly gets much louder and the chandelier increases its flashing.

KAHUNA: Hold on, buds, it's the big one!

Stagehands dressed in black spandex burst through the door carrying red metal buckets with the word *FIRE* printed on them. They douse the surfers with water, then one lone stagehand bolts from the pack, runs straight toward Ike, and heaves his pail. It's a perfect hit. The water is freezing and Ike jumps up off his stool and screams, 'Jesus.'

He wipes his eyes clear to see Bella waving him to be quiet. She throws him a bar rag and indicates that he should sit back down. And he does, mopping his head with the musty-smelling towel.

The action in the depths of the bar continues as the trio of imperiled surfers are replaced by two new beachpeople. One, an older surfer, middle-aged even, his lean body given over to flab and slicked-back blond hair gone gray and white. A hefty beer gut hangs down low over his baggies. He's got those plastic sandals on his feet, the ones that hook between your big and next-to-big toe.

With the old surfer is a young blonde, sixteen, seventeen years old, high school age. She's dressed in an unbelievably skimpy pink bikini and she tosses her mane of hair around like it was a tangle of whips. Something about the scene is familiar to Ike and it starts to nag him before the actors even open their mouths.

> GIRL: God, Daddy, can't you do something about the rain?
> HER FATHER: Miranda, baby, chill out.

When he hears the girl's name, the whole thing becomes clear. He's about to witness some reinvented Shakespeare. It's *The Tempest*. He read it in high school. He saw most of it on PBS a few years back. The big storm. The fairy. The ugly witch's son. The dispossessed duke. The bored young daughter. It's *The Tempest* done as a Frankie Avalon–Annette Funicello beach party movie. *Gidget Goes to Stratford-upon-Avon*. Ike knows they think this is wildly original. He wonders if they've ever heard of Natalie Wood. He's sitting in front of a surfer version of *The Tempest*. And the door to the place is locked.

He gives a soft knock on the bartop and Bella's eyes open. He holds up another twenty and points to the bottle of bourbon on the bottom shelf. Bella rolls her eyes, then nods her head, and Ike hoists himself halfway over the bar and grabs the bottle. He pours himself another shooter and settles back down on the stool to watch.

The play is jumpy, more like a series of old-fashioned blackout skits than a continuous story. The dialogue is all slang, white-leisure-class-teentalk and surfer colloquialisms, monosyllabic, perpetually sarcastic, tinged with a weird falsetto drawl. And by the first act it's almost unbearable. Each time Miranda gasps 'Daddy!' in the exasperated, breathless, eye-bulging whine, Ike belts back a drink. He's starting to feel plastered by the end of the second scene.

And because of this he starts to think that maybe he's missing something, that possibly, as the play progresses, the actors get more chancy, start to go beyond simply translating Shakespeare's English into West Coast beachyak. The pace of the production starts to seem unraveled to him. The action starts to somehow seem more serious and less farcical. And all of these changes seem to be revolving around the entrance of the actor playing Caliban.

Ike tries to pay more attention, but he feels he must be more drunk than he realizes. The dialogue starts to lose its logic, speed up a little, get louder. More than once, the actors stop in midsentence and stare at one another. Ike glances over to see Bella up out of her rocker and leaning on the bar, eyes squinted, giving full attention to the action. Ariel, the spirit, played fully naked by a well-developed adolescent girl, can be seen whispering something into Prospero's ear.

The actor playing Caliban is a real muscleboy, probably about six four with a chest span twice the size of Ike's. He's dressed in a tattered loincloth and he's got a blond head of long Sampson-curls that put Miranda's locks to shame. His body is covered with white powder and he moves in a strange skittish but agile manner, sort of leaping about the stage with the hyper-surety of a chimpanzee and the risky grace of a veteran dancer. Ike can see his Adam's apple doing a weird, overly rapid throb in the center of his neck. He's playing off Prospero, and to Ike, the older actor seems clearly uncomfortable.

CALIBAN: You unrighteous fuck, I hope you get windburn like no amount of cocoa butter will help.

PROSPERO: You're like the most strung-out meat I've ever tuned, dude. You should watch the tongue. I know some cheap change'd give you crabs that never leave.

CALIBAN: This was *my* beach, man. You cruise, hang a bad left on the pipe one Saturday and bang, you cruise in on *my* grains with the bimbette. I'm Mr. Right for the first go-around, def, 'Hey, Callie, join the clambake, babe, hey, Callie, you're the main guy.' But it's all lie-city, man. I'm no Mr. Bonus, *nooo*, sir. You were a righteous fuck to Callie, teach me how to roll with the big curls, the right wax to lay on my board, okay? But now it's just Callie-the-lifeguard, eyes on the water, don't move your ass, and holler when the high tide breaks. I wish you'd drown in the barrel next time out, you shit!

PROSPERO [*angry, but fearful*]: You dog! You mother! Me, who taught you the Prospero-roll, who taught you one-foot balance, who taught you surfer tongue—

CALIBAN [*outraged, screams*]: You taught me the language, and the big score is that I know how to curse! The red plague eat your heart for teaching me the language!

Prospero's mouth drops open to speak, but Caliban suddenly takes a swing and lands a full fist to his gut. Ike can see the big actor lose his wind and sink to his knees. There's a shocked look on his face. Ariel lets out a yell. Miranda appears on the scene, looks down on Daddy, and grabs hold of Caliban's steroid-expanded arm. He flails her away, letting out a bizarre barking noise, then grabs her around the throat and heaves her down on the floor next to Prospero.

'Jesus Christ,' Bella says, 'this ain't in the script.'

Surfers start to flood the stage area. Caliban starts into a yelling, spastic unrecognizable speech, while throwing fellow actors into walls and smashing random props and then regular bar chairs and tables. Ike sits frozen for a second. He hears Caliban yell words that sound familiar but have no meaning to him. Then the words end completely and there's just an awful, high-pitched buzzing sound, as if a hive of crazed wasps were living in his mouth and throat.

Then the blood starts to flow. Caliban is taking full power swings at everyone, catching jaws and noses, cracking bone and tearing open flesh. He grabs Ariel and lifts her bodily into the air over his head, then pitches her against a wall. The sound of her impact stops everything, but for just a half a second, and then Caliban is on top of Prospero, pounding on his head, stomping on his kidneys.

'Do something,' Bella's screaming, and it takes Ike a moment to know she means him. She wants him to act. To help. To subdue this insane son of a bitch in a loincloth.

Ike slides off the stool and watches as Caliban does a replay of the Ariel-heave with Prospero's limp body. Then he notices Ike in the distance and his head begins to jerk and make horrible violent twitching motions. His eyes go into spasms of blinking and bulging and the whole time his mouth is moving too fast to really see, lips opening and closing in an awful, stomach-turning blur.

He starts to walk toward Ike in a jumpy stutter step. Ike begins to tremble, grabs the seat of his barstool, and pulls it up in front of him like some ill-prepared circus act. He thrusts out into the air several times and Caliban makes swatting motions with his hands, still too far away to grab a leg.

Ike tries to hold the stool steady. He yells, 'I'll smash it over your fucking head, asshole. Don't do it.'

Caliban takes one more hopscotch step forward. Ike wheels, smashes the stool through the glass of the locked front door, and throws himself outside, tearing open his cheek and hand on shards that remained lodged in the frame. He falls onto the sidewalk and rolls, gets to his knees, then feet, and without looking starts a wild, panicked, screaming run away from Bella C's.

After several blocks, he looks back over his shoulder, but there's no sign of Caliban. He turns down an alleyway, jogs to the far side of a trash dumpster, falls to the ground, hidden from view of the street. He starts to suck on his bleeding hand, gags, falls sideways, and vomits. He begins to have spasms, his stomach emptying over and over until all that's left to throw up is acidic bile that burns all the way up to his mouth.

When the dry heaves finally begin to fade, he leans his back against the brick wall behind him and tries to reduce all his thoughts to a simple, logical plan of action, of movement. He needs to get home. He needs to get to Lenore. He needs to tell Lenore everything that's happened. The box of mutilated fish. The Bach Room. The box of severed fingers. Caliban's fit. Lenore will know what it all means. And what to do.

He reaches into his pockets but they're empty. All of his money is on the bartop at Bella's. He doesn't even have a dime for a phone. So he'll have to walk back out of the Canal Zone. He doesn't want to move. He'd rather stay right here in the alley, like some kid who's wandered off in a shopping mall, like some camper who went too far into the woods. Stay in one place and let the rescuers come to you, isn't that the rule of thumb, the key to safety?

But, technically, he's not lost. He knows his way back home. He's an adult who's lived in this city all his life. If he can just get started, he'll be home in an hour. If he can just make the first move, pull himself up off the ground and walk out to the main street.

He stays seated. He begins to have muscle spasms in his arms and legs, annoying cramps of tightened muscle that start off as a ticklish throb, but once he's conscious of them, increase to an awful, painful knot. He tries to massage the backs of his calves, tries to make his body calm down and let the muscles unclench. He runs his hands up his opposite arms from elbow to shoulder. The knots reduce back to the quivering, ticklish mode, but then lock there.

So he gets up and tries to walk the feeling off. He moves slowly to the end of the alley, pokes his head out, and looks from side to side, then steps onto the sidewalk and turns left toward the west side. He starts walking near the edge of the sidewalk, using the wall of parked cars, half of them burned-out hulks, as a shield. Each time a car comes down the street, he fixes his eyes on the pavement and quickens his step.

There's an amalgam of dissonant background noise that perpetually changes. Mainly, it's made up of music from the dozens of hole-in-the-wall clubs in the Zone. Weepy, overamplified guitar fades to neo-bebop alto sax, which is overtaken by slightly out-of-tune chamber music which mutates into a postmodern, electronic orchestra of unnatural, machinish sounds. It's never clear exactly where any of the sounds are coming from. It always seems like it's just one more block ahead, but by the time Ike reaches this position, the next noise has taken over and beckons from farther up the street.

And there are images to go with the sounds, glimpses of movement and light framed within the obsolete largeness of the tenement windows on the opposite side of the street. The windows belong to the second-floor apartments above the street-level storefronts and most of them are without shades or curtains. He can see picture after picture of people in the midst of an assortment of common activities – dancing, smoking, embracing, pacing, eating. Everyone he spots seems to be dressed in black, as if the entire neighborhood had agreed to mourn some terrible loss.

Ike thinks the windows are a lot like the succession of comic strip frames in the newspaper. Only this is a long strip that makes little or no sense. And that's probably totally appropriate for the Zone. A living comic strip of the absurd. Live-action Nancy and Sluggo in the grip of post-punk existential boredom. Someone else, maybe even Lenore, might get a real kick out of the window-pictures. Ike just wants to get back home. He wants to find the most direct route back to the green duplex and lock himself inside. He wants to pull some 1930s mystery off the shelf and lose himself in the logic of its investigation. Or even better, he wants to be inside Lenore's apartment. To eat waffles in her kitchen – he'll do the cooking – while she checks the bolts on the doors and stands a confident watch with her Magnum.

He'll tell it all to Lenore as soon as he gets home. He'll run down the whole sequence of events and ask her what it might mean. He'll leave the next step up to her, trust in her experience and general wisdom. It occurs to him now that what he's casually taken to be faults in Lenore's character – aggressiveness, suspiciousness, and, at times, full-blown paranoia – are really probably talents, tools for survival, the very attributes that could ensure longevity and, maybe, peace of mind.

On his right he passes an old Catholic church made of sandstone and stained glass. It's long been abandoned by its parishioners, desanctified and sold by the diocese a good decade ago. Ike was inside once for some forgotten relative's baptism. He was only a kid, eight or nine years old, and all he can remember is the infant's screaming at the water and balm.

Now the place is a nightclub of some sort. It's retained part of its original name – St. Anthony's – but the new owners have added, in orange neon under the original sign, 'Temptation.' There's a bouncer standing before the heavy wooden double doors, a big black guy in leather pants and wristbands, but wearing a priest's shirt and white collar. It must be the uniform, Ike guesses. He wonders how the waitresses dress. The bouncer stares down at him as he passes, the whole time running a finger around the white collar like it was choking him. His tongue comes out of his mouth and stretches up toward his nose, then dips back inside and does a run around his gums, making the mouth and cheeks balloon out. A clicking noise starts to come from him and Ike turns his walk into a jog and hurries past the church club.

He runs a right onto Verlin Ave and slows back to a fast walk. In a doorway across the street, he spots a man and a woman, obviously deaf, speaking with their hands. They're lit by a yellow bulb in a wire-mesh cage mounted above the building's entrance. Ike makes himself watch as, simultaneously, their hands speed up, practically convulse, fingers flying, opening and closing and making forms too fast to be perceived. They're jabbing their hands so close to one another's faces, it seems someone will lose an eye. Ike begins to run again.

Within a block he comes upon two women, both dressed in white leotards, dancers he's sure, brawling in the middle of the street, rolling over and over, clawing and choking each other, slapping wildly, biting, butting heads. Their bodies are covered with dirt and oil from the street. And the sound of an insect swarm seems to engulf them.

He reverses direction, cuts through an alleyway, emerges onto Congo to see two teenage boys facing off on a second-story fire escape. They're stripped to the waist and sweat on their chests actually glimmers in the glow of the streetlight. They're both holding baseball bats, waving them in narrowing circles directly above their heads, mouths open, hollow, taut – the wasp sound gushing forth, echoing off the walls of the brick five-family tenement opposite them.

Ike's in a panic now. He starts to run through backyards, across driveways and parking lots, turning every time he comes to a corner. He sees a pack of dogs, shepherds, leaping up and over cars parked in a club's lot. They let out a sickening, altered howl, lower and louder than is natural, staticky, painful-sounding, like their bodies were forcing out a noise that would eventually rupture their throats.

Everywhere Ike looks he sees people in a state of noncontrol. Every window he views in the distance shows someone's head and body in a jerking, spastic dance. And everywhere, hovering above him, is the noise. The buzzing. The clicking. The air is choked with it.

Finally, he crosses the border out of the Canal Zone, and after a time, he begins to notice the noise has stopped. On the way back home, the streets are fairly empty. There's an occasional person out walking a pet, but they act normal enough, silent but for clearing throats or sniffling noses.

He's still managing a wheezy jog when he comes to the green duplex. The Barracuda is parked out front and he wants to run to it, fall on his knees, and kiss the hood. There are no lights on in Lenore's apartment. He'll have to wake her. She'll yell at first, but he'll make her understand in no time. He'll be as rational and controlled as possible, simply present her with the facts and request assistance. Instruction. Protection.

He digs a key chain out of his back pocket as he comes up the walkway. His lungs are seizing up in his chest, and he feels a knifing pain with each throb. He climbs the stairs and fumbles with the keys in the darkness. There are only two on the ring, his and Lenore's. He lets himself into her apartment, slides his feet along the carpet, maneuvers through the living room without banging into any furniture. He moves down the hall toward the bedroom. As he walks, he debates whether to start calling out his presence, alerting her that it's only her brother, that there's no danger, no need to go for the gun.

But he keeps quiet. He'll wake her with a gentle touch to the shoulder, his voice low and calm. It's safer that way.

The door to the bedroom is slightly ajar. There are shadows from the moonlight outside, making their way into the hall, forming lines and patches of darkness on the walls. He pauses, takes a breath, pushes the door open, and stops dead. There are two forms in Lenore's bed. She's with someone. There's someone in bed with Lenore. A man is in bed with Lenore. And she's sitting on top of him. He's on his back, his knees are raised slightly, and she's straddling him. And they're rocking together. Up toward the headboard and back again. She's naked. Her back is arched and her breasts jut out from her body, angled toward the ceiling, perfectly visible in the blue light of the moon. She's making a low moaning sound. He's in her, Ike knows. Whoever he is, he's inside her. Inside Lenore.

He begins moving backward. Retracing his steps toward the living room. He stops in the doorway, looks at a lamp, and thinks about picking it up, charging back into the bedroom, smashing the lamp's base into the man's skull. He could say he thought she was in danger. He was trying to protect her.

But he gives up the idea without making a move, pulls her door closed and locked, and lets himself into his own apartment. He sets all the locks on his front door, then begins to move furniture in front of it that he can lift without any noise. He moves into the kitchen and performs the same procedure on the back door.

Then he goes into his bedroom and sits on the edge of his bed. His hands tremble. There's a heavy sweat covering his body, but he can't bring himself to wash up. He falls backward onto the bed, but the position is unbearable. He gets onto the floor, stretches out prone, then rolls underneath the bed. Small clouds of matted dust and lint congregate around his head. He pulls his eyelids together, forced as tight as he can, tiny muscles exerted to their limit. He prays for an instant sleep.

27

When Ike pushes aside the furniture and opens the door the next morning, a gust of burnt-toast smoke hits Lenore in the face.

'For God sake,' she says, waving a hand in front of her eyes, 'do you have to charcoal the goddamn bread?'

Ike doesn't say a word. He pulls open the door and steps back to let her in. She comes inside waving her arms, squinting, coughing. She says, 'Let's get some air in here, c'mon.'

He moves back into the kitchen as she cranks open the living room windows. Ike puts two more slices of bread into the toaster and leaves the setting on darkest. Lenore comes in, pours herself a coffee, and takes a seat at the kitchen table. Ike can't decide whether to push the bread down or not. He stares at the toaster for a few seconds, then moves to the refrigerator, pulls open the door, and begins to stare inside.

'Why don't you sit down over here, Ike?' Lenore says.

He turns to look at her. Something in her voice, low and calm, makes him follow her instructions. He takes the seat next to her. She's dressed for work, black jeans, a white cotton shirt, suede jacket, and a print silk scarf tied around her neck, bandanna style. *She looks tremendous*, he thinks.

'We a little out of it this morning?' she says, and it's not really a question. Her voice holds the tone of a benign grade-school teacher asking a shy student if he's forgotten his lunch. Ike doesn't respond.

'We a little out of sorts?'

He shrugs.

There's an awkward quiet as she takes a sip of coffee from her mug. She slouches down in her seat, then tips it backward slightly, balancing in that way that Mom used to hate. She looks younger to him suddenly, still a teenager ready to run endless laps on the school track.

She takes the mug from her lips but continues to hold it up near her mouth. A smile comes over her face then fades. She says, 'Were you in my apartment last night, Ike?'

The swallow he was in the midst of making catches in his throat. He pulls his lips tightly together, but they quiver, so he opens them and lets out a forced sigh. And then, not really knowing what's going to come out, he mutters, 'You look so beautiful.'

Lenore doesn't move for a second. Then her eyes narrow and her head falls a little to the side.

'I look beautiful,' she repeats in the same tone as her brother.

Ike nods.

'I look beautiful,' Lenore says again, now rising upright in the chair.

Ike continues to nod.

Lenore takes a breath and yells, 'I look like shit, you stupid bastard. I look like hell. Look at me, for Christ sake. I haven't slept in six goddamn months. My eyes are coming out of my head. I'm losing weight like there's no tomorrow. "You look beautiful." You son of a bitch.'

Ike is startled into breathing heavy. He gets up and walks back to the toaster and says, 'To me.'

'And when did your goddamn brain die?' Lenore yells, jerking out of her chair and moving over to the counter.

Ike turns to her, bites on his lip, then asks quietly, 'Who is he?'

'So you *were* in my apartment?'

'It wasn't Zarelli, was it?'

'You like that? You get a kick out of spying on me?'

'Have you known him a long time?'

'You little pervert,' she screams.

He tries to stop it, but it comes out. 'You little slut.'

She flies across the small space between them and slaps him, open-palmed but with enough power and surprise to knock him backward to the table. He bumps a chair, tries to gain his balance, and falls to the floor on one knee. She reacts immediately, running over to him, tries to put her arms around him and help him up, starting to cry, 'I'm sorry, Ike, I'm sorry. I didn't mean it.'

He struggles away from her, holds her at a distance with an outstretched arm. She sees the tears coming down his face, his nose starting to run. 'Leave me alone,' he tries to choke out.

They're both crying now, sobbing like kids still half in a nightmare, breath-halting sobs.

He keeps stammering, 'Stay away,' and pushing off her. She keeps trying to hold him, to latch onto his chest like a drunken, messy madonna, repeating, 'No, Ike, I didn't mean it.'

Finally, he jerks free and stumbles to the bathroom. She hears the door lock and then running water. She can't stop crying. *This is pathetic,* she tells herself. *Control this, get a grip here, pull it together.* But her breath is irregular and her head is pounding and the tears continue to roll out of her swollen eyes like there was an endless supply.

She moves back to her chair, sits down, then hunches, shivers, tries to yell over the crying, 'Please, Ike, I want to talk to you. Can't we talk anymore?'

He doesn't answer and she lowers her voice but continues to say the words. 'I just want to talk to you. Can't we just speak with each other?'

Speak with each other.

She tries to shake off the shiver, comes up a little in the chair. The only sound from the bathroom is water pouring into the sink.

She leans back in the chair and pushes a hand into her jeans pocket, the same jeans she's worn for three days now. The same jeans she was wearing when she watched the girl, Vicky, pitch from the phone pole.

She pulls the Lingo from her pocket and stares at it in her palm. A red Q, dusted with a little lint, some of its rubbery skin rubbed away, but still intact. She lays it on the table in front of her and pokes it once, lightly, with her index finger. Then she reaches across the table for Ike's butter knife. She doesn't bother to wipe the knife clean. She lays its blade down on the Q and starts to press. It separates, though she loses a lot of it to powder along the edges.

She lifts one half on the blade, brings it over her coffee mug, and tilts it in. Then she lifts the second half, leans across the table to Ike's mug, submerges the whole knife blade, and stirs.

She withdraws the knife, brings it to her mouth, and runs it between her lips, wiping off excess Lingo and coffee. She lays it back down on the table, lifts her mug up, and takes a deep swallow. There's no perceptible taste.

The sound of the running water stops. The bathroom door unlocks and Ike steps into the hall, wiping his face with a towel. Lenore turns her head as far as it will go to look at him. He brings the towel down from his face and stares back at her, hesitates, then moves slowly back into the kitchen and takes his seat at the table. He rolls the towel and drapes it around his neck like he's just finished a workout.

Lenore lets a few seconds go by. They continue to look at each other in silence. The look on Ike's face tells her nothing. When he opens his mouth, he might fill the room with screams or apologies, rational talk or more crying.

'We're both pretty over the edge here,' Lenore says as slowly and softly as she can and still manage to sound normal. 'Let's just take a second here, okay? Just take a minute and cool down. Both of us. We'll figure out what's going on around here. This isn't like us, Ike. You know that. Let's just slow down and drink a little coffee here and talk like two people who care about each other, all right?'

Ike nods slowly, rubs a hand over his forehead, then nods again and lifts his mug to his lips. He takes a sip of coffee, puts the mug down, and says, 'I don't know what's going on, Lenore. I don't know what's happening anymore.'

Lenore starts to blink her eyes. The kitchen seems to be getting brighter. 'Just tell me what's happened,' she says.

Ike takes another sip. 'The things that have happened at work the past couple of days,' he says. 'I don't know where to start.'

Just the thought of the packages destined for box nine is enough to rattle him. He can picture the pile of oozing, stubby fingers and his heart starts to pump faster.

Lenore takes breath in suddenly and harshly through her nose. Her mouth starts to feel cottony. 'Was there trouble at work?' she asks.

Ike nods rapidly. He begins to feel a dull throb at his left temple. 'These things started going wrong,' he says. 'I was sorting and there were these packages, two packages, and they were sort of damp, sort of wet underneath...'

His voice starts to crack and go high and he can't bring it back to its normal level.

Lenore feels her pulse starting to race a little, but it's different from a kick of crank, unlike the boost from speed. 'There were packages,' she says. 'Something was wrong with them.'

'Lenore,' Ike says, 'I'm not feeling so well—'

'Just concentrate,' she snaps. 'All you've got to do is talk to me here, Ike. Just keep going. You're at work. You open these boxes. Go on, now. Talk to me.'

Ike gets up from his chair and starts to pace the kitchen. His voice makes him sound like some disturbed adolescent playing with nitrous oxide.

'I used the X-acto knife,' he says. 'I cut them open.'

'You cut open the packages?'

He's shaking his head in a frenzy. He says, 'Yeah, yeah, yeah, I cut them open. I opened the boxes.'

Lenore gets up from her chair and starts to walk next to him, like they're a vaudeville team ready to break into 'Me and My Shadow.'

'And you looked inside?' she squawks.

'I looked inside,' he stammers.

'And you saw…'

'I saw—'

'Yeah, you saw, what, what did you see?'

He reaches the sink and grabs the countertop with both hands and his body starts to shake. He wheels around and grabs her by the wrist, pulls her up against him. She sees his Adam's apple pumping nonstop, his lips quivering out of control. His words come out so fast and breathless, she's barely able to decipher them. 'I saw you and that man, you on top of that man, why did you, why did you do it, Lenore, why, how, why, you were on top, he was in your bed, your, why—'

She tries to pull her hands free and when she can't, the anger comes up like a geyser. She pulls back to make him resist, then shoots her fists forward into his stomach. He doubles over and breaks the hold immediately, sucking air but still trying to babble on about seeing Woo and her last night. He keeps repeating the word *why* until it's nonsensical, until it's just some awful, annoying sound, like nails down a blackboard or knuckles being cracked.

Without thinking, Lenore lets her body go into a series of too-practiced motions. She extends her leg across both of her brother's, then reaches around him, gets a grip on his belt and shirt, and trips him to the kitchen floor. He goes down with the force of a much heavier guy. His stomach takes the full impact of the fall, but his chin manages a good whack on linoleum. And it doesn't end there. She's on his back, a knee into the small of his back, a full armlock around his throat so that his head and shoulders are arched uncomfortably backward.

She interrogates him through gritted teeth, forgetting, as quickly as he did, about the events at the post office, the rental box and its contents.

'What were you doing in my apartment last night, asshole? Where do you come off breaking into my apartment? Spying on me. Spying, sneaking around, spying on me, watching Fred and me, spying, spying—'

She hears herself repeat the word and breaks off both the hold and the questions. She remains on his back for a second, trying to slow down her mind, trying to make sheer will revoke the Lingo. But her mouth continues to dry up and the words continue to come, nonstop, one after another. She doesn't let them out. She bites her lips together, closes and opens her eyes.

He shakes her off his back and rolls onto his side. She sees his mouth moving, but doesn't hear a thing. She wants to say, *I didn't mean it, I didn't mean it, I didn't...*

But instead, she reaches behind her back, grabs the doorknob, pulls the back door open, and runs around the house to the car. She cranks the engine and wheels into the street, turns on the radio, and ups the volume.

A talk-show host is ranting on, a diatribe about a recent spate of unrest at the Harrington Projects in Bangkok. She starts to drive and talk back to the radio, bringing short pockets of air to the lungs between words. She hears her speech begin to lose definition, become slightly garbled, not like the soft consonant-dropping of a deaf person, but almost the opposite, like she's enunciating too much, like she's become some Jerry Lewis imitation of a kamikaze pilot, all harsh, chopping sounds from overtaut mouth muscles, and all at a sickening speed.

The words start to pile up like a record-breaking freeway crash, the front of one adjective slamming into the rear of the next noun. And though her jaw and throat both already ache, she knows there won't be any stopping for some time.

ItwaslessthanhalfaQhowmuchdamagecoulditdoandforhow long...

28

Peirce unlocks her apartment door and steps inside, weaves a bit, puts a hand against a wall to steady herself. After a minute, she closes and locks the door behind her, shuffles out of her jacket and shoes, and moves into the bedroom. She leaves all the lights off and stands still at the foot of her bed, quiets her breathing, strains to hear any foreign sounds, any suggestion of noise.

And though she hears nothing, she takes her service revolver from her bag, moves to the closet, pulls back the hammer on her gun, and yanks open the closet door. She fans the line of her hanging clothes with the nose of the .38, then eases the hammer back down into its cradle, moves back to the bed, and feels the strain of suppressed weeping start to well behind her eyes.

She puts her revolver on the nightstand, takes the microrecorder from her bag, and throws the bag into the darkness in the corner of the room. Then she tosses the recorder onto her pillow and takes off all her clothes.

She steps up to the TV set, turns it on, and turns the volume all the way down. She sits back down on the edge of the bed, folds her arms across her chest, and wedges her hands up into her armpits, tries to concentrate on her breathing. She manages to hold back tears by staring at the image on the screen in front of her: a man and a woman, seated at an anchor desk, crisp sheets of paper held tautly in their hands, vague, pleasant looks on their faces, an occasional nod of the head. What can they possibly be talking about?

She thinks if she still had the revolver in her hands she'd put a bullet into the picture tube, fill the room with blue-white fireworks of spitting electric current. The thought gives her some control and she smiles at herself, leans forward and turns off the TV, pulls back the covers, climbs into the bed, picks up the tape recorder, and turns it on.

It's eleven-fifteen, Victor. Forty-five minutes to go. I'm glad the day's almost over. I'm in bed, Victor. Alone. pitch-dark. My lousy little apartment that you had the nerve to call quaint that one time. Remember that one time, Victor? Mr. Mayor? You remember that one lunch hour when I couldn't stand the desk in your office anymore? When I'd go back to work with my hair all smelling like Lemon Pledge? And you took the big chance of a lifetime and actually drove, in public, in my Honda, back to my place and you took so long making sure all the doors were locked and curtains pulled down that we ended up having about five minutes to jump on each other. You went back to City Hall happy, Victor. But I spent the rest of the day writing a report on some pathetic Bangkok bust, frustrated to hell, uncomfortable. Story of this whole thing with you and me. I just turned off the TV, thank God. I can't take it anymore – the eleven o'clock news. I can't stand it. These people sit behind this long desk and look into the camera and tell these horrible stories every night and then smile or nod or sort of shake their heads very slightly. Like their telling about this thing, this horror, has made sense out of it, has summed it up and put it in the past. And the thing is, I see everything up close. I'm a goddamn cop, for Christ sake. And so far I can take it in Bangkok. I can do the job. But I can't take it on TV anymore. You figure it out, Mr. Mayor. You're the brain here. You're the guy that makes the city work, right? And now something's bugging you, Victor? And you can't just come out and tell me what it is. You can't have me down to one of your little stale-donut lunches in your Lincoln Town Car, driving down the expressway, donut crumbs all over the lapels of your gray banker's suit, talking with your mouth full, telling Charlotte everything you know about your enemies on the City Council. Councilor Searle's tax problems. Councilor Adams's questionable relatives. And then we'd park in the rubble of old Gomper's train station and you'd always have to comment about how much room there was in the Town Car. Weren't you ever afraid of someone pulling into the station someday? Some prospective developer checking out the place? Or maybe that just added to the excitement for you. I would've rather been back here at my place. [*pause*] I've been doing a hell of a lot of thinking. Last week someone, Richmond maybe, although it seems too witty to come from Richmond, anyway, they said to me, 'You know what a detective's first priority is?' and I bit and said, 'What?' and they said, 'Pray for confessions,' and I laughed and then caught on that the joke wasn't over yet and they said, 'You know what a narcotics detective's first priority is?' and I bit again and they said, 'Pray for a mute suspect.' And I laughed, I put on the good laugh. That laugh you told me once you thought was exciting and to this day I take that to mean erotic, though I have my doubts. I think I'm a little drunk, Mayor Welby. What do you think Richmond's joke means? That everybody gets a little filthy when the money's that easy? Or does it mean something else? Something obvious I'm just not picking up on here? Richmond said you told him that joke. [*pause*] I couldn't stop and turn off my brain on the ride home from the Synaboost lab. Your little tape recorder job has done something to me that I've been fighting since day one as a narc. This little Panasonic cinched it. I'm full-blown paranoid now. And as much as I reject it, I can't help feeling that this is the most [*pause*] what's the word, appropriate, the most appropriate view of my life right now. Maybe from now on. I think maybe I'm paying the exact price, the perfect price, for hooking up with you, Victor. The funny thing is, I'm ready to fink on myself. At the beginning, right after that briefing with Lehmann and Dr. Woo there, you told me this would be the investigation within the investigation. But as an investigation this whole thing has been an absolute and total failure. I gathered information for you, Victor. I found out little scraps of information. We both think, thought, I thought, that that's all you have to do. There are just two steps – you go out and, with a trained eye, a logical eye, you pick up scraps, clues, links, anything pertinent, then you bring it all back home and piece it together in ways that fit and when you're done you step back and look and you've got the whole, big picture. But this Lingo thing hasn't worked that way, has it? Nothing really led to anything else. For me it just seems to be spreading out more instead of closing in, coming together. [*Pause*] Maybe it's just me. Maybe I'm burned out and I've lost any skill I had in this line of work. That's a real possibility. I'd almost rather that be true than think that… [*Long pause*] Victor. Victor, I've always thought that people read mysteries for a good and simple reason. Because they confirmed, good word, confirmed, they confirmed a way of looking at life. In general. A positive way. Even through all the pages of bloodshed and lies and betrayals and corruption, if you pay attention and follow the link and clues, you come up with the truth. [*Pause*] I am loaded, Victor. No doubt about it. Bed spins. I'm going to have to run for the john any second, I think. Driving home from the lab tonight, coming down the hill from the airport, this is all the stuff that was going through my head. I'm praying, I'd like to pray, that this feeling I have right now, aside from the bed spinning, this feeling that I need to look over my shoulder, won't last. And I'm scared to death that it will. That I'll feel this way from now on. That no one can be trusted. That nothing will make much sense. For me, the problem with this case was that there were too many possibilities and my brain couldn't seem to discard any. Instead, it kept adding more. On the drive home, down that endless airport hill, I kept thinking of other people. You got me started. I was thinking that any one of my brother detectives, sister detectives, you know, that they could be involved. That Lehmann, Mr. Closed Mouth, Mr. Arrogant, that he could be on both sides of the fence. The brilliant Dr. Woo could be behind the whole thing, murdering the Swanns, stealing the drug formula. I even thought it could be you, Victor. The mayor. The guy who knows everyone, controls everything. Why not Victor Welby? Could be Victor Welby. Or any combination of people. [*Pause*] I know it's only been a day, Victor, but what a goddamn day. I'm out of it. I'm off the investigation within the investigation. I'm done. I'm no good to you. I haven't found anything out. I need some sleep. Long day. I'm too tired to talk anymore. I'm

[*End of tape*]

29

It's dusk before she feels free of the drug's effects. She'd driven north, passing out of her native state and jumping on and off all the eerie New England highways that were cut through solid granite hills. The highways have smooth rock walls running on either side of them, rising up thirty feet high so that nothing can be seen but the road ahead. Over a period of time, they can cause a subtle claustrophobia. Lenore noted this as a secondary concern.

For lunch, she'd grabbed french fries from a drive-through burger chain visible from the road. By dinner, she felt safe enough to stop in at a small, lazy diner in a town she'd never heard of. She ordered soup and tea with milk, thinking this would soothe a nervous system so pushed beyond its liberal limits that a shutdown was not out of the question.

By seven, she's back in Quinsigamond. She drives by the green duplex, but finds it in darkness. At ten, she's still seated in the Barracuda, staring up at the back of the Hotel Penumbra, waiting until the top floor's lights go on. She thinks about writing some kind of note and securing it to the steering wheel. An apology to Ike, begging him to forget the past week, maybe the past year, stating flat out her inability to explain both last night and this morning.

She thinks about leaving several notes: instructions on what to do with any of her belongings that Ike doesn't want. A word of encouragement to Shaw and Peirce. Advice to Zarelli to accept his shortcomings and learn to find pleasure in his family again. And something for Fred. What could she say to Fred?

The possibilities make her too uncomfortable to continue, so she scraps the note idea entirely and climbs out of the car. The Magnum is in the trunk, but she's still got the .38 strapped near her ankle. She walks around the block to the front of the building and stops at the revolving door as a parade of Cortez's women file out for the evening. They're all dressed like it was Halloween and everyone chose the same costume.

Looking through the doors into the lobby, she sees Jimmy Wyatt trying to act stone-faced to the last of the women's comments. When he sees Lenore, his hand instinctively jumps to the inside of his biker jacket, but when she doesn't move, it stays there. They stare at each other for a while until she feels he's assured she's not an immediate threat, that this isn't some bizarre assault, then she pushes her way inside.

She gives Wyatt a small smile, tries to make it look like she's been unsuccessful at suppressing it. She holds her arms out and up slightly, like a bored version of halting for the police. But he's not biting. Nothing about her being inside the hotel is going to be playful. His eyes are narrowed on her. She looks away from him to the rest of the lobby. It's been restored beautifully. Everywhere there are Ionic columns shot through with veins of deep green marble. The lobby has a wonderful, slightly freezing feel to it. There's a small rise of three stairs beyond Wyatt that opens out into an empty rest area where people once checked in at the front desk and then waited for the elevators. Huge Persian rugs of dark reds and greens cover the marble floor that's been worn into shallow bowls in spots. Against the walls are couches and chairs, foreign-looking, experiments in furniture that went wrong. And hung above them are these out-of-place pastoral paintings hung in ornate thick gilt frames.

It's not like a real place, Lenore thinks. Then she turns her eyes back to Wyatt and says casually, 'I'm here to see the boss.'

His eyes narrow and she wonders if he's got a pad of paper tucked away somewhere to communicate.

'Could you tell him I'm here?' she says.

He shakes his head no.

They stare at each other. She hadn't counted on this.

'Okay,' she says, 'I don't want you to take this wrong, you know, I want to be clear here. You can't tell him, meaning you're physically incapable, which I'm aware of? Or you just won't tell him, as in you don't want to or you've got instructions not to or something like this?'

He waits until she's finished and simply shakes his head no again.

'Mr. Cortez would want to see me,' she says, lowering her voice. 'It would be in his best interest to see me.'

Now he just folds his arms across his chest.

'I don't want to tell you your job, but I think the thing to do here would be simply to check in upstairs. I'll wait right here. I won't budge.'

It's a standoff. He makes no movement at all. They just continue to look at each other.

'You're limiting my options,' she says. 'You understand that?'

He nods.

'So I'm only left with one avenue here.'

He raises his eyebrows slightly.

'I'm going to have to shoot you in the fucking head.'

He gives a big smile, but she sees his shoulders shift under his jacket and she knows it would be close as to who got to who first.

Then a voice from nowhere: 'That's enough, Jimmy. Show her the elevator.'

It's Cortez. And he's been watching and listening to the whole scene. She should have realized that. Cameras and microphones. Probably in every wall.

Wyatt pivots backward and extends a hand forward like the perfect bellman. She waves him off and says, 'I can find my way up, thanks.'

She moves past him up the three small stairs to the main lobby and turns left to find a wall of three old-time elevators with the traditional arrow pointers mounted above each door to indicate which level the car is at. The door is already opened on the middle elevator and she steps into the gilded cage and looks to press for the top floor, but there are no buttons. Then it dawns on her that this is the express car, the private car for use by Cortez only. Straight to the top, no stops.

The car bucks slightly, then starts to rise and Cortez's voice fills the air.

'What a delightful surprise.'

She feels uncomfortable not being able to project her words in a particular direction, but she doesn't want to make Cortez aware of this.

'In the neighborhood. You know how it is.'

'Actually, no. I don't get out too often.'

'Is that by choice?'

'Actually, that would be hard to say.'

'You've done wonders with this old building.'

'It was a crime. The way I found it. Left to decay.'

'Some things need constant attention. Continual upkeep, you know?'

There's no response. The elevator comes to a stop with a jerk and the doors slide open. She steps out into a small foyer. The doors immediately close behind her, but she doesn't hear the car move. She stands still for a minute and takes in the surroundings. It feels about ten or twenty degrees warmer than in the lobby, and yet it's not uncomfortable. The ceiling hangs a good twelve or more feet high. It's antique – scrolled tin plating covered with a glossy enamel. The walls are natural mahogany, divided every three or four feet into carved panels. The floor is a burnt-rust-colored tile covered by a large, oval, oriental rug. She stares down at the rug, it draws her attention. It's filled with an intricate pattern, a confusing weave that works like an Escher print – it shows a pattern of books that, when viewed from a different perspective, become fat-bodied geese in flight.

'Come, please.' Cortez's voice sounds from nowhere. 'Join me in the library.'

The foyer opens into a large hall. Midway down, there are two sets of double doors facing each other. She faces one set, reaches out, and tries to turn the gold lever-handles. They're locked. She turns around to face the second set and they open for her, revealing an enormous room.

'This way,' he says, and this time she can tell the sound of his voice is coming directly from his mouth, not a hidden speaker system. She enters the library. It's an enormous room, probably consists of more square footage than the entire green duplex, her place and Ike's combined. All four walls are made of built-in bookshelves, floor to ceiling. All of the shelves are empty and covered with dust.

The rest of the room is almost empty. The floor is covered by two gigantic braided rugs. There are no windows. There is one break in the shelving to allow for a small fireplace and mantel. The remains of a fire are smoldering on the andirons. There's a single, low-to-the-ground, overstuffed rocking chair, covered in a faded, soft-gray material. The chair sits facing and to the left of the fireplace. It looks a bit out of place in the room, like it came from a garage sale or had been passed down through several generations.

The only other piece of furniture is something big and bulky that's been covered by a plain white bed sheet. It's pushed up against a wall to the left of the rocker. Hung on the wall above the mantel is a large, iron-looking crucifix, a grotesque-style Christ figure, bent and broken, iron droplets and running lines of blood covering the body. Below the crucifix, resting on the mantel itself, are small wooden boxes standing upright to reveal their contents – a mishmash of pebbles, shells, watch faces, string, eggs, shards of a broken mirror, a doorknob. Lenore has an urge to walk over to them and study them more closely.

'My own feeble attempts,' Cortez says. 'An old hobby of mine.'

He's standing at the top of a wrought-iron platform that rises from a tiny spiral staircase mounted in the very center of the room. Lenore approaches the miniature stairway and looks up. There's an open skylight cut into the ceiling of the building. Cortez is peering into a telescope that juts out of the skylight. He's being pathetically careless, Lenore thinks. *Could he actually trust me?*

'Come up, please,' he says. 'I want to show you something.'

She looks around the room, then climbs the seven stairs and joins him on the circular platform. He brings his head up from the telescope and stares, then, slowly, smiles at her. 'Which one of us can resist saying it?' he asks.

'Excuse me?' she says.

He tilts his head back slightly, puts a theatrical and self-mocking hand on his chest, and says, 'We meet at last.'

'Had to happen sooner or later,' she says.

Up close, he's a little more breathtaking than Lenore was prepared for. He's tall, probably about six five or so, with large eyes that contain blue and gray and green and dominate the face. He has the most ingratiating grin she's ever witnessed, with a small gap between his two front teeth that enhances rather than detracts from his attractiveness. He has a thick, woodsman beard that covers the whole second half of his face, black with random strands of gray starting to break through here and there. His hair is jet-black and a bit too long, she thinks, and he parts it to the left in a big sweeping arc. He speaks in a rich, almost echoing baritone, like a well-trained actor with a natural sense of timing. There's a strong hint of a Spanish accent, but also something beyond that, something clearly more foreign, distant, impossible to place.

'Just like in the movies,' he says.

'What happens when it rains?' she asks, pointing upward with her thumb.

'There is a cover,' he says, not raising his head from the

eyepiece. 'What the architect called a bubble. I've always liked that. "A bubble".'

She looks down at the telescope, and though she knows nothing about the equipment, she'd bet it was a state-of-the-art model, probably costing more than she makes in a year.

'So,' she says, 'is this for real? Is this some kind of prop or are you really into astronomy?'

He can't seem to get away from the self-mockery. 'I'm a man of many interests and many talents.'

'Don't be so hard on yourself. We've got to pump you up a little.'

'The problem is, the sky in Quinsigamond is so obscured by all the light. Cities are horrible places, don't you think?'

'I'm a hometown girl, you know. I've got a soft spot. I'm a city girl.'

'Where I come from, a town called Banfield, you could go into the fields at night and the sky would be infested with the stars. "Infested with the stars" – *plagado de las estrellas.*'

'Sounds like a disease.'

He sighs. 'I have an evil talent for making the beautiful sound horrid.'

She shrugs. 'That could come in useful. Dissuade people from things that you don't want them to go near.'

'There's no need for that. I've always been a man willing to share.'

Lenore doesn't know how to respond. She pauses and then says, 'That's a chapter in the myth that I'm unfamiliar with.'

He laughs, peers down into the eyepiece. 'That I'm a generous man? You've been misinformed. You can't always believe what you hear.'

'Or what you see. Or touch.'

'Or taste.'

He looks up from the telescope and they stare at each other in silence for a moment.

He clears his throat and says, 'By the time I was ten, I knew the surface of the moon better than most children know the village they live in. At twelve I could name most of the constellations. I once asked my mother if heaven was near Orion.'

'What did she say?' Lenore asks, genuinely wanting to know.

'I honestly don't remember. It was so long ago.'

'I would think that would be the type of thing you would remember.'

'Memory is a pathetic tool. It never works the way it should. It's rarely useful. It brings more pain than pleasure.'

'Memory has never brought you comfort?' she asks.

He lets a slow but huge smile grow on his face, then says, 'Not that I recall.'

She rolls her eyes and says, 'Bring out the big hook.'

'Do you want to take a look?' he asks, motioning to the telescope.

She nods, leans down over the eyepiece, and squints. At first she can't see a thing.

'It's not very clear,' he says. 'Too much cloud cover.'

She brings her head back up, unsuccessful. 'What should I have seen?'

'Surface of the moon,' he says. 'Sea of Vaporum. Wonderful name.'

He turns and starts down the stairway and she follows.

Back on the floor, they stand facing each other. He puts his hands on his hips and says, 'You'll have to excuse the way I'm dressed. I believe in comfort at home. And, of course, I wasn't expecting company tonight.'

He's got on a pair of gray sweatpants that bunch around the ankles, a black crew-neck cotton sweater, and a pair of ratty, five-and-dime-store slippers.

'You look fine,' she says, and feels a wince of embarrassment.

'Could I offer you a drink?' he says. 'I'm allowed a single nightcap, myself, due to my condition.'

'Your condition?'

'Addison's disease. I believe your President Kennedy suffered from this also, yes?'

'I really don't know. I'm sorry to hear—'

'Please take a seat,' he says, cutting her off and extending a hand toward the rocking chair. He starts to move toward the fireplace. She follows, and remains standing behind him. He grabs a short poker from the brick patch of flooring that extends a few feet out from the hearth and begins to jab and stir the embers and charred remains of wood.

'Sit,' he says in a soft voice, and she hesitates and then eases herself into the chair. She sinks into its cushions. It's tremendously comfortable and she can see why it would be hard to part with or even alter.

'Because I am usually the only one in this room,' he says, 'there is only the one chair. But I will sit on the floor. Good for me, for a change.'

'You need some books for your shelves,' Lenore says.

Cortez smiles, then says, 'I've often thought this is the main reason people buy books. To fill empty shelves. But these shelves were once quite full. Bursting with volumes, as a matter of fact.'

'Let me guess,' Lenore says. 'You donated them to the literate poor.' She's immediately unsure of the wisdom of her remark. She thinks it's the chair that's given her the comfort to be a joker.

But Cortez enjoys the comment. 'Not quite,' he says. 'I sold them. To a dealer here in the city. Ziesing Ave. A Mr. Beck. Fine store. You should go sometime.'

'My brother's a big book guy. Loves mysteries.'

'They say that indicates a love of logic. Until recently, I suppose. I read mysteries when I was young. Now they just confuse me. I'll tell you an awful secret about myself.'

'I'm all ears.'

'I came very close to burning every book in this room.'

'And why was that?'

'They were driving me out of my mind.'

'Was someone making you read them?'

Cortez puts the poker down and eases onto the floor facing her, close to the relit fire. Half of his face is left in shadow by his position. He sits cross-legged, with his long arms draped over his knees.

'Now, that,' he says, 'is a very good question. No one was holding a gun to my head, no. Of course not. But I felt compelled just the same. By my own nature. I've been a voracious reader since I can remember—'

'But then, we can't trust memory.'

'Again, very true. But still there are feelings. Instinctual feelings. Whether or not our memories hold a great deal of what we'll call "historical truth" matters very little in terms of these feelings. I loved Jules Verne. Did you read Jules Verne?'

She shakes her head no.

'Oh,' he says, closing his eyes and frowning, his head swaying slightly. '*Around the World in Eighty Days. From the Earth to the Moon.* Filled me with pure joy. My father abandoned the family when I was a child. I like to think of Jules Verne as my father now.'

'That still doesn't tell me why you wanted to burn your books.'

He unclasps his hands and looks up at her as if the answer were obvious. 'The joy started to leave. I don't know why. It just began departing. What I had felt since childhood, what I had felt for books, I started to no longer feel. And it became too painful to keep them around.'

'Why do you think this happened?'

He just shakes his head.

'It occurs to me,' she says, 'that we know almost nothing about each other.'

'I think,' he says, 'that we both suspect a great deal.'

'This might be a golden opportunity to clear up those suspicions,' she says.

'You're sure you wish to do that?'

'I don't know about you,' she says, 'but at this point I honestly, absolutely, have nothing else to lose.'

He rubs his eyes and breathes heavily.

'Tell me something,' she says.

'You tell me what it is you suspect,' he snaps back, not angry, but suddenly very serious.

She wishes she were on the floor with him, at the same level, and that the lighting in the room were different so she could see his face more clearly.

'Okay,' she says. 'I suspect that everything they think about you is wrong—'

'They,' he interrupts.

'The department. And the Feds. And the DEA. And Interpol.'

'What is it they think?'

'That you're a very sharp renegade. That you've had a plan from the start. That you're on your way to control of the whole East Coast, and then, maybe, beyond the East Coast. That the Italians and the Jamaicans and the Colombians and all the various Asian cartels are going to have to deal with you sooner or later. Basically, that you're the top dog, so to speak.'

'And this you don't believe?'

'No,' she says, a little nervous. 'I don't know why. I can't even look at their paperwork. I can't even hear about the documentation. Transcripts from a million informers. Something's wrong about it.'

'You think,' he says, 'I'm a puppet of some kind. You think there's someone above me.'

'No offense intended.'

'But this *is* your suspicion.'

Lenore nods. Cortez bites his lower lip and gives a barely perceptible shrug.

'What I'd like to do,' he says, 'is get all the suspicions out in the open before we confirm or destroy them. So here's mine. Certainly, you're a narcotics officer. There's no question about this. For a time, the question was, were you filthy, or, perhaps, did you wish to be filthy? To the best of my knowledge, I wasn't paying you. Mingo's idea was that you were, in his words, a headcase. *Le falta un tornillo.* Your friend in the lobby, Jimmy, he thought you had the makings of a spectacular junkie, which, I must admit, I had to agree with. Tonight, I think something else, something beyond all these things. I suspect you are a woman without a sense of place. You don't know where you belong. And you're drawn to Bangkok Park because of its completely ambiguous nature. Because you think this might be the end of the road.'

Lenore wishes she'd taken him up on the drink offer. She gets out of the rocker and comes down to the floor, sitting in the same position as Cortez, almost mimicking him.

'Okay,' she says, 'I'm a headcase. And I've got an appetite for speed that's on the move. And I think I belong in the Park more than you do.' She pauses, turns more toward him, and says, 'So, your turn.'

'As a younger man,' he says, so quietly she strains her eyes to watch his lips, 'I was a seminarian, and then a medical student, and also a journeyman trumpet player. I grew bored with everything in time. And now I am a fine actor. Tremendous actor. There should be the Oscar, there, up on the mantel. But I'm bored to tears. I'm bored to the point of distraction.'

He uncrosses his legs, rises, and moves to the sheet-covered piece of furniture behind the rocker.

'Come here and see something,' he says, and Lenore stands and moves next to him.

He pulls the bed sheet free like a magician at a children's party. Underneath is what looks like an antique traveling salesman's product case, a big black wooden steamer trunk with fat leather straps for reinforcement. Cortez takes a moment to open it and Lenore sees that it's fitted with shelves for displaying the goods. The shelves here are crammed with old-fashioned books, leather-bound. Lenore leans forward a little to take in the wonderful smell. The titles written down the spines are all in Spanish.

'I thought you got rid of all your books,' Lenore says.

'I got rid of all those books,' Cortez says, gesturing toward the empty bookcases. 'You have no idea what you're seeing, my friend.'

'Old books.'

He shakes his head no. 'There are one hundred books in this trunk. And not one of them has ever been seen by a northerner. Not a single one. Never been seen, let alone read. You want to talk about conspiracies? Here are novels, stories, poetry. From Argentina. And also from Peru, Brazil, Chile, Venezuela, Bolivia, Mexico, Ecuador. From all the countries below.'

He pulls out a volume and holds it in his hand.

'Paraguay.' He reshelves it and pulls out another.

'Guyana.'

He reshelves the second volume and begins to point at spines.

'Colombia, Nicaragua, Honduras.'

Then he folds his arms across his chest and says, 'And, except for this trunk, Cortez's own trunk, none of them have ever traveled north of Juárez. It's our hidden library. The ghost library. The North knows nothing of it and never will.'

Lenore shrugs her shoulders. 'So why are you telling me about it?'

'Because this is my future,' he says. 'This is what I wish to do. I wish to go back home. Like you. For me, it's possible. I want to just disappear. Into the Andes. Into a cave in the Andes. With my trunk. I want to vanish with my books.'

'Why don't you?' Lenore asks.

'All things in time. The instinctual actor knows when to exit.'

'I'll bet he also knows how to line his pockets one last time.'

'Which brings us to Lingo.'

'How much do you know?'

'Not as much as you think. It's already out there. I'm sure you're aware of that. I've been listening to the police radio all night. Such excitement. The city is humming. There was a sample batch. Every parasite in this hotel has dipped into that cookie jar, I'm sure. In another week, the blood will be rolling down the streets.'

'Do you know who's selling? Do you know who smacked the Swanns, who you're buying from?'

'No idea. I hope you believe me on this. I know it's a new company. The sales rep is unusually elusive. Refers to himself as the Paraclete, which, I'm embarrassed to confess, appeals to my sense of the dramatic. But I can't tell you where they come from or how big they are or how they got involved with the Swanns. You see, I'm more in the dark than you.'

'Yeah, I'll bet. Let's try something else. Confirm a hunch for me. Do you know who the Swanns cooked it up for in the first place? I mean, was it CIA or NSA or some other circle of fuckers in mirror sunglasses and wash-and-wear suits?'

'Who knows these things? These kinds of questions are like little Zen koans, don't you think? The answer is really moot. Inconsequential. It's the process of pondering the question that counts. I personally believe in a unified field theory in these matters. Everything interconnected and as important as everything else. You know who I think dreamed up Lingo? I think it was some blind, deaf, dumb, illiterate, incontinent, unwashed streetperson selling pencils from a soup can for a nickel, standing in front of the White House gates. Good an answer as any.'

'Maybe for you. But I've hit bottom. And now I've got to ask questions that I didn't even acknowledge a week ago. Like who is it on the other side of the fence, on my side of the fence, that's been helping you out for a while now? Someone up near the top of the department? Someone up in City Hall?'

'How do you know it's not both?'

'How high does it go? Does it get up to Welby? Does it go beyond him?'

'My guess would be it goes fairly high. But, like you, my friend, I'm just a cog, correct? I'm an errand boy of sorts, yes? A caretaker. That's your theory, right? You have to have the courage to stand behind your theories, Detective.'

They smile at one another. She says, 'I don't think you'd last a week in a cave in the Andes.'

He shakes his head and says, 'That's where you'd be wrong.'

She shrugs. 'You know what you want, I guess—'

'And you also.'

'So why can't we both have what we want? Why can't there be a way that you get the money and the distance? You get to run. All shots fired far over the head.'

'You want a time and a place?'

'You knew that when I came in the door.'

'You want everyone left over after I run?'

'I want the producer. And the broker. I'd say I want the Aliens too, but I'm betting you'd balk.'

'The aliens?' Cortez repeats.

'The people above you,' Lenore says.

'I love that term. But you know how it is with aliens. Long arms and all.'

'You've got quite the imagination.'

'And a strong sense of history. You're free to believe what you want. I know the extent of their power. It's been my experience that what is fantastic up here is simply the boring routine when you get south of the border.'

'In that case, one last question.'

'Go ahead.'

'The Aliens. They wouldn't by any chance be women?'

An enormous smile breaks on Cortez's face. He cups a hand around Lenore's neck and, without actually making any sound, mouths the words 'Of course they are.'

'I'm glad I entertain you so much,' she says.

'I hope it's been a mutual infatuation.'

'Infatuation. That's how you want to define this?'

'You'd prefer something stronger,' he says, voice low, genuinely flirting with her.

'Absolutely. And since you're the one breaking to run, that makes me the spurned victim.'

'You? A victim?'

'And I'm here for some concessions.' She pauses, then says, 'So how about it?'

He starts to close up the ghost library. He sinks to his knees to latch the case and says, without looking at her, 'I'm taking Max with me, you know. You won't be seeing any more of him.'

Lenore is startled. 'You know about Max and me?'

Cortez nods. 'And I don't believe I'm the only one. But a father will forgive a son almost anything.'

'Father? Figuratively, or—'

'Does it matter?' He pauses, looks at the palm of his hand. 'I don't want Wyatt hurt, either.'

'Okay.'

'Mingo, I'm not as concerned about. I've had the feeling lately that if I looked into some of Mingo's off-time activities, I'd be very disappointed. He's caused more of my problems than he's worth.'

'Just keep your people near you.'

He comes back upright, moves in close to her until their bodies are almost touching.

'You'll be free at two A.M.?'

'I think I can make it.'

'St. James Cemetery? Off Richer?'

'Where my parents are buried.'

'The old section. Near the railroad tracks. A freight car labeled "Pachinko."'

'All right. Done. Have you been given the money for the purchase yet?'

'It should be arriving shortly.'

'Then I should be getting out of here. You keep your hands on the cash. Can you set something up between now and the meet? Transportation and all?'

'I've had some loose contingencies in place for some time.'

'Then this is it,' she says, taking an awkward step backward, feeling a little woozy. 'Have a good life, Cortez. Reading. In the caves.'

He rolls his eyes for some reason. He looks sheepish, embarrassed. He seems to her, suddenly, almost shockingly, unsure and young, like he could hold up his hands at any second and tell her the whole thing was a joke, an elaborate put-on. Ike and Woo, the whole narc department, even poor cousin Lon might come running into the library, conspirators in the gag. Everyone might laugh, bottles of champagne could be popped open, music could be introduced to the dusty room, and a party, based solely on a fat prank played on Lenore, could start its march into the night.

Instead, Cortez holds his hand above his head, palm flat and parallel with the crown of his skull, and says, 'Remember, shoot high.'

Lenore stares at him, waiting for something more. Then she gives a single, small nod and turns to move. Cortez puts his hands on her shoulders, pulls her in toward him, and begins to kiss her. At first, Lenore doesn't respond, but as seconds pass and he shows no sign of separating their lips, she lets herself go comfortable, and then she's returning the gesture, applying pressure of her own. Their mouths open, almost simultaneously, and tongues slide around one another and into new territory. It goes on for full minutes, their breathing becoming more and more audible, sucking noises multiplying.

She wants to press on his shoulders and force him down onto the floor. But he stops, draws his head back slowly, then brings his mouth forward, this time pressing his lips to her forehead. He kisses softly now. He tilts his head and kisses her cheek, holding her face in both his hands. Then he steps backward, gives a small bow of the head, like some odd Euro-Latin count, some last-century duke, and he walks out of the library in a modified march, hands down at his side and feet moving in syncopated time.

She stands for a moment, taken back. She realizes she, too, should leave, get back to the Barracuda, get back to the green duplex, get on the phone, and start setting strategy. Instead, she moves to the fireplace, squats down, and hunches in over her knees. She tries to lean close and get any last heat the embers might have to offer. But it's no good. She's got a chill and an ache that's only going to grow. The thing is to keep it under control for the next three or four hours.

That's the goal. Get through a specific period of time. Keep the mind on that simple goal. Continue to perform, to move through the motions. Fulfill the duties, the responsibilities. Do her job.

And, where Cortez is concerned, shoot high.

30

Eva sits on the aluminum fold-out chair in the back room of the Bach Room. She keeps both hands around her glass of ginger ale. The glass is growing foggy with the discrepancy between the heat of her fingers and the cold of the ice cubes. Rourke is sitting in a chair across the table, opposite her. He's trying to make her as uncomfortable as possible, staring at her for long periods of time without blinking his eyes.

In fact, it's Rourke who is uncomfortable, and growing more troubled as time goes by. He keeps biting on hangnails, using his teeth to tear at tiny strips of skin near the base of his thumbnail until trickles of blood run down his knuckle toward his wrist. There's a bottle of Wild Turkey on the table, the cap off, but Rourke hasn't taken a drink yet. It's apparent to Eva that he wants one, and she doesn't understand his abstinence. But for some reason, it gives her some confidence, it signals some obscure assurance that she's made correct decisions, chosen the right path.

Marconi, the bartender, sticks his head through the doorway curtain, looks from Eva to Rourke, then says, 'He's here.'

Rourke nods his head rapidly.

Marconi says, 'He wants to see you out in front.'

Rourke's eyes break away from Eva and look down at the table. They stay focused there for a second, as if there were writing, some kind of microscopic graffiti, on the tabletop.

Then he rises, pushing back the chair with the back of his knees, making an awful scraping noise against the floor. He moves out into the bar and Marconi steps just inside the doorway and stands in the corner watching Eva, his hands together behind his back. He seems frightened just being inside the back room.

Eva asks, 'Is everything all right?' not really interested in a response, but more to prod and jangle Marconi, watch for a reaction.

He says nothing, looks down to the floor in the same manner that Rourke looked to the tabletop.

From out in the bar they both hear a slapping sound, like the flat palm of a hand coming down on wood, onto the bartop maybe. There's an undercurrent of mumbling that can't be made out and then silence again.

Rourke calls Marconi's name and the bartender exits the back room without another look at Eva, as if he might turn to salt with a last glance. After a few seconds the curtain is pushed back and a rail-thin man steps into the room. He's wearing a charcoal suit and a crimson silk tie marked with a splatter of gray dots. It's impossible to make a good guess of his age, but if pressed, Eva would say late thirties to mid forties.

He takes the seat Rourke had been in, reaches to an inside suit coat pocket, and withdraws a pair of small round wire-frame glasses. He makes slow precise movements opening the glasses, holding them up to check for smudges, then securing them on his face. He acts with such care that Eva thinks a wrong move could break both the glasses and the small bones in his nose or behind his ears.

She decides to take the initiative. She says, 'So you're the Paraclete?'

He smiles at her, waits a moment, then says, 'If you say so.'

She shakes her head and smiles back. 'No, no. I need you to say so.'

He breathes in and out, reaches to his face to adjust the glasses, then brings his hands down to the tabletop and folds them together, staring at her and still smiling the whole time.

'I am the Paraclete,' he says.

She nods. 'I'm Eva Barnes,' she says. 'And as you probably

know, I'm the supervisor of the postal station across the street. I appreciate you sparing the time to speak with me.' She hopes her voice sounds ambiguous, gives nothing away. She wants him to be in doubt as to whether she's mocking him or acting in some rehearsed, rigid manner.

'I think,' he says, 'we could both see that the benefits of our meeting would outweigh the risks.'

Right away, it's clear he's taken on the same tone and measure as Eva, and any confidence she'd taken from Marconi's nervousness vanishes. She clears her throat and says, 'I guess my first question is, do you think you're the first person who's attempted to transport illicit materials through the U.S. Postal Service?'

He sits back in the chair and his hands, still folded, fall into his lap.

'Ms. Barnes,' he says. 'I'm really not overly concerned about the originality of the method. Only its effectiveness. Also, it's *your* employee, Mr. Rourke, who approached my people. Not the other way around.'

She knows she's on the edge of starting to panic, that the best thing to do is make her intentions clear and try to get out. She says, 'In any case, Mr.—'

He ignores her try for a name and after a beat she continues, 'There's been some serious offenses committed.'

'Offenses against whom, Ms. Barnes?' he asks blandly.

'Against my employer. Against the Federal Government.'

'And your job, then, would be to report those offenses. To the correct channels.'

'Yes, it would.'

'And, may I ask, why have you not done this?'

'Who's to say I haven't?'

He smiles and waits, then opens his hands, extends them to his sides like some kind of priest, and says, 'Our present situation indicates otherwise, don't you think? This very scenario we're acting out. I have to assume you wish to negotiate.'

She gives up any hope of manipulating the conversation. She says simply, 'I want in.'

'You want in,' he repeats, neither questioning her nor confirming the words. Just repeating, replaying the sounds.

He takes the glasses off, folds them carefully, and repockets them. He stands up, puts his hands in his pants pockets in an attempt to look casual. It doesn't work. He slouches his shoulders and asks, 'Weren't you at all afraid of the consequences of these actions, of approaching Mr. Rourke? Didn't you consider the likelihood that you might endanger yourself—'

She interrupts. 'Who should be more afraid, me or you?'

He starts to walk around the table, brushing at his lapels as he goes. 'I can only speak for myself, Eva – you don't mind if I call you Eva, do you? – but you can't really allow yourself a sense of fear in this field. You have to be able to excise it, or at the very least, suppress it.'

He moves behind Eva, places his hands on her shoulders lightly. He can feel her trembling.

'You have no guarantee that I haven't told someone,' she says, 'that I don't have a partner waiting to hear from me.'

'Thank you,' he says, 'you didn't disappoint. I was counting on that line. How many films have we seen where someone in just your situation speaks that exact line? It's like a verbal archetype. This is what the movies have brought us, Eva. A vocabulary we can all share. We can actually anticipate the words.'

He begins to rub a slow massage from the outer rim of her shoulders to the back of her neck. He feels the skin on her neck going cool and clammy.

'That doesn't make the possibility of me having a friend any less real,' she says.

'What would your friend's name be?' he asks.

'I don't think so.'

'Would he or she be a co-worker, by any chance?'

'I don't think I'll be answering these kinds of questions.'

'You have no family, do you, Eva?'

'Now we're getting way off track.'

'Not necessarily. I know you have no family, Eva—'

Her swallow and her voice catch. 'People know me. There are a lot of people who know me—'

He eases her forward in her chair and runs the flat of his fist down the line of her spine, from neck to lower back. 'Calm down, Eva. You misunderstand me. You assume I'm threatening you. I'm not threatening you. Were I to threaten you' – he brings his hand around to the front of her throat, pulls his extended index finger lightly across the skin just above her Adam's apple – 'you would certainly know it. There'd be no doubt.'

He can feel her muscles tighten under his hands.

'I was simply trying to make the point that an organization like mine can function in much the same manner as a family, extend the same sensation of belonging.'

He runs his fingers through her hair slowly.

'How much money do you want?'

She starts to shake her head. She wishes he were still in front of her where she could see his face, get more of an idea of his intentions.

'I hadn't really thought about an actual, a specific…'

'You were thinking of the bigger picture, yes? You were thinking in terms of belonging, is that right?'

'I don't know. I…'

His hands come around her again, the finger again drawing across her throat, but then his hands descend down her blouse, rub over her breasts. She immediately pushes them away, but he persists, strokes her brow softly, then begins to unbutton the blouse.

'You said yourself, Eva, you want in.'

She stays silent, stares at the blank opposite wall, then closes her eyes.

'Say it, Eva. You want to belong.'

She doesn't speak, but she doesn't fight him either. Behind her back, she hears him shirking out of his suit coat. She hears a zipper sound, the light jangle of a buckle, a shoe bounce off the wall.

Keeping her eyes closed she moves from the chair, rotates slightly until her behind is on the edge of the table, then pushing her feet off the chair legs, she comes full up onto the table and lies on her back. In a second, he's fully on top of her, kissing her neck, whispering, breathy, next to her ear.

'You've made the right choice. You'll be safe now. In the Paraclete's family.'

31

Ike sits in the darkness of his bedroom closet, door closed, huddled up among a rough pile of shoes, sneakers, and work boots. He cradles the radio in his lap, the volume low enough, he judges, so that no one on the other side of the door could hear anything. He presses the mesh grid that covers the speaker to his ear. It has a cold metal feeling, not unpleasant, sort of refreshing.

After Lenore ran out, he'd run to the bathroom and vomited up his whole breakfast until he was racked with dry heaves. Then he'd filled the sink with ice-cold water and plunged his head in several times. He dried himself and retreated to the closet and tried to sleep. When this proved impossible, he grabbed the radio and tuned in WQSG.

An ad for a funeral home goes over, violins fade out, and the voice of the talk-show host speaks again.

TALK-SHOW HOST: Hoo, boy, it's going to be one of those nights again. Is there a full moon out there tonight, Gus? Gus Z, of course, my engineer and right-hand man. Gus is shaking his head no, but you couldn't tell it by the phone calls tonight. Loon city, if you know what I'm saying. Lock the doors and windows, people, it's going to be a long haul till the light of dawn. Hello, Joyce J, from the west side. Talk to Ray, you're on the air.

JOYCE: Yes, Ray, I'm just calling, I just want to say, you've got me completely terrified now and I can't sleep a wink, I keep going to the window, you really shouldn't say such things—

RAY: Sorry, Joyce, my friend, but the truth will sometimes

do that to you. Our lovely little city has gone out-and-out bonkers this week.

JOYCE: Did you find out any more on all that commotion down at the Canal?

RAY: We are still waiting for a callback from Chief Bendix, but I'll tell you, Gus has had the police scanner on since we came into the studio tonight and it's a madhouse out there.

JOYCE: I've locked all the doors.

RAY: And well you might. Our city is in the midst of a real breakdown if the police radio here tells the truth. What is going on out there? I'll give my theory if anyone's interested.

JOYCE: Tell us, Ray, we all need—

The woman's voice is gone with a high-pitched bleep.

RAY: Oops, we seem to have lost Joyce from the west side. Listen, Joyce, keep the dead bolts secure. And you might want to push some heavy furniture, if you can manage it, in front of all the doorways. So the question gets asked, how did we arrive at this juncture? People, you don't have to be some anal-retentive, thinktank intellectual to find an answer. There is a pervading weakness that's crept into our society. It's our own fault and now we have to pay the price. Painful, I know. But perhaps we should have thought of that when we slackened our immigration standards and eliminated the death penalty and tossed unsafe fluoride chemicals into our reservoirs. A little foresight is what I'm speaking about. A need for people unafraid to open their mouths and move their tongues and speak the truth.

Ike turns off the radio. The telephone is ringing in the kitchen. He opens the door, crawls out of the closet, stumbles to his feet, and manages a run by the hallway. He grabs the phone on its fifth ring. A voice is already speaking as he brings the receiver to his ear and says, 'Hello.'

Eva says, 'Just do it. Meet me at the station. Right now.'

Then the call clicks dead and Ike holds the receiver and, though he knows she's already hung up, he says, 'I can't. I can't go out.'

He stands like this for a few minutes, finally replaces the phone in its cradle, then immediately takes the receiver off the hook again and leaves it on the counter.

He moves back to the bedroom, sits on the edge of the bed, hugs his arms around himself, and starts to rock slightly back and forth.

'Lenore, where are you?' he says out loud in a singsong voice. He plants his heels into the carpet and begins a nervous tapping with the balls of his feet. He wants to go back into the closet and listen to the reports of doom from Ray the talk-show host. He wishes Ray would put Gus the engineer right on the air, live, get a new slant, a fresh perspective. He wishes he were with Joyce from the west side, pushing some heavy buffet-piece from an old cherry dining room set down a pantry corridor, toward a rickety kitchen door.

It takes him twenty minutes of self-prodding and abuse to dress and move outside. For reasons of confusion as much as convenience, he's wearing his postal uniform, gray-blue trousers with navy service stripe down the sides, powder-blue shirt with arm patch, the winter jacket, a nice nylon blend, and black Knapp boots with reinforced toes. He also has a can of Mace in his back pocket.

He walks the three blocks to Sapir Street at a fast and jumpy pace. Despite what Ray and Gus have said, the neighborhood is quiet, normal. A single car rolls past him, a woman, alone in an old Chevy, hunched in over the wheel. He sees two dogs, mongrels, jog across the street and disappear up a driveway. At the corner of Breton he passes Alfred K's Quick Mart, and looks in to see an Oriental woman watching a portable TV on the counter as she sells cigarettes to a teenage boy with long, stringy, black hair.

As he walks, Ike keeps looking for signs of something out of the ordinary, abnormal, alarming. But everything on the street looks as it always looks, calm and boring. Uneventful. Status quo. He expects disaster, and the fact that there's no sign of its approach is in some ways disturbing and frightening. He starts a mild jog down the last block to Sapir and starts to wonder what he'll say to Eva. He's decided that no matter what kind of decisions she's reached about the events of the past week, he's going to spell everything out for Lenore. He's going to put it all in her lap and tell her to make the hard choices. He's out. He will not participate for another day in this weirdness. He's handing it to his sister whether Eva likes it or not.

He comes to the corner, turns onto Sapir, and heads for the station. The main streetlight in front of the station entrance is burned out, but in the employee parking lot, he can see Eva's Volkswagen. The interior lights are on, but the car is empty. Ike runs over to it and finds the driver's door slightly ajar. He looks inside, checks out the front and back seats, sees nothing. He leans into the door with his hip, closing it and shutting out the lights.

He doesn't want to get inside the car and wait, though he thinks it's possible that this was Eva's intention. He turns his back to the car and leans his behind against the side, folds his arms across his chest, and looks around the lot. Someone's thrown a newspaper, it looks like *The Spy*, on the ground and pages have separated and are blowing across the lot, until they get stuck up against the station's walls. Every time the wind blows, the newspaper pages make a riffling sound, louder than Ike would expect. He hates the noise, but not enough to go gather the papers together.

He checks his wrist and remembers he didn't wear his watch. He brings his arms down from his chest and pushes his hands into his jacket pockets. Then he looks to the employee entrance next to the bay doors where the trucks load and unload. A light is on inside.

He walks over to the cement ledge where the mail trucks back up to the dock. He climbs up and looks in the small window covered with a wire grid. He pulls on the knob and the door comes open.

First, he sticks just his head into the corridor. He calls, 'Eva,' softly. There's no answer. He wants to let the door swing closed and run back home, worry about what Eva might have to say tomorrow. But he steps inside, closes the door behind him, and calls her name again. He starts to walk down the short corridor. It leads to a set of swinging, round-edged, double doors that always remind him of submarine doorways from the movies. The swinging doors lead into the main workroom, the sorting area, and the cages.

He pushes through and steps into the main body of the station. Patches of light from the moon make it through the front windows and cast shadows off the jutting arms of the cages. Ike stands still until he's convinced that each shadow is just a trick of light blocked by unanimated metal. Then he moves toward the front of the building.

Eva's office door is open. Ike steps inside and looks on her desk. There's no note, no sign that she's been there and left by foot, abandoned her stalled Volks, called away by an emergency or new information. He moves into the main foyer of the station and looks out the window. The streetlight flickers for a moment, but fails to ignite. He wishes it would either stay dead and dark or snap on for good. None of this in-between crap.

Someone left the back entrance open, he tells himself, and Eva's the only one with the keys. He steps back from the window, starts to head for the main doors to take another look at the car. Then he notices something on the floor. Something spilled. A line of liquid. A trail of something dripped, leading to the front entrance.

He keeps himself from bending and touching it, from bringing a sample dab up near his nose for a smell. Instead, he follows the runny line. It breaks here and there, leaves small gaps, then disappears completely in the small vestibule to the right of the entranceway, the small antechamber of post office boxes. Three walls lined with rented cubbyholes with brass faces and individual combination locks.

There are two hundred rental boxes. They come in three sizes – the small letter drawers, the slightly larger 'flats' drawers, and the big, deep boxes, usually used by businesses. Only one of the two hundred is ajar. It's a deep box, positioned at floor level. Ike starts to shake his head as soon as he sees it is open just a half an inch.

And then the smell hits him. Like biology lab in high school. Like a dentist's office. That chemical smell, formaldehyde-like, something like a mask for the odor of decay. Only it doesn't mask, it blends, so that a new smell is formed.

His feet pull him to the wall of boxes and his stomach starts to tighten. He squats down, takes the weight of his body in his knees and thighs. He's sweating everywhere. The back of his throat has taken on a deep burn, an ache. His eyes squint and there's a pain in both his lungs and his temples that seems to alternate perfectly, one asserting as the other recedes.

His hand extends, fingers come up into the underside groove of the box handle. He draws it out, pulls it to him, and at the same time looks at the label on the face. Of course. It's box nine.

The smell hits him full now and he gags. He brings his head forward, makes himself look.

It's Eva's head, independent of the neck, shoulders, the rest of the body. It's severed clean. The eyes slightly open. The eyes are almost squinting at him and he has a slightly subconscious, instantaneous idea that, like some novelty pictures of dogs and clowns that he's seen for sale on roadsides, the eyes might follow him if he moved, changed position. But they're still Eva's eyes, the taut lids he brought his tongue to just hours ago.

It is Eva's head. He's looking down at Eva's head. The hair is matted down to the skull with blood. It's sitting in a round pan, a cooking pan, lined with aluminum foil. The pan is filled, filling, with a mixture of blood and a syrupy green liquid, like a heavy shampoo. Some of the green syrup has splashed onto the inside walls of the box.

It's Eva's head.

And then there's the sound of the double doors swinging open and closed.

32

St. James Cemetery is on the south side of the city. It lies in a shallow valley off Richer Avenue. It's a large cemetery, stretches out almost to the city line. It's bisected, almost perfectly, into two separate areas by the last skinny traces of the Benchley River as it begins to peter out.

The bisection by the river creates a division that seems too beautifully instructional to be coincidental. The section closest to Richer Ave, called the old section, was the whole of the original cemetery. It's been filled to capacity for decades and holds the remains of the oldest of the Catholic families in Quinsigamond who butt heads with the Yankee founders of the city. When the last available grave in the old section was filled, new ground was broken on the opposite shore of the ten-foot riverbed. The new section was an immigrant neighborhood for the dead. The gravestones became ornate, bordered on the superstitious and maudlin, and the names on the stones were often long and blatantly non-Anglo-European.

At the western edge of both sections lies a stretch of tracks owned by the Providence-Quinsigamond Railroad Company. The tracks are part of a route that, like many in the P&Q system, are no longer operational. Rather than expend the cash to rip up the tracks, the railroad has simply ignored them, let them rust and fall under the cover of ten years' worth of debris, fallen and dead trees and branches, supermarket carts and old tires. Along with the track, they left several antiquated freight cars, common, cheap rigs for industrial scrap and odds and ends. The cars have been home to squads of derelicts and drifters over the past ten years. About five years back, some old nomad's body was found in February, dead of exposure, and there was some mayoral talk about petitioning the railroad to remove the public nuisance. But the talk faded and the cars still sit in a mini-forest of scrappy trees and beggar trash.

Lenore sits a quarter mile away in the new section. She's seated on the frozen ground, inside a newly opened grave. Most likely, the burial is tomorrow and they brought a backhoe in today to carve out a hole for the vault. She's roughly twelve feet down and she doesn't know if this is a standard depth these days or if this is a double grave, purchased by someone thinking of the future, making room for the family.

She's lowered herself down by a black nylon climbing rope tied to a neighboring gravestone, a granite number, a simple grayish rectangle that rises vertical out of the earth and is cut with names and dates. She's dressed in the requisite black and she's done all the necessary prep work – planted a mike in the abandoned railroad car labeled 'Pachinko Brothers Bale Wire,' oiled and slapped a fresh cartridge in the Uzi, popped a megadose of crank.

Now she's humming. She's got her two index fingers extended like drumsticks and she's flailing away at her knees in perfect syncopation. There isn't a missed beat, a balked strike. She's keeping a countertime with both her feet. And her teeth are doing a continual bite, grab, and release, over and over on her upper lip.

Images keep passing through her mind, not thoughts, but random flashes, synaptic snapshots of faces and landscapes, lighting for a millisecond, vanishing, being replaced by the next picture. She can't really get a fix on any of them, but it's not like she's making a legendary attempt. She lets them come and go, tries to grab what she can. It's like trying to stare at a series of unconnected billboards set on the side of an interstate that she's burning up in some supercharged Porsche.

Her mother's face. The whiteness of Woo's belly. Cortez's book trunk. Ike's post office shirt, freshly washed and pressed and draped over a coat hanger suspended from the hinge of his bedroom door. Zarelli's plate of manicotti the last time they had lunch at Fiorello's. Her father's arm, slung awkwardly over his face, blocking his eyes, as he lay on the bed, on top of the covers, for an after-supper nap, 1972. Her own body, naked, reflected back at her from the bathroom mirror, her skin looking suddenly gray, dry to the point of flaking away, dissolving into a granular pile on the cold tiles below her feet.

She brings her hands away from her knees, looks at them, turning them over and over, front to back to front. Then she brings her right hand up to her ear, resecuring the small receiver that never fits very well. She hears a ghostlike undercurrent, not static, but more likely the wind pushing through the cavity of the bugged boxcar.

She thinks that there are people, maybe the majority of people, who would be tentative about sitting alone, inside an open grave, in a deserted cemetery, after midnight. Ike, for one. Ike would be going over the edge about now, she thinks. Ike's nerve would have started slipping as he came through the wrought-iron gates.

But it doesn't bother Lenore. The fact is, she has a tough time even acknowledging an idea of the supernatural. Stories about ghosts, demons, ghouls, vampires, zombies – they all strike her as stubborn remnants of a more primitive time. Useless, superstitious fear. A throwback that society can't seem to shake. Generation after generation of people clutching onto memories of these shadowy myths that, like the appendix, we keep being born with, though their use is so far gone we can't even recall it.

There are things to be frightened of in this life. She'd be the first to acknowledge that. The average person should probably be frightened of a guy like Jimmy Wyatt. No question. A mute sociopath known to veer into rage. A guy who could conceivably come at you across a crowded coffee shop some dull morning and jam his fork into your throat. Jimmy Wyatt is a tangible force. He can be seen, touched, smelled. He has a verifiable history of random violence. There are odds that he could cause you long-lasting trauma. A person should fear a Jimmy Wyatt.

The average person should have a rational fear of cruising Bangkok Park at night. Of finding the lump under the skin. Of the bomb raining down on urban centers across your country. Of the banks bolting their doors and your money long gone. Of losing your ability to control the crank, or the men around you, or your hold on a dicey and cold philosophy that you've staked a lot of faith on, that you've used as a reason for moving.

For the last half hour, Lenore's body has been having small seizures of some kind. It's like her nervous system gets this surge of too much juice, too many signals. Her hands flail out to the side. One foot starts to tick in spasm. A corner of her mouth tugs downward. Her shoulders shoot back like a wave has hit her chest.

She has feared this all along and now it's finally arrived. She thinks she should be experiencing at least some slight relief that what she's dreaded is here. The waiting can end. The subconscious, ongoing anxiety can cease. The worst has happened.

She thinks suddenly of Hitler on the last day of his life, deep in the bunker below the Reich Chancellery. She's read that at the end, the Führer was out of it, heavily sedated by his personal doctor, maybe not even completely aware that the ball game was just about over, the Russians just a quarter mile away, their shells arcing that distance and bursting on the ravaged streets of Berlin above his head.

How different. It's just the opposite for her. There's no sedation, but rather a siege of input, a blitzkrieg offense against a tangled, overused system of nerves, so raw from six months of nonstop overload that the nerves are perpetually hyperstimulated, they no longer know any other mode of perception. *I don't need the receiver,* she thinks, *just my own ear. I don't need the binoculars, just my given eyes.* Take everything in and then take some more. *Which is the worse fate,* she wonders, *the bang or the whimper?*

It's like being in a bunker. Only smaller. The Führer's digs were a penthouse suite compared to this hole. Looking at the wall of dirt to her left, she can see earthworms frozen in mid-burrow. Something about this strikes her as wrong, a primal violation of some obscure law of nature.

Still, she likes the location. She's only yards from her parents' grave and it begins to occur to her that this waiting period is a perfect time to speak with them, to send her thoughts into the ground, a simple straight line through the terra.

Isn't this funny, folks, I want to say it's your firstborn. But there was Ike, and though I know one of us had to come first, right now I can't remember who that was. I'm sure you told us. I'm sure we would have asked. The thing is, this makes me wonder what else I'm destined to forget before I join you guys. The thought doesn't bother me as much as I'd have expected. Forgetting, I mean. You know, really, there's a peace to it. Forgetting. There's a consolation in forgetting.

When you die, do your memories cease? I'm betting they do. I just have this feeling. Do you guys have any memory left? Does it leave you instantly, the brain waves cease and zap, that whole lifetime pool of images is excised? Or is it a gradual thing, a fading, a leakage, until there's only one image left, one utmost picture? What would the picture be for each of you? Ma? Dad?

It's so goddamn, excuse me, but so weird what I suddenly flashed on. What the last memory would be for me. What would you guess? Ma? Dad? Listen, it's not what you'd think. You'd expect something significant, right? Something that changed or shaped a lifetime, some event or moment that altered a course, changed a direction, made an impression so pervasive that you grew into a different person. Something that provoked evolution.

But that's not it at all. No way. I'm sitting here, in a cold, empty grave in St. James Cemetery, waiting for God knows what to happen to me. To take a life or two. To end my own. But what I'm thinking about, what I'm recalling, picturing, bringing up, so clearly, so unbelievably clear, in my head is our kitchen in the old house. Our museum-piece kitchen, an exhibition out of 1950s American Television Sitcoms: Linoleum gray-and-red-checked floor, those four metal-legged chairs with the smooth, cool, dull-white Naugahyde backing, the metal-legged table with matching dull-white Formica top, the overstuffed, paisley-covered rocking chair that was Gramma's, wasn't it? And next to it, a little, black, wiry magazine holder stuffed with Life and The Saturday Evening Post. The silver-scrolled radiator in the corner that really pumped out the heat – remember Ike huddling next to it, mornings in the winter? That old white Norge refridge with the heavy pull-out handle. I built my first muscles opening and closing that monster. Mounted on all the walls are those old cream-colored real-wood cabinets with black handles, the inside shelves all lined with left-over wallpaper, that blue and white Colonial design, an early American man and woman sitting at a table having tea. Or I always thought it was tea. And, though I doubt I ever told you, Ma, I always thought the couple was George and Martha Washington.

I see the whole scene in the dim light of a late November evening, like this one. It's five, five-thirty, and you're waiting for Dad to get back from the corner market, you'd run out of milk, I think it was. You'd run out in the morning and the milkman wasn't due for another day. Remember milkmen? Dad comes through the door, whistling, carrying a brown paper bag filled not only with a gallon of milk, glass bottle, but some Corncakes and Old Fashioneds for later on in the night. And as you take the unexpected treat out of the bag, you give him this mock, scolding smile. So endearing. That's the only word that fits now. Endearing.

Ike's at one end of the kitchen table, scrunched up in the chair, reading, lost as always, deep into, what was it – yeah, a Hardy Boys book, The Sinister Signpost. And I'm at the other end, supper plate pushed to the side, doing my math homework, printing numbers, with a pencil, on a white, lined piece of paper pulled from a black-

marbled-cover spiral notebook, all those confetti-ish scraps running down the left-hand margin.

Dad sits in the old rocker, spreads The Spy *open in his lap, the sports page, as you go about the last preparations for dinner. This is what I remember. This would be my last memory to fade at my death: you turn from the stove, casually, whipping potatoes, and ask Dad if he's heard anything yet on the supervisor job that opened up last month down at the station. He doesn't look up from the paper, but answers that, yes, they offered it to him, and he turned it down. I look up from my math homework, I instantly launch into a study of your face, Ma. You pause, then nod, your head bobbing for an extended few seconds, in time to the rhythm of the potato-whipping motion that your hand and arm are making. Dad, you add the last comment, one you'd probably said before: no better way for a man to lose his friends than to become their superior.*

The words still ring, carried by your changeless voice, always, in my head.

Ma, you served dinner. Meat loaf. Dad, you tossed The Spy *on top of the Norge and took a seat. Ike reluctantly, slowly, put aside Frank and Joe Hardy – I always wanted, still want, to ask him why the signpost was sinister. I moved my math text onto the radiator, felt its heat, and put it on the seat of the rocker. We dug into the meal. Warm and delicious as every one you ever served. The night went on.*

All three of us, you two and me – Ike, I think, was probably unaware of the exchange – agreed it was the right decision. For Dad. For my father. I still think it was. But I learned something in that moment, seated there at the kitchen table. And I learned it in that way where it never leaves you, it becomes a permanent, central part of your essence. I learned a truth in a moment of epiphany.

And the truth was: there are people who want love. And there are people who want power.

And it occurs to me now, sitting in this awful open grave, sitting at the same level, in the same ground, where my parents, my flesh and blood, are buried, that the reason this would be the last memory to fade from my brain is that it was the moment when I changed. If you can stand the triteness of this thought: it was the line of demarcation between my innocence and my adulthood.

The standard way to mark that passage, that dividing line, is sexual. Maybe the first menstruation. Maybe the loss of virginity. These were secondary events for me. Because I'd already made a choice. For whatever reason, I was a changed girl. I wanted power. To the exclusion of all else?

You two tell me.

I am so cold right now. I have pushed my body, my nerves, to a point where some kind of collapse seems to be imminent. I don't know what I feel anymore. And I've got neither the energy nor, really, the desire to find out, to find a system that might bring me back, full circle.

A few weeks back, Ike said to me, in his kitchen now, I don't know what we were talking about, but he quotes some writer he likes. He says – 'I believe in the politics of the lamb.' And the stupidity of that statement made me enraged, made me want to leap across the table at Ike, my brother, the last person I have left, and choke him. I can't even talk to him anymore. Ike. Gentle, mutton-headed Ike.

Remember, Ma, a popular term of my childhood – Crisis of Faith. Capital letters. I don't believe in anything anymore, except will. And I'm losing the hold on that. Mother. Father. Words. It's all come to a head. I'm winding down. I've got maybe enough muscle and meanness and piss for one last seizure. And there are some fuckers about to be on the receiving end of that idea that took me, that entered me. Of that word: Power.

A sound cracks in her ear. A door being opened. Large, metal. Into a hollow-sounding interior. Obscuring echoes. Her fingers stop drumming. The deal makers have entered the Pachinko Brothers train car.

She hunches herself up a bit in the grave, brings a hand back to the earpiece, brings her teeth together, and listens:

ROURKE: Okay, listen up. The two parties in this transaction should be here any minute. I don't want any screwups—

WILSON [*exasperated*]: Billy, please...

ROURKE: Let's just run it down. The three of you did a walk-through, right? Okay, and Bromberg's patrolling the new section and Jacobi's got the old?

WILSON [*amused*]: *Patrolling.* For Christ sake, Billy, talk normal.

ROURKE [*angry*]: Talk normal, I ought to smack your head, talk normal. This is not a goddamn mail route, you little bitch. This is not screwing around. You didn't see the two gooks he brought to the bar, okay? Where did these fuckers come from? This was not in the plan. We're his brokers. He was supposed to come alone. Get that goddamn flashlight out of my eyes.

[*More sounds of jostled, echoing metal. Feet climbing up into the train car*]

ROURKE [*mockingly polite*]: It's the chauffeur. Donna, take the man's lantern. That's a beauty, that's like a real railroad job there. Now, give me your hand, there you go. Where's the boss?

MINGO: Give me the lantern.

ROURKE: I get it. Signal time. Like Paul Revere. Wasn't that the guy? Paul Revere?

MINGO: Where's your guy?

ROURKE: Be here any minute. And who do we have... Mr. Cortez. And his associate, Jimmy, isn't it? Here, let me give you two a hand up.

Graveyard's full of bodies tonight.

[*Rourke's awkward laughter. Hollow, metal echo*]

CORTEZ: Where is he?

ROURKE: Expecting him any minute. Once he gets here this shouldn't take a second. I assume, I mean, the briefcase—

CORTEZ: —is none of your concern at the moment, Mr. Rourke. When I see the product, you will see the money.

ROURKE: Of course, sure, listen, I was thinking, maybe the way to do this, just to make sure there are no mistakes and it's all handled professionally—

[*Laughter*]

ROURKE: Why's he laughing? Why's your driver there laughing?

CORTEZ: Mingo, please. Go on, Mr. Rourke.

[*Quiet for a moment. Foot shuffling*]

ROURKE: I thought maybe I'd stay in the middle, here, and you and your people could stay to one side, and then, when they get here, him and his people, they could stay on my opposite side. If that's all right with everyone? We could pass the cases back and forth through me. You know, broker.

CORTEZ: No objection.

[*Indiscriminate noise*]

ROURKE: Bingo, here they are now. Gentlemen, good to see you.

[*Climbing up on metal, movement, coughing, repositioning of bodies*]

ROURKE: Beautiful, so we're all here, tremendous. Mr. Cortez, this is the Paraclete. Mr. W, I'd like you to meet Mr. Cortez.

CORTEZ: A pleasure to finally meet.

PARACLETE: Likewise.

Lenore's whole body seizes up. The voice enters her ear and it's like she's been smashed across the back of the head with a board, a fat, sturdy two-by-four out of nowhere. No preparation, no time to flinch. Just a pure impact against her fragile skull.

It's Woo's voice. Absolute certainty. The Paraclete is Woo. Lenore comes up onto her knees, hugs the Uzi to her chest, starts to rise, and hears:

CORTEZ: Who's the hostage?

WOO: A visual aid, if you will. I thought you might like to see what my product can do.

CORTEZ [*possibly to Rourke*]: I've seen. All over my streets lately. There was no talk of this. There was no mention.

WOO: Yes, I understand there was some [*pause*] confusion concerning the samples that were sent to you—

CORTEZ: Who is he? Untape the man's mouth. This was not part of the plan.

WOO: —but I thought you might like to witness the process, as they say, up close and personal. Our guest for the evening is a former associate of Mr. Rourke. A fellow letter carrier. Mailman, as they say.

She grabs the rope and starts to climb out of the grave, frantic, all panic and no finesse. Back on the surface, she swings the Uzi on its strap around to her back and falls on her stomach. Rourke's sidekicks are definitely out there somewhere and who knows what kind of backup Cortez or Woo has planted.

She scans the landscape, a full circle, but there's not much she can see beyond tree-shadow and gravestones. She crawls toward the base of the nearest tree and looks around, then starts a crouched, small-step run toward the train car. She moves less than twenty yards when her left foot plants into a pile of dried leaves and catches on something buried underneath. She falls to her knees, lets her body go all the way to the ground, then rolls on her side, swinging the Uzi around to her front. She stops a second, stays on the ground, takes a breath, and sweeps a cautious half-circle in front of her with the Uzi's barrel. Then her eyes spot something protruding from the leaf pile and it's another second before she realizes it's a human hand. She leans back to the pile and pushes leaves aside until she finds what she's tripped over.

It's Charlotte Peirce's body.

There's a black hole in the center of her forehead. The diameter is somewhere between a quarter and a half-dollar. There are charred burn marks visible around the outer edge of the hole. The bottom half of the face is obscured by a heavy coating of dried blood. Fat streaks of blood run everywhere down the neck. The bottom lip looks to be missing from the face. Rust-colored, blood-soaked leaves bulge from an uneven gap that was once the mouth.

Lenore spots a small pink and red mound next to the head and avoids looking closely. The odds are good it could be a human tongue.

Though she knows it's a futile gesture, Lenore reaches to the neck and feels for a pulse. The flesh is cold to the touch, already turning into something else. Lenore retracts her hand. She knows there's another, much larger hole in the back of her head. And that a lot of blood and skull-bone and brain matter have exited into the dry earth below.

She freezes for a minute, tries again to concentrate on breathing. But words come through the earpiece.

> CORTEZ: I'm already a motivated buyer. There's no need for a display. My time here is limited.
>
> WOO: Duk [*finger snapping sound*], the tape.
>
> [Muffled, shuffling noise]
>
> [A voice, high, breathless, possibly hyperventilating]
>
> VOICE: Rourke [*gasp*] don't [*gasp*] let this [*garbled speech*].
>
> WOO: Put him on his knees.

Lenore's body starts to shut down. Calculation and strategy run from her brain. Her breathing is inaudible. Her feet feel like stone, like if someone lifted them, they'd break away from her ankle in a soft, granular rain.

They've got Ike. Ike is the guinea pig, the demonstration model. The Paraclete is Woo. And he's got Ike, on his knees, on the floor of an abandoned train car. He wants to stuff Ike full of Lingo and watch the display. He wants to put on a show for a customer.

CORTEZ [*annoyed*]: I'm not interested in sideshows, here. I'm on a very rigid schedule.

ROURKE [*nervous*]: Really, Mr. W—

WOO: Gentlemen, trust me, it is as much for my benefit as your own. I need to believe in a product, to truly get behind it, to know days, weeks, years down the road that I've supplied a worthy item. It's something of a matter of family pride. [*Sharp clap of hands*] Duk, my case.

IKE [*hysterical, wheezing*]: Rourke, you can't, Billy, Donna— [*choking sound*]

ROURKE [*edgy*]: This was not part of the—

WOO [*to his assistant*]: Watch your fingers, Duk. We can't be too careful these days.

WILSON [*pleading*]: Billy—

ROURKE [*through teeth*]: Shut the fuck up.

CORTEZ: With all due respect, sir.

WOO: This will take just a moment.

[*Various sounds, possibly including: a zipper pulled open, subdued male or female crying-noise, throat-clearing, whispers*]

WOO: Rub the throat, Duk. Just like you've done with the dogs. He'll swallow.

She gets to her feet, lets her fingers find and set the Uzi for use, takes deep breaths. Then she starts running, not a sprint but a serious jog, surefooted, planting and pushing off, rhythmic, no undue danger to the ankles, the whole time calculating timing, when she'll reach the open door, who she'll cut down with the first blast. The whole time in her ear there are the sounds of gurgling, gagging, small choking noise.

CORTEZ [*quietly*]: I don't believe in showmanship.

WOO [*mimicking his tone*]: There's nothing but showmanship.

She pulls the receiver from her ear and lets it fall. She makes the leap from the ground to the train's interior in the space of a last running stride. Her presence is sounded by the heavy clump of her feet hitting floor. She comes down in the middle of the whole group, parallel to Rourke and his girlfriend, Cortez to her left, Freddy Woo to her right. All the faces are lit only by the yellow gleam of swaying lanterns suspended above their heads on some unseen hook. They all look like they're badly made up for some shoestring slasher movie. She sees the huge, bald Oriental next to Woo, must be Duk, start to bring his hand around to his back. She pulls in on the Uzi's trigger like it was made of rubber, like the right kind of touch could flood her with pleasure. It makes a siege of firecracker pops, made odd and loud by the acoustics of the train car. She releases the trigger at once. Duk's body is knocked back and down, hits the floor with a sound she knows she'll recall in dreams.

'Spit it out, Ike,' she screams.

Ike's on all fours now, like he was someone's father ready to play Bronco. He comes downward in the front, onto his elbows, his back slanting, shoulders practically touching the floor. His face is obscured. She can see only a thick line of saliva arcing from mouth to floor.

'Spit it,' again, screaming.

She pokes at Woo's chest with the stunted barrel of the gun and says, 'You're a fucking dead man,' then without taking her eyes off him, she takes a step, brings a leg up until she's straddled across Ike's back, brings a free hand down and around to his face, and forces a long finger into the mouth and down toward the throat. There's a fraction of a second of pause and then she feels the heaving start to build in the chest. In a single motion she pulls hand and arm free and dismounts. Ike begins to vomit onto the train floor.

Sounds start to become recognizable. First, there's the halting whimpering from the girl, Donna, interlaced with small slapping noises from Rourke, trying to silence her.

'Hit her again, asshole,' Lenore says, and Rourke looks up, face all shock and fear, to see the Uzi swing toward him.

No one speaks for a second. Lenore lets the situation sink in, then says, without looking at him, 'Here's your big chance, Freddy. You've got people out there. A waiting car. Go ahead.'

Woo says nothing. He looks quickly to Cortez, who stays rigid, arms folded across his chest.

Lenore lets a hand fall down, sweeps Ike's hair up off his forehead, wipes away sweat with her palm.

Woo's mouth opens, closes, opens again. 'There's a tremendous amount of money…'

'Oh, Christ,' she says, almost rolling her eyes.

'More than you would think.'

'I can't believe you can't do better. Mr. Language. Jesus.'

'I think I'm going to be sick,' Wilson says.

'Help her out,' Lenore says to Rourke, looking at Woo. The girl starts to fall toward the floor, slowly, still in the grasp of Rourke's awkward arms.

'Excuse,' Cortez says, clearing his throat and motioning toward the graveyard with a slight tilt of his head.

Lenore exhales, then nods back to him. Cortez lightly touches Jimmy Wyatt's shoulder and the mute picks up the briefcase of money and jumps out of the boxcar.

'You've got to be kidding me,' Woo says, his head hung out past his shoulders, not ready to accept what he knows is about to happen.

Cortez starts to follow Jimmy, then stops for a moment next to Lenore.

'You've got to be kidding me,' Woo repeats, tight-lipped, a tick beginning in his left eye.

Lenore chucks him lightly under the chin with the Uzi barrel.

'Learn some new words,' she says slowly, then turns to Cortez. 'You get to that cave in the mountains down there, make sure it has two exits.'

Cortez nods, puts a hand on Mingo's shoulder, and steers him toward the doors.

'Will the Aliens find you?'

Cortez shrugs.

'You want Wyatt to take care of anyone outside?'

She shakes her head no, stops, shakes her head yes.

He pauses as if he had something more to say, then takes an off-balance step and jumps down from the train car, followed by Mingo.

'Pathetic choice,' Woo says to her.

'There was no choice at all, Freddy. I cut no deal. I don't take one dime out of this.'

He makes a face to indicate how ridiculous this sounds to him.

'Believe what you want. I didn't know you were the producer – the Paraclete, right? – until five minutes ago.'

Woo holds up his hand in a stop sign and mutters, 'Oh, please…'

Lenore cuts him off and says, 'You whacked Peirce, you fuck.'

Woo breathes through his nose and holds up a second hand. 'You're making a terrible mistake, Lenore. There are so many things you just don't know. Your sister detective made some pathetic character judgments. It was her associates who judged her expendable. When all this is over it will look like she was one more dirty cop who made one more stupid decision—'

'A couple things *you* should know, asshole. That diner you hit. That motorcycle chickenshit drive-by. You killed a friend of mine. And your visual aid here' – she strokes Ike's forehead – 'this is my brother.'

Woo goes still and silent. Across the car, Rourke says a weak, 'Oh, shit.'

A small grin finally breaks on Woo's face and he says, 'So now you take me in.'

'Now who's kidding who?'

'I've got people outside. You know that.'

'Great. The Duk-man here will have some company. You can all sit around, play Scrabble in hell. You'll have a real edge, Freddy.'

'They'll have heard the gunfire.'

'I've got a feeling they were told to expect some gunfire.'

'It doesn't stop with me, Lenore. I have friends. There's a great big family. People in position. You know the saying about City Hall.'

'Impress me some more, dickhead.'

Woo takes a breath. 'All your talk about will. All your words. It comes down to this, Lenore.'.

'You know, Freddy, there's a reason the Families put the gun barrel in the enemy's mouth. You know that, right, Freddy?'

'I'm unarmed. Defenseless. A prisoner. You can just execute me? You think so?'

She raises her free hand to his mouth, pinches in the sides like some cliché of an elderly woman admiring a child's face. She turns his head from side to side.

'Courage of my convictions, Freddy.'

She hears the metal-click sound of a safety being snapped off. She steps back slowly and turns enough to see Rourke, on one knee, one arm extended forward, hand gripping a small revolver.

Woo begins to laugh and says, 'Even the mailman carries a gun. I love this country.'

Lenore pivots very slowly as Rourke, caught somewhere between terrified and adrenaline-high, says, 'Don't, do not, just stop.'

'Okay, stupid, just listen. I've got a bead on you right now. I've got tension on the trigger. You might get a shot off. But I'll be firing back. My body jerks back, the weapon fires, I swear to you, this will happen.'

Woo makes his move. It happens in seconds. He goes down and up into her, his shoulder coming under her, knocking the Uzi upward toward the ceiling. A small burst of gunfire sounds and stops. Lenore loses balance, falls backward, hugging the gun into her chest to maintain position. Woo is on top of her, one hand pushing the weapon down against her so she can't get control, another struggling to pull something from the inside of his coat.

Then it's out, an open razor. A long straight razor, a barber's tool from a generation past. Woo manages to get a grip on her throat. He makes a sweep that passes near the end of her nose. The miss charges him up and he pushes harder on her neck, brings the razor up more slowly this time. And his intention becomes clear. The thought gels in Lenore's brain: *he wants to cut up my mouth, he wants to cut out my tongue.*

Now he makes a jab motion instead of a sweep. The blade slides into Lenore's upper lip and at once a rush of blood flows down over her mouth. There's no pain, but the shock of the action gives Lenore enough of a jolt to throw him to the side. He pulls the blade across the back of her hand as he passes. Blood spurts and runs, and she tries to keep a hold on her weapon. Woo gains balance and begins to come at her again, backhand, a wide arc.

There's a round of gunfire, a series of low-caliber pops. She turns to see Cortez, outside the train car, bent in a practiced shooter's stance. The bullets enter Woo's body chest-level. For an instant he makes the helpless, jerking, seizurelike spasms of a man in an electric chair. The body erupting in short, violent twitches. Then he pitches forward and his head lands facedown in Lenore's abdomen.

She rolls to the side, angles the Uzi toward Rourke. But Ike is in the line of fire, a knee planted on Rourke's chest, hands around the throat, coming downward with his head, cracking the bridge of his forehead into Rourke's nose, eyes, skull. The revolver is a few feet away from them. Lenore slides out from under Woo's head and it thumps to the floor. She crawls toward her brother, picks up Rourke's gun, then pulls Ike off him.

She turns back to see Cortez climbing into the car. She watches him toe Woo's limp head until he's satisfied the man is dead. Then he bends down and picks up the briefcase full of Lingo.

'I forgot something,' he says.

'That wasn't part of the deal.'

'The deal,' he says, 'was left very vague.'

'I need it. To explain.'

'You'll find another explanation,' he says, and she realizes his gun is casually pointed toward her. 'That's one of your strengths, Lenore. You're so good with words.'

'Don't,' she says, tensing muscles.

'I'm leaving now, Lenore. Wyatt and Mingo are waiting for me.'

He starts to back toward the door. They stare at each other until he turns and jumps to the ground.

The girl, Wilson, is curled up, weeping, gagging, trying to breathe, in a far corner of the train car.

Ike sways under his sister's hand, falls off Rourke, whose face is a lumpy puddle of blood, torn skin, visible bone.

They sit, their bodies fall into one another. The only sound is Wilson's choppy, eerie, infant-noises and their own attempts at regulating their breathing. The train car is already starting to fill up with a smell, something heavy, primal. Something without a specific word attached to it.

Lenore pulls in some air and tries to speak, but the sounds are unintelligible. Ike looks up at her, crunches up his eyes and mouth, brings his hand up to her lips in a useless effort to stop the bleeding. They both know, at once, it's more a sign of concern than something pragmatic.

Ike takes his hand away, dabs at his pants leg, then reaches around to a back pocket and produces a white handkerchief. Lenore takes it from him, presses it up over her mouth. She knows it will be saturated in a minute.

They manage to pull Wilson down from the car, and the three of them huddle into one another for the walk to the Barracuda.

Lenore lets herself scan the graveyard just once. It's possible she spots two or three bodies, lying prone, refuse left by Jimmy Wyatt. It's just as possible the figures in the distance are piles of clumped leaves that will blow into different formations by morning.

She distracts herself from studying the landscape further. She looks down at her feet as she walks. She tries to keep her tongue tucked in a far corner of her mouth. But her resolve is gone. And the tongue roams on its own, dipping into the mess of blood and open flesh, tasting, against her own better judgment, the flavor of her own juice.

33

It's Thanksgiving morning in Ike's kitchen. The radio is delivering a blow-by-blow of the Main Street parade, an endless march by an infinite number of helium-filled cartoon characters. Super heroes. Comical sidekicks.

> RAY:... And now, passing City Hall in a special seat high atop the lead float, waving to the cheering throng as he goes, this year's grand marshal of Quinsigamond's annual Thanksgiving Day parade, the leader of our fair community, the voice of the people, the city's own Mayor Victor Welby...

Lenore sits in the rocking chair, wrapped in an oversized terrycloth bathrobe that Ike had intended as a Christmas gift. Her legs are pulled up underneath her. Her head is resting on a throw pillow at her shoulder. She holds a mug of steaming tea between her hands, in her lap.

Ike wears an almost matching robe over flannel pajama bottoms. He has white tube socks over his feet. His hair sticks out in the back in birdlike tufts. He has a full loaf of bread spread out on the kitchen table and the toaster's going nonstop. So far he hasn't burned a piece. He's in the process of making bread stuffing for the small turkey that's now roasting in his oven, filling the kitchen with the familiar smell of every Thanksgiving in their mutual past.

They're both a little dopey from Valium and the brandy Ike has added to the tea.

'What a waste,' Lenore says, the words obscured, softened in places by her swollen lips and dozens of stitches.

Ike understands her and shakes his head. 'You do it for the smell. You need that smell.'

'Dr. Z said to stay on soft food and liquids for a week.'

'So what is stuffing?' Ike asks. 'Soft food. Like the epitome of soft food. And I can still eat the turkey.'

'What a sport.'

'Tomorrow I'll make you some turkey soup. Broth. Good for you.'

Dr. Z is a friend from the city clinic who owes Lenore more than a few favors. He sedated Wilson and let her sleep in an empty room, then phoned Zarelli at 4 A.M. What happens from here, tomorrow and the weeks ahead, Ike neither knows nor wants to know. He hasn't slept yet. Right now, he wants only to be in this kitchen, these familiar walls. He wants to move through well-known motions. Movements that involve cooking, eating, feeding.

After they got home from the clinic, Lenore tried to sleep on top of Ike's bed, but got up after half an hour and showered. She knows the Valium is putting off a real meltdown. That there are still very bad times ahead. Shakes, an inability to get warm, days, maybe weeks, of nausea. Maybe visions. All Ike will say about what's to come, he said, as she stepped from the bathroom, the new robe warm on her shoulders, a towel wrapped around her head.

He said, 'We'll get through it, sis. You got all the strength in the family.'

Now, watching her brother cut toast up into small squares, she's not at all sure of the truth of his statement. And she wishes she'd countered with, 'And you got all the wisdom.'

Wisdom. It's a funny word. She doesn't think she could say it, even without the stitches. Certainly not without laughing.

She lets her head roll across the back of the rocker. She thinks about Cortez, months from now. She imagines him sitting cross-legged, Indian style, in the mouth of some cave, ridiculously high in the face of the Andes, a rare book, a novel, open in his lap. He's reading it for the third or fourth time. His face is tanned to a leathery cover. In a notch in the rocks below him, the sound of Mingo telling ancient jokes to a silent Jimmy Wyatt, Henny Youngman one-liners, floats up toward him. Echoes. His aides tend the sheep, bring water. He just sits and reads, moves his hands over the covers of the whole ghost library. Halfway through the day, he begins to read aloud. To Max. He tries to discover the boy's preferences. His likes and dislikes.

She can't help ask. 'What's going to happen when the shock wears off?'

Ike can't answer. He'd like to imagine a moment months from now, he and Lenore at the table working out the intricate plot of a mystery. But instead, the image of Eva's face starts to form. He knocks it away, burns it down, fills himself up with the size of the toast squares, the amount of sage to add, the sound of the parade commentator's voice.

Though it's bodiless, detached, it's filled with such emotion, clearly impressed by this spectacular march down the center of Quinsigamond. It's a celebration. A tradition. Main Street flooded with row after row of marching bands, fire trucks, elephants, lighter-than-air floats of nylon tethers. It sounds like a marvel of color, music, syncopation. The announcer can barely contain himself.

RAY: How can I tell you all out there, how can I tell you? You've got to see it for yourself. Come on down. It's beyond words.